Praise for Award-Winning Author

C. Hope Clark

Hope Clark's books have been honored as winners of the:

EPIC Award, Silver Falchion Award, Imadjinn Award,

and

Daphne du Maurier Award.

"The author immediately plunges you into action and setting."
—Angie Mangino, Medium.com on *Edisto Tidings*

"[*Salkehatchie Secret*] is another hit. Enjoyable story line. Wonderful characters. Multiple story lines. Would definitely recommend."
—Pernette Wells, Netgalley Review

"Riveting. [*Tidewater Murder* is] a first-rate mystery."
—Donnell Ann Bell, Bestselling Author of
The Past Came Hunting and *Deadly Recall*

The Novels of C. Hope Clark

The Carolina Slade Mysteries

Lowcountry Bribe
Tidewater Murder
Palmetto Poison
Newberry Sin
Salkehatchie Secret
Lake Murray Money

The Edisto Island Mysteries

Murder on Edisto
Edisto Jinx
Echoes of Edisto
Edisto Stranger
Dying on Edisto
Edisto Tidings
Reunion on Edisto
Edisto Heat
Badge of Edisto
Edisto Bullet
Edge of Edisto
Edisto Storm
Hidden on Edisto

The Craven County Mysteries

Murdered in Craven
Burned in Craven
Craven County Line

Lake Murray Money

The Carolina Slade Mysteries – Book 6

by

C. Hope Clark

Edisto Bridge Books

EDISTO||||
BRIDGE

Edisto Bridge Books
140A Amicks Ferry Road, PMB 4
Chapin, SC 29036
Print ISBN: 978-1-968423-36-0

Visit Hope at chopeclark.com

Cover design: Debra Dixon
Interior design: Hank Smith
Photo/Art credits:
Man in boat (manipulated) © Jozsef Bagota | Dreamstime.com

:Lmlm:01:

Dedication

Dedicated to Angela Kaye Lane,
who loves me being "the only writer in the family."

Chapter 1

WAYNE'S BOOTS echoed across the barn floor. This venue clocked in at number four, and that was just today's tally. We'd taken a two-day leave from our crime-solving jobs with the feds for this, and we were on our second day of canvassing wedding facilities. Silly me for naïvely assuming when we got engaged that our "I do's" would be an in-and-out, notarize-the-form-and-go affair.

Stupid me for not realizing Senior Special Agent Wayne Largo, a man professionally accustomed to maneuvering amidst the shadows until he could throw the culprit in cuffs, would turn soft and giddy about tying our knot. Who'd have guessed he'd be the romantic?

Last weekend, he'd met me on my home's back porch . . . our home now—he'd moved in once the engagement was solid. "I need you to take off a couple days," he said.

"You got it, Cowboy," I said, my mind thinking more about what we'd be doing rather than where. Again, silly me. I'd thought he'd planned an impromptu amorous long weekend. "Where are we going?"

"We're visiting potential wedding venues. Let's get this ball rolling, Butterbean."

I'd gone along, thinking we'd choose one of, maybe, three places. Then set the date, tell someone like this guy leading us around to make it happen, and clinch those vows.

Oh, but no. After yesterday, I realized I'd totally missed that mark. So had the weather. It was only mid-September, but the day held a distinctly October feel. We'd been to Irmo, Leesville, and now Little Mountain. I'd nixed anything in Columbia. Edisto Beach had been tossed around, but the ocean wasn't my thing. Dark water scared me. However, undeveloped miles of acreage turned me on.

We'd wound around and around off St. Peter's Church Road, venturing into Newberry County to Wheeland Road to find this place. I lived fifteen miles from here and never knew it existed. Amazing how many farmers were allowing their farms to be rented for special events.

Even though developers were gobbling up rural land as fast as they could wheel and deal, this area remained rural, thank goodness. We passed a church to reach Wheeland Farm, Wayne slowing, admiring the basic, period architecture.

"Look at that," he had said, stopped on the edge of the two-lane road beside St. Peter's Church. "Over two hundred years old. That's just plain beautiful, Butterbean."

Plain beautiful?

This man had a lawman exterior and a cinnamon-roll interior, a combination I adored from the moment we'd met. But lately, with nuptials consuming his mind, the softness had taken control.

"And Macedonia Church," he added. "We'll pass it on the way home. A hundred and eighty years. That's incredible, don't you think?"

He'd scouted the area before bringing me. "Are they both Lutheran?" I asked, humoring him, showing I knew enough about the region's history.

"They are," he said. "Once we're wed, we might think about a church. What do you say?"

"Once we're wed?"

"Yeah," he said, not catching at all my inference at the alien formality of his words.

I wanted no ceremonial church wedding, preferring an outdoor, one-with-nature informality. Wayne had conceded to nixing the brick-and-mortar church while warning that he wanted a place that felt sacred enough for vows. I explained how nature was as close to God as one could get. He went along with that.

Currently, he marveled at the overhead design in a barn structure. The end opened up, and a wide wooden cross hung from the ceiling, designed to be emphasized or decorated beyond recognition to suit all tastes and beliefs. Nothing fancy, but my guess was this *barn* had never seen a cow or a hog.

I hollered over to the wedding planner who'd brought us here. "You ever get birds nesting up in there?"

Wayne cut me a glance. The other man looked up, trying to imagine what I asked, before answering, "Never heard of a problem with that."

They ought to call this barn what it was . . . a party factory. An open faux-barn to house people and offer a rustic feel. All these sites ran together in my mind; Wayne couldn't wipe the smile off his face, which reined in my mockery. Poor baby. If the wedding planner showing us around had been a used car salesman, Wayne would've brought home the biggest lemon on the lot.

But I'd agreed to these appointments, and out of love for the big guy, I owed him. Frankly, I found pleasure in watching how thrilled Wayne was with his plans to get that ring on my hand. After scouting so many venues, however, a jaded feeling crept in. Seemed a lot of farmers ran side gigs with wedding, reunion, and birthday celebrations, and they all looked alike. A farmer in Newberry leased his acreage for Spartan races each year, where the most insane athletes ran miles and miles of obstacle courses for medals.

I forced my attention back to our tour, my own personal obstacle course. We'd just seen the loft with dressing rooms for bride and groom complete with bathrooms decorated better than half the historical homes in Charleston. Every place we'd seen had over-the-top decorations ranging from arbors overlooking ponds to a silo bar. Tulle-draped chairs and even Marvel comics themes. Motorcycles or feathers. Ponds, forests, and even a vineyard. They came with catering options. The wedding cakes ranged from cupcake towers to donut cakes or seven-tiered monstrosities.

Lighting in crevices overhead, under the food, and around the dance floor tried to dress up the plainness of the structure to justify overcharging couples like us. Barns too nice to be barns. I'd only seen one small herd of black Angus in the distance here, and a minor chicken operation at an earlier venue. Nothing clucked, mooed, or oinked around a *venue*.

Wayne and the planner strolled out the barn's exit, the gentleman gesturing with his arms, painting the what-ifs for Wayne. My fingers ran over the railing that kept drunk revelers from falling off the balcony and into the pond below.

Think of him.

My sister's words rang in my ears, nagging, accusing me of dodging the *I do's*. That's the last message I wanted to send.

I'd even worn new boots, bought a light sweater, and doubled the mascara in order to make Wayne feel proud to show off the fiancé he'd snared. He'd been so tickled this morning. Now my feet screamed at the too-tall heels I'd been stupid to think would last the miles we'd walk.

I wanted this man as badly as I'd wanted anything in my life, but I wanted him *now*. As in justice-of-the-peace now. Sis was wrong. Not that I could prove it by eloping. Nope. I was stuck in wedding-planner hell.

Ahead of me Wayne continued, in step with this animated director, asking questions I never fathomed and didn't care two cents about. Could the person in the chair twenty rows back hear the vows? What was the acoustics quality for one guitar versus a four-piece band?

Some of these questions felt like word problems on a college entrance exam. *Since the end of the barn faced west to see the vista, how bright did the sun get at eleven a.m., then two, four, and six p.m. for photography consideration? Where were the bad shadows?*

My man had turned into some sort of wedding alien.

I plopped on a bench strategically placed for catching your breath—which also, coincidentally, allowed one to envision yourself on your big day, and fall in love with the place. The planner led Wayne to a wall of ivy that served as an outdoor photo op for guests, continually touching my fiancé's sleeve as if he wouldn't mind having a taste of my cowboy. I pushed down the smidge of jealousy, knowing full well which team Wayne preferred.

Then this guy gave what he thought was a discreet nod in my direction, nudging Wayne. I couldn't read lips, but I imagined his saying something cliché about how beautiful I was, or how I *dreamed* about the big day, picturing myself in my *dreamiest* best on the *dreamiest* day of my life. Whatever he said made Wayne smile.

In truth, my mind was bored, my body sore, and my mood bordered on ugly hangry. Our back-to-back appointments ran through lunch, and no one offered us the first sign of refreshment short of water, Coke, or coffee—all of which fell well short of the calories required to keep my growing impatience at bay. Right now I'd sign with the first venue that fed me well.

Wayne saw through the pseudo-damsel smile I tossed his way. We'd had mini versions of the same conversation a dozen times on the subject of what kind of wedding we needed, and this place had become like all the others. Over the top and too commercial. It did, however, beat a church.

I'd been married before . . . in a church. Fortunately, husband number one was in the ground, killed by a farmer he'd partnered with to kill me—coincidentally the case through which Wayne and I met. My first wedding had been a hard five figures and, in view of that logic, supported that how much you *paid* mattered little in terms of a couple's future.

Wayne, however, had married his first wife in a hormonal courthouse rush. His ex served time in prison now. He'd had to shoot her before she shot him, due to her being in cahoots with hard criminal sorts. He wanted to do our nuptials properly, he said. To start us on the right foot since both of us had gotten it so wrong the first time.

The two men backtracked in my direction, and I scolded myself to sit up and behave. I might be forty-three, but my mother's chidings on *acting a lady* whispered in my ear.

"Seeing yourself on the big day, Ms. Slade?" Mr. Everlasting, or whatever his name was, asked. "I keep wanting to call you Carolina."

Carolina was my first name, rarely used. Kudos to him on not using it since I only remembered his moniker started with an E.

"This place is lovely," I said, though my vision of a lovely place was more along the lines of my backyard overlooking Lake Murray, a barbecue waiting on the patio. We'd say *I do* standing on my dock in way-more-comfortable shoes.

"Makes the top three on our list," I pushed out in decent-sounding sincerity, remaining seated, not ready to stand in these boots.

"Are we getting tired?" His faux pout irritated the crap out of me. "We still have a little more to go, Ms. Slade."

I rose, wondering if my daughter Ivy would take these boots since they were too scuffed to return. "Lead on, kind sir. I assume you've saved the best for last."

Mr. Everlasting beamed, tapping Wayne on the arm for the umpteenth time. "I bet she's a character. Usually, I'm having to control the bride." Another stroke on the arm. "I've thoroughly enjoyed escorting the groom for a change."

I scrunched my nose and drawled, "Wayne's indeed a treat."

Wayne threw me a glance over the top of the gentleman's head, and I threw him back a wink. "I'm right behind you guys, taking it all in."

We wound along the railing to where it curved down to the pond, which offered a pleasant view. At the bottom, they veered left along the well-kept path. I detoured to the right.

The place sported some beautiful flower species, many of the plants decades old. A magnificent assortment of Confederate Roses bloomed red and pink—lush and tall about thirty yards up the slope, accented even more by the backdrop of scattered oaks and hickories warning here and there that they would soon explode into full dress of red and yellow.

Oh, my, those flowers had me. Going all the way back to the Civil War, legend said the flowers soaked up the spilled blood of dead soldiers. Those roses and gardenias were my favorite. Both incredibly Southern. They could be found on half the rural grounds in the state but not mine. I would kill for cuttings off those plants and had the perfect place for them in my front yard. Slipping my pocketknife out of my shoulder bag, calculations told me a half-dozen twelve-inch lengths would work, and begging forgiveness in lieu of permission made the most sense in the moment. Those boys could go five minutes or more before they needed a response from me. They wouldn't notice I had gone.

Under the largest specimen, I hunted for a healthy branch that was not too old. God, these were gorgeous. They bloomed hard, a tribute to their care, and brought back memories of my grandmother's Mississippi yard, brimming with those roses.

With two cuttings in hand, I maneuvered to the next plant. Oh yes, these would do.

One plant with an abundance of red flowers seemed to enjoy being close to the pond, and I sidled my way down to it, promising to limit myself to three cuttings . . . maybe four.

Hey, why not talk to the farmer himself instead of this wedding organizer. We just might concoct a celebration more natural and down to earth amidst these roses.

Stooping, trying to locate just the right baby slip amidst the adult growth, a flash of red orange caught my eye from the pond. South Carolina was noted for a wide assortment of birdlife, and at first, I imagined a cardinal. But my dark water phobia wasn't keen on my venturing too terribly near the pond. No telling what creature lay in wait. We had our share of snakes around here, and this time of year they were ornery.

One more step. Then two. The bright-colored patch seemed more orange than red, tucked into and half-hidden by overhanging bushes and thin slips of water grass. Bright rays bounced off the bobbing water. I was no longer sure I was dealing with wildlife of any kind.

Knife still in my hand, purse and cuttings dropped to the ground, I almost called Wayne, but he had his back to me—jabbering with Mr. Everlasting. No point playing the scared little lady and interrupting them.

I stepped sideways down the slope, as Wayne had taught me to do when confronted with danger, to avoid being as much of a target as possible.

A natural body of water would have sticks and leaves underfoot from which to grab something to poke the object, but the venue was too cleaned up. Sterile, even. Eight feet . . . six feet . . . four feet from the water's edge, the color took on substance . . . cloth. What was causing the bouncy movement?

Plop.

A ten-inch mud turtle slid into the water. Startled, I jerked, making two others follow him. Before I could scold myself for letting them bother me, my slick new boots lost traction and flew out from under me. Having sense enough to drop the knife, I fought to catch myself, but in spite of arms and legs scrambling for purchase, I skidded downhill.

I must have hollered, because Wayne yelled, "Slade? You all right?"

But I had no words. My expensive Tecovas had mired up to the ankle in mud and water, having halted against the arm of a dead man.

My bumping his shoulder untethered him, and he began to float off.

Remembering the body I once found at Edisto Island, I panicked, thinking he'd float away, and I reached for a sleeve.

"Wayne!" I managed to scream before my boots sank further, then more, then tipping me, finishing the job of taking me into the pond.

Chapter 2

REPOSITIONING, I fought to right myself in the muck and the water, clouds of soft brown mud around me. I instinctively sought to balance myself against anything but that damn body.

"Son of a bitch!" Rearing back, reaching for some other handhold, I would've lost balance again if not for Wayne reaching a long arm down to catch the back of my sweater. He readjusted, caught me beneath the arms, and slid me onto dry land.

"Oh shit," yelled Mr. Everlasting as the body seemed to take life and bobble like a cork. He cleared his throat. "I mean . . ." But he couldn't finish the sentence. He stared at the body buoyant about ten feet from the bank and then sank to the ground, mumbling to himself.

"You all right?" Wayne asked me, though his gaze rested on the body.

My heart still pumped a gallon a second, but I willed it to settle, swallowing once to force down the scare. I held up a hand for his assistance in standing, to join him in staring at whoever floated dead in the pond.

"I saw the orange half-hidden and went to check it out. Didn't expect a body to come with it," I said, unsuccessfully wiping at the mud coating me from belly down.

From his six-foot altitude, Wayne peered down. "Did you check to see—"

"If he's dead? He had turtles eating on him, Wayne, but help yourself if you want to wade out there and feel for a pulse."

But wade in he did, almost before I'd finished my sentence. He rolled the body over.

Mr. Everlasting threw up on the finely manicured grass.

Wayne didn't have to check the pulse. My grumpy hunger turned into thanks I hadn't eaten because the dead man's coloring alone would've prompted a loss of stomach contents. Nibbles here and there from the turtles only accented the fact this man was no longer with us and had probably enjoyed the night out here. Wayne rolled the body to its original position, left it, and waded back.

"You're just leaving him there?" I asked, the concept that the man couldn't breathe face down stupidly crossing my mind.

"He's been there a while," he said, pulling out his phone, his thumb hitting the obvious numbers. "The coroner and investigators would want us to leave him in place. Decomp speeds up once out of the water, and any detective would prefer to see the scene undisturbed. The body could've been placed in the water after death, for instance."

In an animated scan of the area around me, I scoffed. "You call this undisturbed?"

He sighed. "Typical Slade behavior to me. On the other hand, the police might be asking why we mucked it up so badly." He turned away, the 911 operator on the line.

I returned up the slope to ease down beside our wedding planner, choosing the side opposite of where he'd vomited, plus a foot or two.

"God," Mr. E said, his new paleness more pronounced than he showed earlier. He didn't seem like much of an outdoors guy. "Not another one."

That remark snared me. "What do you mean *another one?*"

"Same thing happened at a Lexington place a couple months ago, the very week I was sure we'd line up three weddings in a row. Boy did that set me behind."

I wish this man would quit with generalities. Who, what, exactly when, and where. But first, "What do you mean *same thing?* You ran up on another body while showing off wedding locales?"

He laid a hand on his chest. "Oh, no, no. I didn't get to see that one. Thank God."

I waited, trying not to shoot questions so fast, but I stared at him so he'd get the idea.

"Homer Brooks," he said. "Died fishing. Had nothing to do with the farm."

"Where?"

"Over on the Lexington side of the lake. I'm beginning to think I ought to stick to churches." He took in a major breath, held then released it, and the effort seemed to help.

"Do you know this man?"

He nodded in short rapid bursts. "It's Mr. Oakley."

Recognizing the name stole my breath a second. "You mean Troy Oakley?"

I hadn't met Oakley, but I'd heard the name in the halls of work.

My employer was the US Department of Agriculture, the state headquarters fifty miles southeast of here. Wayne and I solved rural crime linked to our federal programs. I did more administrative investigations. Wayne took over when they became criminal.

The planner confirmed the identity with a nod of his head. "This is his place."

Troy Oakley was a good guy, a solvent producer, and, unless I was wrong, a member of the Newberry County Committee of farmers who offered agricultural advice. He was well respected and one of the few farmers keeping their head above water, no pun intended. I hadn't made the correlation that Wheeland Farm was his.

Clearly Mr. Everlasting hadn't noticed the body before, and in his preparations to see us, hadn't looked further than the barn and its wedding amenities. Admittedly, I hadn't seen the body from my bench outside the barn either.

"When was the last time you met with him?" I asked.

"A week ago." His voice quivered. "But I spoke to him yesterday morning to confirm your appointment for today."

I'd obliterated the scene, but hopefully they found one or two foreign shoeprints to ponder. Few people in the country had security cams or even as much as a Ring camera covering more than the front door of their home. Some put deer cams out, but rural land sprawled too much to count on cameras capturing trespassers.

"What time did you speak to him yesterday?" I asked.

"Slade, stop." Wayne was off the phone. "Not our case."

I tipped my chin toward the pond. "Turns out he's one of our farmers."

"That doesn't make it our case. Deaths aren't our bailiwick unless it impacts the services USDA provides."

"But how do we know if we don't investigate?"

"We don't get involved until we're invited. I'll tell them who we are in case we're needed, but in the meantime, leave this poor man alone."

Wayne had clicked into his special-agent self, Mr. Romantic taking a back seat. "For now, we wait. I'll be right back. You tend to Mr. Easton while I get him a Coke."

So that was his name.

Waiting until Wayne was out of earshot, I started to rub Mr. Easton's back in sympathy then realized that doing so would leave a stripe of red mud down the shoulder. The breezes and lower temps that came with fall nights weren't due for another couple weeks, but that didn't stop me from feeling chilled from the wet. I saw no chance this guy would offer his coat. "Care to go inside . . . the barn? I'm rather wet and chilly at the moment."

"Oh, oh, I'm so sorry." He leaped to his feet, holding out his hand for me. "I forgot you're wet. And you've ruined those gorgeous boots I've been admiring since you arrived."

I glanced at his feet to see if they might fit, because if they did, he could have them. Nope. Penguin feet.

Wayne came out of the barn as we headed in, and before we could settle into chairs to absorb what we'd just seen, two Newberry Sheriff's Department cruisers appeared, minus siren. About the time they parked at the barn, the coroner arrived.

Before Mr. Easton could greet them with fluster, Wayne interceded and filled them in. Between his description of the discovery and my grubby appearance, I received a clear double take by the two deputies, and the coroner wore a scowl in response to what I must have done to the area to look like this.

The question of the day was why I had stumbled upon a body, apart and separately from the two men, instead of following Mr. Easton around. Unwilling to say I was stealing Confederate Rose cuttings, I just said I appreciated the water, wondering if the ceremony could be totally outside. Partially true, which made it easy to say.

While Wayne escorted the deputies, two more having arrived in a third car, I chose to wait in the barn with Mr. Easton. He'd been sweet enough to wheel over a portable outdoor heater, another amenity available on the à la carte list in case I didn't choose the package deal.

I shed the boots, propping my wet sock feet up on another chair, removing them from the drafty cement floor, and took a towel from Mr. Easton that looked like he'd just taken the tags off. "How well did you know him?" I asked, no longer having Wayne around to stem my curiosity.

"Mr. Oakley?" Easton asked.

I nodded, recognizing his question on the heels of mine as a means to give himself a second to collect himself. It was a stall most people did when questioned about the uncomfortable . . . or when lying. Why didn't I trust this man?

"Only in a business way," Easton said. "As a wedding planner, I arrange these tours. The owners don't want to be involved with most of them not having a clue how to sell it, so I step in as a broker for the services and softly convince couples, families, and businesses to consider the venue. Therefore, I know him, but we're not friends."

Made sense. I wondered if he charged per showing as well as commission from locking down the reservations. "Does he enjoy doing this sort of thing?" I did a light swoop of my hand to indicate this wedding reception game we played. "Or is this the extra dollars he needs to keep the farm going?"

"Oh heavens, I wouldn't know anything about that," he said.

I waited, though, noticing something unspoken in the lilt of his voice.

"He's normally booked up. I only agreed to see you and your fiancé because he had an opening in November that he seemed extremely eager to fill. Each of these events puts several thousand in his pocket, and he's one who particularly welcomes two bookings per weekend." He seemed to catch himself. "Not that I'd book two weddings in one weekend, mind you. That would be horribly rude. The second event would be something smaller and simpler, like a reunion."

Wouldn't have bothered me. The faster my wedding took place the better. "That level of organization sounds rather hectic," I said, showing him sympathy to keep him talking.

"It certainly can be. Mr. Oakley's a good man," Easton said. "I sense he appreciated the income. Farming isn't as lucrative as it used to be, or so I hear."

I knowingly grinned. "Something I'm quite familiar with. Wayne and I investigate agricultural crime across the state. It's mind blowing how much trouble these farmers get into. All it takes is for the market to tank on a commodity or the weather to go haywire one season and they slide into the red, needing two years or more to dig out. Side gigs like weddings can make the difference between paying bills or having to borrow more money, but they love this dirt so much they'd do anything to keep it. These families have farming in their blood, and that's why Wayne and I enjoy our professions. We aim to keep them in business and not let the seediness of greed and corruption interfere. The folks we serve are true Americana."

"Oh, my," Easton said. "That sounds so . . . patriotic. So, noble."

I'd never been called noble. I held a deep love for country, but nobody had ever seen what I did with agriculture as patriotic. Maybe Mr. Easton had more substance than I'd given him credit for.

I draped the towel higher over me, the heater beginning to make a difference. Wish I had a beer. "Did Mr. Oakley ever talk about selling his land? Or say that these weddings kept him from having to sell? We all know how ravenous and cutthroat developers are in these parts."

I lived six miles outside Chapin, the next town over, and developers had raped the lands around it. The thousands of acres that once belonged to founding families two and three hundred years ago, had been divided once the old patriarchs died and the children became unable to handle the taxes . . . or turn down the obscene monies offered by developers. Money indeed talked, and it talked loudly. Few could afford to turn up a nose at sums that could educate children, pay off mortgages, and remove all worries about retirement.

Out here, however, rural remained rural, at least for the time being. It was precious in my sight, which was why I wanted to marry Wayne out of doors. Near nature. Real nature, not some sculpted garden. A setting more God-made than man-made. Sometimes I thought he saw that, but then of late, lights and linen tablecloths clouded his thinking.

But he did all this for me, and there was something tender about that. No doubt this was what marriage counselors called compromise.

"What does Mr. Oakley grow or raise?" I asked, doing little more than making conversation now, not expecting him to be able to tell a Hereford from a Holstein.

"Soybeans, cotton, and Black Angus," he said. "He has a small herd on grass-fed fields and sells per custom orders locally. Gets way more per pound but turns out to be rather expensive to manage. In addition, he handles Herefords, buying calves and selling them off the standard way."

I reared back with a polite sneer. "Why, Mr. Easton, you almost sound country."

"Grew up on a farm in Fairfield County," he said. "Left for college and never went back. Not my plan, but my parents sold off while I was gone when Dad's health soured. They needed the money to afford my education. After Dad died, Mom combined what was left over from the sale with Dad's life insurance money, and she opened a restaurant. She amazed us all. She's the founder of Miss Lily's Table."

My eyes widened. Mr. Easton was full of surprises. The chain of seven restaurants flaunted home-cooking and stayed busy morning, noon, and night. The owner was Lily Mae Chessereau Easton. "You get her to cater these gigs of yours?"

"Sometimes," he said, grinning at the chance to brag.

Wayne had told me not to interrogate, but I didn't see our conversation as such. Not totally, anyway. Easton's softened mood had opened him up, and I'd be remiss not to capitalize on whatever he knew.

For instance, if Oakley wasn't financially comfortable, the question was why. "How's Mr. Oakley's operation going?" I'd sort of asked before, but we were buds now.

"Funny you ask."

I let him think so.

"His herd is down by a lot."

To that I perked. Oakley had been the man to follow, the small farmer to emulate. "He had that many calves fatted up?"

"No. He sold young and old. I came out here one evening last week to start setting up for the next day's wedding and saw trailers hauling them off. He looked about to cry."

"Did you—"

"Ask?"

I surmised the answer. "Too rude?"

"Yes, ma'am."

Of course. This man's manners were carefully groomed.

The sun had lowered enough to look gorgeous coming through the open end of the barn, and for a second, I imagined it beaming through organza and flowers. This might be the place to think of such things, but it was no longer the time. "Did he have family?"

Easton shook his head. "Sadly, no. The community was his family. Wife died of cancer ten years ago. They never had children."

The all-familiar bootheels on wood caught my ear. "They have a few more questions for you guys," Wayne said.

"The heater's in here," I replied, too cozy to want to return outside into the chill, too sad to see where this farmer spent his last moment, much less gaze upon that gray, puffy carcass.

"The body's wrapped up, about to be taken away," he said, as if he read my mind.

I looked to Mr. Easton. "Want to help me get my boots back on?"

"Be happy to, Ms. Slade," and he reached for the left as I pried on my right.

As we left, I spotted my tracks on the floor. "Oh, I'm so sorry, Mr. Easton. I can come back and clean that up."

Easton waved me off. "Not a problem."

On the way out the door, Wayne let Easton go on ahead. "Did I just enter the Twilight Zone?"

I latched hold of his arm when the air hit us and gave me a shiver. "Just making small talk. And if it's not too late, how about asking Mr. Easton to dinner with us?"

Wayne's puzzled look tickled me, but this was too somber a time to laugh with him. "So, is this venue the one?" he asked.

"Haven't even thought about that," I said, about the time a deputy greeted us and asked more of his questions.

Oakley's death was curious. Whether murder, suicide, or natural causes, I craved to hear more about the organization of this farm . . . and the motives of its owner. Good farmers didn't go down easily, and this one would've been one of the last in this county to give up.

Chapter 3

WE RETURNED to the pond, the potential scene of the crime. From the chitchat, these first responders knew the deceased. Every one of them. I held no opinion on what happened, not having seen much other than the back of the bobbing body. And like most coroners, this one refused to guess before having the science in order. Unlike most coroners, this coroner was a woman.

While she spoke to Wayne and Easton, I looked her up. Board certi-fied in Medicolegal Death Investigation. One of eight so certified in the state. One of only a couple hundred in the nation. She lived on this side of the county, which explained how she arrived so soon.

"Oh, Troy," she said, her gaze following the others as they removed the body bag to the van. Then to me, "One of the most likeable guys you'd ever meet. A lot of widows in these parts would've hooked up with him, but he never seemed to get over Karen."

"Was he having money problems?" I asked. Working with a govern-ment agency that loaned out money and kept up with the agricultural economy, financial issues popped to the front of my mind.

Wayne bumped me.

The coroner shook her head, then corrected herself. "I'm not telling you no. Just saying it's not my place to talk about the dead prematurely. Honestly, I don't understand farming and couldn't tell you a thing about what he did for a living. He was highly respected, though. He mentored the up-and-coming farmers best he could."

"You knew him enough to chat with him?"

"Sure. We all did." Her gaze moved past me and settled on her van. "Anyway, gotta go. I'm sure the deputies can handle anything else."

Didn't take long for them to be convinced we'd literally stumbled upon Oakley and were innocent of any misdeeds. They were almost as eager to leave as we were.

Easton stood to the side, deflated. Not a positive way to end his day, and he'd about given up on clinching a contract with us. I almost caved to getting married at one of his venues, just to make him feel better.

"Not quite sure how to handle my bookings now," he said, as we walked each other to our vehicles. "I doubt I'm legally able to book here anymore." He smiled at us. "Sorry. I'm not so sure the bride was sold anyway."

"I want to get married in my backyard," I said. "I live on the lake."

Everyone for a sixty-mile radius understood that to mean Lake Murray. "You're lucky to be on the lake," he said. "How big a place?"

"Three acres."

He turned to Wayne. "Something to consider, sir. I'd still be happy to plan it for you."

To which Wayne gave an anemic smile. "Appreciate you taking time with us today." He neither accepted nor declined the offer. Then he remembered my request. "Would you like to get dinner with us? I hate parting on this note."

But Easton declined. "Not up to much more than going home and kicking back in pajama pants with a Scotch while watching old Turner Classic movies. There's a Gregory Peck marathon this weekend."

That sounded lonely. "Again, sorry," I said, as he got into his car.

He just smiled, shut the door, and left.

Seated in Wayne's sedan, we waited as Easton drove off in his white Audi—just as snappy looking as its driver. Once he was gone, we sat there taking in the day, unsure where to go from here. The farm seemed to have lost its soul.

"Mark this one off the list," I said, trying to lighten the moment.

"Slade," Wayne said, ending on a sigh. "Have I been wasting my time?"

The question gave my heart a lurch. "As in . . .?"

"*Where* to get married. We were letting the *when* be dictated by the where, but if you never choose a place, we never choose a date. Am I wasting my time?"

That question could apply to anything from the *where* to the *if*, as in *if* we should do this. "You're not having cold feet, are you?"

He shrugged. "That ought to be my question to you, don't you think?"

I felt like a heel. "Let's just find a notary and get married, Wayne, and avoid all this pomp and circumstance. I'm too old to wear white."

"Not sure age has anything to do with wearing white," he said.

"Hey, we're living together. We've been married before. We've dated for three years. Don't you think—"

With each word he seemed to lose steam.

"I understand you want your pretty wedding," I said.

"I understand you don't want a church," he tacked on.

"You want flowers and a preacher."

"And you want outdoors."

We weren't opposites here, just different. "Plan whatever you like, and I'll show up," I said.

His face clouded over. "What a hollow compromise. I'm doing this for you. If you don't like it, I am indeed wasting my time."

I stopped responding, fearful of how much deeper I would dig this hole.

"What would your mother want for you?" he asked.

"She lost that say-so when I pushed out the first baby, I believe. She's more pragmatic than I am. She'd be happy enough if we showed up one Sunday for dinner wearing rings and sporting the same name without her having had to make the trip."

"That brings up another issue," he said. "Are you taking my name?"

"Hadn't given that a second thought. Guess I can." My name was Carolina Slade, with Slade being my maiden name. I'd dropped the old married name of Bridges. I'd always been called Slade and expected to continue doing the same. Frankly, I didn't care.

"Do you have any preference for anything about this union?"

His frustration stung. I'd been too flippant. The cowboy's romantic side was eager to make me his in a manner that would have people wishing they were us. I could read it in his eyes.

But I didn't care what people thought. I only wanted Wayne forever and a day. From his perspective, I wasn't doing enough to make him feel needed.

"Tell you what," I started, being careful with each word. "Pick your three favorite places, outside of a church, and I'll select one. Sound like a plan?" That gave him a purpose with direction, and this way maybe I wasn't so uncooperative. He was trying so hard to make me happy, and he loved me so damn much. How could I show my love in return?

But he squinted, as if there were a catch.

"No catch," I said.

"Let me think on it."

"Fine. Now let me call Monroe."

"Not our case," Wayne reminded.

"But one of our farmers," I reminded him back. "Might not be yours to investigate, but he's ours to be concerned over what he might owe us, and what might happen to the farm."

He nodded. He didn't get involved in the business of the farms and what programs they'd received through Agriculture. That was more my show. His was restricted to the criminal side of anybody under that umbrella.

Monroe answered on the third ring. It was after eight, shadows darkening, which meant my boss and longtime friend was at home.

"What's wrong, Slade?" were the first words out of his mouth.

"Who says anything is wrong?"

"First, it's you calling. Second, it's after hours. You've been on leave, which gave me some sense of peace, but with you calling so late, there's got to be a *but*. Thought you were selecting where to get hitched."

"Well," and I looked at Wayne, who pulled out of the drive and drove on. He knew Monroe, and from his smirk, he could predict the dialog on the other end. "We sort of encountered a dead body on one of the farms," I said.

"What were you doing on a farm?"

"It had a wedding package. We were touring it. I found a body in the pond behind the wedding barn."

There was a long pause. "Of course you did."

"I have a nose for such things."

"You have a cloud over your head, and I get sucked into your storm. By you calling me, I assume it's one of ours?"

"Yes, it is. I've never dealt with him, but I've heard of him. Troy Oakley."

Monroe hesitated. "Wow. I'm so sad to hear that. Heart attack? Accident?"

"Coroner says she won't know until she gets him on her table. I didn't see anything obvious. Wayne didn't either." I looked to Wayne to make sure, and he affirmed with a nod.

"Wayne also says not our case, so I'm just informing you because he's a borrower of our programs."

Wayne affirmed again.

"And you want to look into it anyway," Monroe said.

"That's right."

"What Wayne says goes."

"Monroe, listen—"

"See you in the office on Monday." He hung up.

His agreeing with Wayne didn't bother me. I could change his mind if I needed to. What did bother me was the fact Oakley sold off more than the usual number of cattle then died. Just seemed awfully coincidental. Unless he was in over his head with something, sold off the cattle for it, then did himself in.

I doubted he'd accidentally fall into the pond and drown, so, yes, I had concerns.

Financial trouble? Wrong partner? A stumble into something nefarious?

"Quit trying to make this a crime," Wayne said, as we finally reached Chapin. He passed through town on Highway 76 and turned right onto Old Lexington Road. I lived east of the small town that seemed to be exploding of late with newcomers. Luckily, I lived on a small road impervious to infiltration by the vinyl boxed housing developments. Didn't mean I didn't have to wade through them to reach home, though. If I didn't live on a lake, I'd have sold my place and found fifty acres in the middle of nowhere . . . like Newberry County.

Wayne turned into the long asphalt drive. My home sported three hundred feet of water frontage along three acres, a rarity now, afforded by my dead husband's life insurance payout. He'd made plans to do me in and collect my insurance, having not calculated on his partner taking him out first. He hadn't thought to remove me as beneficiary on his policy. *Voilà*, I had money for a new house.

My debt-free residence made me appear wealthier than I was, and granted, having no mortgage freed up my respectable, but far from lucrative, federal salary. Also, my sister lived with us, taking care of the kids, and Wayne had moved in about four months ago, sweetening the pot. In other words, we did okay.

Between his job and mine, we did do more than okay but, with our schedules, just couldn't seem to get married after a year-long engagement. People were beginning to think one or the other of us had second thoughts, but they weren't aware of the multiple cases we'd pursued, to include one that murdered his partner. Our caseload hadn't cooperated with our lives. Not that we were overly concerned with what others believed. God knows I'd done the opposite of what others thought I should do since my very first case when I learned the hard way that following the rules to the letter didn't always work as promised.

As we approached the house, I noticed the extra car at the top of my drive. "What's Kaye doing here?" I asked, seeing the small Toyota. My sister had one as well, same model but older and just a few shades in color difference. Kaye was Wayne's younger sister.

"She didn't text, so don't know," he said, trying not to show concern. His sister had been in and out of trouble for over a decade, only settling down in the last couple of years, if one could call being assistant manager to a nudist resort *settling down*. It had taken arresting his ex-wife and her cohorts to free Kaye from a life of running from drug traffickers, but her past still kept Wayne somewhat on edge. Showing up out of the blue was what she used to do when she was in trouble in the old days.

Cleaned up and no longer looking over her shoulder, however, Kaye had turned into a fairly cool gal. She adored her older brother and had become tight friends with my sister, with one oddball gravitating to the other. The kids and I had grown into a family of six in a matter of months, and we'd grown closer when Wayne moved in.

We walked inside to the smell of chicken and dumplings. I could cook, but my sister was better at it. Since she had neither an income nor a husband anymore, I let her cover rent with her babysitting, cooking, and cleaning services. I couldn't hold a candle to my baby sister Allegra Jo Slade's sass and quirkiness. Ally Jo was ten times the hoot I was, and my kids loved her to pieces, choosing her side ninety percent of the time in a war of wills.

"Anything left to eat?" I hollered, seeing the kitchen mostly cleaned up.

My sister came from around the bar from the direction of the family room. "Thought y'all would be having some romantic dinner to celebrate your wedding selection."

Wayne didn't say anything, instead went to the refrigerator hunting for leftovers.

"It's in the oven, Cowboy," Ally said. "Didn't want it chilled until I knew for sure if you'd want any."

He thumped her on the head in thanks. "Maybe I ought to marry *you*."

Clasping her hands, Ally batted her makeup-less eyes. "Oooh, you only have to ask me once, sweet cheeks, and I'd make it happen tomorrow." The unspoken being that I'd stalled longer than the average woman would for this six-foot-two, scruffy-bearded guy in boots. The badge and gun only made him hotter, in my opinion, and Ally agreed a thousand percent. Why he chose me was anybody's guess, but we meshed tight enough.

Ally raised a brow. "What happened?"

"We couldn't decide," I said. "Plus, we found a body at the last one. Deleted that place off the list."

With a look of WTF, Ally stretched out hands to the side, then dropped them, shaking her head. "Only you." She took the pot from Wayne and shooed him out of the kitchen so she could fix two bowls for us. "Murder or suicide?"

"No idea," I said. "Keep it low. Where are the kids?"

She tipped her head toward the family room where Wayne had already made his way. "They're in there."

Zack, my precocious ten-year-old, perched on the edge of a sofa cushion, watching Kaye and Ivy, my fifteen-year-old daughter, practicing something in the middle of the floor. The Xbox was frozen, telling me this was something special enough to distract my son, too.

Kaye stood in the open, the coffee table pushed out of the way. "Come toward me, as close as you can get. Brush by but try not to let me feel you."

Ivy feigned nonchalance in an over-the-top manner and strutted past her aunt-to-be, only Kaye grabbed her wrist. "I felt you coming a mile away, little girl. Try again."

I wandered in. "What are y'all doing?"

Wayne answered instead. "I know what she's doing, and I'm not sure I like it."

Zack, unable to keep a secret if his life depended on it, enlightened us. "We're learning how a pickpocket person works." He laughed. "The more we know, the less we will be pickpocketed. Aunt Kaye says so."

Ally peered silently around the bar, probably glad she wasn't the culprit misleading the minors this time, though she'd done her fair share of schooling them on topics they weren't old enough to learn. Like enlightening Ivy on the proper etiquette for a visitor to a nudist resort, not that I'd let my daughter accompany her aunt there. And helping Zack climb trees using steps nailed into them and designed by my sister. I'd come home from work one day with Zack twenty feet high . . . straddling branches and aiming down with a BB gun at makeshift targets as if he were a rodeo rider with no hands on a trick pony. I'd previously laid down the law on shooting animals, so instead, he'd built animal-shaped targets in the woods. Wayne had piled swells of dirt behind them as added insurance against BBs going astray into some passerby's windshield.

Ally had tried to say *boys will be boys* once or twice in her early days with us, but I'd tongue-lashed her such that she hadn't tried since, though Zack could be the talisman for such a campaign.

"So now my children are pickpockets," I said, jaw tight. "I'm waiting to hear the justification on this, Miss Kaye."

Wayne slid onto the sofa beside Zack, returning my son's punch with one of his own. "Have to agree with your mom this time."

"Best to be prepared," Kaye said, not standing down. We appreciated she was way more worldly than the rest of us, having socialized with some incredibly malevolent sorts for years before Wayne brought her back to earth amongst the normal folk. Regardless, I wasn't fond of those skills finding their way under my roof.

"And what brought this up?" I asked, then changed my mind in light of the composition of the audience. "Or we can talk about this later?"

Timely, Ally spoke over us. "Food's ready."

At the kitchen table, Kaye joined us. But not the kids. They knew they'd be bored by adult conversations about adult topics that nine times out of ten they wouldn't appreciate. Ivy disappeared into her room, phone at the ready to converse with girlfriends until bedtime, and Zack donned headphones and resumed a game, his mind disappearing into another universe.

Ally fixed herself a coffee while the rest of us blew on dumplings hot enough to scald feathers off a hen. "Used a little more pepper than usual," she warned.

I didn't care about pepper. I cared about her letting Kaye teach bad habits to my kids.

"I need your help," Kaye said, finally cooling her meal enough to eat.

Wayne put his spoon down. I absentmindedly stirred my dumplings, waiting.

"I've got a pickpocket at the resort," she said.

I laughed. "How does a pickpocket pick people without pockets?"

"They home in on the new visitors," she said. "You've been there. You know how it works. We have a bathroom shower area where guests disrobe and put their things in a locker. The regulars have a regimen. Some stay on site, some in campers, some drive in from the region. Those who regularly visit know to bring minimal belongings. We've had several cars broken into. Graffiti on the guardhouse." She sighed. "I can't take much of this."

"A member or staff?" I asked.

Kaye shrugged.

"But first-timers don't always disrobe." I was rather proud of knowing a little something about nudists resorts. I had paid attention when I'd visited Kaye. "I can't see new visitors bumping up against nudists. There's a big *ewww* factor involved."

"Pickpocketing isn't about bumping into people," Kaye said. "It's about deception and stealth, mainly distraction. Most never realize they've been violated. And you definitely can't say we're lacking in distraction."

"Thought y'all locked those cubicles and kept a master in the office," Wayne said. "Since nobody has pockets to tuck a key in."

"That's right. There's a key in the office, and I keep a key on me. We've been toying with upgrading to keycards, but just haven't had the funds to do it with. But that's not where the theft is happening, Bubba. It's definitely pickpocketing off the people still wearing their pockets."

"If you don't mind my asking, where do you keep the key on you?" Wayne asked.

Kaye gave her brother an impish grin. "Around my neck, brother. In plain sight."

He hadn't been out there. Once upon a time when we were attempting to find Kaye who'd hidden out at the nudist resort, Ally and I had been forced to go native in order to fit in. Wasn't fond of the experience, but I complied. The memory popped up in a dream every now and then. Nude at work, nude in class, nude in the grocery store. . . .

"What are they taking?" he asked.

"Wallets mostly."

Who chose to pickpocket a nudist colony other than someone who was regular enough to recognize the naïveté of its visitors? They had to be a member or employee. "You need a security guard."

Kaye dove into her cooled dumplings. After a couple bites, she nodded. "You're right. We can't afford it, though. They can barely afford me, giving me room and board in lieu of half my pay. I won't get rich, but I can't complain. I like the place. It's private."

The rest of us were just happy she had a regular address and no criminals hunting her down.

We focused on our bowls, each, I'm sure, with a different image of how a pickpocket worked in such a facility.

"I'm asking a favor, sweet brother," she finally said.

He hesitated, looking out from under hunkered brows, unsure what to expect.

"I was hoping you'd play security guard for a couple weeks. We've been hit six times in two weeks, so I was figuring another two weeks would be enough time for them to do so again."

Ally busted out laughing, and admittedly, I fought to hold back the bite of dumplings in my mouth.

"So, I'm to hang around a lot of buck-naked people for two weeks and watch for a thief." He scowled at the concept. "I'd stick out like a sore thumb amidst all that bare skin. Your thief wouldn't do a thing, Kaye. What are the odds that the one time I come as a visitor, your pickpocket would appear."

"True. You can only get away with being a visitor once or twice. After that, you'd sort of be *undercover*," she said.

Ally and I busted out laughing.

"Without cover," I said, laughing until tears rolled down my face.

The panic in Wayne's expression made us laugh long enough for our bowls of dumplings to go cold.

Then it hit me. "This is September, people. I sense some . . . shrivel, and fewer guests."

"On the contrary. It's an active time of year. There's an indoor heated pool. And parties. We play trick or treat in October, sponsor a fall 5K run, serve Thanksgiving, and there's always Christmas. Holiday decorating happens on more than a door or a tree."

"There you go, Cowboy," I said, wiping my cheeks with a napkin. "Find a costume."

"Oh, you can't cover up. You just decorate," Kays said.

"Okay . . . just wear a utility belt and sunglasses and go as a cop," I said. "Nobody will be the wiser."

Ally got this impish expression. "Remember that single guys are rarely visitors, and people are more likely to see them as pervs. Wayne can't go alone. Have the victims all been couples?"

"They have. Except one lone woman. No single men," Kaye replied.

The laughter got raucous, the kids peeking out, wondering how much we'd had to drink. I, however, wasn't as amused as everyone else, who were all now laughing at me.

Chapter 4

I WOKE THE next morning and the morning after from dreams of being caught naked, much like the nightmares I'd endured two years ago, but the mortification of them dissipated at the fresh vision of Wayne doing security for Kaye's nudists. I'd go through the humiliation over again to watch that.

He hadn't agreed, but he hadn't refused either. His sister was important to him, and she didn't ask favors often.

With the weekends being prime time for guests and members, and the weather a balmy seventy-five degrees, Kaye returned to the resort with the question still in the air. That's how South Carolina temperatures rolled. A firepit in the backyard one evening and floating on the lake the following afternoon.

On Sunday Wayne and I revisited wedding possibilities, only he didn't have quite the same pep in his words. I needed to fall in love with something then cut him loose to put the deal together. Time to tell him I loved fall colors, lemon cake, and Southern rock to dance to. I drew the line at a formal dress, preferring something reusable that I could wear for someone else's wedding. I wasn't good at shopping for clothes, however, and I had nobody in my wheelhouse I trusted to just go pick some out for me.

Ally was redneck to her core. Kaye . . . I was just afraid of what she'd choose. My friend Savvy would insist on sucking all of me in with shapewear, if not with the dress itself, certainly chosen to tighten body parts and amplify sex appeal. Then there was Callie Morgan, the police chief of Edisto Beach. Her fashion choices traveled closer to my ways with maybe a hint more style. Yes, she was the best choice for help—practical taste I could live with.

Sunday was her only day off, though. I wasn't disturbing that, so I made a note to call her tomorrow and see what she recommended.

I'd walked my three acres three times this weekend, envisioning chairs here, music there, a cake under a canopy to avoid the acorns falling like rain like they did this time of year. Not much cost. Easy to plan, but

Wayne wasn't in sync with that, and I suspected because it was my place, not his. He might not even be aware of his hesitation or the why. Surely there had to be something relatively easy that wasn't a cheap social hall or an ostentatious cathedral.

Today we weren't talking very smoothly about the matter, and I'd left him to his thoughts, afraid to cross him. The trick was giving in without his realizing I was waving the white flag. I should've just picked one of the ones we'd already seen. Too late to do that now.

With the day so warm, I'd found my way to the back porch, coffee in hand and playing Wordle on my phone while reliving Troy Oakley's tragedy. I looked forward to talking it out with Monroe at work in the morning, with hope he'd let me dabble into details, interview the locals, take a gander into financials. We needed the coroner's report, though. That sort of dictated where I should focus. The guy could've had cancer, OD'ed on pills, and blacked out on the pond bank as he spent his last moments surveying the land he loved.

"I already solved it in three tries," Ally said, plopping into the black metal rocker beside me.

I paused; my finger hovered over my fifth guess on Wordle. She'd seen my puzzle effort over my shoulder when she stepped outside.

I put the phone down and leaned back, sock feet on another chair. We were grilling chicken this afternoon, and the grill master had gone to Food Lion for last-minute items. Between Ally loving the kitchen and Wayne the grill, my food responsibilities fell more along the line of choosing where we ate out once a week.

"You better make up your damn mind on this wedding crap, Carolina." She was the one and only person allowed to call me that. To use *Slade* was to reference me by her last name, too, and she said it felt weird. My parents used *Carolina* since they gave it to me, but they lived a hundred miles south. I didn't have to listen to them every day.

"I know," I said through a sigh. "I'd just go to the courthouse, but he won't have it, and I'm not spending a fortune in lace. Give me a picnic. Or better, let's have a cocktail party with heavy hors d'oeuvres. This time of year there's so many football games that it's almost a sin to do it on a Saturday anyway unless we did a football theme."

"Jesus, listen to you. You did all the right things with your wedding with Alan."

"*Right things* don't make a marriage right. I was divorcing him, re-member. Plus, he was trying to murder me. Don't even go there."

"The right things about the wedding y'all had. It was correct in every way except for those maroon dresses. I hated those things."

She was right about the bridesmaids' dresses. What was I thinking?

"You love Wayne to pieces, and he's crazy about you, so what's the deal?"

I couldn't say. I wanted this done and over with for reasons I couldn't pin down. "Don't like being the center of attention?" I said, ending with a question mark.

"People are beginning to talk."

"Want me to elaborate on how little I care about that?"

"No, I already know, but think of Wayne. Maybe the talk matters to him."

I didn't want to argue that. She might be right.

"I'm waiting for him to come up with another list," I said.

"Why not give *him* a list? It might show that you're serious about what makes him happy."

"I really just want to elope, Ally. What's wrong with that?"

She leaned in. "What's wrong with telling the world you love this man? What are you afraid of?"

But I couldn't say. Honest to God, I just couldn't say. Standing in front of people, putting on airs . . . that just wasn't me. Wayne was me. Why did I have to have a show to prove it?

I WAS MORE THAN ready to head to work on Monday. My role as Special Projects Representative, short for administrative and civil investigator within the auspices of the US Department of Agriculture, ran hot and cold. I had no arrest authority. When things pivoted to criminal, I turned the cases over to the Inspector General's office, i.e., Wayne Largo in these parts. Sometimes we worked in tandem, and other times the IG took cases from me after I'd worked my ass off on them. Wayne hated those cases since I hated being left out of the loop, making for difficult evenings at home.

Wrongdoing didn't happen on a schedule, so my days could be irregular, as could his. My assignments came directly from the hand of the State Director. In our state, that was Monroe Prevatte.

"Mr. Prevatte wanted to see you as soon as you came in," Whitney said from her desk outside my office. Blond and in her late twenties, she was ridiculously loyal and had been known to hide issues from Monroe in times of my misdeeds . . . or hidden agendas. Monroe could never see or entertain the different possibilities I found fascinating in every case, but neither did I think on his political plane. I thought politics often clouded his judgment. He thought my judgment ran rather one-dimensional . . . in whatever direction gave me a case to investigate.

Monroe liked to play life safe and with certainty. His methodical work ethic and dedication to the agency had merited him the State Director's assignment a couple years ago. I'd have never guessed he'd be decent at the job since there was so much partisan manipulation involved. Such an appointee rarely made it through more than four years since they were selected at the pleasure of the President. As in the United States President. As soon as those politics changed, so did the State Directors across the nation because politics meant selective budgets, favored communities, and appeasing constituents. One party did it one way. The other party did it another. Leaders like Monroe walked a tightrope between treating clients properly while appeasing senators and representatives, in addition to keeping the governor from getting pissed. No two politicians ever danced the same dance.

You couldn't pay me enough money to operate in those circles.

Monroe's secretary gave me the all clear. I knocked and then poked my head in the doorway. "You ready for me?"

He smiled. Of course, Monroe always welcomed me warmly. He'd have married me if Wayne hadn't cut in line.

His office was immaculate as were his clothes. Prematurely white, he held bragging rights for that thick, wavy head of hair though he wasn't quite fifty. Before assuming his current role, he dressed Lowcountry-ish with nice loafers or deck shoes, no socks outside the office. His wardrobe was khaki and button-ups. Tanned year round. Handsome.

Now, however, he sported a couple of Armani suits as well as other designers I couldn't name . . . again, those circles so foreign to me. I bought the best Dillard's had to offer off the rack, preferably during seasonal changes, on sale. Used to be JC Penny before they closed.

His ties popped. I mean seriously drew the eye down to them, and don't get me started on the shoes. He became higher-caliber eye candy when he started earning the money to pay for "sartorial elegance."

"Close the door," he said, which I was already making moves to do. It was the only way we could drop the pretense and have straight talk without the constraints of rank. Some of my assignments didn't need to be heard by others in the lobby, either.

"You look nice," I said, pulling out the chair closest to his desk, again admiring the tie. A jewel-toned turquoise against a soft gray shirt and a medium-gray suit. Made his white hair just gleam, especially in a dark room full of cherry and mahogany.

"You look nice, too," he said, that warm smile traveling up into blue eyes that carried most of his charisma. I knew him from over a decade of having worked alongside him, our roles equal. But the man was shy, letting his looks and his work ethic speak for him.

"Whitney didn't mention anything pending," I said. "Something new on the table?"

"Tell me about Troy Oakley," he said, not sitting back in his chair like he normally did in our meetings. Instead, he had cleared the papers off his blotter and rested elbows on it, those blue eyes staring into me like I hadn't told him everything. I was stymied since I wasn't holding anything back.

"We . . . I found him floating in a small pond on his farm," I said. "The coroner took him away. Nobody mentioned foul play or anything to indicate scandal. Why no *How's the wedding coming?* or *Did you make any progress on the plans?* Why's the dead farmer the first topic of the day when on the phone you said listen to Wayne and let it be?"

He looked down at his notepad. His notetaking habit was worse than mine in that he wrote while he talked. In his job, documentation could weigh for or against you, but he couldn't help himself. Notes beat trying to remember, and both of us had gained the advantage in court cases when our contemporaneous notes outweighed someone else's foggy memory.

I could tell from my vantage that he'd covered three quarters of a page in scribbles, but I couldn't make out the words.

"Received a call from the CDM in Newberry," he said, using our abbreviation for Community Development Manager, the managers who ran our programs on the ground in each county. I'd been one for years in one of the busier counties, before my first case put my name on the map and promoted me to Columbia. "He'd heard about Mr. Oakley," Monroe said, "and was rather beside himself."

Al Blanchard was the CDM. South Carolina had forty-six counties, and some CDMs oversaw several counties, so most of us could rattle off the names of each office's manager.

CDMs were close to their farmers. They were often neighbors, sitting next to each other in church, the local diner, the bars, and at ballgames. "Al would know Oakley well," I said. "Death of a close acquaintance could be rather shocking."

"Al was off Friday," Monroe continued. "He returned this morning to a message on voicemail from Oakley." He looked down to his pad and read.

This is Troy. We need to meet about a problem I'm having. Similar to that boy over in Saluda. Call me when you get this. Don't care if it's the weekend or the middle of the night. You know I talk anytime. We need to shine daylight on these sons of bitches.

That last part. . . . "Damn."

"Can you call the coroner?" Monroe asked. "Ask the status of that autopsy? There's no family, so I doubt anyone's going to get in your way."

"I could try," I said, almost as stunned at the phone recording as I was at Monroe asking me to pursue something that was clearly suited to Wayne's expertise. My authority stopped when anything had the least scent of malfeasance or criminal behavior. This request would walk a mighty fine line. Oakley's type of demise could dictate whether this case was mine or Wayne's. Given the deceased's recent contact with our office, however, we'd more than likely go into the investigation as a joint venture. And Monroe's clout could let the coroner know how important this was.

"You would carry more weight," I suggested. "They might not listen to me."

"Use your wiles," he said.

Now I was really intrigued. This was Monroe ordering me to be myself in my most creative manner, something he normally had nightmares over.

"Can you talk to the CDM today?" he said, his way of nicely giving me an order.

"I can."

Monroe seemed nervous. Surely there was more. He continued to reread his notes in silence. I gave him about half a minute then couldn't stand it anymore. "What aren't you telling me?"

"He's the fifth farmer we've had die in as many months," he said. "Once you speak with CDM Blanchard, speak with these others." He handed me a typed list of the farmers' names, addresses, and the CDMs and counties associated with each.

People died. Farmers as a whole weren't young—half of them were over sixty-five, and the job took its toll. The rate of suicide amongst farmers was over three times higher than the general population. But depression wasn't a subject farmers spoke of. Mental illness held a stronger stigma in rural communities, where there was little education and even less mental health care.

Back in my earlier years, I'd had a twenty-four-year-old heir to a farm blow his brains out with a shotgun. A friggin' shotgun. The guy happened to be over six feet with arms long enough to pull the trigger. His father, who'd just handed over the farm to the boy on his birthday, was never the same. In the end, the family determined the son had watched his father struggle for the kid's whole life, and he hadn't wanted that life for himself. The father died five years later, still farming. Stewards of the soil didn't give up the ghost easily.

"I told the Newberry CDM you'd be in touch today," Monroe added.

Guess I had my orders. "Anything specific you want me to delve into?"

"All the normal questions about why and how this happened. Then you'll talk to the others. We need to know if this is coincidentally suicide or something nefarious. We don't need agriculture smeared in this state with the stench of a crime wave or rumors we lean on our farmers so heavily as to send them to their grave."

Ah, the press. The image. Thus was the role of the State Director. "Who's leaning on you, Monroe?"

"Only one chief of staff thus far," he said, sarcasm clear. "But there will be more if we don't find a logical answer for five deaths. Three of these farmers were small, but two were larger and well known, one in Lexington County, which means more attention."

"Why is this your problem? Why not the Inspector General's office? We aren't the only agency in a farmer's life."

"Be glad it is us. What if our people are looking the other way or, worse, pressured them?"

The *or worse* angle took me aback. It shouldn't have. A chunk of my job was internal investigations of our own employees. You couldn't point fingers at the criminals if your people's hands were dirty.

He continued. "I'd rather call in the IG on a problem I'd already studied rather than them come to me with a problem I wasn't aware of and consider us to blame. Be discreet. Please. I cannot express that enough."

I understood. If a situation had gotten out of control under Monroe's nose, he could be released from his position. But he also couldn't be caught personally digging around without giving this situation even more attention.

"I get it, Monroe. Trust me," I said. But the question had to be asked since he had reservations about IG involvement. "Can I at least use Wayne as a sounding board?"

Monroe might have pined over me when Wayne won my hand, but he highly respected the lawman's investigative abilities. I rarely pursued a case without running it by Wayne anyway. Who declined access to free legal expertise?

"I'd rather you didn't," he said.

That was a big fat no.

"May I ask why?"

"The fewer people who get involved the better. We should've studied this three deaths ago, if you ask me."

"Why didn't you?"

"Some looked like accidents so one wasn't an issue. Two gave me a second thought, but not long. Three, however, gave me pause; accident or suicide, the number was higher than the norm."

He'd put his head in the sand instead of calling me, but he was correct in that accidents happened on farms. But five deaths in as many months was rather disturbing, and now it had grown into a problem.

I'd do my research. I'd do my interviews. I'd have to function on the down-low, though, and not make any sort of sweeping entrance into these county offices. When I entered an office, people tightened up, suspecting an investigation right off the bat. Word spread. Files were cleaned up. My appearance usually meant something had gone wrong or someone had done wrong, and I was the person appointed to take out the trash and put things back to right.

This time required prudent and measured behavior. I could hear Wayne or Ally laughing about those words used in any sort of description of me, but the simple fact Monroe had pleaded with me to handle this for him and had begged discretion in the asking told me to do my best.

Not the best time—right before a wedding—to omit Wayne, but Monroe and I went way back. He wouldn't ask me to leave out the lawman unless there was a dire need to do so.

Chapter 5

I CLOSED MY office door. Whitney had become accustomed to this being my notice to tell visitors I was not in or already had an appointment. She understood I wanted time to think, research, or phone folks, usually on a case others need not be aware of.

Putting slow piano jazz as background noise, I turned to stare out my window. With my office ten floors up in the Strom Thurmond Federal Building, its view covered many of Columbia's landmarks. The Trinity Episcopal Cathedral, the gold dome of the Greek Orthodox Church, the Colonial Life Arena, and—while I could spot where it should be but couldn't see from so high up—the Tunnel Vision Mural. Up this high, the wind made the state and American flags whip furiously over the State House today. The building's flag display was now minus the infamous Confederate flag from a decade ago.

It wasn't a bad city, and not big and sprawling like so many other capitals. We were a small state, but our history made us loud and rowdy while at the same time filled with Southern charm. South Carolina was a juxtaposition of the redneck and the genteel, never shying away from a fight but respecting manners and tradition.

Many people wanted to live here now, but once they arrived, having chosen the state for the weather and low property taxes, they struggled to understand the culture they'd chosen was not like the one they'd left. In my area, they gravitated to Lake Murray where real estate values had exploded. People bought boats when they'd never driven one before, and forty-year-olds partied on their new water like they'd been released on spring break. We loved our lake, but Wayne and I tried to avoid boat time on the weekends due to the wild array of the inexperienced and the increased danger on the water. We never boated at night unless we simply floated in our cove, chilling.

Change and growth could be depressing, but such were the facts of life. Made me grateful for what I had, for sure. The family, the home on the lake . . . Wayne.

This growth also had the developers both in-state and out, clamoring to fill it up with houses to satiate the appetites of these newcomers. Most of these developers walked all over the old residents, and quality of life was beginning to suffer in pockets where insufficient infrastructure existed.

Putting the problems of growth from my mind, I turned around in my swivel chair and laid out the paper Monroe handed over, the list of five farmers and their respective CDMs. I doubted there was another copy.

Five farmers in four counties. From the most recent to the oldest, Troy Oakley in Newberry. Dewey Anderson in Saluda. Homer Brooks in Lexington. T.J. Candleman in Lexington as well. Merle Lester in Richland. Their deaths were separated by anywhere from two to six weeks.

Unsettling.

Newberry, Saluda, Lexington, and Richland were Midlands counties that touched the fifty-five-thousand-acre Lake Murray. Prime counties for development. If the subject wasn't such a tender issue for me, I might not have noticed so quickly.

Other facts jumped out at me. The CDM for Lexington had two farmers on the list. And the CDM named Delores Bell, in Richland, hadn't been in her office more than a couple weeks before she had a dead farmer. Might be nothing. Bell had also been the CDM in Craven County. Without even the announcement of an opening, Monroe had transferred the woman to Richland. Transfers were made for three reasons: promotion, demotion, or lateral transfer for personal reasons. Bell wasn't promoted, and she wasn't demoted. A personal reason could be anything from family issues to fatigue of the same county or the county's politics turning against her. Impropriety sometimes came into play.

CDMs didn't rotate counties often. Their feet usually were planted in agriculture of their own, or they were related to it. I'd have to talk to Bell about the death in nearby Richland County, and I'd get a better feel for her transfer at that time. Might not matter, but one never knew until one asked.

Without more details, the farmers' names melted together, though. Time for face-to-face interactions and conversations to embed them in my head. With Bell being the CDM for the local county, the manager with the oldest death on the list, and possessing an office just a few floors down from mine in the building where I worked, my gut told me to start with her, but Monroe's exact order was to meet with CDM Blanchard in Newberry first.

If Monroe was this disturbed and wanted me to delve into this, I would, and I would also adjust my process according to his orders. I didn't like the don't-tell-Wayne part though.

More than once Monroe had cringed at my coloring outside the lines when we worked alongside each other. We often asked for forgiveness after the fact, or rather I pushed him into doing something for which I took the heat afterward.

This Monroe, however—in spite of the politicians urging him to operate more loosely, to hunt for loopholes—fought even harder to play by the book. Politics and stringent regulations rarely mixed; however, Monroe walked the line swearing to make a difference in what agriculture meant to this state.

Politics corrupted, altered, and misled the best-laid plans, but my job was to protect Monroe. I would do my utmost best in the field. He would run interference on the political side.

Start with Oakley, he'd said, but I doubted the coroner had worked this weekend on the body. My call might offer some catalyst to move Oakley closer to the top of the coroner's list, though.

My call went to an administrative type who put me through to a technical type who stated the coroner had not gotten to Mr. Oakley. I left my name and number and a small message that would connect dots. I was the lady present where they found Mr. Oakley, and now I was the lady with Agriculture interested in what happened to one of its constituents. In rural counties, agriculture still meant something.

Time to search online and agency records for each of the farmers. To confirm how they died, first. Next, to get a feel of who they were in the public's eye, what type of enterprise they managed, and what family they may have left behind. Were their farms still active or were they being dissolved? Were they reputable or was the community breathing a sigh of relief they no longer caused trouble?

The average soul didn't realize the butt-in-the-chair work that came with investigations. Whether federal, state, or private, an investigator pounded a keyboard before they left the office and spoke with persons of interest. Then strategically sorting that new human-driven data would indicate how to choose the next interviewee or offer insight as to how to approach the whole investigation, how to slip up on the situation before anyone knew what was coming.

Slip up sounded dodgy, but everyone lied. Investigators did their homework, approached the parties involved, and fed them as few facts as possible, just enough to prompt an unadulterated response. Enough to lead them to talk but not enough to hint as to what was right to say. Many investigators played dumb. Some got forceful, which, in both Wayne's and my experiences, didn't work nearly as well. Cooperation both ways usually took you further.

I had learned how to investigate through trial by fire, in my original bribery ordeal with Wayne. Having come up through the agency's ranks as a CDM, understanding the job on the ground gave me the background I needed to run an investigation differently and sometimes smarter than conventional approaches taken by the folks who didn't bleed agriculture. Internal folks often thought—mistakenly—that I played at being an investigator. I didn't *play* at anything. I tried to read them within minutes of sitting across the table from them, sussing out the appropriate levers and triggers needed to get the task done.

Underestimating me only armed me better.

Around one, past a lunch which came and went with my nose deep in research, Whitney tapped on my door. "Mr. Prevatte wants you in his office. Says he needs an update."

"What? He just gave me this assignment this morning."

She shrugged, knowing she'd had no choice but to interrupt me for the boss's request. She could always pick her battles, never wasted time justifying the obvious and never hesitating. If the agency had the budget, I swear I'd groom her to be my assistant investigator, but Agriculture's coffers went toward farmers and rural communities, not the staff. Plus, unofficially, they banked on my connection with Wayne a lot of times. Free skilled labor.

Again, I tapped on Monroe's door. This time I held the pad of paper with all the scribbles. "You called?"

"Yea, close the door. What did the coroner say?"

I pulled out my same chair and sat. "Monroe, I called, but she hasn't seen to him yet. I'll wait a day or two. I want her cooperating, not dreading my calls."

He fell back in his chair, disappointed. "What the heck have you been doing all this time? What other cases do you have? I told you this was priority, or at least thought I did. When I hand you something I want it done pronto, Slade."

I fought not to get angry at the friend and reminded myself to respect the boss. "Been studying the farmers. How they died. What the press said about it. How the obituaries read. Looking up relatives I'll need to meet. Going through our records of what these farmers specialized in."

He listened, but he seemed to only half hear me.

"I was about to do something similar with the CDMs," I said. "I'll start with CDM Blanchard in Newberry, then I'm considering seeing CDM Bell in Richland, because she has the oldest case. I'd also like to hear why she transferred from Craven County."

"Why?"

"Why . . . what?"

"Why does it matter why she left Craven?"

"Goes to frame of mind. Tells me more about what she's made of when it comes to how she dealt with the farmer that died in her county."

"Most committed suicide," he said. "That might save you some trouble."

No, his words saved me zilch. I'd validate everything, regardless of who told me. We didn't know how Oakley died anyway, so when he said most, that meant . . . three? Versus the five he said before?

"Are you sure?" I asked. Neither he nor the agency needed the reputation of pushing farmers over the edge, so why assume they had?

"I wouldn't mention suicide if it wasn't a serious possibility, Ms. Slade."

Uh oh. He'd used *Ms.*

"Has anyone looked into this before me?"

"You're my only investigator, so who else would you be referring to?"

"Anyone, Monroe. You, CDMs, whoever."

He sure was pissy.

Once again, I explained myself. I'd determine what the farmers were like and had in common. How solvent were they? What trouble, financial or otherwise, were they in? How was their health?

"All the deaths occurred in counties around Lake Murray," I said. "These counties aren't noted for particularly large farms, but they could still have problems. I'll check all of them the best I can."

Monroe focused on me, as if his future was in my hands, and I was puzzled as to what I wasn't being told.

"If I had Wayne, we could make better time," I said. This situation could quickly escalate and be out of my hands if even one death was questionable. For me to pursue this case without Wayne's knowledge only made for potential ill feelings later. Passing a case over to him once it got out of hand could make my professional as well as home life exponentially worse. Guess there was a reason couples didn't work together.

"Let me ask him, please."

Monroe almost looked like he might.

"No," he finally said. "I'm not handing the IG a case that could wind up being nothing. He has to report to his bosses, and then there's a record for God-knows-who to read." He released a long breath. "I'm sorry. We've done investigations together, Slade, and I realize your brain processes don't mesh with mine in these things."

Finally, agreement.

"Go do as I've asked. Report to me daily. And don't tell Wayne."

He was losing sleep over this but not telling me really what *this* was. "What are you specifically hunting, Monroe? I'll focus more on that. Otherwise, I'm entering this cold and uninformed."

His pause was intense. "I need you doing this cold, Slade. It's how the politicians will receive it, and I don't want you accused of following my direction to cover up."

He was ordering me how and when to do this investigation, while telling me to do so independently and open-minded. I hoped this yoyo didn't continue, because it could be interpreted as a cover-up. Especially if he was holding back information I needed for context.

Was Monroe more anxious about unearthing the wrong, or distressed over how to diffuse the blowback? Or was I uncovering what needed to be covered up?

Five deaths in that small of a population, in the same profession. The number of suicides wasn't like we had the equivalent of a stock market crash and despair, but this was an outlandishly high figure in a short period of time.

Surely Monroe hadn't become the stereotypical bureaucrat he'd sworn never to become. I didn't know what I'd do if he had. He'd been my best bud for years.

BACK IN MY OFFICE, I scanned the skyline again, more concerned about Monroe than the view. To make him happy, I needed to head to the field and see people. I felt almost handcuffed.

Taking a half hour first, I researched CDM Blanchard's personnel file then did a Google search for whatever he'd done that merited online mention. Same age, give or take, as his farmer, Troy Oakley. Blanchard had worked as CDM in Newberry for a couple of years, having assumed the role after the death of the woman before him. He was born there and had lived in the Prosperity zip code for years. Degree from Clemson, like most of us. Specialty Ag Econ. He fished. Sure he did. He lived a mile from a lake noted for its striped bass tournaments.

His wife taught in the nearby middle school. Children were grown, none of them living in the county that I could tell. He was a member of the Rotary Club and the Zion United Methodist Church.

Better to meet him elsewhere than in his office. That would stir up the rumor mill within the ranks. He didn't need that.

I called. "Hey, Al, this is Carolina Slade. Any chance we can meet about that phone call from your farmer?"

"When and where?" Good. He was eager.

We agreed on a small restaurant in Prosperity, farther from his Newberry office but closer to his home and mine since I had no intention of coming back to the office afterwards.

While gathering my notes and taking a second to jot questions in my phone, my cell rang in my hands, giving me a start.

Then I did a double take. Since when did my mother call during work? Daddy, yes. Mom, never. She always claimed she had to overcompensate for Daddy's indulgences. He was responsible for all our flaws. She taught us our assets.

Ally and I were pretty damn independent. That was most assuredly the asset apple that fell from Mom's tree.

"Mom? Everything okay?"

Thoughts of Daddy having a heart attack, or someone being diagnosed with cancer ripped through me. Mom never called to ask, *How's your day?* or *I was just thinking of you.*

"I just spoke with your sister."

God help me, I wondered who called whom first. It mattered. It really mattered. So help me God, if my sister called my mother . . . and that call prompted this one. . . .

"Oh yeah? How's she doing?" I asked, thoughts of Ally drawing out my snark like a magnet in a bowl of paper clips.

"Don't be that way," Mom said. "She was concerned about you. I asked questions, and now I know."

Still no mention of who called whom. "Now you know what?"

"You're having cold feet, Carolina. I swear, I kept my mouth shut with that last husband of yours when I should've told you what I thought. A total waste of humanity. You find a man who's decent and you can't figure out where or when to get married? It's not like you don't know how to do this, girl. And you don't need a thirty-thousand-dollar ordeal to make it happen."

"Mom—"

I couldn't get a word in edgewise as she relived all the negatives of my past husband. "Mom, please . . ."

A knock sounded on the door, but the party didn't wait for me to issue an invitation.

"Hey, Monroe."

I'd muted my side of the conversation. She kept talking, still on speaker.

He frowned at the treatment I'd given whoever was on the end of the call.

"My mother," I explained, to which he frowned deeper, because Monroe treated his mother like a princess. That's because she was five foot nothing, as adorable as mothers come, and doting. Mine came closer to being a Russian tsarina. Coincidentally, her name was Catherine . . . like the Great.

"Slade? Did you hear me? Tell me you didn't just put me on hold."

Quickly, I replied. "No. Sorry, Mom. Just had someone walk into my office."

"Well, tell them you're busy. I only have about ten minutes before I have places to be."

The creases eased out of Monroe's forehead and prompted a smile.

"Mom, it's my boss. Mind if I talk to you later?" I didn't dare tell her she'd been on speaker.

"Just promise me you'll nail down this venue ASAP, Carolina. Don't string this man out. You won't get another chance. You already have a job that I don't feel is good for you or the children. And I don't care if he hears me."

"Will call you later, Mom."

"When you do, make sure you have the details. Unless you don't want us in attendance, but honestly, if you showed up married one day, that would make me happy enough."

She hung up faster than I could.

I was rather mortified that Monroe heard that, but I neither explained nor apologized. Instead I asked, "May I help you?"

He started to say something, a mild smirk on his face, then didn't, and I appreciated his casting aside whatever it was. I preferred straight talk right now, and not about my personal life.

"I hear you're going to see Al Blanchard," he said.

"Wow, that was quick."

"He's nervous and wanted to make sure I sent you."

"Why else would I be going?"

When I called someone in the state, it was universally understood that I represented the State Director in ferreting details of a difficult situation, thus, the reason people feared me coming. No amount of sweet talking and polite manners disguised what I did for a living, and that was checking out things that had seemingly gone wrong that the State Director wanted to correct.

"Him calling makes me wonder more about him, boss."

But Monroe shook his head. "He's feeling guilty about not returning the call before Oakley died. That's all."

Few people double-checked behind me, and fewer still had the balls to call the head boss and ask him to validate my visit.

Then, God help me, I had a thought I wish I hadn't.

What if Al Blanchard called Monroe to get his story straight? What if he asked the State Director what he was supposed to say? There was an RDM between the CDM and the State Director. A regional manager, one of five in the state, handled a pod of county offices to add a layer between the ground dealings and the state office. Monroe hadn't the time to manage problems at the county level. Suddenly I wondered where was the RDM in all this? Why jump the chain of command and call Monroe?

All employees were taught by the Office of the Inspector General, Wayne's people, that when offered a bribe, to contact the OIG itself and skip the chain of command. But there was nothing in the books about a CDM skipping the RDM about a farmer dying.

Monroe had just become more of a person of interest to me.

"Is he okay with me coming?" I asked.

"Absolutely," Monroe said. "Glad you're going out there today. Glad to see you getting started."

Like I hadn't done a thing until that phone call. Another erroneous assumption that investigators only worked face-to-face without preliminary analysis.

I hoped this fresh awkwardness wasn't reflecting off me, but he seemed only focused and satisfied that I was *on the job.*

Great. Now I lived on two time clock countdowns. One to investigate these farmers' deaths while discreetly studying if my boss had gone awry. A second to get married. Work squeezed me on one side and personal on the other, and with my best friend Monroe in the middle of both. I had nowhere to vent frustration. And I'd been banned from discussing this with Wayne.

Damn, now was as good a time as any to make that call to Edisto Beach.

Chapter 6

ONCE ON THE road to Newberry, I put in the call to Edisto. With it being the middle of the afternoon, I almost didn't expect my friend to answer.

"Oh, my goodness, you're the last person I expected to hear from today," she said, and sounded genuinely pleased. Refreshing compared to the rest of my day.

"You're not busy, are you?" I asked.

As the police chief of Edisto Beach, Callie Jean Morgan managed a force of six officers, and her job ran hot and cold just like mine. In September it was still warm enough in South Carolina for the rentals to be fairly full. I wasn't sure how consumed she would be in her day considering crime in her neck of the woods was dependent upon tourist volume.

"Nothing going on much," she said. "You married yet?"

My theme song of late. "Can't find a place."

"You waited too long. The good locations book up a year in advance. The offer to come down here still stands. I have a beach, plantations, river fronts. How many people are you expecting? A hundred? More?"

For a Carolina girl, I was not a fan of the coast. Although visually satisfying—and I didn't even mind the bugs and snakes, which were in abundance with the humidity and jungle warmth—nobody put me on or in dark water. Though my home offered a fantastic view of Lake Murray, you didn't catch me wading its edges, and I cringed at the thought of looking over the side of a boat. Nobody should trust swimming in water that creatures bigger than you called home. Lake Murray had catfish practically my height and I wouldn't wade there, so why the hell would I be caught dead in the ocean?

"You don't have to swim to get married," Callie said, fully aware of my phobia.

"I'd just as soon not be reminded of it." Time to change subjects. "Headed out on a new case. Before I get there, I need to ask a favor.

Would you mind buying my wedding dress for me? You're the only one I trust not to screw it up."

I wondered if I'd dropped the call for a moment. "You there?"

"To be honest, I've only bought one in my life, and it was a suit. Then there's shoes and underthings."

"Sounds perfect," I said, almost feeling I could tick one box in this wedding escapade.

"Wait a minute. I didn't say I'd do it."

"You're turning down the bride-to-be?"

"I'm not your size, Slade. How am I supposed to know if it fits? And what is the color scheme?"

True that. She was barely five feet tall, and I had forty pounds on her. "Color? Something neutral that you think matches me. I believe I'm supposed to be a fall color gal. Sound right? Make it something I can wear again, not collect dust in the back of a closet."

A chuckle through the line promptly turned into laughter. "Outdoor or indoor wedding?"

"I don't know. Let's go with outdoor."

More laughter. "I bet Wayne is having a fit with you."

"As are my mother, my sister, and my future sister-in-law. My daughter gave me suggestions, but I'm not sure a fifteen-year-old represents my tastes."

"Might make Ivy happy if you chose something she recommended, even if it's only the bouquet."

"Bouquet?"

"Gotta carry something."

"I actually don't, but if she wants to pick out flowers, I'll pass her to Wayne. He's the one wanting all this."

"What's wrong with your backyard overlooking the lake?" Callie asked, and I wanted to drive all the way to Edisto and hug her neck for the suggestion.

"One would think," I said, and the *humph* on the other end told me she didn't want to get in the middle of whatever I was in the middle of. But if she bought this dress for me, I could prove to Wayne I was making positive strides.

"Charleston would have better stuff than Columbia, right?"

"Not necessarily, but I haven't shopped for something like that for years. But sure. I'll do it. What's my deadline?"

"A week?"

"Tight but doable. Sizes?"

"Dress ten. Shoes seven and a half. No spike heels but no old-lady clunk heels either. Nothing open toed."

"Jewelry?"

Oh, hadn't thought of that. "If you see something that would match that you can't say no to, get it. If you don't, I'll make do." Might ask my mother. Or I might ask my sister to ask my mother. That was even better.

I'd left the interstate and traveled Highway 76, headed through Chapin which meant I was ten or twelve miles from Prosperity and the restaurant where CDM Blanchard suggested we meet. Not much time.

"What's your case?" Callie asked, and I really wished she were with me for this interview.

My training focused on internal, mostly administrative, investigations. Range certifications and service weapon quick-draws were not required. Not what I did. Not who I was. But though not a gun-toting, badge-wielding law enforcement officer, I'd gathered more than the average experience in some dangerous investigations alongside Wayne, with the scars to prove it. More than most of his counterparts, to be honest.

As he was so quick to say, however, I stumbled more than stalked. Tripped through rather than sculpted my path. He had said I possessed somewhat of an instinct, but he would quickly tack on a disclaimer about not having enough real training to be safe. And he might have used the phrase *stupid lucky* a time or two.

In other words, I could be a hazard.

But he still used me and backed me up when needed. Only this time I couldn't rely on him for backup.

I approached Little Mountain and lifted my foot off the gas. The small town wasn't fond of speeders.

Callie raised her voice. "Hello? You're still there because I can hear road noise."

"Listen," I said, not sure where to start. I had maybe six miles and a hell of a story to tell, and I still hadn't interviewed the first witness.

"There have been five farmer deaths in as many months. All in counties that front Lake Murray. Our managers ought to be familiar with each one, so it falls in my lap to interview them and ensure nothing's shady or out of sorts."

"No patterns, you mean," Callie added.

"Right. But it's early days. My boss is worried about the department's image."

"Rightfully so."

"And he doesn't want Wayne involved."

"Oh, ho," she said, voice rising on the end. "Because he loses control if Wayne finds anything."

She nailed it. Guess training did matter. Edisto underestimated Callie, forgetting she had fifteen years of time as a decorated detective with Boston PD before she crashed and burned and came home to the South Carolina coast. Edisto was a cakewalk compared to what she'd seen and done before.

"Well, you know how to do interviews," Callie said. "Wish you had Wayne, but you can handle this."

"I'm stuck in the middle."

"Between . . .?"

"Monroe and Wayne. Work and home. Can't decide how to tell Wayne."

"Thought you were told not to."

"Yeah, but I have to at least tell him something. We discuss work, even if we aren't working together. And this one he's sort of familiar with." I quickly told her about finding Troy Oakley.

"Hmm."

"Yeah. Hmm. You ever kept work secrets from Mark?" Her live-in guy was retired SLED, the state's investigative division. He'd seen action. He still carried a bullet in his leg. They hadn't tied the knot either, but they didn't seem to care.

"Don't take this wrong," Callie started.

"I'm braced. Go ahead."

"Mark and I are both law enforcement. The dynamic is different. We aren't as much into the details because they go unsaid. They're understood. And he's fairly decent about waiting until I'm willing to talk. Then there's the peace he has of knowing I can handle myself."

Bingo. There it was.

"Don't get pouty on me," Callie continued. "Wayne worries about you, and he should. Hearing what you're doing is a way for him to judge your safety. You're not armed. You're not . . ."

"Trained?"

I'd entered the town of Prosperity with my dander trying to rise. I slowed and pulled to the side to finish our conversation. Roma's Pizza was on Main Street in the town limits, a town that took three blinks to travel through. I'd hoped for Hawg Heaven Bar-be-cue on the other side of the limits, but they only opened Thursday through Sunday. A lot of Southern barbecue places did. But I rarely turned down pizza, too.

"I'm almost there, Callie. Gotta run in a sec."

"Slade," she said, "right now, just get your head straight for your interview. How well do you know this man?"

Though he'd lived there for ages, Al had been in charge only two years. "Enough to speak to him at meetings," I said, releasing a cleansing breath, doing what she said. "It isn't a formal interview. It's getting a feel for things. He received a call from his dead farmer, and he's asked to be heard. He's clearing his conscience, Monroe says."

"Passing the responsibility on to someone else," she said. "Good. Go enjoy dinner with him. Make the man feel better while learning where to take it from here. What are you eating?"

"We're in a mom-and-pop pizza place. Roma's." She'd calmed me down, and I eased back onto the main street. "They have great stromboli. Hey, thanks for the offer to dress shop."

"No promises on the results," she said. "I'm not a high-fashion guru by any measure."

"Which makes you qualified to handle *my* wardrobe. Thanks for listening." I parked the car but wasn't anxious to end the call.

"Go with your gut, not your heart, Slade. Don't get in your way. Trust me. I know."

She did. She had enough past for any ten people in law enforcement, but she remained sane. We clicked, and I counted myself awfully lucky we did.

"One more item . . . make sure you think hard before telling Wayne. And how you tell him if you do. If he gets a whiff of anything that connects with cases he already has, and you kept it secret, it appears you chose to protect Monroe."

I hadn't thought of that. "Thanks. I'll see where this goes. We're in baby stages here."

Parked on Main Street, my spot was two doors down from the restaurant entrance, and I was five minutes early. I couldn't tell if my guy was here or not.

I texted our home group, consisting of Wayne, Ally, and me. *Meeting an employee at Roma's House of Pizza in Prosperity. Don't plan dinner for me. Shouldn't be late since I'm close.*

Then I grabbed my notepad, set my phone to mute, and left the car. Inside, the lights weren't lowered with it being four thirty in the afternoon, making Al Blanchard easy to spot. He sat toward the back at a table for four with an oilcloth cover, a glass of water before him.

He rose when I approached. "Haven't seen you in a while," he said, holding out a chair. I accepted and scooted up to my place.

"No. And to think we live so near each other." That's how monstrous the lake was. You could live on it and not see the majority of its inhabitants for years. "Have you ordered?"

He shook his head. "Waiting for you. I usually get Williams' Special."

I scanned the menu for it.

"Chicken spaghetti with all sorts of stuff on it," he said.

Tipping my head, I hunted for something else. The ads might say Greek and Italian, but at the bottom of this menu I noted Jambalaya. Guess any restaurant cooked what they were good at. I held a weakness for pizza, but when the waitress arrived, I ordered the Special Stromboli. Partly because I liked a loaded pizza, and this was close to it. Partly because the menu warned it took fifteen minutes to cook, and I wanted the time to talk to Blanchard.

He declined a beer, and from the look of the waitress, that was unusual.

"Are we okay meeting here?" I asked.

"Yeah. This is my place. I've met community members, farmers, and the preacher here, in addition to my wife. They know it's where I do business as well as socialize."

Good. Being female often made meeting a man in these small towns a brow-raiser.

I'd written out the farmer's phone message Monroe dictated to me, and now seemed as good a time as any to bring it out. "Mr. Prevatte gave me the message that Troy left for you." I turned it around for him to read. "Is this right?"

He read it, lips moving a little, then nodded. "Can't believe I didn't check my calls on Friday. I normally do, but we had a weekend with family, and I just . . . I felt . . ."

"You don't have to explain why you didn't return a call on the weekend, Al. Now. What's this mean here?" I pointed to, *We need to meet about a problem I'm having. Similar to that boy over in Saluda.*

"What's the problem in Saluda?" I asked.

Peering at me like I was mentally shortchanged, he went from puzzled to concerned.

"Hey," I began, but stopped speaking and moved back as the waitress set down my iced tea. I leaned back in once she left. "People may think I keep up with everything in the state, but I don't. Not unless it merits my kind of attention. We both understand what that means. If you think my questions are because I'm uninformed, that's fine. Educate me. I'm all ears, and my ears might as well be the State Director's." I added Splenda to my tea and waited for him to catch me up to whatever was going on.

"A borrower of ours in Saluda hanged himself," he said. "About two weeks ago."

Wow. I tried to remember what I was doing around then to not be aware of that. I'd been in Atlanta, at a federal training class put on by the Inspector General for the handful of people like me across the country. The death must not have been a shock or someone would've notified me. Still, I was a little put out that nobody had.

"What did that farmer have in common with Oakley?" I asked. Newberry and Saluda Counties butted each other, with their eastern corners having the lake in common. Not a lot of lake, but enough to make that acreage valuable.

"They knew each other," he said. "Not tight friends, but close enough. Both managed cattle and the standard beans and corn, sometimes cotton. Dewey Anderson lived across the Saluda County line, between Big Mans Marina and Highway 378."

I did logistics. Oakley and Anderson resided maybe fifteen miles apart, both a stone's throw from water frontage. As a matter of fact, one had to cross a piece of the lake to get from one to the other.

"So what's the problem?"

"Pardon?"

"The phone message. Oakley said you needed to meet about a *problem*. Similar to Anderson's."

He gave me a slow shrug. "I'm not completely sure. I would've run over to his place and asked him in person, except . . ."

We both understood why that hadn't happened.

"Was Oakley having money problems?"

"Not really. I mean, he wasn't rolling in it, but I wasn't sending collection letters on his government loans, either. A year ago, he started that wedding rental, and I've seen several farmers do that and make enough on the side to balance the ledger. No idea what he meant when he referenced being similar to Anderson other than what they farmed. I can't speak to Anderson's situation, though. You'd have to contact Cathy Risher, the CDM over there."

We covered Oakley's farming history, family history, and social history. Blanchard swore up and down the man was solid, and he refused to believe the farmer did himself in. He preferred to believe in an accident. "I'd accept murder over suicide," he said.

He couldn't say much about Anderson, again referring me to the Saluda CDM. "He was going through a divorce, I heard."

For an hour, he described the plusses of Oakley's life. His volunteerism. He'd even run for county council once, losing by a handful of votes, deciding afterwards that he couldn't afford the money it took to run again. Instead, he raised his hand for Agriculture's County Committee. He held a position in his church and served as local president of the Rotary Club. "He always said politics sucked you dry or stole your soul," Al said. "He retreated to activities that allowed him to give back without costing him. Said the community was his family since he had none of his own."

"He had nobody?" I found that such an anomaly. Most farmers came from farming and at least lined up someone in a will to assume the land, whether they farmed it or not. I'd never fathomed them having nobody. "Not even charity?"

He shrugged. "My guidance and advice, as you well know, doesn't involve requiring a will or asking what was in one, but we did discuss what he might do. Troy was in a quandary about how to bequeath his place, but he mentioned leaving the farm to group of young farmers if they could form a legal coop group. He liked working with young farmers."

"I heard." The coroner had said the same at the Oakley place. "Would be nice to know if they ironed out those legal wrinkles before he died."

Again, a shrug. "Guess we'll find out soon enough, won't we?"

"You know his attorney?"

"Sure. Same as mine. In Newberry."

Good. "Think you could ask him who might be the beneficiary?" The attorney might speak more openly to a familiar. The request from me meant a federal investigation, and maybe that didn't need to be spread so quickly at this point in time.

He agreed to and to follow through with me. From there on, we spoke of Oakley's sense of humor, his good will, and how much he'd loved his wife Karen, who died of kidney failure at the age of forty-eight almost a decade ago. Talk gravitated toward the politics of who we worked for, then finally, as we completed our meal, we resorted to the weather. For Blanchard claiming to be so familiar with Oakley, he told me little more than the average citizen might be aware of. He just wanted to get this phone call and guilt off his chest, but he'd also given me just enough intel on Saluda County to pique my interest to head there next.

He reached for the ticket as we cleaned our plates. "We ought to do this more often."

I went for my wallet. "You don't have to buy my meal."

But he waved the waitress to the table and quickly handed over the ticket and his credit card. "No, you took the effort to see me right away, and accommodated me by meeting away from the office. You're a good egg, Slade."

I cocked my head, grinning. "Despite what others say?"

He laughed. "Some, but surely you realize that trash talk comes with your job description. You're like the IRS auditor appearing on your doorstep unannounced."

"Fair enough," I said, enjoying this man's personality. "Seriously, though. If you ever want to do this with our spouses, give me a call."

"Spouse? You tied the knot?" he asked.

That was news that would've traveled fast . . . if it had actually happened.

"Still engaged," I said, showing the ring. "We've been canvassing places to do the deed." I took a second to ponder whether to say the next, concluding there was nothing secret about a simple fact. "I was the one who found Oakley. His farm was on our list of places to rent."

CDM Blanchard leaned back as if I had COVID. Most people don't experience stumbling upon a body. "Bet you can't get that image out of your head."

I'd seen worse, but he didn't need to hear about the others. "It does stick with you."

He leaned in. "I've heard you've seen some incredible things in that crazy job of yours."

I bit back the words, *You wanna see my scars?*

"People get testy when money's involved, or when they get backed into a corner," I said instead.

"Anything get dangerous?"

"A few times."

He waited for me to share. Took him a moment to realize I wasn't going to. "I hear you've snagged a real IG agent for a fiancé," he said instead. "Bet that makes for some bizarre talk around the dinner table."

Over these couple of years of crime solving, I'd learned our employees fell into two categories when it came to what I did. The first consisted of people like Blanchard, the curious. Like with cops or soldiers who'd served on the front line, they wanted war stories, the grittier the better. The second category—consisting of most of our employees—felt I was too radioactive to dare ask for details, much less invite to dinner.

I preferred the former. The more you shared with them, the more they shared with you, and it didn't take much from me to have them falling all over themselves in their aim to please. Blanchard had shed light on a few things, like Oakley knowing the neighboring county's farmer who'd committed suicide. So, as a reward for him, I pulled out a couple of lightweight stories, disguising some facts. That made him happy.

Then we were done.

My original plan would've been to talk to Delores Bell, the CDM in the first county on the list of counties that experienced farmer deaths. The oldest case. Monroe changed that. Now, however, after listening to Blanchard, I wanted to run over to Saluda, but it was too late today. Dare I drop in unannounced in the morning? Cruel to shock employees that way. Nope. Best to leave a voicemail this evening then show up on the heels of their arrival to the office in the AM. I didn't want this CDM across the table from me to have time to call that CDM across the water and coordinate stories.

Chapter 7

A YEAR'S WORTH of cases ago, I'd learned to keep a keen watch when I drove, front and back. A time or two I hadn't kept myself aware of my surroundings, and someone had caught me unawares. Experience and Wayne's teachings had changed my habits.

CDM Blanchard hadn't had time to call anyone and probably wouldn't, but I was on a new case, making me watch my mirrors.

Blanchard had enlightened me about Oakley in Newberry and then Anderson in Saluda. I hadn't told him about my orders to check out all five farmers and their CDMS, nor that our mutual boss was unnerved by the deaths. Those in the field had to remain confident in management. Blanchard would've freaked at being a name in an investigation and then spread nervous gossip across the state—probably in the short seconds it'd take for me to make it to the car—thanks to texting. This way I had done nothing more than calm a CDMs nerves about one of his client's missed phone calls.

Oakley's death should make the evening news, maybe online media. I did a search and found nothing, but news spread more slowly in the country, and oftentimes, city people didn't care what happened *out there.*

I'd searched for "farmer" and "suicide" with a broader search across the state and found nothing. Obituaries on the other three deaths didn't mention cause. Not a lot of press. It would take a very nosy reporter with nothing else on their plate to do a search about farmers' deaths or the stress of agriculture. Maybe Monroe and his political peers wanted to get ahead of something that wasn't there.

That was my job, too. To see what a problem *might* be, even if the problem didn't materialize.

Before leaving my parking space in front of Roma's House of Pizza, I had called the Saluda office, my message saying little more than I'd see them in the morning. Someone would have to be diligent if they bothered checking voicemail after hours from home on the off chance they'd need to be informed of something before arriving for work. Then I called Whitney's voicemail and told her I'd be out tomorrow and if Mr.

Prevatte inquired as to my whereabouts, tell him I was on the case.

Word spread in fiber-optic speed these days via so many methods, with nobody caring how accurate it was. To most of these people, I was walking trouble when in fact I was trying to keep trouble from kicking in our doors.

I rather liked that image of my work. Wished others saw my job like I did.

Thanks to meeting in Prosperity, my trip home didn't take twenty minutes, a welcome change. The eruption of homes in the small towns of South Carolina came from everyone wanting a piece of fabled Southern hospitality, and the infusion of souls made travel between Columbia and home an hour-long ordeal. We were being forced into the rat race that people moving in had wanted to leave behind and only brought with them, unfortunately. The locals were finding the change hard to swallow.

Pulling up in my driveway a few minutes later, my hopes of absorbing the peace and relaxation of the lake flew out the window at the sight of my son scrambling out of the branches of a hickory tree and dropping at least eight feet from a lower limb. God help me, I was going to have to build the kid a treehouse to keep him from breaking a collarbone. He'd already broken an arm from bouncing on furniture three years ago, and that was within arm's length of his babysitting grandfather. The kid was walking trouble . . . more so than his mom was accused of being.

I parked my truck with a lurch and leaped out. "Zackory Thomas Bridges! Get your butt in the house. Now!"

I'd lost sight of him but heard him scrambling through the trees and pine bark beds to my right. Then, somehow, he reappeared to my left, and I'd never seen him make that thirty-yard sprint and get past me.

"What is it, Mom?" he asked, hands empty, when I was sure he'd held something, likely the BB gun, when I spotted him on my way in.

"Where's the gun?"

"What gun?"

But I could read this boy. He'd find some way this evening to backtrack and collect his toy. How long would it be before I wouldn't be able to read those sky-blue eyes? Already he walked the line between charismatic and problematic like a pro.

I pointed to the house. "Just get inside."

Following him in, I called for my sister. "Ally Jo?" The kitchen smelled like chicken pot pie. I adored chicken pot pie, but I was too stuffed with stromboli to eat again. Or so I told myself.

My sister's voice sounded in the hallway leading from Ivy's room. "What did I do now?"

"I caught Zack two stories up in a tree again."

"Zack?" Ally hollered.

He peered out from behind the sofa, where he'd slipped in to grab the Xbox remote. "Yes, ma'am?"

Ally put her hand out. Zack relinquished the controller. "The whole night," she said, and he didn't whine or ask for explanation.

He would've given me fits.

I wasn't sure whether to be glad to have Ally in my house or sad she had a firmer rein on him than I did. Wayne was even better with him, and for a quick nano-second, I regretted the fact the kids had no father. Then just as quickly, I reminded myself what he'd been like.

I started to ask where Wayne was, but remembered I'd come home early.

"I take it you've eaten?" Ally headed to the oven, taking out the most gorgeous, golden-crusted casserole dish. My stomach said no, but my nose went on high alert at the aromas of chicken, sage, rosemary, celery . . . and that buttery flaky crust.

Hands in mitts, she shifted the heavy cast-iron skillet from the oven to the glass topped range to let it cool. "Wayne's eating out with Kaye," she said, removing ceramic bowls from the top cabinets.

He hadn't told me. "That's good."

"She's trying to win him over about Clay River."

"Did she take him there?" He'd never been to the nudist resort. I would've died to have seen the lawman's expression.

She chuckled, no doubt having the same thought. Ally used to go there regularly, still did on occasion. "A drive-by maybe? Not sure." She doled out the pie, the scoops steaming just short of boiling. It would be a minute before the kids could eat.

"What were you doing in Prosperity?" Ally asked.

"Clandestine meeting with an employee about a dead farmer. Had a meat lover's stromboli for dinner."

She winced. "That's some heavy eating."

My belly agreed, but still . . . the smell of the pie in that skillet.

Ivy appeared out of nowhere, going to her aunt. "That smells really good."

"Ought to. I'm damn wonderful in the kitchen, little girl."

Ivy peered over at me, a weird grin on her face.

"What?" I asked, feeling my cheek, looking down at my blouse, wondering what part of dinner I might be wearing.

But instead of pointing out tomato sauce on my collar or cheese on my sleeve, Ivy held up my phone. "Gotcha," she said.

My hands immediately slapped against my pants pockets. Empty. "How did you—"

"I've been practicing," she said, handing the phone back.

My appetite waned as I forecasted calls from the school about my daughter pilfering items from book bags and coat pockets of students, or worse, teachers. My brain carried that thought further—into who would be impressed by such behavior—and flashed visions of black-leather jackets and chains. My daughter on the arm of a biker, or worse, driving a motorcycle. Skipping school. Robbing convenience stores.

I'd almost rather she smoked weed.

Ivy laughed witnessing her mother at a loss for words. "I haven't married the devil, Mom. It's nothing but a hobby."

"Collecting Pokémon cards is a hobby."

"Not to girls my age," she said, taking her bowl of pot pie to the table.

"Like pickpocketing is the current fad?"

She acted as if she didn't hear me.

The aroma brought Zack into the kitchen. "Did she get you, Mom?" he asked. "She's been practicing on me and Aunt Ally ever since we got home from school."

I stared laser holes into my sister's eye sockets.

Ally passed by me with Zack's dinner and his glass of milk. "She's good at it, Sis. Let her have this. It's totally innocent."

"Sure, yeah, that's reassuring." I fought the temptation to dish out my own bowl, poured a glass of water from the tap instead, and followed my family to the kitchen table.

Everyone dove in, while I analyzed my daughter through a different lens. Seemed she gave me all sorts of lenses to see her through these last two years. I didn't like it.

She giggled and hit her brother. "Mom's freaked."

Zack laughed. "Yeah."

"Maybe y'all ought to teach your mom how to do it," Ally said.

Did I want to learn? That seemed to endorse the craft, and was that what a mother should do? I imagined a principal listening to my daughter making excuses about being caught, her spouting back, "My mother does it."

Both kids stopped eating, studying me almost as hard as I studied them.

"Nah," Ivy finally said, returning her interest to her dinner. "I like being one up on her. Might come in handy one day."

If she'd been older, I might've called her something a mother shouldn't call a daughter.

DRESSED IN MY pajama pants and ZZ Top tee, I curled in the corner of my sectional sofa, making notes of how to address the CDM in Saluda tomorrow. On the way home I'd thought and thought about how to start the interview and never could get past the discomfort of meeting in the office, so I'd made another call and asked her to meet me at the Anderson farm around nine. That would allow her time to get both my calls, rearrange her day, and drive to the site.

The questions would be similar to those put to Al Blanchard. They might've spoken to each other, too, possibly during her drive to meet me. If I'd had a whisper of what was going on with this investigation as a CDM, I would have made that call if I were in her shoes.

The questions would be somewhat different, too. Who found the man? Had he acted peculiar before he hanged himself? Who remained on the farm and what were their intentions in continuing the operation? Had the coroner confirmed the farmer had hanged himself?

Speaking of coroners, I hoped the Newberry one would complete a lot of her work by the close of business today. She had my message, so hopefully she'd call me. If I had Wayne on my team, she'd be more likely to call him with him being Mr. Badge and all.

Next my mind jumped back to Oakley. CDM Blanchard would try the Newberry attorney in an attempt to learn who inherited the Oakley place. Someone had to feed the remaining cattle, and assumptions would be that chore belonged to the heir or the executor. In the Saluda case, there was at least a wife if the hanged farmer was in the throes of divorce.

Investigators usually started with the corpse and worked out from there, which I'd done in Newberry, physically and figuratively. For the Saluda case, I'd be forced to gather information from others.

Regular cops had handled these situations, mostly sheriff's deputies, few of them versed in agriculture other than knowing farmers grew stuff and owned a lot of land. Rural living was one thing. Agricultural living was another.

Each sheriff's office was limited to their county, too. They'd have no desire to delve further than their home turf, and nine times out of ten, they went with what looked obvious. If it looked like suicide, they'd go with it. If it looked like an accident, they'd go with that. Murder was the last resort in their decision tree.

Monroe Prevatte, however, had a bigger scope of responsibility—the entire state of South Carolina—and his responsibility became mine. We saw these deaths through a wider lens. Seeing more than the occasional incident enabled one to spot trends. In other words, I had a better chance at feeling an itch the deputies would not.

Part of that itch would be felt because I was subject-matter expert on these people. Farmers didn't start or cease farming on a whim. They were devoted.

While the death rate was higher than expected, I didn't believe I would've jumped to conclusions as quickly as Monroe did. But I didn't function amongst politicos, either.

The chime sounded as Wayne entered the house from the garage. With Mr. Lawman having moved in, we had acquired even more security than before. Alexa was not allowed, but motion sensors and cams were in place at all the strategic points of my three acres, to include down at the dock in case someone tried to steal or sabotage the boat. Never crossed my mind that someone would drive off with someone's boat, but once he installed the devices, I noticed three thefts on local social media.

"How'd it go with Kaye?" I made no mention of Clay River resort, but, honest to God, I wanted to ask if he'd gone commando or not. The funny thing about that place was the unexpectedness of feeling just as awkward being the only person in clothes as you would have felt naked. But one had to get naked at least once to understand.

"Stupidest damn place," he grumbled, passing me toward the bedroom.

Interesting. Either he'd taken the job or had agreed to. If he'd passed up the request, he would've come in with a kiss to my cheek and a routine browse through the kitchen to see what he'd missed for supper.

The bedroom door shut, then the bathroom door, and then I heard the little squeaky *whoosh* noise that happens when our shower is first turned on, which told me he'd gotten in to bathe.

Though we often shared our day's news while changing clothes or through the shower ritual, this time I let him be. Clearly, he wrestled with Kaye's situation. No point in interrupting via my presence, making him feel like he had to ask about my day, the day he wasn't supposed to know anything about. No point breaking Monroe's request to keep

Wayne in the dark barely twenty-four hours into the case.

I put away my notepad, hiding it beneath my purse and denim jacket in a chair by the bar. If he saw it, he'd ask what I was working on.

The shower went off quicker than expected. "Slade?" he hollered.

I went in, rehearsing what to say. Talk about my pickpocketing kids. Ask what he thought about Clay River. I entered the bathroom "What?"

"I forgot to get a towel. Can you hand me one?"

Heart pumping a little at the reprieve, I grabbed one from under the sink and handed it over the glass-walled shower. "Someone's distracted," I said.

"Hmmph," he grumbled, taking the towel, drying his hair with enough fury to pull it out by the roots. "You've been to that place?"

"You know I have, Wayne. Without clothes. Once."

He practically gnawed his words. "You know what she's asking me to do?"

Like I had no idea. "I can't imagine."

He released a fair share of expletives, and I listened for twenty minutes to what Kaye had asked of her big brother. He gave angles and alternatives, but the trouble was, for him to be involved, he had to disrobe, per his sister. And this man, standing nude before me, wasn't having it.

Finally, he had nothing left to dry and the whirlwind ceased. His hair combed back damp, clothes in his hand, he stopped cold. "I am so sorry," he said. "How was your day?"

I fought for the laugh not to sound forced. "Nothing like yours, for sure. Ally made chicken pot pie for dinner. Want me to fix you some?"

Chapter 8

THE NEXT MORNING Wayne left well before I did, since my first appointment was in the field. He kissed me goodbye without delving into more. My work for Monroe was still safe and secret.

"He sure was on a roll last night," Ally said as I fixed my travel thermos of coffee. The kids had already left for school. "Almost heard him through the wall."

"These walls are practically soundproof. Were you in Zack's room trying to listen?"

"Maybe."

"In his closet with a glass to the wall?"

"Give me some credit. I hear better than that."

"He's in a lather about his sister," I said, just now seeing that his sibling issue would keep him from inquiring much into my business.

Ally shook her head. "You two are total prudes not wanting to go to Clay River. Go help Kaye and be done with it. You've seen each other naked." She hesitated, smiling. "He might like it."

"No, he won't. I didn't like it when I went, hunting for Kaye that time."

I didn't understand the so-called freedom of displaying private parts of anatomy. My body came with shortfalls, but, admittedly, the bodies I'd seen at the resort had even more. Even in his late forties, however, Wayne's physique was worth the ogle, but that wasn't the point. He didn't want to put it on display. Ally didn't get that. Kaye most assuredly didn't get it, because she thought she'd died and gone to heaven living at that place.

After twisting on the thermos top, I grabbed my purse and notebook and headed to the garage. "It's between him and his sister. Don't get involved."

"Has he asked you to do this with him?" She'd chatter all the way to my car door. Some days I worried she didn't like being home alone.

"No, he hasn't." I tossed my purse and notebook on the passenger seat before sliding in.

"You heard Kaye," Ally said. "She needs him to be half of a couple. Single guys look like pervs."

I reached for my keys, trying not to pause at her truth. Wayne hadn't asked. A light came on—a day late, but still, it came on. He was just as indignant about me showing off my skin as much, probably more, than showing off his. Frankly, I wasn't so sure I wanted to share him with others, either.

And, to me, there was an ick factor to a brother going buff in front of his sister.

"Well, let them iron it out," I said, checking my phone. Five past eight. "Gotta go. GPS says it'll take me forty minutes to get to my appointment."

"Where are you going?" she asked.

A routine question, and it wasn't like she really wanted to know, but Ally wasn't known for keeping her mouth shut, and I didn't want some slip in front of Wayne later. "A farm out in the county," I said, not referencing which one. "Then back to the office. Ought to be home the regular time tonight."

That satisfied her. I backed out of the garage and headed to Saluda County.

GPS didn't direct me back through Prosperity, like I thought. Instead, it took me down St. Peter's Church Road, then Wheeland Road. With a heavy dose of déjà vu, I passed Troy Oakley's farm, trying to focus more on today's dead farmer than last week's. A hard left onto State Highway 391 took me toward the lake.

Lake Murray ranked as one of the cleanest lakes in the state. It was fed by the Saluda River, which was fed by various tributaries going all the way up to the North Carolina line. The dam was massive and used to be considered an engineering feat in its day.

Out here, however, the lake branched into tinier fingers, more little coves, and took on a woodsier, out-of-the-reach-of-town character. Almost enough wilderness character to make one think civilization would never come this far. Homes were smaller, cozier, rustic, with most homes small enough for blue collar to afford even though the American dream seemed forever a challenge these days. The closer you drove your boat toward the dam, however, some thirty miles east, the larger the houses, the smaller the lots, and the more insane the property values. A one- and two-million valuation was not uncommon.

COVID had woken up people nationwide. Folks all over decided to live their lives with more emphasis on desires and dreams. No more wasting time. The lower taxes, balmier weather, and lower cost of living around this lake, as compared to where they came from, didn't hurt Lake Murray's appeal either.

The rural ambiance did my soul good. Chapin used to possess this same green, minimal-traffic, slower-living quality. Prosperity and Little Mountain, small towns nearby, were even feeling the pinch of the population boom now, and per public records, developers had begun buying up family land for future use like they had near my home. Such shifts caused shocks in a community, especially each time a farmer died and the family chose not to continue the struggle.

I crossed a bridge at Big Mans Marina, known for its holiday celebrations, crawdads, burgers, and beer. One could pull up a boat, park, and place an order at the small diner, noted by an old and incongruous Shoney's Big Boy statue facing the lake. Wall-to-wall boats filled slips from Friday through Sunday, and the diner stayed fairly busy most days during the summer.

My GPS showed the Anderson farm halfway between here and the Saluda traffic circle. That crazy traffic circle. No place in the Midlands had had a traffic circle in the last fifty or so years except for Saluda. One story was the Doolittle Raiders practiced their bomb dropping over Lake Murray during World War II, onto selected sites on the uninhabited islands. One plane strayed, however, and dropped the makeshift bombs of flour bags on and around that circle. That's the sort of tale I hated to see disappear, but disappear tales did with development.

Lost in thought as I enjoyed the scenery, I almost passed the farm's entrance marked by a nondescript black mailbox at the end of a two-rut drive. Driving a quarter mile in, I came upon a white-siding farmhouse—like any of a hundred scattered around the state—with black roof and green shutters. An array of pecan and willow oak trees around it sported trunks almost three feet across. No sign of a car.

Preferring to park under an oak in lieu of a pecan, preferring the autumn oak leaves over the potential pecan sap that might mark my car. I stood in silence and listened for signs of life.

The shade carried a slight chill, and I wrapped my denim jacket closer around me before closing my eyes. The tangy aroma of the pecan's leaves and nut hulls carried a memory of fall. My father used to climb up pecan trees when the nuts were just beginning to ripen, and he'd jump from limb to limb, doing a joggling up-and-down movement to make a tree give up its wares. Nuts had dropped like rain around us, sometimes clunking my sister and me in the head. We cared little since we got paid ten cents a pound to fill a grocery sack. Mom put pecans in everything that time of year, and what she didn't cook with, she froze.

A small wind blew through, but the nuts clung tight to branches. It was still a little early for them to fall. Drying, dying leaves overhead rustled, eagerly awaiting a stronger breeze to set them loose, again, not quite ready. The golden yellow made the whole place light up. Squirrels chittered overhead at me, not happy at my disturbing their peace.

The house appeared desolate enough. Nobody had come out asking if they could help me, or worse, what the hell I was doing there. I was about to knock on the door then peek in windows before tires popped a few rocks from where I'd come in. A white government car made its way up the drive. Unless someone was willing to make themselves known, the CDM and I would be alone, it seemed. I'd have loved to talk to family, but I'd make do with a more laid-back chat with this lady.

A woman older than I parked and exited the car. "Cathy Risher," she said, her hair short, above her collar, the color at a crossroads between gray and salt and pepper. Her khaki slacks and a light-weight turtleneck under a corduroy blazer gave her a safe but still in-charge appearance. The ankle boots looked way more comfortable than mine had been at the Oakley place.

"Carolina Slade," I replied, accepting the handshake. "Just call me—"

"Slade. Like Cher or Madonna."

Cute. "Yet I can't carry a tune worth a damn. How are you?"

She sighed as if that meant something, maybe because we were at this place. She had a middle-aged solidness about her.

"Good, good," she said. "So," and she peered around the grounds, as though to make a point. "It's just going to be us. Hope you weren't expecting his family. The kids are grown and live out of state, and the wife had already moved out, having filed for divorce. She's already sold the pickup and a car." She peered around, as if seeing the place in her mind's eye rather than how I saw it. "The farm is out of business. I hear negotiations are already in the works to sell it, but that's gossip."

We both knew, however, that gossip about land deals, especially for farms, usually wasn't far from the truth.

"Another farmer or a developer?"

"What do you think?" she replied, telling me the latter.

"And the equipment?" I asked, like I would about any farm. Newbies in the field with agriculture were usually assigned the task of accounting for chattels and equipment as grunt work, but when someone died, it had a way of walking off the farm if the CDM's office didn't get on top of the situation.

Risher ran a hand through her bangs, pushing them away from her face after the wind had shoved them in her eyes. "She's already had it picked up for auction. Not sure the date, but the auctioneer understands we hold a lien on it. We'll get paid."

The common assumption would be that I came out here, concerned about Agriculture recouping its loans from the sale of assets. Since the CDM was in charge of that, she probably thought the death prompted me to double-check that she'd done her job.

"Tell me how he died," I said, having already done all the proper nodding at what Risher had done to salvage the farm's value. She'd worked longer than I, with a solid reputation for managing her farmers. Like the other CDM, she was from the county she managed. That kind usually ran a tighter ship. They had to. They could put their hands on all the skeletons in all the closets. She went to church with these people and saw them in every social setting.

Risher motioned to the barn. No hesitation on her part to go see where Anderson had offed himself. The body was gone, I told myself . . . a couple of times.

One end of the barn, a sliding door, already open about three feet, let us in without effort. She found a switch, but nothing like in a house. Just enough light to dispel the blackness and give us a soft glow with shadows.

No odor. At least not of a body. The stereotypical scent of hay, seed, fertilizer, and oil clung to the siding and rafters. A cologne many of us loved. I let my gaze stray enough for evidence of the death . . . stain on the floor, noose from the ceiling . . . then told myself to grow up and do my damn job.

It was difficult not to envision what someone had run up on that day.

"Who found him?" I asked.

"One of the hands," she said. "Anderson was living alone by that time, and apparently strung himself up sometime during the night."

Without asking a dozen questions, I pieced together the situation. His family grown and gone, his wife divorcing him for whatever reason. . . . "Why'd she leave him?"

"Why do you think?" Risher said.

I picked up a piece of straw, breaking it in my fingers. "Got tired of the lifestyle or found another man who wasn't a farmer?"

Risher gave a melancholy grin. "Right on both counts."

"So, he wasn't sick, hadn't let the farm go, hadn't changed his routine enough to warn someone, huh?" Anyone working in agriculture comes across suicide sooner or later, the rate so much higher than the general population, but still there were signs. Most people stayed too busy to notice or wrote off the changes as someone just working too hard, but hindsight usually made the signs clearer.

"Nobody saw it coming," was all she could say.

That's normally what everyone said.

"Tell me about him."

She didn't ramble nor babble, just described a man she felt sorry for and had watched from afar, hoping he would find his way back to what he loved by relying on friends and redirecting his life.

Nothing else to look at, so we wandered back outside to enjoy the beautiful day and shake the ghoulish feel of the barn. Outside, a pole barn, rather neat and clean for a working farm, stood on a rise about three hundred yards further back, facing rolling woods on the far side of an ambling hay field. No equipment under it. Newer than the rest of the outbuildings and set far enough back to be separate and distinct. A separate road led to it from what must be another entrance further down the highway.

"Was he leasing for weddings and reunions?" He certainly had the setup for it.

She nodded. "It's the thing now. City people wanting to be country. Country people wanting to stay rural. I came out here for one a few months ago. A niece of mine rented the place, and when you hang chiffon and flowers around that structure, it takes on a fairy-tale look."

I could see that. "Guess that business folded pretty quickly after his death."

"I hear everyone who was scheduled wants their money back now. Would you want to have your party on a place where somebody strung himself up?"

That was a big nope.

We talked acreage. How much was open and how much wooded? How far was public water and sewer from here? Where were the schools? All of which told me how eagerly a developer would elbow their way in versus someone buying the farm for agriculture.

I didn't want to tell her about Oakley's death right across the line in Newberry County. Not until I unearthed a few answers.

"I understand that Mr. Anderson and Mr. Troy Oakley in Newberry were tight friends," I said.

"They were," she said. "I've met Oakley. Sounds like the model farmer."

"He mentioned something about having a problem, something similar to your guy, Anderson. Any idea what that might be about?"

She looked puzzled, and I realized I hadn't made myself clear. "He left a voicemail for Al Blanchard, telling him to call him about a problem he had similar to your Mr. Anderson."

The woman wasn't stupid. "So why doesn't Al go see him?"

She was going to make me say it. "Because Oakley was found dead on his farm Friday. Al didn't get the message until yesterday, Monday."

She didn't gasp as expected. That's what being seasoned in this work did to a person. *Or she already knew.* "Poor Al," she said. "I'll give him a call. And if it's okay with you, I can brainstorm with him to see what our two guys might've had in common other than a friendship. Is that okay with you?"

"That would be wonderful," I said. "If y'all get a feel for anything, no matter how small, please, give me a call. I can meet you anywhere. I live near Chapin, so no inconvenience at all."

She took my card for easier reference.

She opened up more as time went on, and we spent an hour and a half discussing her farmers, development, the future of agriculture, and the rising taxes putting a strain on landowners. How her county had changed since she grew up aiding her grandfather raise chickens. I'd have enjoyed lunch with her, but I didn't want to take up her day. I'd sprung this visit on her last minute, and she surely had obligations.

Soon she went her way, back toward Saluda. I headed the opposite direction, back toward my neck of these woods that I hoped would remain in trees for as long as possible.

Chapter 9

SPEAKING WITH two level-headed CDMs inspired me. They were saddened that their farmers had passed, and equally saddened at what might happen to the acreage, and I was right there with them. Made me happy to work with like minds . . . sad about what we shared concerns about.

Urbanites appreciated the colors of fall across a rolling hundred acres, or the scent of a freshly cut fescue hay field in the summer. And no scene matched a cotton farm with bolls popped open, or a rambling meadow where Angus calves, red and black, nursed at the sides of their mommas. The aroma of a barn where a hundred years of farmers had stored their harvests, or feed for their stock.

The scent of farm silage ranked up there with lavender to me.

But what these city folk didn't understand was that their relocation to this environment, so many cramming into the space that wasn't made for many people, in the name of enjoying it and becoming a part of it . . . ruined it.

Halfway home, I'd teared up at the memories of the many farms I'd assisted in remaining afloat, and I sadly wondered how many of them ultimately gave up, replaced with God knows what.

I felt more motivated than usual this afternoon about preserving agriculture in a state that relied on it, which made me pine more over the two we'd just lost. Troy Oakley in Newberry and Dewey Anderson in Saluda weren't just farmers lost, but they'd also been friends, per Al Blanchard. That was coincidence enough in itself. Anderson's death seemed centered around divorce and its resulting depression, driving him to take his own life. But what was it that Oakley had said to Al Blanchard about that farmer?

We need to meet about a problem I'm having. Similar to that boy over in Saluda.

Anderson in Saluda hanged himself and had personal issues. Oakley was single; the community labeled him as a model citizen. What possible problem would they share?

I'd made notes on my phone and was itching to glance down at them while driving, to reread the list of farmers, CDMs, and counties, along with my thoughts thus far. While I would've interviewed folks beginning with the oldest case first and worked my way forward, Monroe's pressure had pushed me to do the opposite. Number five, then four. If I continued in this direction, the next was farmer Homer Brooks, overseen by CDM Jerry Crown in my home county of Lexington. His office was in the courthouse, about eighteen miles from my house. I knew the mileage from having gone there to straighten out my car taxes when I first moved to the area.

But that meant skirting outside Irmo, then crossing the dam, and then navigating the choking flow of vehicles that entered and exited the county seat. I wondered if he'd come to me, in Chapin. That would lessen the stress of meeting with me, too. After my having met with Blanchard and Risher, and their likely telling a soul or two, he would be suspicious that his name was next, and so would his staff. He'd hopefully be curious and eager enough to meet up sooner than later.

As I had with CDM Cathy Risher, I phoned CDM Jerry Crown, asking if we could meet today, or tomorrow, preferably off site of his office and a far cry from mine in Columbia where there were even more snoopers on the tenth floor of the Strom Thurmond Federal Building.

My call went to voicemail, and I slowed driving, cruising through Little Mountain again, following the speed limit. If Crown checked often enough, I might be able to work in a meeting with him before close of business. Per the dashboard clock, he could be at an early lunch.

I slowed more, then after a quick thought, pulled over and turned around. There was a lunch opportunity here. I didn't often get to this small town, and with it being the noon hour, I had an excuse to hit Little Mountain Antique Mall. They served wraps, salads, burgers, and such in the cafe on the bottom level. Chickens ran around in the back. I spotted a little bantam rooster almost every time I'd visited.

As I parked, I could almost taste the jalapeno cream cheese and cranberry salsa of my favorite sandwich on the menu. On a Tuesday, the place wasn't busy, so I made a point of walking in the front as an excuse to shop the antique booths on the way to the stairs that led down to the café.

I took my time, meandering through depression glass, century-old tablecloths, and cameo brooches. I limited myself to no more than a monthly visit to the immense, wandering warehouse of antiques, because I would drop a hundred dollars before I could reach the café. I had a dozen different antique plates on my wall already. Four assorted chicken statues over the fireplace.

Uh oh.

I stopped at an oak armoire, the tint having darkened with age, the style wrapping itself around my heart. My grandmother had a similar bedroom design in her Mississippi farmhouse, if not the exact pattern. Tentatively, I turned over the tag. *Twelve hundred dollars.*

That was a rather pricey impromptu purchase. Not something you just happen to buy on the way to grabbing lunch, so I cut a deal with myself. If I hadn't talked myself out of it by the time I finished lunch, and if someone else hadn't snared it—like a piece that large would disappear in a snap—I might just . . . oh, but how to get it home? I'd driven my F-150 Super Crew, but no way I could load it. I'd need Wayne. Then there was the fact I had absolutely no idea where to put it in the house.

The aromas from the downstairs kitchen called my name, pulling me away from the piece. By the time I found a seat, I'd decided if Jerry Crown hadn't called by the time I'd placed my order, I would go back and rethink the purchase. No. By the time I finished eating. That would give me more time to mentally move furniture around the house.

The waitress took my order and had returned with iced tea when my phone vibrated in my pocket. No caller ID I could immediately recognize, but the Lexington prefix caught my attention.

"Carolina Slade."

"Ms. Slade? Jerry Crown. You know, it makes my heart jump to hear your voice in my messages. What's wrong?"

"Have you had lunch?"

"Eating it now," he said. "Afterwards my afternoon is rather booked, but if I need to, I'll cancel."

My guess was the CDMs had communicated.

"Mr. Prevatte called me as well," he said, "but I assume you're aware."

"Sure am."

No, I wasn't. *What the hell?*

Who was running this investigation? Monroe or me?

"What time would be better for you this afternoon or in the morning?" I asked, though tomorrow wouldn't bother me at all. I hadn't done quite as much research on this guy and his farmer. I could see him in the morning and line up CDM Delores Bell of Richland County in the afternoon and make Monroe think I was genius knocking out this investigation so fast.

I'd heard nothing exceptional nor derogatory about Jerry Crown, so I expected no problems. Delores Bell, on the other hand, had a bit of a cloud over her name. She'd transferred from Craven to Richland for some whispered reason about a relationship, but in my opinion, women got labeled more than men in our world over that type of gossip. One never could tell fact from fiction unless the fact or fiction involved you personally or you had the investigation of it. Having been the subject of such rumors myself, I wasn't too quick to believe whispers. I verified before I walked in on someone with those kinds of questions.

"The morning, if you don't mind," Crown said, bringing me back around.

I could go with that and even go one better. "Meet me at nine in Chapin at The Coffee Shelf. It's in a little strip mall in the town limits. That'll save you the traffic boondoggle of getting there during rush hour. They don't do hot breakfasts, in case that's your preference, but they do homemade pastries and any kind of coffee you want."

"Works for me," he said.

Worked insanely well for me, too, being a hardcore fan of their lattes and cinnamon rolls.

Settling back in my booth as the waitress placed my turkey wrap before me, the tension in my shoulders eased. I would relish an afternoon of seclusion and online research after calling Delores and scheduling her for tomorrow after Jerry Crown.

The jalapeno cream cheese was insanely tasty, and I was about to pop the last bite of the wrap in my mouth before I realized I hadn't thought twice about that armoire. To avoid succumbing to the temptation of buying it on the way out, I exited the back door, sidestepping around that little bantam rooster who thought briefly about giving my calf a peck.

In the car, I called Delores Bell's office number. She was uniquely located of all the CDMs. Her office was in downtown Columbia in a little office on a separate floor from the rest of us in headquarters. We were on the tenth. She was on the second. I saw little of her, and unless she had a serious situation with a client, she had no need to come up those eight flights of stairs. We often forgot she was down there.

Had the reassignment been for her benefit or to crucify her for some misdeed? Nobody wanted to work near us headquarters types. Never having visited her, I assumed she kept her head down, did her job, and remained purposely invisible.

But even as small as her office was, she must've been too busy to answer her phone, so I left a message for her to get in touch, asking for a meeting any time after lunch tomorrow.

Okay, time to decide whether or not to dare that horrid commute back downtown or to work from home, the latter clearly preferred. I dialed Monroe's line while seated in the antique mall parking lot, to give him his report and take measure of whether I could avoid coming in.

Two ladies in smocks and elastic-waisted pants, each old enough to be my grandmother, tottered holding onto each other as if a breeze would knock either of them over had they been alone. They clung to their oversized purses on their outer sides, providing balance.

Kudos to them for getting out and about. The day was as perfect as a Carolina fall could be. Temperature around eighty, no wind, the sun glistening off everything it touched. The warmth made it quite comfortable, such that I had a smile on my face when the secretary answered.

"He's not at his desk, Slade. Can you wait? He said for me to retrieve him if you called."

"Um, not really necessary."

"Oh, no. He said come get him. Please hold."

Monroe was still obsessed. He had called Jerry, and sure as heck, he'd call Delores Bell the moment I told him I wanted to see her tomorrow. He'd make her call me back ASAP, if not meet me after hours.

Monroe picked up. "Slade? How's it going?"

"The CDM in Saluda was great. She answered all my questions. It appears the guy was depressed over his divorce and hanged himself. The ex is already liquidating the estate, but the value should more than cover what he owed us. CDM Risher expects the farm to go into the hands of a developer, but she had no facts on that. Just community talk."

"So, nothing we did made him . . . do that to himself?"

"Not that I can tell. Nothing she can tell."

"What was the problem he mentioned on the phone call to Blanchard?"

"No idea," I said.

Monroe went quiet. "You have no idea or he had no idea?"

"Blanchard didn't, therefore, I don't. Neither did Ms. Risher. Whatever the two farmers shared was between them, and Oakley didn't get the chance to enlighten Blanchard."

"Well, that sucks."

I had no response to a remark that didn't normally make an appearance in Monroe's vocabulary. I wasn't so sure the reference to the joint problem between the farmers was worth probing, honestly. Might've been no more than disappointment over the price of beef.

"What about the others? What have they said?" he continued.

"I'm in Little Mountain, Monroe. I gave Cathy Risher the whole morning in Saluda. That leaves CDMs Jerry Crown and Delores Bell. He's meeting me at nine in the morning at a coffee shop, and she hasn't returned my call."

"We'll fix that," he said.

"Monroe, please stop."

He did, for a second or two. "What?"

"You're freaking me out here at the intensity you're splashing on this. What aren't you telling me?"

"Nothing."

"Now you sound like someone getting interviewed and telling half the story."

Another pause, only he didn't come back so amiable this time. "You think I'm lying, Ms. Slade?"

Again, like yesterday, he threw my formal name at me, and that couldn't be labeled but one thing, in my opinion.

"Are you using your title and sudden formality to intimidate me?" I said, probably one of only a couple people who could get away with that remark . . . especially in the tone I delivered it.

"Are you forgetting I'm your boss?" he countered.

"Would you talk to anyone else like you just spoke to me?"

"Would you sass your boss if it were anyone but me?"

The back and forth was contagious . . . and getting us nowhere.

"Monroe . . . just please stop."

He did. Now what was I to say that didn't crank this argument back up?

"For me to do an honest, transparent, thorough investigation, let me off the leash. You assigned it to me, saying I had to discover everything on my own, no cues from you so that I didn't appear tainted by you. However, here you are fussing about how I'm investigating, and I have no earthly idea why. Anyone other than me would think you sounded guilty of something."

He cleared his throat. "I was trying to expedite the effort."

"It looks worse when you push. What if I find enough to catapult this thing to the Inspector General? That means they'll interview you . . . then me. And if any of the parties involved gets scared or nervous and points a finger at us, claiming we used our friendship in an attempt to corroborate an outcome, we're screwed. I'll lose my authority to do investigations. You'll lose your job." I snapped my fingers loud enough for him to hear. "Just like that."

"So what are you saying?" he said, not completely chilled but better.

"I will talk to Jerry Crown tomorrow. Hopefully, Delores Bell as well. I'll do more research, maybe going back to the CDMs for a second round. The families of the deceased may have something to say. But . . ." I trailed off on purpose.

"But?" he asked.

"But I need to be given a week without you breathing down my neck. If this business looks about to blow up, then I'll make a beeline straight to your office. Otherwise, I do my job."

He sighed into the phone. "That's difficult."

I didn't like the sound of that. "Why should that be so hard? Even the worst of the worst of your political brothers and sisters would expect you to do your due diligence and investigate. If they were you, they'd stall for weeks, if not months, hoping it would go away."

Another throat clearing. "You're right. Take whatever time you need."

"Thank you. Now, I have a request."

"Ask." Good for him for trying to appear open at least.

"If I need assistance, if things start getting murky, may I bring in Wayne?"

"No."

"Not even off the record?"

"No. Not without my permission."

I had to stop there, because my next question would fire him up again.

What if I found that Monroe had a connection to any of these people and any of these occurrences? At that point, unfortunately I would have to make my own call, because if Monroe as State Director appeared to have been even slightly affiliated or had used influence when it came to these people, places, and happenings, I'd have to go to the IG myself. He'd have zero say-so in the matter. And regardless of how it turned out, we'd never be friends again.

Chapter 10

I COUNTED MY blessings working from home when kids were in school, and I didn't want to be interrupted by nosey coworkers. Especially Monroe. He allowed me the latitude to do so when needed, as long as he could get in touch. These days he wanted to get in touch a little too much.

My study wasn't fancy, maybe ten by ten, but it was private with a desk and chair caught on sale from Staples. Kids drawings hung all over, tacked straight into the sheetrock.

The best thing about my study, though, was that it was mine and not to be disturbed. Even Wayne tapped on the door first. The room was supposed to be pure unadulterated work.

I preferred my personal time, however, in the out of doors with its lake view. A small garden sat to the side of the property, and one day, we hoped to build a chicken coop. Three acres was almost big enough to live off of, if one was so driven to pour that much sweat into crops and livestock, but there was something about a lake that detracted one from wanting to work very hard. I'd already let it get too late in the season to plant a winter garden.

The kids were at school, and Ally understood the seriousness of my work and left me alone, short of bringing me a cup of coffee. Her personality could drive one looney some days, but there was no doubt she loved being aunt, housekeeper, and babysitter to us, and we loved having her. My mother was beyond happy that she didn't live on her own any longer. Her divorce didn't even have an alimony clause in it because the son of a bitch she parted ways with was unemployed and so far in debt he'd still be paying with Social Security checks. Besides, she didn't want to be attached to him in any way. We agreed on that.

Door shut, coffee on a coaster, I dove not into Agriculture's files, but into the Internet for my next visit tomorrow. Farmer was Homer Brooks from Lexington County. Social media showed he lived on his farm halfway between Gilbert and Lake Murray. Clearly, he played hard on that lake, on a separate ten-acre playground he owned where he had four-wheelers, fishing gear, and assorted man-toys. A playground with water frontage.

He farmed the same as the others—beans, corn, and cattle—but had vegetables as well. I could say this investigation had a type, but more farmers fell into this category than any other in this state. Facebook details led to many lake events such as boat parades, striped bass outings, and, of course, the annual Fourth of July fireworks show one could see for a dozen miles around. Even with tall pines on my place, we could see the biggest and best explosions, and we sat five miles from the island where they were ignited.

This was the man whom wedding planner Easton—while seated on the grass and trying not to throw up—had referenced with his *not again* comment. Therefore, without research I already knew Brooks earned part-time money hosting weddings. Brooks's farm and lake place appeared to be paid for. Maybe he'd inherited his real estate. Out of all the properties I'd seen thus far, his held the most potential for development, being closest to populated areas and the accompanying employment.

Ultimately listed as accidental, his death had been considered a homicide and a suicide in the early days, if one listened to the gossip and shallow notices in the weekly papers. He'd taken his Sea Ark bass boat out, alone. The boat had been found minus its owner about two hours after his wife pled for friends, family, and neighbors to hunt for him. He hadn't phoned to check in, a safety habit his wife had mandated and he'd honored.

Cause of death was drowning. They found his body submerged not far from the boat. His wife swore up and down that he in no way contemplated taking his own life.

No CCTV or Ring cameras in the middle of a fifty-thousand-acre lake, so accident it was.

As the papers said, Brooks had a wife. A grown son lived nearby and helped run the farm when he wasn't running his local hardware store. A grown daughter was a nurse in Greenville. Three grandchildren, per the obituary.

There was another Lexington County deceased farmer, T.J. Candleman. He worked on the same side of the county as Brooks, but ten miles away. Methane-related accident. A hog farmer, he was tinkering with the pump next to a pond of hog waste and fell, quickly overcome by the invisible fumes. He was announced dead on arrival of hydrogen sulfide poisoning.

This one I was familiar with. It made the news. Arm-chair environmentalists fussed about the dangers of methane to the atmosphere, to global warming, to the human diet. Mostly critics were from out of state, because South Carolina believed in pork barbecue like sinners believed in being saved on Sunday.

The two Lexington cases were within two weeks of each other.

Sitting back, I pondered the odds of these cases. The commonalities, the exceptions, and the statistics. Those of us in agricultural management kept up with those.

Farm fatalities were down the last five years, but then, farmland was being gobbled up and more farmers retiring. A hundred thirty or so deaths annually in recent years, which is what made our five around Lake Murray stand out so much. Suicides were about ten to twelve percent, depending on who you talked to, but the truth was, one couldn't tell if a farmer fell off his tractor on purpose or not. If he—and they were overwhelmingly men—didn't outright hang himself or slit his throat, who knew? Stigma made a coroner lean toward accident if they couldn't label the death clearly suicide.

Then I shifted to CDM Jerry Crown and scrutinized him. If I'd learned anything since becoming Special Projects Representative, it was that you looked in all directions for misdeeds, beginning with those closest to you.

I'd learned this from the outset of my investigative life. When I'd phoned in a farmer's bribery attempt three or four years ago now, the IG sent Wayne. He appeared at my home on the weekend, taking two hours to interrogate me.

I was livid. I was sarcastic. I was scared out of my mind. He received my cold shoulder for a while, but only until I realized the close study of me, the whistleblower, was necessary in order to conduct a sincere investigation. The whole deal was worthless if I wasn't on the up-and-up.

Since then, after my training and a ton of experience, I'd learned to look hard at those close to the difficulty, even those openly cooperating and representing the good guy side of things. They had to be clean for a case to be made.

Therefore, these four CDMs merited study. Al Blanchard thus far was clean. Cathy Risher cleaner still. Jerry Crown lived as close to me as Blanchard. We'd been at some of the same meetings, and he hadn't been in any trouble I was aware of. But he didn't break records anywhere either. Average, in terms of making grants and loans. Average, in ensuring his clients paid money back. Average, in community interaction and protecting the name of federal Agriculture in his jurisdiction. That averageness meant I'd never looked at him before, which is what being average did for you. It kept you under the radar.

Which meant I would look at him closer.

Jerry Crown had worked in six different county offices throughout the state and was originally from a small county known more for its state parks and forestry. His first assignment was in an office that combined two neighboring small counties. He was promoted to CDM a few years later. He served in a couple of other counties as CDM, again, small offices, then Lexington. All in all, using the same earlier description of him, average.

At this stage of his career, he clearly had no desire to manage a leading agricultural county. He appeared comfortable in the shadows earning a stable income doing what didn't rock many boats, no pun intended.

Lexington, however, had a uniqueness of its own. It was known for a lot of peanuts and had enough acreage for CDM Crown to have to work harder than his other stomping grounds. Also, his county abutted Richland County, seat of the capital, and boasted the most water frontage on Lake Murray. An award-winning school district or two made the appeal for homeowner relocations to Lexington strong and the temptation to convert farmland stronger. Many of those issues weren't exactly a foremost concern for a CDM, but one should stay on top of said issues in one's jurisdiction.

Crown's farmer Homer Brooks owed little to Agriculture for his loans and probably had the means to pay us off. The CDM, however, wouldn't want the farmer to pay him off, for statistics' sake. The faster your customer base dwindled, the faster you could be relocated, or your county combined with the one next door, which could eliminate your job.

The Brooks death occurred two months ago. Other than the flurry of news during the week Brooks died, nothing monumental was noted since.

A knock sounded on my study door, and Ally poked her head in. "Hate to interrupt."

"What's up?" I said, snatching readers off my nose.

"Are those reading glasses?" she asked, a smirk spreading.

"Only for in here," I said, lying. Mid-forties had me riding the fence of needing glasses for reading, and I kept a pair in my purse, one in my office, and one in my study, here. "What do you need? I'm prepping for a meeting tomorrow morning."

Instinctively, I glanced at the clock to see how much longer I'd have before the kids barged in and, of course, how long before Wayne came home. "The kids get back in, what, a half hour?"

"Well, Ivy does, but . . ."

"But what? They ride the same bus."

"They don't want him riding the bus."

Uh oh. Impish Zack could push buttons, but in a fun way. Teachers hated disciplining him because they loved him. Unfortunately, his charisma had allowed him to get away with a few antics during his elementary years, scarily fast becoming his middle school phase. "He's not some sort of threat. Not his little silly self. What am I not hearing, Ally?"

"They said someone has to come to the office and pick him up and meet with the assistant principal. Since you're home, I wondered if you wanted to tackle this or if you wanted me to go in your stead. Wasn't sure how important your work was. You don't come home much, and you seemed entrenched in whatever it is."

I swiveled around, my attention snared. "You're not telling me why he was banned from the bus, or why we have to check him out through the assistant principal."

"He picked a kid's pocket and got caught doing it."

At first I counted my blessings it wasn't something worse. Then I counted my blessings that he hadn't practiced his craft on a teacher. Then, however, I wanted to kill Wayne's sister Kaye for sharing the skill and choke Ally for allowing Kaye to hold the lessons under my roof. Guess the only person I wasn't angry at was Wayne.

"I'll get him," I said, slamming folders shut and moving them into my tote.

"If you need to work—"

But I was already shaking my head. "Oh, no, Sis. I want this little boy to fear God himself when he sees me instead of you."

One could read the fear on her face. "Don't be too hard on him."

Ordinarily I'd admire the motherly instinct. She'd missed the mark this time letting him learn this new skill of his.

"I've got to hear the evidence first," I said, standing to leave. "I take it Ivy is still on her way home, via the bus. Has she been made aware she won't be seeing her brother?"

"I'll take care of that now," Ally said, and quickly left.

I left the house with Ally on the line with the middle school office. Some days I swear I had three children instead of two.

Zack's school was just over three miles from my home, but with it being close to let out time for the schools, traffic was a bear. Mothers lined up an hour before time, vying for the closest spots up front for reasons that made no sense to me. I often wondered what they did for that hour, while other moms, probably those with more children to pick up or jobs that kept them busy to the last minute, careened to the back of the line two minutes before.

Today I was one of the lucky ones who could pass every one of these car poolers to the parking lot, land a slot not fifty feet from the front door, park, and waltz in. The receptionist would have my son ready and waiting. If this meeting didn't take long, I'd be out and gone with son in hand before the last half of that line reached school property.

Head held high, I strode into the office.

Zack's red hair was easy to spot behind the counter, not in front. He looked confined and awaiting sentence.

Didn't take the receptionist long to escort me into a private office.

"Please bring my son in," I said.

"We'd rather you meet Mr. Strong without your son first," she said, like I ought to know better.

"Well, I'd rather not meet with Mr. Strong without my son first. You bring him in, please, or I miss the meeting."

What was it about education that brought out the worst in parents? Or at least me. My guard went up the moment Zack handed me even the most innocent notice from his book bag, so being asked to come into the principal's office only armed me to the hilt.

Mr. Strong and Zack arrived at the same time, and I pointed for Zack to take his seat. Mr. Strong wasn't nearly as symbolic of his name as one might expect, no taller than I, missing half his hair, and a waistline that told me he enjoyed sitting behind a desk.

Zack knew better than to speak, his eyes wide at seeing me instead of his aunt.

We dispensed with the niceties quickly. "Zack has been pickpocketing students," Mr. Strong said.

My stare at my son melted him into his chair. He said nothing, meaning he was guilty as sin.

"Are you aware of his . . . talents?" Strong asked.

"He has a family member who visited recently and showed him," I said. That's all the man needed to know.

"Well, we believe this is the first time he was caught red-handed. When this situation flared up, other students came forward."

"How many?" I asked.

"Four," he said.

I glared harder at Zack who melted deeper.

"What did he take?" I asked, still lasered on my son.

"Key rings, Pokémon cards . . . money."

"Seriously, Zack?"

He wilted further. "I gave it back. I wasn't trying to steal. I just wanted to show what I could do."

"In other words, show off."

He had no response.

My attention shifted back to the principal. "Did he steal anything?"

"No, but it's just a matter of time."

I could see the principal's point, noted the appearance, but I also knew my son. Nothing malicious about him, but how did you explain that to an administrator in charge of, what, eight hundred kids of all shapes and sizes and behaviors instilled from an array of home environments? What if one of Zack's *protegees* decided keeping the money made more sense? What if a bully forced Zack to work on his behalf? My brain spiraled, but no point making Zack's reputation worse.

"The resource officer spoke to him," Strong said, "but we didn't see the need to involve the law. However, in light of this situation, we ban him from riding the bus, where we're sure temptation is even greater in such a cramped space."

"How long?" I asked.

"A month . . . this time."

I could live with that. Zack could, too. And Ally Jo damn sure could. "Anything else?" I asked.

"The next time, we consider getting social services involved," he said.

That was a bit over the top, in my opinion. I swallowed a wad of fear and anger, hoping he didn't see me do it. If he'd said, *Get law enforcement involved*, I could've lived with that. Either Wayne or I could've talked to said law enforcement and explained the innocence of Zack's latest endeavor, but social services was another story.

We left the office, the car line down to its last dozen cars. While I'd waltzed into the school unaffected, I left having been taken down a peg, hoping nobody there recognized that we'd just gotten scolded.

Zack walked a half step behind me, slid into the car without a whine and buckled up, on guard while waiting for his private moment of discipline. More than one, actually. That was the deal when you had three adults in the household. The mom, the caregiver aunt, and mom's special agent fiancé . . . all three with stock into what happened. Each of the three with a different viewpoint and different spins on discipline.

Zack was fully aware I watched from my rearview mirror. He looked anywhere but at me.

"What were you thinking?" I asked.

"That it was a target-rich environment," he mumbled.

Whose son was this? "Say that again?"

"It's what Aunt Kaye said when she taught us. Pickpockets go for a target-rich environment. A group of people who don't pay attention, so they don't see it coming."

Oh, my friggin' gosh. What was I raising here? I wished he learned his math half as well.

"You knew better," was all I could say at the moment.

"But I—"

"Shut it!" I wanted him cringing in silence in that backseat. I wanted that three miles to feel like forty.

It did. For both of us.

I checked my rearview again for Zack, instinctively scanning behind, then using my mirrors on the side. A white SUV followed about a half-dozen car lengths back, and I wondered if that mom had ever had to pick up her child from the principal's office for all the car line to see.

Chapter 11

ZACK SPENT HIS entire evening in rotation with inquisitors, to include his sister once the adults got through with him. Ivy craved details, and I wanted her to cross-examine him as much as the rest of us, so that she didn't get any ideas of demonstrating her newfound abilities at her school. Whether innocent or not, playful or not, I wanted her to understand that if the wrong kid was tapped, the wrong adult saw, the wrong teacher misunderstood, any wrong move could create trouble she didn't need. Nor did her family.

Ivy and Zack would remain pent up talking until bedtime, avoiding adults, so Wayne sat with me in the living room. Ally watched a show in her bedroom, like the kids, dodging me. She understood loud and clear that her permissions and oversight helped cause this. Wayne vowed to deal with his sister.

"Lucky you," I said, sipping on a coffee under a lap blanket. "All you had to say was how disappointed you were in him."

Wayne nursed a small bourbon and water. "You're welcome."

"Yeah, but that means I issue the lecture. That makes me the bad guy."

He gave me a soft half grin. "You're the mom. It's what moms do. I remember my mother's scoldings way more than my dad's."

Frankly, I did, too.

God, don't let me turn into my mom.

"Why were you working from home?" Wayne asked.

"I'd been in Saluda County. Took lunch in Little Mountain, then since I had no other appointments, chose to work from home versus fighting that Columbia traffic." I tried to focus on the television, reaching for the remote.

"What're you working on?" he asked.

There it was. We ended a lot of days asking about each other's cases. The new ones, the closed ones, the ones in the middle. A few of Wayne's I couldn't be read into, being criminal and out of my jurisdiction. *Open investigation. Can't say.*

I could get away with spouting that as well, but not with Special Agent Wayne Largo. Nobody could crucify me for telling him, and he knew it. This time, however, my boss had ordered me not to talk to him, and that meant he was off-limits. "I was checking with the CDM on a farm that's going out of business." *Truth. Just not all of it.*

He took that no problem. "Have you heard from the coroner?"

Heck, which one? But he'd only know of the one from Newberry. "Who says I called the coroner?"

"The coroner."

Damn, I forgot that he spoke with her, too. "No, I haven't heard from her. She tell you anything?" *Note to self, call her again tomorrow.* Surely by now she had something for me.

This was how we spoke in the evenings. The back and forth. The sharing.

"Why'd you call her to start with?" he asked. "I already had."

"Monroe asked me to. Somebody has to start probate. I have the CDM talking to Oakley's attorney this week as well. Somebody has to keep those cattle fed and watered until we get our money."

I didn't mention the other dead farmer cases, and luckily, the conversation went such that I didn't have to lie. The lawman had no idea about anyone but Oakley.

Wayne tipped his head in understanding. "Have you made me a list of places you might like to get married at?"

Where the hell did that come from?

"I," then I stopped. Was I supposed to make a list?

"Ally told me she suggested you make one," he said.

Crap, she did. I could ask if I was fighting both of them now about this, but this ought not be a fight. A wedding was supposed to be a united front and conversation mixed with compromise and love.

I almost tripped up and said I was busy on this case, the case he wasn't supposed to be aware of. So, what was I able to say and not make it sound like I'd made it up or was trying too hard to be right?

"Your brain is short-circuiting," he said. "I smell it burning."

"I'll get you a list of more places in a couple days," I said. "And the Oakley death reminded me I needed to check on some farms that have ceased operation, to make sure we get paid from the estates."

I was rather proud of that answer, to be honest. "Want me to call your man Easton?" I added, wanting already to speak with the wedding planner about the dead farmers, to see what he knew of their deaths since he was already aware of two and seemed to have his ears open in the farming community. "Without Mr. Easton, I need to do some digging on those wedding places on my own."

Wayne shrugged. "He's as good as anyone, I guess."

Yep. Call Mr. Easton in the morning.

"You know," I said, feeling emboldened at Wayne's acceptance of my answers. "I've been thinking . . ." Actually, the idea had just flashed to mind. "We have the license. We could knock out the formality with a trip to the notary of your choice . . . even a preacher, if you like, then just hold a celebration. Maybe a pig pickin'. Or, and this is even better, take that wedding money and turn it into an expensive trip. Ever wanted to go to the Azores Islands?"

He shook his head, no longer smiling.

His temperament almost got under my skin. "Doesn't it make more sense to use that money to have a memorable time at someplace incredibly special? A trip that we'd remember the rest of our lives?" The idea made perfect sense. "There's such a thing as too much wedding, don't you think?"

I realized everything I said ended in a question and he wasn't answering. He waited to respond until I quit asking.

"I want to show off our vows." His voice spoke those few words slow and low, with enough emotion to show I'd gone too far. Coffee gone, he rose, despite it being an hour early for bed.

"I'll call Easton," I repeated.

"Don't do anything you'd rather not do," he said, going to the kitchen.

Damn it all. I tired of being the bad guy. I could understand that in disciplining Zack. I wasn't open to it with Wayne.

But this wedding business made him downright pouty. I said I'd do whatever he wanted. He wanted me to want what *he* wanted and help in pulling it together. I didn't know how to do that. I just cared that we did wed, in whatever fashion got the job done.

"You're being a bit childish about all this," I said, loud enough to reach him in the kitchen.

He came back around the bar and stopped, keeping distance between us. "Slade . . ."

"I don't get it, Cowboy." My hackles went up, but not before seeing his had already done so. "I cannot make myself get excited over a lavish affair when a party will do. We're talking thousands of dollars. Tens of thousands, maybe. You want to strut down some aisle and speak promises in front of a hundred or more people when these vows are meant to be between us." I stood, coming closer. "You're asking me to compromise. Yet you aren't willing to."

"We aren't getting married in a church," he reminded.

"Okay, then. You want my preferences? I want nothing more than carnations or daisies for flowers. I hate open bars when I'm paying for them. I prefer a dress I can wear for some other occasion, and shoes that I can dance in. Finger food versus a sit-down meal, and it can come from Publix for all I care. Have two food trucks if you like. And I don't want people spending a lot of money buying new clothes. The music can be from a Spotify playlist."

I'd just surprised myself. That had to be the most input I'd given him since we started talking details.

"So, you want cheap."

No, he didn't say that. "Are you calling me cheap? If that's how you see me, then, whatever, maybe that's more my style. Is that a problem? You don't like the idea of marrying a cheap woman?"

That last part came out a little louder than expected.

Cheap. Amazing how powerfully that word had wedged between us.

About six feet apart, we stood at odds. Honestly, I'd said I'd do whatever he wanted, but he wanted me to want it. When I told him what suited me, he found my choices without heart.

Cheap.

"I'm going to bed," he said.

"Go right ahead," I replied.

He left.

No way I wanted to go to bed now. Time to check on the kids, then grab a book so the television didn't keep anyone up.

This wasn't good, and I had no idea what to do other than the one task we agreed on: call Mr. Easton tomorrow and ask him for ideas on venues. Wherever he showed me, I'd pick one and decide it rocked my world. From there, I'd ask Easton about flowers, catering, and I didn't care if the food came from his mother's restaurants or not.

My head hurt. At least Wayne hadn't pushed as to what I was doing. And we had put the fear of God into Zack about pickpocketing. The night wasn't a total wash.

I crossed fingers that I completed this case without Wayne's inquisitive nature getting wise. Fingers crossed that Zack behaved. Fingers crossed that Ivy learned from Zack's mistake. Fingers crossed that Mr. Easton came through with something to suit our needs.

I was fast running out of fingers.

Damn. I could've at least asked him about his sister and the nudist colony. Somehow the night's conversation had turned into an all-about-me session.

WAYNE ROSE EARLY and went to work before I stepped out of the shower, with his shouting, "I'm gone" over the sound of the water. By the time I dried, the kids were gone, too, with Ally driving them both since Zack was banned from the bus.

Like yesterday, I lucked up avoiding the commuter traffic to the capital city with a one-on-one with a CDM in the field. I had asked to meet Jerry Crown at a coffee shop in Chapin, on the opposite side of Lake Murray from his office. I beat him to The Coffee Shelf, arriving ten minutes early. I ordered my plain latte, large, with a half hit of whip on top, and a square of coffee cake. The coffee flavorings I refused added a couple hundred calories I could not afford, but a latte tasted better than plain house coffee.

In the time I waited, I wandered around the books. Bookstores had closed all over the midlands of the state, but this coffee shop owner loved to read, so she had a remarkable assortment in her small inventory, some of which belonged to local authors. Many of her coffee flavorings were named after literary characters. Even Zack and Ivy loved the place. Ivy claimed she'd grown to love coffee, as if the "Charlie Brown" with its peanut butter flavoring and chocolate drizzle was coffee. She dreamed of being a barista, which I wasn't allowing for another year . . . assuming the grades were worthy.

Jerry Crown walked in about the time I found a table near the bookcases, making me put my book purchase away. A little after nine in the morning, a lot of the rush was gone, with only a handful of retired gentlemen seated against the opposite wall, rowdy enough to not hear what anyone else in the room said.

I started to rise and order Crown's coffee as a courtesy, but he shook his head and handled his own. Took him a while to decipher the menu, resorting to a house coffee with room for cream and a cinnamon roll slathered with enough icing to paint a wall. Made me wish I'd ordered one.

"How's it going?" Crown said, seating himself.

"Not bad," I replied. "Yourself?"

"Can't complain." He sipped his coffee, finding it hot so he put it back down to rest and dove into his roll. "So, we're talking about Homer Brooks?"

"And T.J. Candleman." I liked someone who cut to the chase. "I heard about Candleman in the evening news, but I was out of state when Brooks's accident went down. Murder, suicide, then accident, huh? Some shrewd detective work there. The suicide slant sounds rather gossipy to me."

Crown sighed and shook his head. "Damn journalists. Someone who knew someone told some two-bit reporter looking for a break that Homer Brooks had been worried about being followed. Also, someone heard that people had been knocking on his door trying to buy up his land, like that's anything unique. He wasn't willing to sell. Not with a wife, two children, and three grandchildren to leave it to. Especially the ten acres on the lake. You know how it is. But they tried to make it sound sinister before the coroner confirmed otherwise. Don't you live on water?"

I nodded.

He snickered, sarcastically, which probably meant he didn't have that luxury. "You ever get those phone calls or mailings trying to coerce you into selling?"

"Yeah, I have three acres, and I get them in the previous owner's name, too."

Anyone willing to sell usually broke up the land into as many small pieces as possible since a half acre sold about as much as a whole. If the place had over a hundred feet of frontage, it was entitled to a dock. There-fore, the lake had accumulated quite a few pie-wedged pieces of prop-erty, with front yards barely wide enough to place a driveway, but the back as wide as possible.

"So, Brooks was getting inundated with said calls?" I asked.

"And mailings, but he told me someone hounded him in person."

"Any idea who?" I asked.

"He didn't know, or at least didn't say to me."

Um, that didn't make sense. "Someone harasses him, and he doesn't bother finding out who they are?"

"The people kept changing, I think, but they had the same spiel. He would ask who they represented, and they wouldn't say unless he was interested in talking price. He told some to take a hike. He told others to go to hell. He swore he was being followed, and another met him at his boat ramp, refusing to leave until Brooks accused him of trespassing. Some walked right into his barn and onto his fields. He started carrying a firearm. Must have been a dozen or more in the three or four months before he died."

I leaned in. Talking about someone getting stalked and possibly killed within earshot of the old guys enjoying retirement across the room wouldn't be polite or good investigative practice. "Is that why they thought he might've been murdered?"

"Yeah. He also found messages in his mailbox, asking for a price, over and over. His son was pursued at the hardware store."

"Harassment without it being threatening enough for the sheriff's office to get involved," I said.

He lowered his voice. "Someone killed his wife's dog. On his farm. A Boston terrier. Found it behind the barn with a note attached with just two words. *How much.*"

"Say what?" The visual was a little much. I didn't go to movies that focused on animals of any kind. "How was the note attached?"

"You don't want to know," he said.

No, I didn't. "Surely the sheriff got involved then."

Crown shook his head. "They came out. They wrote up a report. They advised him to install cameras. That's when he called me. That's when he called everyone he knew, telling them what happened and asking if they had been approached by any of these same people. Some of the other farmers had been asked if they were interested in selling, but not to that degree. I asked around, but you know how it is. So many are wanting to move down here to God's country they're trying all sorts of ways to talk people into selling, so everyone, including the authorities, just wrote it off as someone fishing for a real estate deal. Either that or they didn't have any hard evidence to make an arrest."

These stories explained the murder rumor, but not the suicide. "Why did anyone think he killed himself?"

He'd finished up the roll and sipped his cooled coffee. "Oh, his wife had a fit about that. The coroner nixed that pretty quickly, too."

"But why consider it at all?"

Crown scowled. "Because he had lung cancer. Stage three. Maybe four. He had an end in sight, I know that."

Oh. Damn. "Did the people wanting to buy the place know that?"

"Have no idea," he said. "But he didn't keep it secret."

"What made them decide it was an accident?"

"The trauma on his head matched the edge of the boat. He still had a fish on his line, and they assumed he slipped trying to reel it in. He wasn't found far from the boat, in about twenty feet of water."

Not to discount law enforcement, but in agriculture, when given the choice of accident or suicide, you went with the former, and it was done all the time.

"So you're checking out farm deaths," he said. "Heard I'm not the only one you've talked to."

I gave a tight grin. "No, you're not."

He nodded. "Hey, I'm out of coffee. I talk better with something in my hand. Give me a second?"

"Sure."

He seemed to be doing okay, which made me feel a hint better about him. Like when cops asked for samples of DNA, the ones who offered to cooperate weren't the guilty parties.

He returned with plain coffees for both of us and another cinnamon roll for himself, tossing sugar and creamer on the table for me, just in case. He offered me half of his roll, which I declined, then he went on talking.

"His son and wife will continue farming. They didn't want to make any major decisions otherwise atop of his death, plus, because he died from an accident, his insurance is paying off rather handsomely." He paused. "Or so I heard. With them not being behind on their debts with us, and their debts being small to begin with, I haven't done much inquiring."

My concern was the land grabbers. "Are those real estate people pestering the family?"

"Don't know, but I'm sure they are," Crown said, his cinnamon roll gone in four bites.

"Sad," I said.

"Yeah." He licked then wiped his fingers. His eating manners could stand correction. "If I were them, though," he said, "I'd dump the place. That's literally millions of dollars if sold to the right developer."

That's why historical families sold thousands of acres to dozens of developers. The smell of money. Crown was an average civil servant without an inheritance who probably dreamed of what looked like easy money. Some farm families had heirs with the same mindset. They hadn't had to work to buy, to develop, to pay the taxes on real estate so that it could increase in value and provide insurance for future generations. Sometimes those who were told since birth of said inheritance simply waited for the right funeral and the opportunity to cash in. Splitting the money umpteen ways, they enjoyed the wealth . . . ultimately leaving their grandchildren little to nothing.

Except not the Brooks family. Mr. Easton popped to mind. He whined that day on the side of Oakley's pond as if Brooks's property was no longer available for weddings. He seemed to think Brooks's death had ended that side gig as well. However, Crown made it sound like the family was going to give things a go, in Homer Brooks's honor.

Time to call Easton like I'd promised Wayne. I bet Easton would hug my neck to learn the Brooks wedding venue might still be viable. And to be nice, I might just go out there with him and give it a look . . . you know, in case it could work for Wayne.

"Wait, before we wrap up, tell me about Candleman," I said. His has been the odder death.

"He was alone. He was poor. He was an argumentative moron," Crown said.

I reared back a little. "What do you really think, Jerry?"

"I'm sorry." He looked down and shook his head. "You have to be careful around hog collection ponds. They'll kill you in a second. He was stupid enough to find that out."

"Any talk of investors harassing him?" I asked.

Crown chuckled. "Like Brooks, Candleman carried a side piece. The difference between Brooks and Candleman, however, was that Candleman would use it. Word spread fast in the real estate community that you took your life in your hands trespassing there. That and it being a hog operation sort of lessoned developers' interest."

But I knew better. People assumed a hog operation made a piece of land undesirable, but a developer could take almost any type of dirt and turn it into someone's palace.

Chapter 12

CROWN AND I parted ways from the coffee shop at eleven. Too early for lunch, I headed to the office in Columbia, the traffic toned down this time of day. Watching all sides of me, on an interstate that had lost its mind in recent years over lane construction, I noticed a white SUV, an Explorer maybe, behind me. While I patted myself on the back remembering to remain aware of my surroundings, I also knew one could be followed by a white car every day for a month, and it never be the same car.

On the way in, I called Mr. Easton, got his voicemail, and left a message. The cocky man still seemed to merit the *Mr.* when I thought of him, though I couldn't say why. "Please call me back. I'd like to look at a few places and make a list for Wayne to choose from, kind sir."

That didn't sound right, so I added, "He's tied up with work, and besides, I have some good news for you about the Brooks's wedding venue. Thanks."

As I pulled into the parking garage, my phone rang. Expecting it to be Easton, I answered quickly. "Hey, Mr. Easton."

"Sorry, Ms. Slade, but this is Anna Price, the Newberry coroner."

"Oh, sorry, I was going to call you today."

"I figured. Spoke with your other . . . not sure who he is to you . . . Agent Largo?"

"Yes," and I chuckled once. "We work together on cases, but we're also engaged. It's complicated."

She didn't giggle back, so I assumed she preferred getting to the point.

"Anyway," she continued. "Mr. Oakley hasn't had any relatives come forward, and since there's an open investigation in which y'all are involved, I decided it's okay to share."

We weren't involved together in this investigation, but, hey, I'd take the opportunity. "Much appreciated. We want to ensure that the farm and Mr. Oakley's assets are handled properly. Has an attorney come forward with the heir?"

"The attorney is the executor," the coroner said. "Not aware of the heirs. Not my business."

Good, at least we had an attorney of record, but I wanted to hear more from Ms. Price. "Any news as to how Mr. Oakley died?"

"Well, that's the thing," she said. "He was a diabetic."

I was hearing hesitation. "Which means?"

"He drowned after what appears to be an overdose on insulin," she said.

That might sound innocent to some people, but it hinted of darkness to me. I'd evolved over the last few years into seeing criminal behavior first. I was proud of that, most of the time.

"In my limited knowledge," I said, checking out the guy who'd just parked beside me in the parking garage. In a white car, no less. Though a stranger, he seemed innocent enough as he locked up and left. "That sounds rather . . . unusual? I mean, diabetics have a handle on what to take and how much to take, right?"

"Absolutely," Ms. Price said. "But not all of them make the best choices. There was also alcohol in his system. No two diabetics handle alcohol the same, and if he wasn't careful, he could've gotten hypoglycemic. That would have disoriented him. He might've not remembered if he'd taken his insulin, or how much, and that's when mistakes happen. Honestly, that's as much as I can say for him, because what actually killed him was drowning."

My mind darted with what-ifs. What if he'd been enticed to drink? What if someone had on purpose overdosed his insulin? Or escorted him to the water and pushed him in? If Oakley hadn't been considered such a stable individual, I could've given in to the accident option, but my gut weighed in on the perverse or degenerate ways things happened, too.

But the coroner knew Oakley. I didn't. "Being familiar with him as a person, I mean, you said you recognized him on sight and had spoken to him several times," I said. "What do *you* think?"

"I'm not allowed to do anything but follow the science, Ms. Slade."

Try again. "Does this type of behavior sound like Troy?" I used the familiar name to make this personal.

"No, but accidents happen."

"Would he—"

"I'd rather not guess, Ms. Slade. Is there anything else I can do for you?"

Not wanting to piss her off since I still might need her, if not on this case, then another, I concluded my questions. "No, and I appreciate you returning my call. Did you tell Agent Largo, or should I?"

"He knows," she said. "So do the sheriff's department and the estate attorney. It's been a pleasure, Ms. Slade."

We hung up, and a stillness fell over me, and a sadness. I really wasn't sure what to make of all this. In light of Oakley's friend hanging himself over in Saluda, and Brooks drowning in Lexington, I didn't feel right settling for Oakley's death being a simple stumble into the pond. He seemed more responsible than that. Who would want him dead, or if he had a dark side, what would make him end it all?

He had sold off most of his cattle per Mr. Easton. That could be a sign.

I really didn't want to think of a bunch of farmers being suicidal, like Monroe feared. But considering there were rarely over 150 farm deaths in the entire country, meaning three deaths per state per year, not taking into account the sizes of Texas versus Rhode Island, or Alaska versus Connecticut, five deaths in five months in our little state was on the high side. And that included all types of deaths.

We were just talking around Lake Murray.

I needed more intel. CDM Blanchard had said Oakley wanted to leave his farm to a young farmer coop, which was in the fledgling, if not planning stage. Oakley would surely arrange his legacy before intentionally doing anything to himself. I dropped the CDM a text.

Check on the status of the young farmer coop, please. Did they make it into Oakley's will?

I would have called the attorney myself, but with his being both the CDM's and Oakley's counsel, CDM Blanchard could use his hometown personality and more easily get the information.

That took my daily list of to-do items down to two now that the coroner call and my meeting with CDM Crown were behind me. What remained on my plate today was to connect with Delores Bell and get the story of her farmer's death. Next, get Easton to carry me out to the Brooks farm in Lexington and talk to the family, to get a feel for that man's mindset when he accidentally fell out of his boat after having fished his entire life. How badly were people harassing the man to sell? Any idea who they were?

Were they sure he was alone on that boat?

CDM Crown told me the gist of what led up to Brooks's fishing debacle, but he didn't talk as if he knew Brooks well. Guess the responsibility lay on my shoulders to check details out myself.

I LEFT THE PARKING garage, and entered the federal building, climbing the first four sets of stairs. Embarrassed that someone familiar would hear my huffing and puffing, I exited the stairwell and rode the elevator the rest of the way to the tenth.

Unfortunately, Monroe's secretary's desk was strategically placed to give her a clear line of sight to the agency's glass entry door *and* the agency personnel's comings and goings. She waved as I came in. I acted like I didn't see her and darted into my office in hopes of avoiding Monroe.

No such luck.

Whitney took a phone call before I could plant my butt in my office chair. "Ms. Slade?"

I moaned. "He wants me up there, doesn't he?"

"Yes, ma'am."

"Anything come in while I was out?" Hopefully something I could use to shorten my visit.

"An update from the IG on that case you passed on to them last month. They don't see any substance in it," she said.

That case wasn't splashy enough for their taste. I hated it that they got to pick and choose their cases when I didn't. I trudged over to Monroe's office, wondering if I could remind him that he had agreed to give me space.

"Heard you spoke with Jerry Crown this morning," Monroe said before the door closed behind me.

"He called you." I sat, placing my notepad on the table. I'd decided to document my days, and my meetings, especially with Monroe. He'd have a fit if he understood my reasoning was due to doubts about him. What he told me, when and how he told me to do my investigation mattered. If something big popped up and bit us in my turning over rocks, I wanted all bases covered.

Such documentation could make him or break him.

When he gave no immediate response, I glared. "He called you because you told him to once he met with me."

He didn't deny the accusation, because it was true.

Monroe was fast impeding an investigation. If we found nothing of substance, no problem. One criminal find, and I worried how he'd react and what I was supposed to do with that.

My phone rang. Mr. Easton. "Um, I've got to take this. Give me a second?" But I didn't wait for an answer, instead, stepping away to the far corner of the room, at least twenty feet from Monroe's executive chair and hearing. "Hello?"

"You called, Ms. Slade?"

"Oh yes. Any chance you're open this afternoon?"

"For . . .?"

"A trip to the Brooks farm in Lexington. Did you get my message?"

A throat clearing. "I did but found it odd. Are you sure that venue is still open for business?"

I was going on CDM Crown's information which wasn't absolute fact. Whether or not the farm was active, which meant the wedding barn as well, needed to be confirmed. We could do that together. "Pretty sure, but I thought, hey, I have a reason to go there for my job and since you've met them and I haven't, I felt you could make introductions. As a bonus I could take a peek at the wedding venue while we're there. What do you think?"

He left some silence hanging. "Are you using me?"

Unexpected. "Using you? How?"

"To do your farm-checking stuff you do . . . to make them think you aren't?"

How had I given that impression? "No, I'll be up front with why I'm there. Do they have reservations about you? Is that why you're hesitant?"

His chuckle wasn't lighthearted. "Let's just say you weren't too excited about any of the addresses I showed you last week. You may have thought you hid your disdain, but trust me, you didn't. And I was just being nice about your boots. They looked uncomfortable as hell."

Whoa, listen to Mr. Easton. And he dodged my question.

"Some of that attitude was more for Mr. Largo instead of you, Mr. Easton. But if you don't want to go, that's fine. I'll vet it on my own."

"Humph."

A sigh, and I could almost see his animated body language.

"I can always strategically place cows and hogs around the place to give it the appeal you desire," he said, then he *tsked*.

Taking a quick peek around to see my boss told me to quickly handle my call. Holding him up could interfere with a lot of moving parts with our agency.

"Mr. Easton, I have to see this venue for work reasons. But my fiancé asked me to come up with my own list of places for the wedding, and using you made the most sense. I sort of wish we could revisit the Oakley place again, to tell you the truth. I had an idea of how to use those Confederate roses."

"Hmmm."

Honestly, there wasn't a farm out there I couldn't approach on my own, but I never turned down a way to make approaching a farmer easier.

"Well, call me back if you change your mind. I have someone waiting for me. You have a nice day."

"What time this afternoon?" he said.

This was lunch hour, and I wasn't sure how long Monroe would be. "Three?"

"Three it is. Are you calling Mrs. Brooks or shall I? My last connection with them was for them to say all weddings were on hold."

"Then let me," I said. The wife would be more worried about the government visiting than the wedding planner anyway, and his tagging along with me was less disturbing than me tagging along with him.

Hanging up, I skirted back to my boss.

"Making time for me now?" he asked, just as sour as Mr. Easton.

"That," I said, to clear the air, "was a man who knows a lot of these farms and will soften things when I visit the Homer Brooks farm this afternoon."

"We don't need people to make introductions for us."

Jesus, Monroe.

"No, we don't, but I don't like pestering people. The easier a situation is approached, the more someone speaks to me, and the more I dig out of them. It's more than just interrogating people across a table."

"Who is this man?"

"Just someone who does business with the farmers. Call him a CI." Monroe had worked alongside me enough to understand CI was a cooperating individual one needed to bridge a gap.

Putting the pad down, I steepled hands and stared at an old friend, debating on whether to tell him I might attempt to squeeze in a meeting with CDM Delores Bell on the second floor. Then I thought better of it. What was even odder was he hadn't asked what my plans were about her.

Chapter 13

LEAVING MONROE'S office, I walked to the glass door and exited the agency, without a word to my clerk. As loyal as Whitney could be, I didn't want her to be knowledgeable of where I was going to give her plausible deniability in case Monroe asked.

And I took the stairs.

Nobody passed me on the steps to the second floor, and once there nobody recognized me or me them. It was sad how we isolated ourselves to our floor of employment. Government creatures could remain insanely chained to our habits. I made the appropriate right, left, left turns in the hallways to reach CDM Bell's isolated office, the farthest from the elevator and nowhere near the main traffic of the floor.

Either this was the cheapest rent for the Richland County branch of our agency, or this CDM was paying a price for something she'd done. Did she deserve to be close enough to be watched, yet far enough to give her the tiniest sense of autonomy? A lot of what-ifs as to why CDM Delores Bell had been moved from Craven County to Richland, and something told me only she and Monroe truly understood the decision.

Her door was locked and sported a sign saying someone would be back at two. I was rather surprised. Government offices were pretty strict about remaining accessible to the public during normal hours. She had a clerk, and if the clerk was out of pocket, surely someone from our tenth floor could have covered. While this was the smallest county office in the state, little hairs stood up on my neck. I was feeling rather avoided.

I considered my schedule. It would take me forty minutes or so to reach Mr. Easton at the Brooks farm in Lexington County, and I only needed half that to get there during a time of day when traffic flowed easily. If I left now I'd be at least thirty minutes early. *Lunch was suddenly back on the agenda!* The building's canteen being only two floors up, I took the stairs again. The coffee cake from this morning long digested, I pondered what type of sandwich still left this time of day might be worth eating. Government bureaucrats ate like starved coyotes, swooping into the canteen at lunch, cleaning out the favored items first.

Moseying through the propped-open double doors, I assessed the seating area, which held only ten people in a room that could seat two hundred. This federal building housed two thousand people, and during virus season, I scheduled as much time in the field as possible. The circulated air in the place spread flu like smoke at a campground. COVID was years ago, but a few souls continued wearing masks when too many people could be heard sniffling and sneezing. General Services, which managed the building, swore up and down the air was fine. Nobody believed them.

Sooner or later everyone crossed paths in the canteen. Here was where you saw directors, clerk typists, technicians, and engineers. The room leveled the playing field, and anyone could be found seated with anyone.

Delores Bell was in the far east corner, reading a book.

Darting into the food area, I snatched whatever sandwich my hand landed on first—keeping my eyes on the exit so she didn't get gone—then a bottled water. I paid, telling them to keep the change, but no, the government didn't do that. You had to endure the counting out of nickels and dimes.

Then I sauntered through the room, as if seeking the most comfortable spot to spend my lunch hour.

"Well, here you are," I said, sliding into the opposite side of the booth from Bell. The slick vinyl let you slide five feet, worn smooth by thousands of bureaucrats, probably from before I was born.

A rather tiny lady, Bell put her book away, tucking a tress of dark hair with minimal wisps of gray, behind her ear. She had it in a lone cute braid. She was my age. She appeared stunned until she tucked that away, too.

I had about thirty minutes before I needed to leave to meet Easton.

Bell's lunch wrappings had already been wadded up; her glass of tea was down to ice. "Good afternoon." She forced herself to look at me. That told me just what I thought. She was hiding out here.

Unwrapping my sandwich like I'd meant to be here, I played it simple. "Went by your office and saw the sign." *In other words, why weren't you in your office?*

"My clerk's out," she said. "And I had to eat."

I raised a brow. "I left a message we needed to meet, and Mr. Prevatte called as well, I believe."

Her gaze dropped to her hands, and she focused on collecting her lunch detritus. "He did. He just said that you were in headquarters today, and I was to be available."

Nevertheless, she was here instead of her office.

We'd beat up that topic, so I bit into my sandwich.

Good God in Heaven, what the hell was this? Chewing up what resembled spam from a can, I lifted the top slice of white bread. Little green pieces of something dotted a pink, pate-looking substance. Not enough mayo to improve the flavor.

Delores chuckled at my reaction. "Never get the ham salad. Comes from cans that probably expired during the Korean War."

Spitting it out, crunching it back up in its wrapper with the rest, I sat back and resorted to my bottle of water. "We need to talk."

Her humor disappeared. "Have I done something wrong?"

I bit back saying something about the simple fact I had to run her down and instead smiled innocently. "I'm researching farmers who have died, wanting to check on the status of their farms and their loans to us. It's a project Mr. Prevatte put me on after we had another one die last Friday in Newberry."

She scowled. "How many have there been?"

"Five in five months," I said. "That I'm aware of."

I waited. She waited. "Where are the others?" she finally asked.

"In chronological order, the counties are Richland, Lexington, Saluda, and Newberry," I said, using location instead of names.

Squinting a bit, she quickly unsquinted, as if I couldn't see her attempt to figure out the connections.

Hell, I didn't have the connections yet, but if she had an idea, I was all for hearing it. "What are you thinking, Delores?"

"Five. That's a lot. I'd heard . . ." But then she stopped.

"Heard what?"

"I'd heard about mine, of course, then the hanging, the drowning, and the hog pond. Who's the Newberry one?"

"Troy Oakley," I said. "Cause of death yet to be determined."

I recognized her thought processes trying to decipher something. Either that or I was overthinking this.

"Tell me about the one you had here, in Richland County," I said, aiming to work my way backwards since that's how fate had been directing me since this whole investigation started.

"Mr. Prevatte said—"

She stopped, showing no desire to complete the sentence. I prompted her. "What?"

"He said to just answer your questions. That everything would be all right."

Interesting about that last part. Unless he said something like, *If you're truthful* everything would be all right.

"I'll reword," I said. "How did your farmer die?"

Opening my phone to my note app, she watched my hands. "Taking notes in my app," I explained. "No paper."

"Which farmer?" she asked.

I stopped typing and peered up, caught unawares. "There's more than one?"

"Oh," and she reddened. I mean, really turned red-faced. "Who were you here to talk about?"

Huh, right. "How about you tell me about all of them. How many are there?"

"Can you not type and just listen?" she asked.

"I'd rather you just answer the questions." She wasn't a taxpayer. She was an employee. I held the trump card here.

"Is this a formal interrogation?" she asked.

"Does it need to be?"

"I don't really know, Ms. Slade. You're rattling me."

Then I did something I don't often do. I pulled out my makeshift badge, an embossed plastic affair embedded in leather. It looked like a real badge but held little authority other than it solidified my position as an extension of the State Director in any investigative matter. I rarely used it, especially with employees. It felt bullying to me, but sometimes episodes called for it to make an appearance.

"First, Ms. Bell, I do interviews, not interrogations. That's what the agents do when they arrest you. Second, if you don't like doing this informally, by all means, let's go to your office and turn it formal." I didn't tell her we eventually would wind up in a formal meeting if this case got weird. For now I was simply fact-finding in the name of Monroe.

Only having seen this woman from the opposite side of a room in a meeting here and there, I'd arrived with no real opinion of her until she dodged our meeting today. A strong opinion was damn sure trying to form now.

"Delores, we are in the canteen, and to anyone who walks by, we are sharing lunch. If you want this to be behind closed doors and recorded, I can clear my afternoon right now and make that happen. I'm not trying to threaten you, but you seem to want to dodge me, which only makes me look at you harder. Almost like you need an attorney or representative to advise you before you pick your words. Am I wrong?"

That seemed to be a lot for her to digest. Now I was wondering which meeting was more important, this one or the one with Easton and/or Brooks. One would have to be rescheduled in order to do the other justice.

"Tell me about Merle Lester first," I said, using the name of the dead farmer in her county, bringing the purpose of this visit around.

"His tractor ran over him."

All I'd heard was he'd died in a farming accident. Nothing in the papers said suicide or accident, and murder had been ruled out. So, again, the unspoken assumption had been accident.

"Who found him?"

"His son."

"Jesus," I said, without thinking. "How old is the son?"

"Twenty-eight," she said.

"Was the farmer behind in payments?"

"No. He owed very little as a matter of fact." She mentioned him by pronouns only, as if we continued some need for secrecy by not mentioning his name.

"Was he having mental problems?"

She thought then shook her head. "Not to my knowledge."

"Had you talked to him much?"

Again, shaking her head. "Never met the man, honestly. He wasn't behind in payments and therefore, wasn't high on my list to see as a relatively new CDM here."

Which made her little help with Lester. Tractor rollover was the number one killer of farmers, making up half of farm deaths. Slopes, mud, sharp turns, and high centers of gravity could turn a tractor over on the driver in a blink.

A farmer definitely would know how to make it happen if it was suicide, but there were better ways on a farm to end one's self.

Each farmer, thus far, had issues totally different from the others. Only the hanging pointed to suicide, and he'd had marital problems.

For continuity's sake, I asked what I'd asked about the other four. "Anyone pressuring him to sell his land?"

"No."

"You said you'd never met the man, however you are aware no one had been pressuring him?"

"You tricked me," she said.

"No, I just asked you what I've asked the other CDMs. Call them to confirm if you like."

Her eyes expressed a quick array of expressions.

"Ms. Bell. Either you'd met him and learned that he was talking to people about his land, or you didn't meet him and had no clue. Which is it?"

"He came in once or twice, but I never went to his place."

She'd squeezed out a little truth.

"And what about him selling his place?"

"He'd been asked to sell several times. He's on a river with frontage on a decent highway. Prime for development. This is Richland County, so you can imagine how the taxes were jumping up on him. He wasn't a wealthy farmer nor a wealthy landowner, just a lonely man who farmed a hundred acres and was worried one bad season would do him in."

"See there?" I said. "You know way more than you thought you did."

Ms. Bell had secrets. I could smell them on her. Whether work-related or personal, she held them tight to her chest, and the fact she'd been relocated for unknown reasons told me they might have originated in Craven County, where she'd transferred from . . . maybe away from said reasons.

"Sounds like a sad situation with him," I said, trying to be sympathetic.

She sat back like she'd thought of something. "You want to know the ironic part of it all?"

"Tell me."

"He was starting a side gig," she said. "He'd built this pole barn affair where you strung lights and draped material to look like something mystical to rent it out for entertainment. He hadn't even had his first event. Some say he had depression issues. Some say he was stalling the inevitable."

"The inevitable?"

"Getting out of farming. He was alone, working himself to death. Some say he drank."

"Tractor incidents are usually accidental."

"Or they can look like accidents. It's all messed up, in my opinion," she said.

Yeah, it was, but not for the reasons she thought. That meant the commonality of four out of the five deaths I looked at was weddings. And developers wanting to buy their land.

Let's see how many more thoughts she could come up with. "What's happening with the farm?"

CDM Bell shrugged.

"You're with Agriculture. It's your business."

"Not my business yet, I meant. Not if someone pays off his loans with us. Surely, he had insurance . . ." She faded out.

"Ms. Bell," I said, calling her out. "You rattle off what people think but don't sound like you can confirm much of anything. You knew this farmer, or you didn't. And with him dead, you need to find out how the estate is being handled."

"I've said enough already," she said.

What the heck?

"I'm not a tabloid journalist, Ms. Bell. I'm an appointed investigator directed by your boss and mine, Mr. Monroe Prevatte, to delve into these issues. To avoid talking to me, to hold back information"—I leaned in just a smidge—"is to put your job in jeopardy."

I'd never had to recommend someone be demoted, transferred, or fired for clamming up like this. I could, though.

"Yes, but I spoke out of turn. Cheesy gossip, true or false, is destructive."

Not to a dead man without family.

CDM Bell had ten years under her belt from her personnel file, having worked with the Clemson Extension Service for a decade before. She should be a better quality employee than this, which made me want to know as much about her as the farmer.

"Mind my asking why you transferred from Craven to here?"

Her whole being stiffened. "Yes, I do. If you don't know already, then maybe you weren't meant to know."

Oh yeah, this CDM merited some serious digging into.

But I wasn't picking a fight with her. Not yet. I closed my note-taking app and checked the time. The half hour had come and gone. I had enough from Bell for the time being, enough to make me want to come back. "I have another appointment, but we need to talk again."

Her expression tried not to harden, but her jaw gave her away. "Any idea when?"

"Not certain," I said, suspecting that Ms. Bell might start taking take her lunches someplace nowhere near the federal building.

"On that note, I need to unlock the door to my office." She didn't wait for my response, collected her lunch wrappings, and strode off without a goodbye.

Twisting in my seat, I watched her leave. She did a slight stutter-step at the double door entrance, clearly recognizing someone out of my line of sight. Her smile melancholy, she headed in that direction. I got up and fast walked to the nearest trash can and dumped my own wrappers, but when I reached the door, she was nowhere in sight. I trotted to the elevator, but no sign of her nor whomever she greeted.

I almost returned to see if she opened her office as she should have, but I was pushing the clock when it came to meeting Mr. Easton at the Brooks farm.

I'd have another go at her on another day . . . another day soon.

This time the elevator ding called my name. I had to scurry to my vehicle, hoping traffic and lights were in my favor for the entire thirty-five miles ahead.

Chapter 14

HONEST TO GOD, Mr. Easton pulled into the Brooks farm drive about sixty yards in front of me. My car showed the dust of being on the road, but his shined like it had come right out of a car wash.

This farm appeared more diverse. Along the highway I'd passed fields of stubble where corn and soybeans had been, but once I pulled up to the Brooks's house, I spotted fall plantings of collards, turnips, and spinach, maybe rutabagas, in the most beautiful, well-tended rows that went on forever toward a backdrop of woods. Not a weed in sight.

Behind the house, three large, assorted barns covered about six acres, but off in the distance, toward the east, I spotted what was likely the wedding venue. They'd lined a wide one-lane, well-groomed path with loropetalum bushes, and while that evergreen held no flowers this time of year, the maroon foliage created a striking contrast against the fall backdrop of everything else. Come spring and summer, those bushes would pop dark pink or lavender, and if managed properly, would bloom for months, making for incredible photo opportunities.

The siding of the wedding barn itself, even from my quarter-mile distance, stood proud and maroon as well, trimmed in beige. Soft gray clouds of the day offered a crisp photogenic moment.

This place was amazing. Easton thought he'd lost access to it when Homer Brooks died, which was why it hadn't made Easton's list for Wayne. Wouldn't that be a hoot if I came home with a locale nailed down, thanks to a fluke.

In my admiration, I almost didn't see Mrs. Brooks walking toward us. Mr. Easton did, however, and closed the distance quickly, hand outstretched. The main reason for the visit was for Agriculture, not him. Hopefully he remembered the secondary reason we were here was to be addressed more subtly. I had to be careful how we dealt with that.

"How do you do, Mrs. Brooks?" I advanced for a handshake. "Nice to meet you."

The woman was sturdy. Not overweight but her bones had enough meat on them to fill a size sixteen. A working woman. Hair in a graying shag, she wore jeans like she was born in them, boots like she learned to walk in them. "Ms. Slade."

"My condolences about your husband. I understand that he was quite revered in the area, and from a cursory glance at these fields, he loved his work. Very nice place you have here."

"Come on over to the trees," she said, where black metal tables and chairs sat in three clusters to handle a dozen people. Though cool enough to sit in the sun, the tables were placed to be in the shade, for the six months the heat could become miserable. A pitcher of something sat on a tray that also held cookies. The closer we got, the more homemade they looked.

"Sit." She motioned to the prepared snack. "I imagine y'all might have some questions about how things will be managed around here with Homer gone." She came to the point with confidence, her voice softening at the mention of her husband.

We let her sit first. Mr. Easton waited to sit last.

She filled our glasses with what turned out to be cider; the cookies turned out to be ginger snaps, and they were indeed homemade. Moments like this made me love what I did. While I was a troubleshooter for my agency, I liked to think that being a woman softened things a bit at times like these.

The wife started. "You're here for a status on the farm's plans?"

"Well, I am," I said. "You know Mr. Easton and probably can guess his purpose. Happenstance had us both needing to see you. We combined our trips. Hope you don't mind."

She was maybe a dozen to fifteen years older than I was. Maturity, widowhood, and status as matriarch of the property warranted my full repertoire of manners.

"I can walk around and come back," he offered quietly, playing second fiddle. I almost felt like he and I had developed a slight bond after our chat at the Oakley place under that portable heater, a towel draped over my damp lap while he empathized about my boots.

Mrs. Brooks shook her head and launched into talking to set the record straight. "We're keeping the farm. My name is on those loans, so life continues business as usual."

"Yes, ma'am," was all I said, because she clearly wasn't through. Easton's brows bobbled at me when Mrs. Brooks wasn't looking. This could evolve into a financial discussion he wasn't privy to. "Um, ma'am, if you don't want to speak in front of Mr. Easton."

"Our markets are still supportive of us," she continued, ignoring me, leaning over to refill our glasses when they weren't half empty. She pushed the plate of cookies closer. She was accustomed to taking charge.

"Our crops haven't missed a beat. Our employees and seasoned help are, as they've always been, loyal. Even more so with Homer gone. My son Roy has stepped up, but he was actively involved before anyway. He owns the hardware store in Lexington, and he upped the hours for his assistant manager to make up for being here more. My daughter-in-law does the books."

Wow, Mrs. Brooks had her act together, but nothing had been said about the wedding business. Maybe she hadn't decided, but surely, she realized that Mr. Easton was present to learn that one way or the other. For some reason she omitted that topic, which only brought more attention to it, in my opinion, since she'd been so articulate and firm about everything else.

For a while we sat and enjoyed our cookies and cider, speaking of crops.

Mr. Easton cleared his throat.

"I realize you're sitting there," the woman replied, glancing at him before setting her gaze on the wedding barn. "And it's why I didn't talk dollars and cents in front of you. None of your business." Mrs. Brooks turned to me. "I'm surprised y'all came together. Is there something I'm missing?"

Mr. Easton started to say something, but I interrupted. How could I word this? Hell, might as well call it what it was.

"Truth is, ma'am, I'm engaged, and I met Mr. Easton at another farm. He was giving us a grand tour of several wedding venues in the four-county area, and when he mentioned he didn't believe he could show us yours with Mr. Brooks's demise, I said I had to visit you anyway. He asked to come along. I saw no harm in it as long as we didn't get into personal data."

She seemed to accept that, but she did have the good sense not to say much more.

Maybe it wasn't a good idea to come with him after all. My bad.

"Mr. Easton," I said, turning my attention to him, "could you give us a moment?"

He nodded and left, and I waited until he was far enough away. "Sorry. Didn't mean for things to get awkward. But with him gone, mind if I ask if you will continue that sideline in terms of the farm's income? Between you and me only. Tell him only if you like."

"Haven't decided," she said. "Honestly, I don't trust that man."

That caught me off-balance. "Has he done something to make you wary? Might help me in my dealings with him." If he had done anything off-color with her, who knew if he'd done the same with all these others?

"No." She dragged out the word. "Just my sixth sense, and I've learned over the years to listen to it. So if you're here to hunt for a venue for your own wedding—"

"Ma'am, let's forget Easton is even here. My apologies." I shifted quickly. "But I am thrilled to meet you and see how amazing you are handling things. Everything. You're impressive. I wasn't just here to check on your loans. I wanted to see if there's anything we can do to assist you in making this farm a continued success."

That earned me a slight smile. "Apology accepted," she said.

Whew. My decision to invite Easton wasn't all that bright in hindsight. It had, however, shed questionable light on him. Something about him rubbed Mrs. Brooks wrong. To be honest when I first met Mr. Easton, I wasn't a fan either, which made me wonder why I'd discounted my instincts. Wayne's frustration over selecting a wedding place might have muted my judgment.

From there on, Mrs. Brooks explained what happened to her husband. He often fished alone, the sport being his favorite pastime. The boat was his normal boat, one he'd had for a decade at least, that he kept maintained and well-equipped. He checked in periodically while on the water, to ease her mind or to address a problem on the farm. Most people fishing had a safety plan in place to keep those on land informed.

"The cancer made him focus more on what was important, though he had a fairly good grasp of that before," she said. "He fished more. He shifted more responsibility onto Roy. He spent more time with the grandchildren. And he tied up his affairs in tight order, giving him and me some peace of mind."

"And then people tried to talk him into selling the farm," I said, echoing what I'd heard.

"Like damn vultures," she said. "Three or four times a week someone called or knocked on the door, like this farm couldn't function without him and would fall into ruin shortly after his last breath. Well, this is a family farm in the truest sense, Ms. Slade, and the best way we can preserve his memory is to keep it operational and tell developers to go to hell. Homer was working on a conservation easement for most of it, and my son is well aware that's how this land will be handled. No damn subdivisions." She sucked in a lip, peered off toward the woods, and added, "And they're not killing another dog."

I didn't ask what would happen if they tried. All farmers wielded weapons to ward off dangers.

You go, Mrs. Brooks.

Hands were busy on the place in spite of this being a slower time of year, and one of them interrupted us asking for guidance on replanting a flooded-out spot in a field. Then another interrupted. The widow was being called back to work.

A couple more questions. "Are the developers hounding you now?"

She scoffed. "They try. One even said Homer had agreed to sell . . . verbally. I told him where he could stick that agreement since I had agreed to nothing, and my name was on the deed. They harassed the ever-loving hell out of him, Ms. Slade. Probably one of the reasons he was so diligent in getting his act together to depart this earth." She gave a sarcastic chortle. "And the sons of bitches then thought I'd cave to pressure, afraid to be alone out here all by my little lonesome self."

The following laugh wasn't humorous. "They were accustomed to such dealings. Like watching a human snake." She put her cup on the tray. "Do you need anything else?"

I'd taken up enough of her time, and Easton grew impatient pacing the lane leading to the wedding barn.

I excused myself with ample thanks and a final apology. She seemed to be in a better frame of mind, However, she barely waved at Mr. Easton before carrying her tray back indoors. I motioned for him to follow me in the cars, telling him and his puzzled look that we'd pull over somewhere along the way and talk.

Chapter 15

IT WAS AFTER four, and traffic had increased. I took Mr. Easton to a Waffle House, ignoring his wince at the ambience when we walked in the door. Coffee was good here, and that's all I needed. That and a booth in the corner to talk to him about my new concerns.

"I can't remember the last time I've been in one of these," he said, looking around like something would crawl up his sleeve and infect him.

"Don't be such a snob." I ordered my coffee, telling him to inform the waitress what he wanted. The place was three-quarters empty, not quite time for the dinner rush.

He did, then remembering I'd tossed that gunky sandwich at lunch, I also requested a small bowl of grits and a piece of toast.

The waitress left and I leaned in toward Mr. Easton, the small table allowing me to just about get in his face. "I should not have met you out there, but it did open my eyes to something."

He leaned in, eager to hear a secret, like we were best buds or something. "What?"

"I don't think you lost that farm over Mr. Brooks dying," I said. "Mrs. Brooks doesn't like you. Care to share?"

Stiffening in his seat, he drew a hand to his chest. "Seriously? I'm pretty good with wives." He thought for a second. "I had no idea."

"Not believing that for a second. Anyway, listen, are you an anomaly being familiar with all of these farms or are there more like you running around these parts doing what you do?"

Giving me a side-eye, he pursed his lips. "No, I'm not the only one, but I am the most active," he said. "Let's say I've made a good business freelancing these opportunities. The farmers make money, and I run the gigs, them watching from the side."

Mrs. Brooks and her gut feeling about him worried me. "Any chance you said or did something that made her dislike you? Or her husband, because I sense those two were pretty damn close."

"I cannot imagine," he said, but I sensed that calculating business head of his knew better.

"Somehow, I believe you *can* imagine, Mr. Easton. Humor me. What might you have said to give yourself a . . . a stink?"

He scowled at my use of the word I'd purposely chosen to get a rise out of him.

He scrunched up his cheeks to where they almost touched his eyes. "I may have told someone that Homer Brooks was dying of cancer and might be amenable to selling. I took pictures of the place and made friends with the wife, or thought I had. I was hoping that she'd give my friend first crack at a deal when it came time . . ."

He ran out of steam watching me shake my head at his audacity.

"And they killed her dog in an attempt to make her cave. You ought to feel proud."

"I didn't kill the dog."

"No, but you practically set it up. Thanks to you someone went after the farm, Mrs. Brooks stood her ground, and they took her pet. Doesn't take long to put two and two together. I'd hate you, too." Wouldn't be difficult, for sure.

"That wasn't my fault," he mumbled.

"Which do you make more money at, Mr. Easton? Wedding planning or unofficial commissions from pointing developers to tracts of land owned by desperate farmers?"

The waitress set our coffees before us, then my grits and toast which no longer looked palatable. I put sweetener in my coffee and made Easton watch, waiting.

"It's not quite as seedy as it sounds," he said.

"What's the difference between a little seedy and a lot seedy?"

"That's harsh."

I pushed the grits aside and rested elbows on the small table. "How many farmers do you do business with. I mean, wedding-wise?"

"Twenty-one."

Stunned at the quick response, I thought maybe he did make a living at this. "How many farms have you steered to developers?"

"In what length of time?" he asked, serious as a heart attack.

"Good heavens, since you started."

He thought. "Seven."

Those grits would have come up if I'd eaten any of them. "You mean you have singlehandedly directed land-grubbing subdivision developers toward handicapping the farming in the Midlands."

I grimaced at him. He showed his share of disgust in return.

"How many acres does that amount to?" I asked, madder with each word.

"I don't really keep track . . ."

"How many acres?" I repeated, loud enough for two waitresses and a cook to look our way. I didn't give a damn.

"Four thousand seven hundred," he said. "In five counties."

The number left me speechless. Then it hit me that he'd operated in more counties than I thought. "Name the counties."

"Lexington—"

I began to think I barely scratched the surface in my knowledge of him. "More than just Mrs. Brooks in Lexington, I take it. Who else?"

"Not sure I want to say."

"What other counties?"

"Not sure I ought to tell you."

"If you don't talk to me, then I'm forced to talk to a lot of farmers to get the information. That just might kill both your wedding business and your sleazy real estate deals. But . . . it's your choice."

"Saluda, Newberry, Kershaw, and Richland."

Four counties around Lake Murray, counties I was already looking at, plus Kershaw, which boasted Lake Wateree. That area attracted people almost as much as Lake Murray.

A chill rushed over me at what he was doing, and his timing in doing it. I couldn't help but mentally run down my case list.

Troy Oakley in Newberry County. Drowned after an overdose of insulin. I knew firsthand that Mr. Easton managed weddings on that site.

Dewey Anderson in Saluda County. Hanged himself after his wife filed for divorce. Mr. Easton managed weddings on that site, too. "Did you tell people about the Saluda place?"

"That place was gonna go sooner or later. Had to be slick on that one."

"You aren't doing yourself any favors talking like that. What does that even mean?"

"I wouldn't be discrete if I told you, huh?"

Homer Brooks in Lexington, the place we just left. Drowned after a cluster of an investigation which debated whether he was murdered, committed suicide, or fell by accident, atop the fact he was dying of cancer. I already knew he'd been pushed to sell . . . and Easton held weddings on his place.

Lexington County farmer T.J. Candleman didn't sound like the nicest guy, wielding a weapon at those wanting his farm before dying from methane poisoning at his hog pond. That made the news. Maybe Easton had confronted him about the option of doing weddings. I could almost see him pushing the guy in except Easton would be a coward at the sight of a weapon.

"Why no weddings at the Candleman place?" I asked.

"It was a pigsty," he replied. "No amount of tuille, flowers, and lights would make amends for what you had to drive through to reach the venue. No view. Ample stench. He pissed me off flaunting a gun at me. The accident was opportune, in my opinion."

"You're owning that opinion about a dead man?"

"He was easy to not like."

Then there was Merle Lester in Richland. Died under his tractor. "By any chance did you know Merle Lester in Richland?"

"Oh, that was sad. Yes, I did. Wonderful man."

I'd already confirmed Mr. Easton's wedding-planner world had involved Newberry and Lexington. "You used these farmers, didn't you?"

"You give me too much credit. Not all of agriculture sees the advantage of sidelining. And most of them I only knew well enough to plan weddings, usually from a distance," he said. "T.J. Candleman was an idiot and not worth the trouble. Some of them aren't."

"You'd sell their land in a heartbeat."

He held up a pointed finger. "Correction. I'd recommend their land to someone. There's a difference."

I sensed he was damn active, widespread, and successful at what he did. Now to point out why I was in this line of questioning to start with. "That's a pretty high death rate for this area, don't you think? You might want to redefine your business model."

"The model works perfectly well, Ms. Slade. I plan weddings, a pure joy for me, or I sell the real estate and put a little change in my pocket."

Had to hand it to him. He had some sense of a plan, and he seemed to be making it work. I hated that it eroded agriculture and aided developers. "What if they do like Candleman and send you packing? Convenient he died."

Easton's animated sigh and subsequent *tsk* spat a drop on the table. Chagrined, he quickly wiped it up, frustrated with his loss of manners. "I don't go around killing people, Ms. Slade. That's insulting. Talk like that could hurt my business, so please keep it to yourself or I'll consider it slander."

He could threaten all he wanted to. First, it wasn't easy to sue the government. Second, he wouldn't want the notoriety. Frankly, neither did I. Monroe would have a cow if this case blew back on him. He was already worried about what politicians thought. "Who're the farmers in Kershaw?" I said instead, but then I blurted, "Any of them die, too?"

He did this little head toss thing. "That's it. I'm not telling you a thing more. I've said too much already. You're not going to let me handle your wedding now, are you? I bet you could talk Mrs. Brooks into using her place. I saw how you admired it."

Honest to God, the man didn't give up! I wanted to reach across the table, grab him by the collar, and throw him to the tiled floor. "Are you kidding me?" Then I took a mental half step back. Had he been playing me? Giving me enough intel in the hope I'd feel obligated and consider hiring him?

He capitalized on my lack of words. "I make a living either directing developers to potential sales or planning weddings. Sometimes reunions, though I prefer weddings. Either you use me for your event on your place, let me find you a place to hold the ceremony on, or I'm done with these shenanigans." He leaned in this time. "You're more high maintenance that you think you are."

After a stunned moment, I gave a lone, caustic laugh. Days ago my big mouth had told him I already had a place on the lake. "You're from another planet, Easton. Do you even have a real estate license?"

"Don't need one."

Unfortunately, he was right.

But good Lord, I wondered how often he'd snared or hassled farmers, and how many. Then I had to wonder how many had died that we weren't aware of. I hoped none, but the odds of that—after this conversation—unsettled me.

I pondered Easton's upscale Audi and his clothes, which weren't off the rack. His leather loafers, not from the mall. He was the heir to a seven-store restaurant enterprise that was renowned for its success. One would think him too wealthy to cope with pouty brides-to-be, finger foods, and dressed-up barns.

Why wasn't he doing this in the city? His mother could cater there much easier, but I quickly answered my own question. There weren't *bird-dog* real estate commissions in the city.

"Is your mother funding your lifestyle or are you operating on your own, Mr. Easton?"

He threw his thin white paper napkin, the one he'd snatched out of the metal box anchored at the end of the table, but the tantrum fell short. The napkin slid across the vinyl and floated to the floor.

He crossed his arms. "We're through, Ms. Slade. I don't want your wedding. And I'll see to it you don't book any of the farms in the area, either." Taking a second to study the benign napkin statement he'd tried to make, he left it on the floor, slid free of the booth, and strutted to his car.

I let him go. On the positive side, a very tiny positive, he'd narrowed down where Wayne and I could get married. On the work side of things, he'd helped me spot a trend between hungry developers and wedding venues, but unfortunately, a trend that the average federal investigator would laugh at given I couldn't hand them an issue that involved Agriculture. None of these farmers was behind on payments to the government, and when they died, agriculture got fully paid.

And nobody was complaining but Monroe.

What was I missing?

Wayne had to hear this . . . nope. I stopped that thought. This wasn't quite to the level of a criminal investigation. But that's exactly what I used Wayne for, I argued with myself. With him I weighed and measured when a case did or didn't need to be shared.

Monroe wouldn't fire me if I did, or would he? Depended on the resulting embarrassment, I guess. Monroe had been my friend too long a time to up and cut me loose.

However, if he wasn't being on the up-and-up with me, and he had done or said something wrong that painted him into a suspicious corner. . . . No, I really couldn't see him going to the dark side. Why would he mind me taking things at this point to Wayne unless there was more here than met the eye . . . my eye?

Control. Because if Wayne saw more than I did and snatched this investigation away, even I'd be mad.

But when I got home, what did I say? How would I act when Wayne asked how was my day? How many times had I thought that today? Which explained why I still sat in a Waffle House at the end of a workday.

"Well, I pissed off the wedding planner who swore to blacklist me from all the rural wedding venues in a five-county range, Wayne, but that's okay because many of them seem to be dropping dead at an alarming rate anyway."

The waitress filled my cup again, and I molded deeper into my booth seat to let rush hour come and go . . . to think.

The longer I didn't tell Wayne, the madder he'd be when he found out. And how was he not to think I'd sabotaged our wedding plans again when I couldn't tell him the truth?

Chapter 16

BY SIX, I HAD no excuse not to leave Waffle House and go home. Floating in coffee, I took a long pee before heading in that direction, caffeine-wired and uncertain where this case was headed.

Thus far, all I'd found was coincidence, a lot of sad people, and an opportunist making a buck at every turn . . . every bit of it legal as far as I could tell. Ergo, I wasn't mandated to tell Wayne.

But I wanted to so badly I could taste it. There was a dark element to all of this that had me wary.

Easton's dripping arrogance made me want to go to Wayne out of pure spite, and his words kept running through my thoughts. *I just bird-dog. I don't buy the real estate. I just tell them where it's at. I get a commission if the deal goes through. That simple. Might as well capitalize on the opportunity, because if the land sells, I'm out a wedding venue anyway.*

I understood fully what *bird-dogging* meant, and it wasn't illegal. Still, there was a creepiness about what he did.

What did I tell Monroe? The case had gotten deeper, but remained disjointed and might not be a case at all based on how he defined it. The assignment had been to see if the dead farmers were connected, and if Agriculture had a hand in the environment that led to their demises. In the list of five, they'd indeed been connected . . . through Easton, but what did that matter?

I'd give anything to have that arrogant bastard's overall list of farm clients, past and present, so I could paint a better picture of who and what he was. Not sure what I'd do with it with no authority over him, though. There were no public records of how many weddings he had planned, the places he'd planned them, or even the real estate he'd directed buyers to, because he didn't formally broker any deals. I had no power to look at his tax records.

He'd broken no laws, which meant Monroe's orders not to tell Wayne were still valid.

Monroe would take the facts Ag wasn't out any money, there were no suicides, and nobody could confirm any criminal activity as good enough to shut things down.

If I told Monroe of my results he'd shut me down. The creepiness factor, however, was just too large for me to want to quit.

Still, if Monroe said to drop the case, then who said I couldn't talk to Wayne then? That was awful thin ice to stand on, though.

Having chosen the busiest time of day to go home, a long string of traffic snaked as far as I could tell. The red Toyota directly ahead of me braked hard, again. Instinctively glancing behind me, tensing for a bang into my rear end, I breathed a sigh of relief that whoever was behind me—another of the ubiquitous white SUVs—hadn't hit me. Damn it, traffic was worse than I thought, and even taking back roads I traveled twenty miles under the speed limit. Yep, the Midlands area was exploding.

Traffic crept back up and I eased forward. Not to the speed limit but better than nothing. Inching cars made my mind wander. I had developed a distaste for Mr. Easton and should have gone with my initial gut instinct on Troy Oakley's farm. When was I going to learn that gut instinct mattered?

He didn't even merit the *Mister* anymore. Just Easton, like a perp, and I envisioned him as someone who had somehow aided and abetted death. It was as if he had this radar for finding land opportunities via the bad luck of others. He was like a cat in a nursing home, smelling when someone was about to die.

I didn't like the son of a bitch.

And crap, we were back to ten miles per hour on the two-land road.

Why are you in a hurry? Thought you wanted things to remain slow and rural?

Recognizing my ill mood, and smart enough to recognize my spirits reflected more than Easton, more than traffic, but a compilation of worrisome thoughts about situations with Wayne, Zack, my sister, and Monroe, I took ten long deep breaths. *Choose calm.* Choose to coast home instead of letting traffic derail me and send me home to spread this sour mood over everyone else.

I kept studying my mirrors. Side, side, rearview. Side, side, rearview. Though moving slow, in an accident-ripe situation, would take more than my vigilance to keep me safe. One driver looking a second too long on his phone, bored at the creeping, mentally straying like me, would turn this two-lane crawl into a ten-car fender-bender.

That white car remained on my butt. Close, like within two feet, then the driver let a three-car distance build between us. Windows too tinted, the visor down too low for me to make out the driver, I tapped my brakes, making them also have to brake, putting a few more yards between us.

That was tacky, meaning me. But I swear, the car looked similar to those I'd seen following me. A white SUV. Easton drove a white SUV, but it was an Audi, and this car didn't look like his.

Made me wonder if that's why some people chose white cars. So they couldn't be identified. I wondered if I hated all white cars because Easton had one.

I'd been tailed before, though, which is why I studied my surroundings. Back then, however, my tail had been a black SUV which had stood out like a sore thumb.

Finally, the pace picked up, and I was able to reach my turnoff. The white car got off when I did, but so did a dozen other vehicles, and I felt stupid being leery.

Until I lurched forward.

What the hell! The damn driver had bounced off my bumper.

After jamming my foot to the floor to avoid hitting the car ahead, I peered quickly into the rearview mirror, unable to make out the driver. With a deep sigh of disgust, flashers on, two tires in the grass, I eased out of the string of cars to the side. Getting out of my truck, I shut my door, hugging the vehicle, waiting for the other driver to do the same so we could come to a meeting of the minds on what was to be done.

I wanted his name, damn it.

But the truck sped up. *What . . . what the hell?*

"Hey—"

I shut up as the driver came straight at me. With a spin I sprinted to the front of my truck. Taking a dive, I prayed for enough force in legs I now fervently wished I'd worked out, to reach safety. My eyes clenched, waiting for metal to knock my bones into the next county over and all my worries to be over. Sliding atop gravel and asphalt, I came to a halt, under my own power, thank God. But a whiff of air made me cringe, telling me I'd been missed by inches.

The SUV rumbled, growling loud in my ear, revving its engine for a sprint up the side of the road to surpass the line of cars. At the head of the line, it tore right, away from where most of the other traffic was going. The engine whined taking the curve at twice the speed limit and drove out of sight.

Another pickup pulled over ahead of me, and as I rose to my knees—shaky at best—before standing, a young man about thirty rushed to assist. "Are you all right?" He felt the need to hold me under the elbow, and I flashed him a nervous smile, itching to hug someone. To tell the truth, I almost did.

A quiver ran through me. "Jesus, they just tapped my bumper. I probably would've said no problem if he had stopped, but . . . did you see what he just did?"

"Yeah," he said. "Crazy. One would think he was aiming for you." We both watched the traffic continue, nobody else stopping.

I brushed grit off my forearms, wincing at the rawness I wasn't willing to look at. After a mental once-over, I found nothing seriously wrong. My jitters subsiding, the most serious damage appeared to be a tear in the knee of my khakis. There'd be a bruise there tomorrow.

"Damn, guess road rage is real," the young man said. "What're you going to do?"

I shrugged and shook my head. "Didn't get his tag."

"Me neither." He studied the traffic, making obvious note of nobody else stopping. "Clearly none of these morons did either."

This time I did hug him, which caught him unawares, but I needed to thank him.

"You're sort of shaking," he said. "Sure you don't want me to call someone?"

No more than five miles from the house, I told him no. "I'm practically home, but I really appreciate the gesture. Tell your momma she did a good job with you."

To that he beamed. "She'll appreciate that since I was her problem child." Then he tipped his billed cap at me, which amazingly, I'd just noticed, held a Clemson logo.

"Take care," I said. "Go Tigers." To which he grinned and left.

In those few short miles home, I re-lived the tap over and over, each time with a different outcome . . . me under a tire, me bounced off a fender, me smooshed between theirs and my vehicle. Scrapes, broken bones, cracked skull, crushed ribs . . . and worse. I'd lathered myself into a bit of a state by the time I parked in my drive, not even remembering how I got there. I was breathing faster than normal, and I couldn't even remember how long since I'd parked.

A tap on my window brought me around.

I closed my eyes, praying it wasn't Wayne. When I opened them, of course it was.

I rolled down the window. "Hey."

"What's wrong?" he asked.

"Why does anything have to be wrong?" I said, fumbling for my purse.

"You've been out here five minutes." His stare was analyzing, and I tried not to cringe at the scrutiny he was so adept at.

Had I been sitting here that long? Surely not.

"Zack was arrested today," he said.

"Is he okay?" I asked, wondering how the hell I was to tell Wayne about the white SUV without going into the rest of my day, because he would ask, and he would inspect. He would dissect each movement, and each word I said. He was too good at his job, but for some damn reason, I continued honoring Monroe's order.

Wayne reached for the handle. "He got ten years."

But all I could think about was the disappearance of the door standing guard between us, then him seeing my arms, my torn knee, and no telling what else I hadn't noted.

"No parole, which I found rather harsh," he added, facing me head-on.

"Parole . . . what?" Then I realized what he'd done. "Quit messing with me. Got a lot on my mind." Naturally I hunted for Zack in the tree again, seeing nothing of him, though that didn't mean he wasn't well hidden. Or had Wayne been halfway telling the truth about my son getting caught again.

"Is Zack—" I slid out of the truck, and for God's sake, my hurt knee gave out on me. Wayne grasped me under the arm.

"He's fine," he said, but he failed to ask for an explanation for the rest. Instead, he ensured I was stable on two legs then shut the door, following me inside.

"Change clothes," he said. "Had dinner?"

He acted like nothing was wrong. Maybe I'd overthought this.

In the bathroom, I shut the door, locking it like that wasn't weird if Wayne decided to come in. I stripped down. Yeah, the slacks were toast, my knee bloodied and already swelling. Both elbows and some of both forearms had lost a couple layers of hide. They weren't oozing red, but they'd weep on anything long-sleeved. Then there was the bruise on my chin.

Well, shit. Like he hadn't noticed any of that.

What did I tell him about the accident, or the attempted murder, however you looked at it. Or how things went with Easton. Or the inevitable simple question of *How was your day?* when it was clear as mountain water that my day had been anything but good.

I took a shower to think about it. A longer-than-expected shower from the knock on the bathroom door. "What are you doing in there?" *Ally*.

"Chopping wood," I yelled back.

"Well, I fixed you something to eat, and I don't like it getting cold. Get your butt out here." Then she left.

I'd have to face one or the other of them, and both could read me like a Bible, so I shut the water off. After careful toweling off and a few bandages, I threw on loose flannel lounging pants, slippers, and one of Wayne's long-sleeved henleys so nothing rubbed my wounds much. I hadn't realized I'd chosen comfort clothes until they were already on and I was halfway out of the bedroom.

Nobody stood around, no noise in the kitchen. Not even the kids seemed present until I heard bumping in a bedroom down the hall. So out the sliding door I went, knowing full well that's where everything was. They'd turned on the porch heater to dispel the slight chill, and the small table between the chairs Wayne and I normally claimed held steaming leftover bowls of pot pie and corn bread under a cotton dish towel.

I thought I was going to cry and wasn't sure why.

"Eat," Ally said. "Wayne waited for you. The kids and I already ate."

They were being manipulative but in a sweet way, and they knew that I knew it, but there was nothing for me to do but eat the food while it was hot.

Wayne and I hadn't gotten three bites in before the squeak of the sliding glass doors sounded behind us. Nobody seemed surprised but me.

"Kaye," I said. "Want something to eat?"

She already had a bowl in her hand. She assumed a seat at the table next to Ally. Instead of pondering what was going on, I ate my pot pie, staring out at the water.

Little soothed me more than the view of Lake Murray. My cove was two small coves in off the deep water and had the extra calm one would expect tucked away from boat motors and Jet Skis. No wonder everyone wanted this. No wonder developers capitalized on that desire. Rule of thumb was water frontage held a thousand dollars per linear foot value. I had three hundred and fifty feet . . . and three acres to go with it.

This was heaven. And it was paid for. And I had a happy healthy family living alongside me and a fiancé I would kill for. Just let an Easton or developer knock on my door.

But despite my piece of heaven, my mind recognized something was up. What was this? An intervention? A gang up to convince me of something, or worse, inform me of bad news?

"Where's Zack?" I asked.

"In his room," Ally said.

"Grounded?"

"Not today."

Thank God for that. I didn't need another Zack issue.

"And where's Ivy?"

"With him."

Okay. My tension eased a smidge, but something was up, or amiss, or sneaky. "Then what the hell is going on?" I asked, a gaze resting on each one for a couple seconds to spread the request around.

Kaye pointed her soup spoon at my leg. "You're bleeding."

"Yeah," Wayne said, setting down his bowl, leaning over to study it. He slid the pants leg up, and sure enough, blood had bled through the bandage. He dabbed it with his napkin. "And by the way, Butterbean, don't even think I missed the dent in your truck's bumper."

Blowing out, I stared back at the water, wishing its magic could take me away from this. If my peeps continued, I sensed myself about to be busted. Trouble was I had so many things to be busted about of late that I wasn't fessing up to any of them until point-blank asked for specifics.

Kaye spoke first. "I need your help." She paused, attention still on my leg. "Do you need to tend to that for her, Bubba?"

The delay of my interrogation was killing me.

Ally leaped up first, ran inside, and returned with the kitchen first aid kit. She handed items to Wayne who took care of the wound. "What did you do?" he asked.

"Finally!" I yelled, and Ally about fell backwards, the wrought-iron railing of the porch the only thing holding her up.

Wayne hesitated with a quick glance but went right back to putting adhesive tape across the gauze. "You'd tell us sooner or later," he said, sitting back and admiring his work. "That ought to do it. We'll change it again before bed." He wadded up the debris.

"Okay, what are y'all up to?" I said, standing to make my pants leg shake down. "You're holding me to task over something, and before you ream me for whatever it is you believe I did, I'd at least like to be given your suspicions and the benefit of the doubt."

Ally shut the first aid kit and tossed it on the table. "You wear guilt like a banner, Sis. Who says we're blaming you for anything?"

Wayne looked skeptical. "Was the truck accident your fault?"

"No!" I said, insulted. "I'd been investigating a farm in Lexington, then Easton and I had a fight because I believe he's a sleazy prick, and by the time I'd found the nerve to come home and tell you I'd pissed off your wedding planner, it was rush hour, and all those crazies jammed up the back way I took to get home. Then a guy I think was tailing me, hit me from behind. When I pulled over, he tried to run me down, and I leaped out of the way and tore my pants and scraped my elbows."

I stopped for a breath, only then noting stunned expressions around me.

They expected none of this, which meant there was something else amiss. Hell, I wasn't saying another word.

Kaye spoke. "We were going to ask you to come to Clay River tomorrow, but that suddenly sounds like nothing compared to this. What's going on, Slade?"

Wayne didn't have to echo his sister, but his expression told me he waited for the answer.

"Oh." The blinds parted a little as one of my brats peered through. "What's this about Clay River?"

Ally laughed. "Ain't gonna work, Sis. You already started. Explain your day first."

"At least let me finish eating," I said.

"Fair enough," Wayne said. "We've got the whole evening."

I picked at the bowl in my hand. One of my favorite dishes in the world, and the flavor had gone the way of my confidence.

Chapter 17

ALLY CLEANED UP the dishes quickly. Now I had to face my familial adversaries on the back porch. The sun had dipped too low to see the water, the chill seeping through our clothes, so Wayne turned up the heater.

I could simply say I was handling an investigation and get rid of Kaye and Ally, but that would be telling Wayne I was investigating, and he'd want to hear the details.

"I'm visiting the farms of dead farmers," I said, which was the truth.

"To see how they will continue running?" Bless her, Ally tried to act interested in my work. This time she'd said the right thing.

"Exactly."

Kaye, however, could think outside the box from her days staying one step ahead of drug dealers. "So why would that make someone rear-end your truck?"

"I don't know that it's connected. I could be overreacting?" Then I recalled what the young man had said at the accident. "Maybe it was pure road rage due to the traffic backing up. They just hit my truck and didn't stop, panicked, and I had to leap out of the way."

Wayne asked a few other questions, like were there any identifying scuffs or dents on the SUV, was there anyone else in the vehicle, and had I noted any peculiar parking stickers on the culprit's vehicle. Was it a regular tag or something personalized with a different pattern? Maybe even something commercial?

His questions made me think. "It was not a new model. Three, four, five years old at the most." What else? It came awfully close to me, and while seething, I'd watched it take the right turn out of sight.

"It had a SC Sheriff's Association donor sticker on the back bumper," I said, amazed at recollecting that.

Wayne gave a half smile. "People donate ten dollars, get a sticker, and think they've bought a get-out-of-jail-free card when they get stopped."

"That doesn't work?" Ally asked.

We'd have laughed except she was serious.

Wayne grinned his bless-your-heart reaction to her question. "If there's one sticker, there are likely more," he said to me. "Think harder. You might even nab part of a tag."

"There was another sticker. Light blue and white." I squinted, thinking harder. The sticker felt familiar, but I could not place it. "Tag . . . normal three alpha and three numeric. Nothing custom. Might have started with an M."

Never thought I'd remember that much, honestly.

"Call the highway patrol?" he asked.

"No point," I said. "No tag. No description of the driver. Only one guy bothered to stop, and he didn't get those either. The SUV was long gone."

I could see Wayne's disagreement. Maybe I should have filed a report in case the driver repeated said behavior, or in case he came after me again. Stranger things had happened to me. Police forces in six counties had paper with my name on it related to chases, accidents, tickets, and so on.

Was I onto something in my questioning people about dead farmers? Easton had been anything but discrete in his motives and accomplishments, but what about the developers? No, I was jumping to conclusions. Easton hadn't had to time to sic developers on me, like he even had a reason . . . at least that I was aware of.

I'd thought too long.

"What aren't you saying, Slade?" the lawman asked.

Blowing out long and hard, I hoped he'd understand the shaky ground I walked on. I started to ask Ally and Kaye to leave the porch, but I didn't. They knew firsthand what I did for a living, and both had seen me in action. They'd seen Wayne in action. They'd been in action. My mother had just about strangled me for letting my sister get shot in the leg.

I went with a general overview. "Monroe feels badly when farmers die, leaving the farms at risk. He has asked me to visit the last five incidences and take note as to what happened to the farmer, what might have led to it, and who will be taking charge from this point forward." There, I'd made that sound as administratively benign as possible. Sounded downright benevolent compared to what I'd handled before.

Wayne studied me, measuring for what I was leaving out.

"Y'all don't shut down these farms, do you?" Ally asked.

"Quite the contrary," I said. "We'd rather they stay alive. But farms aren't cheap to run, and farmers don't always leave behind family willing or capable to run them. It's how subdivisions are born." I pulled out a reference she could relate to. "Like Palmetto Forest?"

There had to be three hundred houses in that development only a mile from our property. Thank goodness we lived on a side road that could not be developed, so its oaks and hickories, gums and pines remained, with my Lake Murray cove touching the backs of a half-dozen homes. What once was a drive with cows, deer, and wild turkey in open fields, now had retention ponds and vinyl-sided wonders. Broke my heart.

"Can we move on to Clay River?" Kaye said.

"Yes, let's do that," I said.

Wayne didn't ask me if I pursued an actual investigation, and he allowed the conversation to move on. He might ask later. He might wait and see. There were a few lines we tried not to cross between his work and mine, respecting that we were lucky to be together, and didn't need to damage the relationship with intrusive curiosity that might delve too far. Unique situation, to be sure.

The wrong question would make me lie to Wayne or betray Monroe.

"Go ahead about Clay River," he said, holding the glance he gave me an extra second to relay he might understand the difficult hill I stood on and the possible reasons behind my careful answers.

"Okay, Kaye. The floor's yours." I was more than ready to change the subject.

Wayne sat back, turning things over to his sister, but his posture told me he wasn't relaxed with what was about to be said, either.

"Since I've taken over managing the resort," Kaye started, "I've worked hard to make it meaningful, respected, and attractive. Not just for the local day-trippers who want to drop in at any time, rent a cabin, or hook up a camper, and not just for members, but also for travelers. Instead of an Airbnb or VRBO rental, they can find us through the national association, call and make a reservation for a weekend, a week, or whatever time they need in their travels. I've increased the campsites, and we've added a lot of events. A week doesn't go by without at least a game night and potluck or cookout event. Our membership has grown by thirty percent, with potential for more."

"Thirty?" I was proud of her. "Kaye, that's wonderful."

She didn't smile openly often, but she did at my compliment. "We have our first big wedding this weekend. If you still need a venue, I'm your inside girl."

Ally busted out laughing. "I'd kill to see that! Mom and Dad . . ."

She all but rolled on the floor. "Oh, and the kids. Oh my gosh." She cackled until Wayne reached over and threatened to tip her chair. "Sorry," she said, wiping away tears.

Kaye, however, was still proud, happy to be amidst family and talking issues. She'd been alone for so long. While on the lam from dealers, she'd made her way to the South Carolina Midlands from Atlanta and hidden out at Clay River, ultimately taken under a wing by the owners. Ally had made friends with Kaye at the colony, and I'd gone out there attempting to talk Kaye in for Wayne. Yes, all three of us ladies in the nude. My education and experience with a nudist colony greatly surpassed that of the average person.

However, the whole mess had escalated when Wayne's ex, a DEA agent turned rogue and, obsessed with finding Kaye, had turned to the dark side at the temptation of serious money. The affair had exploded into violence and kidnapping near the cabins and in the woods leading to the river itself, with Wayne ultimately shooting his ex, who was doing time right now . . . permanently crippled. He and I rarely mentioned her anymore, but he managed to visit her once a quarter. I couldn't deny him that. I'd gone at her to protect my sister. He'd shot his sister to protect me.

The ordeal had welded this family together, but understandably, Wayne hated the place, though he recognized that Kaye asking for assistance meant she had no other avenue to trust.

"You guys are aware of the problem I've had with theft in the last three or four months," she said. "Some of the first-time visitors still in clothes get pickpocketed. Now I've got lockers being broken into, cars violated, and graffiti on the guardhouse. A colony's reputation is tenuous."

"Shame you're having to be so wary when the place is supposed to be so free," Ally said, then, ever the housekeeper and hostess, she shifted. "Anyone need something else to drink?"

Ally left. Kaye lost her smile. "Someone who's been a member for years has suggested that I had to be suspected as part of the problem." She reached for her tea, only to realize that's what Ally went inside for, refills. "The owner asked me what else I could do. We have a great relationship, and she hasn't said she'd let me go, but everyone understands that if a colony develops an untrustworthy reputation they are done for. This is the owner's retirement, y'all. I can't be the one who lets the ship go down."

Kaye wasn't a softy, not by a long shot, but she paused there. "I've worked hard to find a place to put down roots, and to find a job I love, to boot . . . well, it's just a lot to lose."

Living at and running a nudist colony wasn't for everyone, and after the owner lost her husband in the mayhem that took down Wayne's ex, she didn't have it in her to run the place solo. Kaye had partnered with her, ultimately allowing the owner to borderline retire. She'd risked a lot relying on Kaye, a woman with a criminal record. If Kaye lost this, she'd lose her mind . . . or disappear like before.

Kaye had fought hard to be respectable, feel respectable. She was grounded enough to manage a business, with people skills. Wayne loved her to pieces and was insanely relieved to have her nearby. She and Ally were practically besties. Their personalities were miles apart, but each reinforced the other.

"I take it you're worried about the wedding, and your unknown thief seeing the event as ripe for picking?" I asked.

"Yeah" she said. "And I'm terribly sorry about Zack. I had a talk with him. I hope you don't mind."

Of course I didn't mind. Zack's judgment to practice in front of his friends wasn't her fault. The teacher and other students who instantly labeled him a thief had overstepped, in my opinion. I wasn't worried about Zack. His homebase of discipline was solid, and I twirled my forefinger in the air to take this conversation further. "What's the plan?"

"I took Wayne to Clay River . . ." She halted, watching her brother who sat rather stoically, his sock feet propped on a short table nearby. "I refreshed his mind of the layout. I mean it's been a long time since he's been there, and it was under such different circumstances."

Yeah, we all got that.

"I have several options here," she continued.

Wayne tensed a smidge.

"I can act like I've hired security in Wayne, but he's limited. He has a career."

I understood. "And hiring real security isn't sustainable financially."

"Right. I started to have him visit as a guest who's passing through, having made a reservation on the national site. We get those all the time, in all shapes and sizes."

Wayne listened. He'd already spent the day with Kaye and heard all this.

Ally returned, and Kaye waited for her to distribute refills and take her seat. "The kids are trying to listen, you know."

"Big surprise," I said. "Go on. You're wanting Wayne to be a guest.

Long enough to tempt the pickpocket."

"Well, Wayne had a better idea," Kaye said. "Sure, he can be a target, but why not wait until the wedding, so his appearance won't stand out. He'll just be a friend of the groom or something."

Wayne's set-jawed silence told me he'd accepted. I kicked his chair. "Good on you, Lawman."

"He needs a partner," Ally said, wiggling her brows. "You know how lone males stand out too much." She giggled. "I've offered. Been dying to see this man naked."

Wayne's complexion reddened. "I understand nobody cares about what you look like out there. Or so y'all tell me. Like walking barefoot or drinking out of the lake, it's supposed to be natural and nobody thinks twice about it."

"Right," Kaye said. "You don't think about it after a while."

My mind ran scenes of the place. A naked Wayne and Ally in the pool, at the river, along the nature walks, along the cabins. She'd fussed over my guy since the first day she met him, and while I trusted her completely, the fact she could check this box off her bucket list didn't sit well.

"Or you could go, Slade," Kaye said, before I could begrudgingly volunteer. "I'm asking in person because this is important. It's asking a lot of you and my brother because this is not your lifestyle."

I thought about it a second. I'd be with Wayne. That would be weird, but it was doable. "When on Saturday?" I asked, my jaw now as tight as Wayne's.

Ally snickered from her corner.

"Noon. With this being September, we capitalized on the warmest part of the day. Being on the weekend, it shouldn't interfere with your day jobs, should it? I mean, you two haven't been obsessed with a big case or anything, right?"

I nodded in agreement. She rose and walked over to embrace me in a hug.

I had a membership at the local recreation center and had used their gym equipment a time or two, but too late now to wish I'd done way more than write them a check. I'd be flaunting whatever I had the way it was.

Sighing in resignation, I reached over, and patted Wayne on the thigh. "You game?"

"Going through the motions," he said, as monotone as he could be.

Kaye stood. "Good. Now, let's talk pickpocketing. Not just how to spot it but how to pull it off." She held up my phone.

"Hey," I said, patting my baggy flannel pajama pants.

The kids cheered from inside, apparently still skulking at the blinds.

"All it takes is a hug," she said, tossing it back at me. "Now let's go inside and practice getting light-fingered. Tonight and tomorrow night ought to at least sharpen your senses." She turned to Ally. "When I come back tomorrow, I like spaghetti, by the way. Just saying. With mushrooms."

"Meatballs or ground?" she said.

"Surprise me."

Ally hugged her. "You got it, girlfriend."

The kids waited at the hallway entrance, hell bent on watching the lessons. Meanwhile, Wayne and I stood in the living room, waiting for our instructor, both of us now determined that Kaye would not pull another successful pilfer maneuver. We were too experienced, we thought. Too keen.

"Here's your wallet, Bubba," Kaye said, coming toward us, returning his credentials. "And here's your . . ." she held up a little notebook and started to open it to read its pages.

"Oh, the hell you get to read my journal," Ally said, swooping in to take it away.

I'd never feel safe in my house again.

Chapter 18

THAT NIGHT, EVEN Zack and Ivy got into the lesson, and it made me uneasy that they had mastered pickpocketing way better than Wayne and I. During one engaging demonstration, Zack pulled one over on Wayne, and the whole lot of us fell out in laughter. My heart filled watching this group so enjoying each other. However, we were bonding over criminal activity. How ironic was that?

During one particular moment, when Ivy attempted a new move from Kaye, Wayne intently studying for his own benefit, I pointed to my phone. "I need to take this," I said, leading them to believe I'd received a text. Nobody questioned.

Fully cognizant of my family's keen ears, I moved out onto the porch where the only noise was sleepy ducks. I called Monroe.

"What time is it?" he answered, caller ID telling him it was me.

"Eight thirty, old man. If you were in bed, I need to set you up and get you a social life."

He grunted. "I'm not in bed. I'm enjoying myself for the first time this week, alone, with a meat lover's pizza, and a rerun of *Guardians of the Galaxy*. The second one. It had the best soundtrack."

"That just sounds sad," I said. "You should come over here more often."

"I'd go insane under your roof for long. Your sister, your kids, they are versions of you." Out of the office, probably in sweats and socks, he'd dropped the boss façade.

"Love you, too, Monroe. Now, do you want to hear why I called?"

After-hours calls were not unusual for me, even more so since my friend became my boss. There was something about slowing down and thinking harder that gave me ideas and made plans, or pieces of plans, come together. Before Monroe rose to power, I hesitated to call like this, not wanting to blur the lines between co-worker/friend, and, as he might perceive it, a friend with benefits. We'd never gotten that far, which he had been known to say was his fault for not stepping up to the plate when my marriage went south and before Wayne staked his claim.

"Go ahead," he said, with food in his mouth. Yep, he was relaxed. Hopefully he would still be so after this call.

"I need to speak to Delores Bell in more detail," I said. When I'd run her down in the cafeteria, she hadn't been totally cooperative, and my gut said she'd tried to avoid me. "Would you phone her in the morning and tell her to be available, say, around eleven? I have some calls to make before. If she could rope off between ten and noon, that would be best."

"Why?"

"What do you mean *why*? To do your investigation, that's why."

"Didn't she tell you about her farmer?" Yep, they'd chatted.

"Loosely, but I barely caught her in the canteen for thirty minutes. But you already know since I suspect you were the one waiting for her outside those double doors when she left. I tried to catch up, but you skedaddled pretty fast."

Silence. I'd gone out on a limb on that last part, but my educated guess was that Monroe had been that person she'd lit up seeing, like a trusted friend. She hadn't been in the Federal Building long enough to have too many close friends, and I suspected Monroe had rescued her career somehow. Her unspecified problem in Craven and then a sudden transfer to an office right under the State Director's nose told me she was trouble enough to be watched or a close ally to the boss. Either way, she'd received special attention.

Since he said nothing, I did. "I've learned enough from the other three CDMs to have more questions for her. Our spontaneous meeting in the middle of a cafeteria was not conducive to serious questioning."

No more smacking. Only the sound of Sam Cooke singing *Bring It on Home to Me* in the background.

"Any reason you don't want me to talk to her?" I waited then decided no point giving him the chance to say the wrong thing. "It looks bad if you're keeping her off-limits, Monroe."

"I'll tell her to be available," he said. "She's a good person, Slade."

"Not saying she isn't." I gave him a pass, since I didn't want to let this conversation cross into something moody or regrettable. "I'm being beckoned back inside. The whole family's playing a game, and I said I'd only be gone a moment."

"Go on then."

We hung up.

There. In spite of today's craziness with the Brooks farm, Easton, and the fender bender, my thought processes about tomorrow's agenda had gelled. In spite of Kaye's request to attend a nudist wedding on

Saturday and pickpocket training, I'd formulated what to do in the morning. Afternoon's plans depended on how the morning went.

I knew one thing, though. I wouldn't be around after the Delores Bell interview for Monroe to call me in and pick my brain.

THE NEXT MORNING, I rose earlier than usual, a pure anomaly for me, and beat Wayne out the door. I even left before the kids went to school. The milder traffic almost convinced me to do this more often, but common sense said I'd set the alarm clock for this new routine and promptly snooze it five times until I was back to the norm . . . ten minutes late to the office.

I could've worked from home, but in light of CDM Bell's interview around eleven, I might as well do my research from my desk. Whitney was told to say I was ever on the phone and take messages.

I delved into searches into deaths of farmers in the Midlands of South Carolina in the last year. I Googled a half-dozen different ways. With and without suicide. With and without the words *rural, farm, agriculture, accident,* and *murder.* Two more deaths came up, but they were smaller farmers. I found nothing about changes to their farms. Technically, they were outside the ring we considered the Midlands.

By the time I'd exhausted my searches, office hours had begun across the state. Kershaw County was first up. I had never met this CDM, which meant he kept his head down and never got in trouble. He was mid-career, nowhere near retirement, and experienced enough for his word to have value.

During twenty minutes on the phone, I asked point-blank if any of his farmers had died unexpectedly in the last year. None. So I took him out two years. Still none. I asked him if he was familiar with Easton. In name only, he said. He heard the guy specialized in country weddings, and a few of his farmers did business with him. No opinion on him.

With the workplace hopping now, I called five other CDMs, taking my circle of counties out another ring. Two farmers had died in the last year. The ones I'd found in my searches. One almost a full year ago, the other about eight months. Both from natural causes, with both farms still in operation under different family members.

My ear now cauliflower-swelled from two straight hours on the phone, I turned my chair to peer out the tenth-floor window, thinking. Ten twenty a.m. I had breathing room before meeting CDM Bell in her second-floor office. I hoped she was there. She'd know better than to hide in the cafeteria, and if she took an early lunch downtown someplace, I'd be pissed.

Doing a slow sip on a coffee—part to settle into my plan and part to spark my brain to life for this interview—I analyzed what I had already researched, collected, and deduced, to have it on the edge of my thoughts. Mentally on my toes.

Whitney tapped on my door. "Ms. Slade?"

"Don't tell me," I said.

"Yes, ma'am. Mr. Prevatte asked that you see him."

Sighing, I had just a few short minutes to decide what to do here. If I honored his wishes, he'd make me late. He'd want to nail down what I was going to ask Bell. I'd refuse to tell him, and he'd fuss. We'd go back and forth, then he'd demand I see him immediately after I left Bell, to see what was said.

Telling him details was risky. The more he learned, the more he interfered, which did not look good for him. Why the hell was he so blind to the obvious? He needed to let the case run its course, so that it appeared absolutely legitimate.

"Did you write down he called?" I asked Whitney.

"Ma'am?"

"Is there a note?"

She got my message, disappeared a couple seconds, and returned, handing me a yellow paper. I tossed it on my desk unread.

"You delivered the note," I said. "Yes, you handed it over while I was in my office, but you didn't see me read it."

She nodded in full understanding and returned to her station.

The time came for me to head down to Bell's office, and after a bathroom stop, I took the stairs down, not wanting to converse with whoever happened to be on the elevator. Also, something told me if Bell dodged me, she'd take the stairs.

Halfway expecting to find a sign on her door like last time, I instead found her main door wide open. I entered, her office technician welcoming me with a smile until her brain synapses recognized who I was . . . the Special Projects Representative from the State Director's office who never showed up without a problem in tow.

In an office small enough to be heard from one end to the other, the technician buzzed her boss and said under her breath, "Ms. Slade's here." Like I couldn't hear.

Few of the field staff understood the depth and breadth of what I did and didn't care to learn. The job had been created for me by Monroe's predecessor, and the average employee had never heard of such a thing, so the wariness made sense. In their eyes I was a recruiter for IG cases, helping give agents like Wayne an inside track to anything marginally wrong.

You loved me or hated me, depending on your need at the time.

CDM Delores Bell had no need for me, so I knew what to expect.

"We'll take about an hour or so," I said once Bell appeared and welcomed me. "Is your office okay, or would you like me to find us a meeting room up on the tenth floor?"

I predicted the answer.

"My office is fine," she said, fighting to smile, striving to hide that she hated my existence right now. Most people chose their own office where they felt secure, unless they had an office full of nosey people, like in one of the larger counties, in which case, they wanted to be someplace away from the eyes, ears, and whispers of staff guessing what was going on.

Door shut, Bell put her desk between herself and me. "Why did Mr. Prevatte have to call me, Ms. Slade? You could've made an appointment."

"Sorry, didn't mean to make you nervous by him doing that. I only had this time frame to speak to you, and after the office was closed the other day, I wanted to make sure you had time to schedule coverage. That's often how my job works, Ms. Bell."

I jumped right into the Merle Lester death, the Richland County farmer who died when his tractor overturned.

"Was Lester in financial trouble?" I asked.

"You asked me that the other day."

"Oh, then refresh my memory."

"He owed enough not to have the money to pay us off, but he easily made his payments," she said. "He seemed to know how to farm well enough. He wasn't very big, mostly doing the work himself with a few hired hands and his cousins during the busy times."

We discussed what he farmed, how many times she'd been to the farm (once), and how many times she'd held conversations with him (twice, one of those to schedule the meeting at the farm). Not enough to be very familiar with the man, and with his not being a problem, he'd be near the bottom of her list of priorities. Add to that she'd only been in Richland for five months, the very time frame Monroe had asked me to cover.

"Did he have personal problems? Like health issues? Depression? Family difficulties?"

"Didn't know him well enough," she said, taking no interest in my story.

Okay, fair enough. "Any chance he was being pursued by real estate entrepreneurs?"

"What do you mean?"

The question wasn't hard. I repeated it another way. "Was anyone pushing him to sell?"

"He mentioned it," she said. "Only in passing, like it was a commonplace thing around here. He didn't know me well, so why would he confide in me? If he didn't offer, I didn't push."

"Your job is to get familiar with these people, Ms. Bell, to better assist them in being successful." She hadn't asked me to call her Delores, and I wasn't doing so without that invitation. The way things were going, I preferred keeping this formal.

"Do you believe this push to sell reached the level of harassment?" I asked.

"Have no idea," she said, watching me jot notes. I hadn't brought a recorder. Recorders were for when you needed facts on record and already had a good inclination of what they were going to say . . . or admit to.

"Do you know a man by the name of Garrett Easton?"

Her eyes widened, not in a stretched-out sign of fear, but in a bare split second of recognition. A reaction she quickly regained control of. "I'm not sure. Vaguely rings a bell, but I can't place him. Who is he exactly?"

"Let me put it this way, was Lester holding weddings on his farm for extra money?"

This time her eyes darted. Yeah, she knew Easton.

"I may have heard of him doing some of that. Again, I just moved here, Ms. Slade."

"Then I take it Merle Lester knew Garrett Easton?"

"I assume so," she said.

Which opened the door for me to ask, "Have you met Mr. Easton?"

"Okay, I remember who he is now."

She wasn't very good at this.

"Can you explain the circumstances under which you met?"

Her eyes darted again. She was searching for an answer, which meant it wouldn't be complete truth. Truth was easy to say.

"He came in and introduced himself the first week I was here. Probably why I didn't recall him right off the bat."

"What did he want?"

"Just to introduce himself. The conversation didn't last five minutes."

Her guard went up, stiffness in her body language. This *forgettable* man apparently left his mark.

"Nothing more than an introduction?" I asked.

"No." Spoken like she was glad that was all she had to say, hoping that was the end of the topic.

"Did he ask anything of you?"

"Um, no."

"Did he threaten you?"

"No," she said, without questioning as to why he would do such a thing. Small red flag there.

She had an adversarial air about her. I wanted to know why.

"Why do I have the sense you are holding back?" I asked, stopping short of saying she lied. I saved that word for harder conversation later.

"I'm answering your questions," she said. If that wasn't deflection, nothing was.

"You didn't deny. Are you holding back? Do you need me to repeat the questions, and we try this again?"

Bell clammed up, and up went arms across her chest.

"Let's try something else," I said. "Why did you leave Craven County?"

"If you were allowed to know, you'd already know, wouldn't you? Mr. Prevatte said I never had to discuss that to anyone, and we'll just leave it at that."

Chapter 19

CDM BELL HAD practically told me to go F myself when I asked her why she had to leave the Craven County office. No employee had done that to me before.

"Excuse me?"

"Not up for discussion," she said.

"What happened in Craven before you moved here is not a difficult question," I said.

"And it's not applicable to my work in Richland."

"That might be my decision to make."

This disagreement by her bordered on childish, and her reaction made me all the more intrigued. The first death on Monroe's list originated here, in Richland County, under this particular CDM's oversight.

Odds were that happenstance drove the timing since she hadn't been here long enough to instigate or be wary of Merle Lester's death. On that, she'd responded well enough.

But at the mention of Craven she shut down, turned defensive, and snared my interest more. Also, the fact that Easton had come in and introduced himself before she'd had time to warm her chair gave me more to digest.

She didn't like talking about Easton. I was reading more from what CDM Delores Bell wasn't saying than from what she was, and with every second I sat there, the less she liked me. I tried to clarify. I hated applying pressure, but they'd warned me when they trained me that there was a time and place for doing so. I saw no other option here.

"I am the equivalent of Mr. Monroe Prevatte walking into your office," I said. "I function under his permission, per his order. Section Eight of the US Department of Agriculture Handbook requires cooperation with an investigation, or you risk your career."

"That pertains to federal agents," Bell replied. "You're not an agent. You're a hybrid. You can't even arrest me."

"You want to push that theory?" My pressure rose, and I told myself to cool my jets. Yes, I could damn well get her fired, but I wasn't going there. I started to say I'd take this back to Monroe, basically ratting on her, but that wouldn't help either. She felt she had his blessing for reasons I didn't understand.

Taking myself down a notch, I was determined to give her another chance, to avoid being considered a trouble-making instigator myself, versus a facts-only investigator. "Until today, I hadn't thought much about what happened in Craven County," I said, "or I would've looked at your file. Let me explain myself better. There are rumors, I get it, and you're looking at someone who's endured her share of gossip and inuendo in her career."

She sat there, arms a little looser but not removed from their crossed position. "The State Director didn't say only speak to this person or not to speak to certain people. He said, point-blank, I never had to discuss Craven County," she said.

She'd dug in deeper. Monroe and I would have to chat about this. I wasn't wanting to discuss much with him at the moment, though. The more he knew the more he tended to get on the phone with someone, cast opinion, maybe even redirect the investigation. In hindsight, I should've made my own appointment with CDM Bell, like she said.

"Okay, then," I said. "Let's go back to talking farms."

Her arms came down back into her lap. Not bright, because now's about the time an agent tightened the screws, coming out of nowhere to do it . . . when the guard came down.

"Let's go back to talking about Garrett Easton. Was anything else said to you the day you met him? Other than an introduction?"

Bell seemed confused. "Like what?"

"Like anything. Just tell me what was said and you're good."

"Nothing else was said."

"Did he do business with other than Merle Lester?"

"I don't know."

"Do you trust Mr. Easton?"

A pause. "Don't know him well enough."

"What happened with you in Craven County?" I came back and asked one more time.

"Not required to say," she said.

Unbelievable.

I clenched onto objectivity, the key requirement of becoming a superlative investigator. It wasn't about what she thought of me or what I stood for. The point was to come to factual conclusions on the evidence collected. People often got more in trouble not cooperating than confessing, in trying to outthink an investigator. It almost never worked.

This experience, however, tested me. She trusted Monroe. They were connected somehow, and for God's sake, I hoped not in the way creeping into my thoughts.

If Bell was correct in her assertion that Monroe allowed her this secrecy, then I had three assumptions to choose from. First, Monroe simply was covering the agency's reputation. Secondly, he might just be a good guy, which he was well known for, helping this CDM put down new roots in a new place, overcoming something unfortunate in her past. But third, and I hadn't wanted to think this, was that he had interest in this woman that spread further than the nine-to-five office routine.

That would open a particularly nasty can of worms.

"Ms. Bell, do you have anything else to add to this interview?" I asked. "Remember, if you do, and haven't disclosed everything, you're possibly concealing information that could be relevant to the investigation."

"No, I have nothing to add."

"Will you be calling the State Director once I leave?" I added.

"Not your concern," she said, probably feeling empowered, falsely thinking that I would worry what Monroe thought about me after having pressured a woman who felt rather armor-plated. Frankly, I hoped she did, because that would show Monroe how his phone calls and personal interference impeded an investigation. There was time to correct this, but the time wasn't now. I wanted all the information I could gather before I sat down with him again. An investigator tried to learn the facts before confronting people who needed to confess them.

Pulling details out of Bell was like extracting teeth, and, therefore, I didn't trust what she said. I stood and closed our meeting with a warning. "It's easier to talk to me than a real IG agent, Ms. Bell. I hope you get a decent one, because that's probably the next party you'll have to speak with."

Holding out my card, I gave her my stare. She took the card from my outstretched fingers, trying not to touch me in the process, trying harder not to make eye contact.

On that note I left. In the stairway, I hesitated, wondering whether to go up to the tenth floor and access Bell's personnel file. The transfer papers would all be there, with the reasoning easily being something mundane like *career potential* or *personal improvement*. A lot of personnel issues were disguised and ignored unless you wanted to penalize the employee, with the justification that making minor mistakes a permanent, indelible part of employee history was cruel and unnecessary.

A lot of my past wasn't in my personnel file, that's for sure.

That cumbersome interview had filled little more than an hour. My stomach growled, a reminder that my day had started earlier than usual. Going upstairs to my office, however, would drag out a meal longer when Monroe pulled me in for questioning.

A different option took shape in my mind. It would take up the rest of my afternoon and evening, and I would miss out on Kaye's second pickpocketing lesson, but it would allow me to acquire a better history on Bell while giving me someone in particular to bounce ideas off of. Hell, I might even spend the night. Texting Whitney I'd be gone the rest of the day, I told her to tell Monroe I had face-to-face meetings that were impossible to reschedule, and I would remain in the field at least the rest of today if not tomorrow. That would put over three days between a confrontation with my boss and me.

I'd give Monroe the benefit of the doubt for the moment, but I intended to keep out of sight for the time being. That would be best for all parties concerned, especially for me. I needed my head on straight. An investigator had to look past the familiar to see the facts, even if those facts condemned someone you were close to.

I left the parking garage, headed toward Interstate 26, running through a drive-through for a burger before heading east. GPS put me in Craven County in a comfortable two hours, giving me ample time to make phone calls. Talking while driving wasn't the safest way to run people down, and neither was eating one handed, but time was of the essence, and I wanted my thoughts and plans in order.

MY CALL TO Wayne went to voicemail. In my worries between work, the wedding, and my son's criminal antics, I hadn't asked which case consumed his attention these days. Something local, for sure, because he'd been coming home every night. That made my choice to travel to the Lowcountry all the more bitter with him at the house without me. That already happened too often, one or the other of us in some distant part of the Carolinas while the other was home, which was part of the reason we'd postponed our wedding plans so much.

I glanced in my rearview mirror, and damned if there wasn't a white SUV about six lengths back. What were the odds . . .? I'd be seeing white SUVs on every highway, at every light, on every corner. What would a shrink say about that? I hoped it didn't mean my imagination saw Eastons all over the place.

Slowing to the actual speed limit from the ten miles per hour I'd been exceeding it, coincidentally the SUV slid over as well. I slowed to the minimum allowed, but my tail kept the same distance.

Few would happen to be going to Jacksonboro, South Carolina, like I was. I'd made the decision on the fly. I continued, doing the speed limit, noting my friend behind me every couple of moments.

With my phone on audio through the truck's speakers I almost made another call to Wayne, to tell him I wasn't alone on the road, but that would only make him worry and me sound needy. My message to him already said I'd be in touch later, from the lower end of the state.

Made another call, this time to Ally, who answered, bless her. She always answered. She took my notice in stride, having heard from me like this before. She offered to tell Kaye on my behalf to save me the trouble, and I thanked her. For the most part she was a good sister.

My next call went to my buddy and wedding wardrobe savior Edisto Beach Police Chief Callie Morgan. I hadn't spoken with her since crying on her shoulder about Wayne and wedding and what to wear. God, the wedding had become the furthest thing from my mind these last couple of days.

But an overnight stay required a bed to sleep in. Edisto Beach was an option, but thirty-five miles further than I'd planned to drive this afternoon. However, I needed Callie's ear, and an evening with a friend would be a balm. Here was a friend who had mad investigatory skills, with whom I could exchange ideas, and who would let me vent.

"Hey you," she answered. "This is Wednesday. Thought I had at least two more days to pick out your ensemble. If I hurry, I might get to Charleston tonight, though. Y'all move up the date?" Then she stopped. "You're not calling about the dress, are you?"

"No." I was halfway to Orangeburg, the traffic thinning this far from the capital. The white SUV drove way back, sometimes disappearing behind another vehicle. About the time I'd consider it gone, though, it or one like it would reappear, but who knew? Never close enough to see the driver. I'd slow, and they'd slow. With Orangeburg just ahead, I could slip off one of the three exits and see if they did the same.

"How's the case?" Callie asked.

"Ongoing," I said.

"Tell Wayne?"

"Nope. He suspects I'm in the middle of something, but he has no clue as to what. He's even backed off asking me about wedding venues, but then I also pissed off the wedding planner he'd been working with, so there's that."

"Sweet move there, Slade."

"The wedding planner's screwing around with my farmers," I said. "I don't trust him as far as I can throw him. He fired me when I accused him of raping and pillaging land for profit. Then he said I was too *high maintenance*."

A staticky sound came across the phone, then a breath, then a long, drawn-out cackle.

"Did you just spit a laugh at me?"

She couldn't stop laughing long enough to answer.

"Seriously? You think I'm high maintenance? My clothes come from department stores and LL Bean."

Her laughter slowed, but I could hear tears in the effort. "Oh, that's choice," she said. "You might not be high maintenance in the strictest sense of the word, but that's one way of describing you. And that was a rather harsh accusation, don't you think? *Raping and pillaging?*"

I peered up in my mirror. The SUV was back, in the slow lane but keeping pace. "Well, it's true."

Callie chuckled once. "Does that mean you're back to square one for a venue?"

Road noise sounded in the phone, so she was driving, too. A male voice spoke in the background, and she responded, asking him to give her a minute. Could've been a radio mic.

"I need to check on this situation, Slade. Can we talk later?"

"One last thing. I'm headed south, to Craven County, to do research on one of our employees. If you get the chance, call me back. Maybe we can meet up for dinner."

"Right. Gotta go. Chat later." And she was gone.

US Highway 601 was a mile ahead. I sped up in the fast lane, as if I had to eat up asphalt to get someplace. Then at the last minute, I cut across the slow lane, onto the off-ramp, and followed it up. Instead of stopping anyplace, however, I gave myself a few seconds at the top, then reentered the interstate on the other side, to see what the SUV would do.

Back on, I drove the speed limit, hoping they proceeded east going a little faster than the limit as most drivers were prone to do, putting distance between us. Not seeing them ahead gave me some peace, enough peace to return to contemplating the reason I was even on the highway, and I made another call. This time to the current CDM of Craven.

His last name was Jackson, first name Malachi. An old-fashioned first name and a last name that represented genealogy going back to the Civil War. There was a reason the county seat was called Jacksonboro. Monroe must have decided when Delores Bell left that he best replace her with someone the county agricultural community would trust, a hometown guy versus the outsider woman. I would've done the same thing. What about that couldn't he just tell me?

A lady's voice took my call, telling me the CDM was in the field, but once I told her who I was, she offered his cell phone. He answered on the second ring, a deep baritone, melodious and clear. "Malachi Jackson. Can I help you?"

"Carolina Slade from the State Office, Mr. Jackson. I take it you're out of pocket in the field?"

"Yes, ma'am. My clerk texted you'd be calling. The farmer I'm spending the afternoon with moved a few yards away so we could talk."

This might not work. "Can he hear me?"

"The farmer is a she, but no, she can't."

Bad on me assuming a stereotype. "I'm headed down to Craven."

He paused. "May I ask what is so urgent to appear last minute like this? Is something wrong?"

"Nothing on your end," I said. "I'm following up on a few things, and a couple of them led me to your county, back to your predecessor's time. I'm going to ask you something you might not want to hear, but I do need to pick your brain."

His pause went longer this time. "I'll do the best I can." He sounded like he was moving, and the noise went from the airiness of outdoors to the vacuum interior of a vehicle. "Go ahead," he said.

A road sign announced county highway 33 a mile ahead.

"Are you familiar with the reason CDM Delores Bell relocated from Craven County?"

For a second I thought I'd lost the call. "Mr. Jackson?"

"Um, I'm here. Not sure that's something I ought to be discussing. I mean, I learned nothing from Ms. Bell herself, nor the State Director when he offered me the job. I'd been an assistant in Charleston, and this was an opportunity for me to step in as a full CDM. With Craven being my home county, I wasn't asking why, if you catch my drift."

"I'm sure you've spoken to others in the county . . . and your office staff."

"No, ma'am. I avoided the topic like a virus. Didn't want to be that kind of guy, not in my first supervisory role."

His response painted him the good guy and me the gossip monger. Like CDM Bell, CDM Jackson would be wondering why I didn't have a grasp of the facts with me being so close to the boss and with access to so much internal and personnel information. I couldn't tell him or anyone else in the agency that I could not go to State Director Monroe Prevatte right now. That could get misconstrued on an exponential level.

I gave him a more open-ended question. "You may not know much, as you say, but what do you know?"

"She was in a car accident with one of our farmers. He died. She didn't. Less than thirty days later, she transferred to the Midlands, and they put me here."

Nice summation. "Which farmer?"

"Edmond Jackson," he said.

"What date?"

He gave it to me as I passed under state highway 33.

"Time of day?"

"Eleven p.m."

"Was he killed instantly?"

"Yes," he said. "She went to the hospital, but they released her the next day with a mild concussion and other minor injuries. That's about all I know, Ms. Slade."

Meaning, that's all he wanted to say, but he'd told me enough.

"Thanks," I said. "I'll let you get back to your farm inspection. Chances are I won't come by your office, so don't change your schedule."

"I appreciate that," he said. "You have a good day." He wanted off the phone.

We hung up.

I cruised along, grateful for the traffic, and even traveled a few miles without hunting for a tail. Up ahead, the biggest Orangeburg exchange appeared, not big for most cities, but busy for the town of fifteen thousand or so. The town hadn't grown or decreased in forty years, its families just replacing each other with offspring.

I crossed under the overpass, the motels and restaurants more for travelers than the local residents, and I cruised on, periodically searching my rearview mirror.

A white SUV sat on the off-ramp, waiting. I didn't get two hundred yards before the driver put it in gear and got back on the interstate. They sped up until they were six or eight lengths behind me then coasted, matching my speed.

I'd had enough of this.

Chapter 20

IF MEMORY SERVED me, a minor exit would soon appear ahead, with a Pilot gas station truck stop with witnesses and cams. Moving to the slow lane, using my blinker to give plenty notice of my intention, I called the next number on my to-call list, in the hope she'd go along.

She answered, and I loved that my number was apparently in her contacts list. "Hello? Is this Carolina Slade?"

Quinn Sterling was a private investigator, pecan farmer, and Low-country heiress whom Edisto Police Chief Callie and I had met on a couple of investigatory occasions. We liked her, a lot. She was a bit of a spitfire and her own person. The Sterlings were Craven County royalty, but she wasn't hoity-toity. The woman exuded the confidence that came with law enforcement, atop the assurance that came with wealth. She owned a hell-bent attitude on righting whatever wrong that crossed her path, and in her home county, she had a lot of clout to do it with.

There weren't many Sterlings left, which was rather sad, making her and her uncle, the somewhat tainted sheriff, a concentrated notoriety in that neck of the woods. She knew everything there was to know about Craven, and she was my original point of destination. Right now, however, I needed her to bear witness to what was about to happen.

"Hey, I'm headed down to see you," I said. "Assuming you have an hour open. About a case that originated in your arena with one of our people. CDM Delores Bell?"

She waited a second or two. "I know of her. And sure, I can meet. More than an hour or two, as well, if you like. When do you expect to—"

"Hate to interrupt, but I sort of need you to listen in on a conversation I'm about to have, if you don't mind." I took the off-ramp, cruised to the stop sign at the top, and waited to turn left, watching behind me to ensure the SUV still was on my scent.

"First, where are you?" she asked.

"Exit 159 on I-26. Homestead Road outside Bowman," I said, turning left. "Stopping at the Pilot Station to gas up and see who the hell is stalking me. They got off when I did."

"You alone?"

"Yep, thus, my call to you."

She could've asked where Wayne was or why I called her instead of him, but in the economy of time she didn't. "Keep your phone in your pocket once you get a picture, assuming you can do so without causing a fuss. However, I'm suggesting you not do this being alone."

I pulled into the station and cruised to a pump. "Explain later. Thanks. Hang on."

Stepping out, I thought of my .38 in the glove box. My Concealed Weapons Permit in my wallet made me legitimate to carry it on my person, but here, at a gas station where a dozen cars gassed or waited to gas up or pulled in to grab snacks inside, I didn't feel it wise to wear it and antagonize whoever would crawl out of that SUV. For the same reasons, they'd be less likely to pull theirs out either.

At least that's what I told myself about three times.

The SUV pulled up to a pump two stations over. I hooked the gas nozzle up to my truck then walked straight over, waiting for some six-foot-something beast of a Neanderthal to unfold from that front seat and call me a paranoid, peri-menopausal female.

With cameras designed to catch anyone stealing gas, hopefully said beast had visions of little more than intimidation, but the driver remained inside, the windows tinted dark enough that I couldn't make out individual faces. Rather than tap on the window, I chose to walk around the front, hunting for dents from my last highway mishap, and found none. Had to be another vehicle. That bang would've left damage, and not twenty-four hours had passed since, meaning not time enough to get it fixed.

But this clone had followed me all the same. Wayne had told me to recall tags and stickers. This tag began with an M like the other. Three letters and three numeric, and I wished I could remember if the patterns were more similar. A sticker referenced the Columbia Chamber of Commerce, but when I studied the other end of the bumper, there was that same blue and white sticker the other SUV had. I might have not read it before because of how fast that bastard had made their escape, but this one popped out at me in total recognition.

The background was a periwinkle blue, the white a lily. The brand of Miss Lily's Table . . . a South Carolina Midlands household name.

Lily Mae Chassereau Easton, aka Mr. Easton's mother. That string of restaurants would have at least one vehicle per restaurant, and leave it to her to have them all white.

But Mr. Easton—*damn it, he doesn't deserve the Mister*—drove an Audi without stickers. White, but not one of the fleet. This one, and I was almost positive the other, was an Explorer.

My on-guard status about meeting a beast dropped from Code Red to Amber. I returned to the driver's door and rapped on the glass.

At first nothing happened. But in the little bit of waiting, my pulse amped back up, pumping into my temple. I'd built this person to be a two-hundred-fifty-pound redneck in jeans who lifted farm implements on and off a tractor's hitch with one hand, throwing sacks of feed in a wagon with the other. Now not so much, but that didn't mean they might not be dangerous.

Whoever it was, though, better be willing to explain why they or their counterparts had tailed me for days, because I'd given up on believing all those white cars in my mirror since Sunday were coincidences.

The window went down. "Can I help you?"

Words escaped me.

Her hair dyed an auburn shade to lessen her age, the woman was old enough to be my mother. Her makeup was impeccable, like she was headed to a wedding, or maybe a board meeting. Her pants suit was stylish for her age. Almost stylish enough for mine.

"Why have you followed me all the way from Columbia?" I asked.

"Honey, you must be mistaken. While I have come from Columbia, I'm headed to Charleston. Might you be headed there as well?"

The voice was a firm voice attempting fragility. I heard the effort and developed an instant dislike.

"My name is Carolina Slade," I said. "And yours is . . .?

"Lily Mae Easton," she said.

You may have heard of me didn't come out as expected. Instead, she sat patiently, waiting to see what I wanted. When I didn't move out of the way, she spoke. "Would you mind moving so I can put gas in my car?"

"You're not owning up to tailing me?"

"Young lady." Her hand rested atop the open window, gel-painted nails a subtle pink. She hadn't fried up hashbrowns or washed a cast-iron skillet in a long while.

"I'm just trying to get to Charleston," she said. "If I'm too late, my son is going to have an utter fit. He didn't think I ought to be on the road alone as it is." Then she brightened up, like she'd had a revelation. "How about this? You gas up my car, and I'll pay to fill up yours. That way I can stay safely locked in here. Does that work for you?"

What the hell?

"Dear, are you okay?" she asked when I stood there like an addled duck not knowing which way to the lake.

"Have you not heard of me?" I asked, using the very words I had expected to hear from her.

She leaned in like she needed to in order to hear better. "Repeat it for me?"

"Carolina Slade. You are Garrett Easton's mother?"

She lit up. "Yes, why yes, I am. You know Garrett? Have you been to one of his weddings?"

This pretense was killing me. "No, ma'am." Her age made my manners still fall into place from rote training at my mother's knee. "I work with farmers. I keep running into him." Why was I trying to temper how I knew that opportunistic son of a bitch?

My thoughts spun through comments like: *My farmers die when he's involved*, or maybe, *He's a damn bird-dog land-grabber, single-handedly destroying Midlands agriculture.*

She handed me her credit card. Then I did something I never expected to do; I filled her tank. As I handed back her card, she grinned like a grandmother about to serve your favorite pie. "Oh, no, honey, go use this to fill up yours."

"No, ma'am. I can't do that."

Her brows raised, and she gave me a tight grin. "You're a good woman, Carolina Slade. I'll tell Easton to cut you a deal if he winds up planning your wedding. You drive safe and have a good day." Her window started up.

Shit, I hadn't taken her picture. Snatching out my phone, I held the button, uncertain how much of that auburn-dyed head I'd caught in my stupid, cumbersome effort.

When I glanced back at my car, someone stood there, resting on my bumper, irritated that my gas had stopped pumping.

"Coming," I said, but pivoted back around to knock on the glass again, to get a better picture.

Mrs. Lily Mae Chassereau Easton drove off. I took pics of the car, but she didn't drive in a little-old-lady manner. Instead, she swerved around two cars and reached the road, not stopping long enough to look both ways. Then she was gone.

She knew about my wedding. And she damn sure knew me.

Wouldn't be surprised if she'd had a weapon in that car, the little phony.

"Slade?" The tinny voice sounded from my hand.

Jesus, I forgot about Quinn. "I am so sorry," I said. "Did you hear all that?"

"Um, not sure what I was hearing. She sounded like someone's grandmother. Why was that important, because I assume it wasn't dangerous."

I sighed, returning the nozzle to the gas pump and getting in my car. "She was not as innocent as you think. Hey, listen, if you aren't available to talk this evening, I can ferret out a few others to get what I need. I could go by the Agriculture office, and I might just go straight to the sheriff's before they close. Surely, they would—"

"Honey, I would see you regardless, but I'm not sending you to my uncle the sheriff. Hell no. Just come on to the house. No, wait a minute. Want to meet at Jackson Hole?" She referenced the local diner that belonged to her friend's mother. A booth in the back was as close to an office as she got for her PI work.

She had me. The place had the best damn food. "Sure, Jackson Hole is fine."

We hung up, and I returned to the interstate with an hour ahead of me, maybe less. There were three different ways to get to Jacksonboro, two of them taking two-lane roads through small towns. Ms. Easton might have that little-old-lady thing going on, but I wasn't taking chances. I took the longest route, staying on interstate as long as I could, avoiding the isolated reaches of rural counties.

She made no other appearance behind me, as far as I could tell. She either beat-footed it to Charleston, or that was a lie and she returned to Columbia. I'd been thinking all this time that some beefy six-footer had rammed me yesterday. She had staff. Some of those staff might be big beefy six-footers. I did sense that ol' Mother Easton wasn't as diminutive and innocent as she played, even if she had talked me into pumping gas in her car.

WAYNE CALLED ME about twenty miles before Jacksonboro. I told him where I was and would inform him where I laid my head tonight, facts that would provide the most immediate satisfaction for him.

I said nothing regarding Mrs. Easton. Opening that subject would lead to the case, and while he wouldn't talk about it in front of our two sisters last night, the longer I stayed on the phone, the more likely he'd dare to try and pry me open about what was going on.

"I assume you'll enlighten me when the time is right?" he asked.

"Yes, sir, I will."

His silence told me he hoped that time was now, but when it wasn't, he moved on. "So, Mr. Easton is out of the picture when it comes to wedding, huh?"

"Yeah, I sort of slipped that last night, didn't I?" Thank heavens I hadn't slipped anything else.

"Yes, ma'am. Is he in your investigation?"

I never said there was an investigation, but no other explanation justified my quasi-clandestine behavior. Wayne felt me out, and the longer we stayed on the phone, the more he'd use his *trained* skills. And he was much better at it than I.

"Wayne," I said, with a pinch of warning. It beat saying, *I can neither confirm nor deny.*

"Then drive safe," he said, giving up the attempt. "And keep me informed . . . whatever that means."

That was his way of saying, *Call when you need me.* He loved being the white knight, and he hated being in the dark. I loved him enjoying the role, but I didn't dare let him play it too often. My independence ran deep, and we played this game more times than I could count. I liked to think it kept us balanced.

We hung up. The restaurant wasn't a mile ahead off Highway 17, maybe two blocks back, if you could call them blocks in this rural community. This would be my third time here, and I'd learned that this place was the heartbeat of the town, if not the county.

I walked in around four thirty, already mentally tasting a tea and a bowl of that fried okra. Truth to tell I'd been tasting that appetizer since talking to Quinn. The diner's owner had a way of cooking it so that you didn't feel guilty eating something fried. It certainly wasn't greasy.

Miss Lenore must have been told I was coming. "Miss Slade?" she asked, greeting me as she wiped hands on her red apron.

"Yes, ma'am."

"Quinn is on her way." She sat me in the same booth I'd eaten at before, ensuring I sat on the side facing the kitchen. *The office.*

The tea came before I could get settled, and two sips into my tea, out came the okra. And before I got four pieces of it in my mouth, a triangle beam of light shined in from the front door, and Quinn arrived.

She had three or four inches on me in height, and I wasn't short. I had six or seven years on her, and I wasn't old. A voracious mane of red hair was tamed in a braid down her back; her mile-long legs covered the ground between us quickly. While she was certainly presentable, I'd bet those jeans and boots were well accustomed to wearing mud.

Quinn slid into the booth, facing the door, as I assumed Miss Lenore habitually ensured since I'd been seated on the other side. Quinn snared two okra pieces from my bowl and had hardly swallowed them before Miss Lenore brought her a bowl of her own. They smiled something unspoken, and the owner left.

"Pleasant surprise seeing you," Quinn said, blowing on the too hot food. "How's Wayne?"

She'd never met him except from a distance during a particularly hot moment when he dropped me off at Jackson Hole on the way to an especially dark meeting with his higher-ups, his truck barely stopping long enough to spit me out. Texts since then had made her realize he was the real deal and awfully near and dear to me. Add to that he had Callie's respect, and Quinn was satisfied.

"He's fine."

She slid a knowing wink at me. "How're the wedding plans?"

How many times would I have to say this? "Can't agree on a place."

"So I heard. You ought to just go to the courthouse and get 'er done."

"Um, not his way," I said. "To me this affair is between him and me. To him, it's his announcement to the world."

"Awww," she said, smiling through another bite, then another, waiting for me to get to the point of the meeting.

"I've been followed for a few days, but I couldn't tell by who. Today, however, gave me a clue or two. Wait, let me back up. First, my boss put me on this assignment to see if a cluster of farm deaths were suicides but also whether their demises could be tied to our agency and its people. He's rather anal about appearance, and he asked me not to mention the assignment to Wayne. Second, as a part of this deal I pissed off the wedding planner guy we'd been talking to. The wedding planner's name kept popping up during my investigation, which makes no sense. He's a sleezy opportunist in my book, but otherwise, I can't see him breaking any laws."

That drew a frown from her. "Any chance he's involved?"

"The wedding planner?"

"He's clearly a person of interest. No, I'm talking about your boss."

I rested my jaw on a fist. "That's one of my dilemmas. Not sure. Until I am, I don't tell Wayne. Once Wayne knows, it might get snatched out of my hands."

She nodded at that, took another bite. "It's five o'clock. Wanna grab dinner while you're here?"

Of course I did. I told her to order for me, and she just held up two fingers to Lenore behind the counter-turned-bar.

"What's with that grandmother thing on the phone?" Quinn asked. "Are you having family issues or is this something I'm not quite seeing?"

The gas station stop hadn't made sense to her. Mrs. Easton had sounded rather delicate to the unknowing ear. "She's the mother of the wedding planner."

Quinn patiently waited a second. "You're the worst storyteller in the world, or I'm still missing something."

I started over, going at the explanation chronologically. Our dinner appeared somewhere in the middle of it. Dinner consisted of chicken and dumplings, the special of the day. Pure comfort food, which I could use about now.

Quinn listened. She had perked up in recognition at one point, but she let me finish my story. "You're down here checking on CDM Delores Bell's part of all this then?"

"Yes. I just hadn't expected the tail along the way," I said. "She can say all she wants that she was headed to Charleston, but that was her butt going on and off the Interstate with me. She's a sly bird."

"The question is why?" Quinn said. "Why her personally? I sincerely doubt she was the one to rear-end you on the way home."

I swallowed my bite quickly. "Why not? She owns a fleet. She might not want people knowing about her son's involvement turning over land."

"Is he working for her?" Quinn offered.

"He talks like he flies solo," I said.

"And Craven County . . .?"

"As odd as this sounds, my boss sort of defined the cluster of farmers to study, and the CDMs who dealt with them. They are all Midlands oriented, on Lake Murray. I'm the one who strung the case down here after talking to Bell. She's the only county manager I can't totally account for. The others have clean slates, but she's harboring some sort of secret . . . beginning with what happened to her down here. With you involved in both agriculture and law enforcement, who better than to ask for history on this woman? I would normally talk to the local sheriff, but in this case—"

"Yeah," Quinn said, taking one last bite of dumplings and washing it down with her tea. "I'm your girl. I knew the farmer. Frankly, I knew Ms. Bell, and together they indeed had a story to tell."

Chapter 21

QUINN STERLING and I had finished dinner at Jackson Hole and were about to be served coffee. "Nothing against your coffee, Lenore, but I'm taking Slade to my house to talk."

Lenore smiled in a way that could only be described as motherly. "No problem, baby. Y'all be safe."

Waiting until Lenore left, I protested. "Here's fine, Quinn. I wouldn't want to impose." My mother had taught me that line along with a dozen others from her repertoire. "Plus, Callie was going to meet me here."

"Okay, then let me," Quinn said, her thumbs texting at the speed of sound, a gift I didn't possess. My hands typed like I had ten of them . . . thumbs that is.

"There, I've diverted her to my place. Now . . ." She kept typing. "Give me one more second . . ." She finished. "There." She put away her phone. "Come on. I love Miss Lenore to heaven and back, but there are too many ears in this place in the evening."

She didn't live far, she said. Less than twenty miles, which to her was a hop and a skip. Rural areas could feel that way. At first I tried to imagine how much she knew of the farmer and CDM Bell, then surmised she probably knew as much or more than Monroe since she was ingrained in agriculture in these parts. She had to be familiar with every farmer and everything the local CDM did for them. Quinn would also have access to every level of gossip thanks to her homegrown legacy and to all law enforcement activity thanks to her uncle the sheriff. Add to that an investigatory background with the FBI gifting her the ability to understand on a higher level than most, and she had to be a wealth of information. I patted myself on the back for the impromptu move down here. Let's see if I thought that way a few hours from now.

My agenda was limited. Saturday was that wedding at Clay River that Wayne and I had to attend as a couple. Nude, if I read things right. Tonight best be work only, not a hen party.

As the miles went by, my mind wandered into how a wealthy farmer like Quinn, with three hundred years of legacy behind her, lived. Did she enjoy a *Gone with the Wind* type of plantation home? Or a more modern brick affair with all the bells and whistles one could install in a kitchen, the guest baths, security, and so on. She acted confident but not snobbish. I didn't read her as a lady who demanded a home gym, spa, and wine cellar controlled by facial-recognition biometrics technology. Maybe the farming kept her feet planted in dirt deeply enough that her head wasn't lost in the clouds of the wealthy.

We passed through two ancient brick pillars and a wrought-iron gate accented with the letter S, telling me not to assume too much too soon. She led us through, leaving the gate open.

We cruised past trees then an open ten-acres field, almost a mile down a drive that took us to a manor of dated brick, surrounded by pecan trees that stretched beside and behind it as far as one could see. Quinn parked and motioned for me to pull beside her truck. "Callie's on her way," she said. "Come on inside and bring your bag. You had planned to spend the night, right?"

"I sort of figured I'd drive on to Edisto, but—"

Quinn was shaking her head. "Callie's staying, too. Give her thirty minutes to get here." She took us through the garage, into the house through a mud room where she tugged off her boots and proceeded in socked feet. I liked her. No airs at all. Nothing in the least about her was airs.

I kicked off my shoes in kind, wishing like hell I'd worn newer, less stretched-out socks that threatened to show through in the heel.

She ushered me into a guest room upstairs, the first off a hall with several. I dropped my bag and purse and came downstairs, stopping on the landing to marvel at the massive den. A desk in the corner was riddled with work materials. The leather in the furniture and the pecan-paneled walls wowed me. As I continued down, I ventured to the three sets of glass doors that framed the pecan acreage outside. "Love what you did with the place," I said, when Quinn came up with two cups of coffee.

"Family before me did it. Let's sit out back since the weather's good," she said, not waiting for an answer.

Soon we rocked in chairs on a flagstone porch. A hundred-plus trees filled my view. "And before you take that first sip," she said, "that's goat's milk in there. The mother of our foreman raises goats as a hobby, and it's about the only milk we drink anymore. You'll find it easier to digest than cow."

I sipped, noting the difference but not disliking it. Thus far I hadn't seen another soul around the place. "Surely you don't live out here alone?"

She gave a soft laugh. "There's a crew of a couple dozen. They've gone home, because they've been working since dawn. The nuts are about to fall, so I'm saving the overtime for then."

Oh gosh, I knew that. I stopped rocking. "If I'm taking you away from your work—"

But Quinn palmed the air for me to relax. "If I can afford that crew, I can afford to take an afternoon away. Besides, Jonah has things under control."

"Your foreman?"

She bobbled her brow. "And my fiancé."

I laughed. "That works. When are y'all getting married?"

"No idea," she said, head against her rocker. "He's always here. His mother lives right over there." She motioned off to the right. "Can't see it from here."

"Jonah isn't pushing you to set a date?" I really liked that old-fashioned name.

"We'll address that soon enough. The whole county has seen us married since we were teenagers, honestly, so we're practically wearing rings now." She cleared her throat. "Anyway, about your case . . ."

"Let's wait until Callie gets here if you don't mind. Tell me more about Sterling Banks."

My purpose for the delay was three-fold. To allow Callie to arrive so I didn't have to explain things twice, and secondly, to really get a feel for the agricultural influence Quinn had on Craven, and it on her. Lastly, I just loved agriculture. I'd never had a client that cultivated pecans to the point of making a sustainable, if not highly successful, enterprise.

With that, she rose, grabbing some well-worn sneakers from the corner. "I can't talk about it without enjoying it," she said, lacing up the shoes as I ran back for my loafers. We then traipsed into that magnificent grove. For a half hour, she spoke of pecan cultivars, how much Jonah did, with her clearly proud of him, and we even walked past the goat pen, the goat herder off doing her pecan duties.

Living on Lake Murray was grand, but oh my gosh, living on acreage like this sure held appeal. The historical aspect gave it such richness.

"We've gotta go," Quinn said, glancing at her phone. She started a fast walk toward the manor. I almost had to run to keep up with those long lanky legs. "Callie's waiting in the drive."

With that news, I was willing to trot. Callie waited, having slipped into jeans and a long-sleeve tee before leaving the island. She held out arms to me, and I hugged her hard in return. Then she shook Quinn's hand, who used the opportunity to draw the five-foot-nothing police chief into a hug of her own.

There was something about this trio that just spoke strength to me.

Quinn threw together a dinner of pork loin sandwich, leftover field peas, and a pecan pie   for Callie, something she seemed to take for granted, cooked by the goat herder, aka Jonah's mother, and we gathered around the kitchen table. The view out the front was beautiful in its own right but not as magnetic as the back, enabling us to talk.

Quinn refilled our coffees, letting Callie eat at her leisure. "Let's cover this baby from the start. Where exactly does it start?"

"When I slid into a pond and bumped into a farmer's body," I said.

"I like it," Quinn said, not taken aback in the least. "Nothing like opening a mystery with action and a hook."

For a half hour, I covered everything in generalities. Each farmer, from the ones I visited to the ones I researched to the ones the CDMs had to explain. What I believed was factual and what I wasn't sure about. I dared speak openly about Monroe, from how we went back a dozen years to his feelings for me to his difficulty with adapting to the changes that came with the role of political appointee. How he drew me into this case, and how he now tried to steer it. How he worried about it yet seemed not to really want the results. Ultimately, I admitted to withholding some of my findings from him and debated when the time was right to inform him.

They gave me appreciative nods and didn't disagree, which rather enabled me, to be honest, which felt way better to me than conversations at work, or even at home these days. I needed to be validated by my own kind, which I considered these two ladies to be.

Then I launched into the CDMs and their jobs. Callie, not being in agriculture, didn't understand their roles so I had to explain. Quinn understood what they did quite well. They were judged, promoted, and fired based upon how well they aided farmers and kept them from breaking the rules, because farmers had bad guys in their ranks like every other profession, and the seclusion of rural areas often gave them better odds of pulling off nefarious ways. With money came the sorts who found loopholes to take advantage.

"How's Wayne?" Callie asked, in her nice way putting him on the table, meaning how was he handling this?

"He doesn't like not knowing," I said. "He doesn't like me not settling on a wedding venue. And he isn't quite happy I'm down here. Ooh, that reminds me. Hold on a sec." The text message about where I was spending the night went out to him.

When I looked up, both women were staring at me. "Let's talk wedding," Callie said.

"We're not here to talk wedding. We're here to talk case."

"We can do both," Callie said.

"Sure. We've got all night and into the morning, don't we?" Quinn added.

Unexpected wasn't enough of a word. "But I . . . I don't want to waste Quinn's valuable time. We're gathered to solve a problem. We should—"

"Slade, pick a place you think he'll like and be done with it," Callie said. "Act like it's wonderful, and you're thrilled he loves it, only you choose something you know he wants. You've been married before. You know how this works."

I had to laugh. "My first husband tried to have me assassinated. I might not have the best track record of *how this works*."

"Do you want to marry this guy?" Quinn asked.

"Of course she does," Callie said.

"Then what's the holdup?"

"She's scared of public display, I believe," Callie answered. "She's been with this guy for, what, three years?"

I nodded.

"And she lives with him?" Quinn asked.

"He lives with her and her two children and her sister. Even his sister is a part of the group."

"Damn," Quinn said. "If you all get along well enough to commune like that, the venue ought to be nothing."

I pointed around the room. "Like what you have going on here?"

"We don't care where," Quinn replied. "But this is about you, not me. Tell me about your man."

But Callie spoke up first, explaining who Wayne was and how he'd come into the picture. I let her. Finally, Quinn concluded with a sassy look at me. "Not seeing him as the one with the problem, girl."

My *tsk* came out loud, clear, and intentional. "From someone who's never been married?"

"From the private eye in the room. Ask the police chief over there. Bet she agrees."

Squinting, I had to set something straight. "Because I don't hold or never have held a badge does not mean I don't have the chops to—"

"Shut up, Slade," Callie said, with Quinn almost in unison saying the same thing.

They were on my side, and I should shut up and just address the elephant they were trying to get me to see. "I want him to be happy, but I don't want to be forced into a fanfare," I said. "I just want to be married. Honestly, I don't want to plan the damn thing, and he doesn't want to plan it without me. Why can't we just love each other, get a ring, and do this? I've planned a fancy wedding before, and it was so damn wasteful."

My answer came across rushed, a bit of spilling the beans. My two friends sat back, not disturbed about my respond or worried for me, but more satisfied than anything else.

"That's what he needs to hear," Callie said.

"Says the woman living with a man she's totally compatible with but hasn't discussed tying the knot?"

"We don't care if we do or not," she said. "Mark isn't Wayne. I'm not you."

I turned to Quinn. "And says the woman living with a man as well, who is likewise a perfect match, but cannot set a date?"

"Hard to work it in the schedule around here. We stay busy."

"Yet you drop everything for me," I reminded. "Seems easy enough to do for a simple *I Do*, don't you think? Besides, ladies, I've already told him to make this simple. He wasn't having it."

We weren't that much different. I just happened to have the man pushing the most at the moment.

Quinn stood and walked to the kitchen counter, clearly changing the subject. "Coffee, tea, or the good stuff? What'll it take to tackle Slade's case?"

Chapter 22

IT WAS TIME TO talk case and drop the marital advice. We had a wonderful location, we'd had a satisfying dinner, and the whole night stretched before us. If Callie wasn't on the wagon we'd have defaulted to wine to solve all the world's problems, but instead, we went with iced tea and moved our discussion to the den. We had an entire evening to grapple with this, and I was intensely grateful. These women were smart. They made me feel smart.

Though we traveled with laptops, Quinn handed us notepads. "Let's dissect this thing, but first, let me fill you in on Miss Delores Bell."

We assumed seats in the den in chairs and a sofa way too comfortable to not get relaxed, so I sat on the edge of my cushion. "She won't tell me what happened here that resulted in her transfer," I said. "Monroe's reluctant to talk about it."

"She screwed him," Quinn said.

My stomach dropped. "Monroe?"

"Oh, sorry, no. The farmer. Edmond Jackson," she corrected.

"Edmond . . ." I wrote the name down, then paused. "Jackson, you say?"

"Yep," Quinn said. "He was black and she was white."

I kept waiting for some hammer to fall. "That's not so unusual. Was he married?"

"Yes, and apparently in a bad relationship," Quinn said.

"You may not be aware, but was Bell making it easier for him to get federal money?"

"First you have to grasp the culture down here," she said. "There are still some dinosaurs, but more so, the Jacksons are a tight-knit clan. You tackle one, you tackle the rest. There's a bloody bunch of them, and it's incredible how their personal business gets spread within their ranks. He was cheating on his wife, and most weren't happy about it. The Jacksons are everywhere. Lenore, at the diner, married a Jackson. Her son, my buddy at the sheriff's office, is Tyson Jackson. They date back as far as the Sterlings. They tend to judge as a group."

"Still, you can't tell me the Jacksons have never seen adultery," I said, dubious.

Her tone turned from one of gossip to one more solemn. "Word was the farm started suffering. The wife kept the scandal quiet at first, prompted by her family because Edmond was dating the money lady. Delores Bell was the woman who opened and closed doors to programs that kept that farm and others like it afloat. Think about it. Who bites the hand of the banker?"

Having met Bell, I bet she didn't even realize the picture she painted or appreciated the power she had wielded. If I learned in any way, shape, or form that she had used her power for personal gain, sexual, financial, or otherwise, she was toast. I'd see to it.

This was the sort of thing I investigated when it came to employees up to, above, and including those at the CDM level. How had I been kept out of that loop? Damn, Monroe.

Quinn popped the footrest up on her recliner, and it rose with nary a squeak. Even her recliner was top shelf. "They dated at night, thinking they were hiding the fact from people, but that's a hard trick to pull in Craven County. Turns out, they usually met in her office, which I found rather . . . ignorant."

"Stupid," Callie said.

I leaned forward. "Seriously?" They'd taken their amorous behaviors onto government property?

"Full-bore affair on a sofa in the Agriculture office's back room," Quinn said. "They'd also been seen on some dirt roads in her SUV. Some say they cruised to Savannah for her to have an abortion, but nobody's confirmed that, and I doubt anyone can."

My mouth dropped open. "I . . . don't know what to say." New and different images of Delores Bell came to mind that were a far cry from the lady I found hiding in the cafeteria with a book.

If I'd been Monroe, I'd have fired her.

This affair infuriated me. Not just the carnal one, but the fact it was kept secret from me. This kind of business eroded the public's trust in us. Why had Monroe kept this under his hat, and why had he not trusted me to investigate?

"What am I not getting here?" I asked. "That woman has been protected and ushered away into a tiny office far from here where she'd won't be seen ever again by Craven people, and not many Richland people. Richland is a low-volume county. It ought to be combined with Lexington, to be honest, and between this and the deteriorating caseload due to Richland's urban growth, we just might in the near future."

Callie touched my arm. "Let Quinn finish. We'll ask questions in a minute. Level head and all that."

"Sure, sure, go on," I said, waving my hand.

Quinn had sat patiently through my brief rant, but now continued. "Bell was smitten, and to be honest, Edmond was a decent-looking man. The affair went on nine months to a year, depending on who you talk to. Then one evening about six or seven months ago, very late and close to eleven, one of the local farmers decided to move one of his big tractors between fields like they often do to avoid blocking daytime traffic. He met them head on. Edmond likewise thought there'd be no traffic to recognize them. One or the other wasn't watching what they were doing on the road, but it's not like a tractor can make fast maneuvers. Edmond was killed instantly, thrown out of the truck. The other farmer was catapulted as well, but he only ended up with cuts, bruises, and a broken shoulder."

"And Bell?" I asked.

"She was found unconscious by someone nearby who heard the crash. She'd been wearing her belt, and they say her being half drunk saved her. Edmond's blood alcohol was through the roof."

"Have you met Bell?" I asked. "Do you believe all this?"

"I have and I do. Met her several times. At local meetings, then in her office when my farm qualified for a small reserve program. She seemed okay, nothing standing out one way or the other. A little abandoned looking maybe? Mousey for sure. Trust me, I did a double take when the rumors started, but I didn't see a need to get involved. In hindsight, I wonder if a good, old-fashioned whistleblower action might have kept him alive. Affairs are private, but—"

"There's no but about it, Quinn." My brashness even gave myself a start, and I took a backstep. "Sorry."

Quinn handed me a folder. "Here's the accident report."

She answered my questionable gaze about how she got her hands on it with a quick, "I know people. You mentioned Bell on the phone. When we left the diner to come here, I texted *my friend* to drop it off here. Just roll with it."

Callie watched my stunned wonder and gave me a smirk. "Remember where you are, Slade. This is Craven County."

I gave a *humph* and took the report, no more questions asked. It read as she described, minus the affair part. They'd been traveling together. They'd been drinking. Edmond Jackson had not been wearing a seat belt. Nor had the tractor driver. Bell was damn lucky she only got a concussion and bruises per the pictures showing twisted metal and a truck that would never be repaired.

But I needed more, like what happened afterwards. The kind of thing that wouldn't be in a sheriff's accident report. "Then what?"

Quinn nodded in understanding. "She was off work for two weeks, so she must have taken a solid lick. Then she returned, per the scuttlebutt. As farmers went in to tend to business that had gone lacking, the news spread wider. She tried to behave business as usual, clearly failed, then she was gone, replaced by Malachi Jackson, a local who'd been working in Charleston. He got a promotion out of the deal, I believe. Whoever made that call made a good one, replacing one tainted Jackson with a golden one."

"Yes," I said, welcoming one thing positive. "Monroe did all right there."

The timeline fit. Bell was transferred to Richland County from Craven, most definitely detouring her career path but salvaging her career as a whole, the lesser of evils. I made a note to research her personnel file to study how they worded everything compared to what I was hearing now.

"She would've never come on my radar except for Monroe asking me about the five dead farmers," I said, almost talking to myself. "Nothing said they were all suicide, so why was he concerned they even might be?"

I was feeling my leg pulled, or that I'd been pulled in to find something hidden.

Writing aided my thinking processes, and I made note again of the farmers to give me easy reference, beginning with the oldest, in chronological order. I spoke some as I wrote.

Edmond Jackson—died in a truck crash with CDM Delores Bell at his side in Craven County. Not suicide.

Merle Lester—died under an overturned tractor. CDM Delores Bell in Richland County. Ruled accident. Could have been suicide with nobody able to prove the difference.

Homer Brooks—died fishing on Lake Murray. CDM Jerry Crown in Lexington County. Almost declared suicide but changed to accident.

T.J. Candleman—died in methane gas incident. CDM Jerry Crown in Lexington County. Declared accident but, like Lester, could have been a suicide, but nobody wanted to go there.

Dewey Anderson—hanged himself. CDM Cathy Risher in Saluda County. Definitely suicide.

Troy Oakley—insulin overdose after overdrinking. CDM Al Blanchard in Newberry County. Accident or suicide. Too soon to tell but probably leaning accident after listening to the coroner.

Again, why was suicide even mentioned?

I showed the list to the other two. Callie wrote them down. Quinn handed it back, either putting it to memory or not feeling the details urgent enough to waste the time. She had me here for that.

"What's the common denominator of these six farmers?" Callie asked. "Assuming we're counting Jackson in Craven."

But Quinn was quick to alter the question. "Does Edmond Jackson even factor in?"

"Not at first blush," I said. "But the CDM herself does factor in, so we have to keep him in mind."

Callie nodded. "And you aren't prepared to query your director about all that."

"Not until I learn more. He's being too weird, and he'll complicate things." I paused. "Might even take me off the case." Monroe had swept a scandal under the rug, but also promoted a qualified man into the role who would do right by the county and protected a woman's career; not that I'm sure I'd have done the latter, but he seemed to start off doing the right thing. "Too iffy to draw him in, but why call me in the first place if he was involved in anything shady?" I was puzzled.

I turned to Quinn. "Do I want to talk to the sheriff?"

"No," she said. "Not this sheriff."

Callie spoke up. "You'd stir things back up for Craven County, Slade. Until we understand the reasoning behind all of this, don't make a move where you can't predict the outcome, at least within some semblance of reason."

"That and Monroe has no idea I'm down here," I added.

The room went quiet. Callie threw out an idea or two. Was Bell related to someone important who was pulling political strings on their relative's behalf? Did Bell have something on someone, someone high enough to pull her own strings and salvage her career? Someone akin to Monroe.

I drew a complete blank to both those questions. I didn't think so, but then, I hadn't been made aware of Bell in the first place, had I?

None of this had started, the deaths, I mean, until Bell was relocated. And what was the deal with Monroe's keen interest in something that should be two layers of management beneath him?

I hadn't noticed my doodling until the room went quiet, all of us thinking about what-ifs. I did it all the time, and had done so again, with the addition of personal scribbles of arrows to triggers like *mediocre manager* or *solid good.*

Callie returned to her earlier question. "Whether you count Edmond Jackson or not, what is the common denominator? Why those?"

The question I'd asked of each of the Lake Murray-area farmers occurred to me. "Was the Jackson farm used for wedding events or reunions?"

"No, that isn't done much down here. Too far from urbanites. Is that a real deal up there around Lake Murray?"

"It is," I said. "And it was done or attempted on every single one of these farms." And with the wedding planning topic came one name. "Remembering me mentioning the name Easton?"

Quinn turned her head, as if it made her think better. "As in that grandmother who tailed you, and her son?" I'd mentioned the Eastons at the diner, but we hadn't gone into great detail about each farmer and each case until here at the farm.

"Yes, Lily Mae Easton of the Miss Lily's Table brand. "

Callie chimed in. "I've heard of her. Mark has spoken of her and how efficiently she runs her restaurants." Callie's significant other was the manager of El Marko's Mexican Restaurant on the beach.

Quinn waited for more.

"Unless she had a good doppelganger, Mrs. Easton was the lady who followed me on the interstate."

This was the first Callie had heard of this. We just hadn't had the time nor been on the right topic to discuss it. "Why would an old lady who owns restaurants in Columbia tail you that far out of town?"

"Maybe . . ." And a thought began to form. For a moment I thought it through before saying it aloud. "Maybe Mama Bear didn't like me giving her baby boy a hard time. She joked that maybe he could cut me a wedding event deal before she drove off, so they've spoken. I met Garrett Easton when I slid into the pond and met that dead farmer. Wayne used him to scout out venues. All my dead farmers had wedding venues or had been approached about having one, and Garrett Easton was the one who dealt with them."

I turned to Quinn. "Has Garrett Easton ever come down here?"

The heiress looked a bit stymied, so I pulled up some of my research from my phone. I had done an online search for his wedding business.

Of course I'd found him on Facebook, Instagram, Twitter, and LinkedIn. I clicked on the easiest to pull up—Facebook. His picture appeared big and bold, with him dressed fit to kill and beaming bright for his camera closeup and caption which promised he'd provide you the best day of your life.

Quinn lit up at the picture. "I have seen him."

"Where?" I asked.

"Where else do you ask for information around here without dealing with the sheriff? At Jackson Hole," she said. "He was talking to Lenore, and she turned him over to me. He was looking for the Agriculture office."

My heart kicked up a notch. "How long ago?"

"Six months ago," she said. "Give or take a week."

"When Delores Bell was still here?"

"No, about a week after she left."

Chapter 23

I MUST HAVE had *stymy* written all over my face. Quinn had just confirmed that Mr. Easton once made an appearance in Craven County, hunting for information on Delores Bell, and Quinn had seen him.

"Why would he be asking about Bell after she left?" I asked. "He went out of his way to meet her during her first week or two in Richland. She says it was a basic introduction, but now I have serious doubt."

"Well," Quinn said. "I might have fed him some information."

"I'm listening."

"I informed him she was no longer in the county. When he asked if she'd moved to Richland, I said that was what I'd heard and then wondered why he'd asked for her in the first place. When he asked if she'd left under scandal, I told him I wasn't in the business of spreading gossip. I could've offered to research her for him, but I hate that sort of PI work. Besides, he ought to be asking her. He never would explain why he wanted the information other than he was a businessman in the Columbia area and liked to be knowledgeable of who he did business with." She scrunched her nose, accenting those freckles. "His quest wasn't passing the sniff factor with me, so I generalized, told him where the Agriculture office was, and sent him on his way. I assume he went there, but honestly, Slade, if he talked to enough people around here, someone would have told him about the affair and accident. It's not a secret."

"Well," I said, still rubbed wrong Monroe never told me. "Outside of this area, it was kept low key."

"But that's not the takeaway of all this, is it?" Callie said.

"No, it isn't," I agreed. "Easton's name is in the middle of these farmers' business, and most of their acreage, after their deaths, wound up in the hands of developers after Easton doing his *bird-dogging*." I didn't have to explain the term to these ladies.

"Troy Oakley's farm in Newberry may be next if his will doesn't leave it to a young farmers' cooperative, which reminds me I need to check on that. Homer Brooks, the farmer in Lexington, had a wife and son who carried on like he never died, a move Easton didn't see coming. They had the best land for development out of all of them, even acreage right smack on the lake."

Quinn held up her coffee cup as if to toast. "Good for them."

Callie remained relaxed on the sofa, making little movement other than the occasional taste of her coffee. She was the quietest of the three of us, the more internalized . . . Quinn the most outspoken. I liked these two balancing me out, validating, and correcting me. I hadn't gotten involved with law enforcement until at an age too old to join their ranks, so I took what I could, doing internal cases and sharing the more critical ones with the Inspector General. Some days I loved the duality. Other days I hated being the lesser.

"Easton smelled leverage," I said. "He had a new CDM he wanted to know intimately before she learned what he was up to with developers."

Callie spoke up. "What happened to the CDM before her?"

I hadn't thought of him, and I should have. "He retired. They were going to combine that small office with the Lexington one until Delores Bell came along."

"How convenient," Quinn said. "I've got to say I'm not feeling much love for your boss, Slade."

I nodded, sad at how this appeared. This case was inching closer and closer to Wayne's territory. I thought I was closer to Monroe than this.

"He screwing her?" Quinn asked.

"I would've told you Monroe was honest as the day is long until all this. I can't sincerely say he's not sleeping with her. Not anymore."

I told myself I wasn't jealous, but a piece of me was. He'd always carried a torch for me, and I'd never reciprocated. He'd kissed me a couple times, but always in the heat of some situation without Wayne around. One time Wayne walked in when Monroe had dared make his move. Took them a while for Wayne to come around to Monroe after that, but he did. Especially once Monroe made it clear he'd back off.

Still didn't mean I didn't love Monroe in a friendship way.

Quinn rubbed her socked feet together, as if she had an itch. "We only know about Easton researching Bell because she was new. Have any idea if he did the same to the others?"

"They've been entrenched in their counties a while. Maybe he didn't have to. But regarding Bell, it's clear to me, after studying these others, that he had some gig, scam, line of work, whatever, going on he didn't want interrupted," I said. "I didn't label him that smart before. Maybe I was wrong."

Callie chuckled. "Who could look menacing amidst flowers, organza, lace, and hors d'oeuvres? He sounds almost like a cartoon character, Slade. Someone like that flies under a lot of people's radar. Is he operating solo or in cahoots with someone? I mean, is he shrewd enough to scout these farms on his own and make sales happen, or does he have a partner?"

Quinn sat up in her recliner. "Wait. Ever considered he had a hand in killing these guys? You know, to make the farms sell?"

I held up my list and pointed for them to look at theirs. "The oldest, that we know of, is Merle Lester who died under his tractor."

"Is the property being sold now?" Quinn asked.

"Yes."

She continued. "You and I know that tractors are easy to overturn. If the man wanted to off himself, he could do it. And if someone wanted to push him to do so, they might have. Someone could've forced him to turn wrong as he evaded them. Who knows?"

Callie frowned at the concept. "There are easier ways, Quinn."

But I understood what Quinn was saying. "Not if you didn't want embarrassment," I said. "Not if you wanted it to be considered an accident."

"Who cares about embarrassment if you're dying?" Callie said.

"Farmers," Quinn and I chimed together. Quinn pointed to my notepad. "Who's the next one?" Her understanding of agriculture was refreshing.

"Homer Brooks," I said. "The big Lexington farmer."

"The one with the strong wife. The one who died while fishing in Lake Murray."

"Yes."

Callie studied her list. "The one where they killed the wife's dog? The one they first thought murder, then suicide, then an accident. Not like anyone was out there to see, was it?"

"What she said." Quinn nodded slow then a couple times faster. "T.J. Candleman. Methane gas poisoning. Easy way to die. Like the Brooks guy, call it murder, accident, or suicide and who's going to know the difference? A coroner would side with the family and the least controversial if it could go one way or the other. If a single guy, again, go with what's easiest to rest your laurels on."

"The next guy, the guy who hanged himself, was already depressed," I said.

"I'd help his ready-to-be-divorced wife push him over the edge," Quinn said. "Tell her she could collect big money if he either quit or died and the place had to sell. Depends on how big a greedy bitch she was and how hard she pushed selling in family court."

My heart was steadily dropping through all this. We described a scheme that caused death in a variety of ways, hiding murder.

"The last one," Callie said, "overdosed with insulin after overdrinking."

"And everyone says this was unlike his personality? What if someone . . .?" I stopped there. Troy Oakley likewise would be difficult to prove with no motive to declare nor a witness. Everyone liked him. He had no family craving his money. "There's no way to prove any of this," I said. "In pushing this school of thought, we hand the case over to Wayne. I cannot investigate questionable death, and from what I see here, the IG's office is more than likely to decline if we go to them. Monroe would be furious with me, and ultimately the case shuts down."

Callie shook her head. "That has to be frustrating doing what you do without real authority, Slade."

That earned her a loud scoff from me. "You have no idea."

She laughed. "Oh, I've seen you enough times to spot the rub. Can we move this to the porch? I'm stiff sitting in this overstuffed couch."

We did, only once we stood, we craved to walk more. We strolled the huge pecan grove in the dark and wound up at Windsor, the tree house Quinn grew up in, and once we'd glanced at the water winding beside it, a little fearful of getting too close in the pitch of night, we actually climbed the stairs into the house.

She tugged the cord to a lone lightbulb, casting shadows on a childhood history of how Quinn and her two buddies, Jonah and Ty, grew up. There were three chairs, consisting of a rocker, a bean bag, and a rigid straight back, and Callie and I assumed our places once Quinn chose hers. We sat there for a while, admiring the hodgepodge of memory items, hoping the change of scenery would joggle our thoughts.

But we wound up with nothing but rehash of the same, and we accepted the fact we might as well default to the hen party we'd thought ourselves too good for earlier in the day.

In the morning, we dragged ourselves awake, leisured over breakfast, which Jonah's mother arrived to prepare, and languished over coffee having not much else to do short of disburse. Such a joy to be waited on like that, but such a sadness in the parting.

"Found this," Quinn said, holding out her hand. "It got too late to go over your truck last night in the dark, so I gave it a going-over this morning."

A small tracker.

I kicked myself for not checking on my own. "Where?"

"The wheel well, like any amateur would do. Let me keep it if you don't mind. Got a truck going to Savannah this afternoon. Let's see if someone finds their way to Georgia before realizing they've been misled."

"Doesn't have to carry Miss Lily's logo to know where it came from," I said. "Appreciate it."

It was going on eleven. Each of us had gotten antsy over our awaiting day jobs. I went to leave first with the furthest to travel.

"Wish we could come help," Callie said after we hugged our goodbyes.

"I have not exactly met your Mr. Wayne," Quinn said, "but my suggestion is to tell him, Slade. He has tools, and . . ."

"Skills. I get it," I said, smiling at this woman I wished lived closer.

Callie got in another hug. "What's your next step?"

"Talk to Monroe or talk to Wayne. Either way will piss someone off at me, but that's inevitable. Nothing I haven't experienced before. Thanks so much for the help." I laughed lightly. "Now you've got me thinking murder."

"Without the first piece of proof," Quinn reminded. "Don't go ruining your career staking a flag on this. You risk sounding like an idiot screaming murder at a bunch of people who don't see it."

"I might just look at wedding venues tomorrow," I said. "Clear my head and ponder how to approach Wayne so he won't be so upset over being left out of this case."

"Sounds like a plan," Callie said.

With that, I left, not in a hurry to return to this mess. I even stopped off in Ridgeville, just off the interstate. Being in the Lowcountry, I had to at least stop and say hello to my parents.

Thinking of Daddy made me smile. Thinking of Mom made me sit up straight. But thinking of home still warmed my heart. I texted Whitney to put me in for a day off.

Took me under an hour to reach the homestead. They still owned twenty acres outside of Middleton.

I might've missed Kaye's pickpocketing lesson last night, but I told myself not to do so today so I scheduled my visit for two hours, three tops. Daddy was over the moon, never reluctant to welcome either of his girls. Mom fussed about the lack of advanced notice, and I definitely didn't tell her I spent the night in Craven, but her smile shined genuine.

Part of me wanted them up near Lake Murray. The other liked the distance. Mom was a power to be reckoned with, and if she were within ten miles of Ally Jo and me, we'd be horsewhipped into submission to a schedule, vacations, and God knows what else. The garden I'd stalled in starting, she'd have tilled and planted in two days, with assigned chores to each person to keep it managed. Yeah, these two came with a mixed bag of emotions. I did apologize for showing up without the kids, though. My folks were perfection at grandparenting.

But time crept up on us quickly, and I hit the road again, loaded with pound cake from the freezer and an assortment of garden vegetables the woman managed to throw into an instapot in time for me to leave.

I arrived home a little before six, earlier than my normal days, and Ally was thrilled at the food delivery.

"Kaye coming?" I asked, poking my nose in the oven for whatever my sister prepped for dinner. Nothing.

"There's leftover spaghetti in the fridge from last night," she said. "Kaye wasn't happy you didn't make her pickpocketing lesson, but she schooled Wayne and me like crazy. You're at a disadvantage to all of us now. You'll have to beg on your knees for us to teach you, and you can expect anything on your body to get swiped over the next few weeks."

"Been working on a case," I said.

"We get that, but still, Slade, she's anxious about this wedding at Clay River tomorrow. She wanted us on our toes."

Now I felt like crap. "I'll have to make it up to her." Though I wasn't sure how. I'd agree to most anything now.

Ally looked wary. "Any chance you'll miss the wedding? Please say you'll be there. It's around noon, and she needs us." The little sister scolded the older.

"I'll be there." I had evaded thinking about this event with nudity involved. Security or not, Wayne would be awfully awkward. I wasn't thrilled about attending in the buff, but it might make Wayne feel better to have me there. The kids weren't attending because of the nudity but more so because we adults attended the event to work, not go for the entertainment, with no time to babysit. Ivy was old enough to tend to Zack for that length of time, and Zack would be harshly instructed to behave for his sister . . . without access to his BB gun.

Eating my leftover spaghetti alone since Wayne had gone to his headquarters in Atlanta today and presently drove home, I moved to the porch overlooking Miss Murray as she was often called.

Canadian geese sounded more rampant lately, and it wouldn't be long before the loons and coots would arrive, chasing fish in the cove. Too warm for frogs to be rowdy. Not cool enough to put snakes in the ground.

I let the calm of the lake sweep over me, but it didn't take long to feel rather amateurish on this investigation, especially after consulting my law enforcement gal pals. All we'd done was expand the what-ifs into devious options. As I scraped the last noodle in the bottom of the bowl, I decided to talk to Monroe on Monday. He had to accept this had to be run by the IG, though I didn't see them wanting it. By Monday afternoon, I'd be busy elsewhere, on some other misstep or employee misjudgment. Chalk this one in the cold-case column, a no-case in Monroe's mind, and a what-were-you-thinking case for Wayne.

No longer distracted by what to do next for the job, I pondered a place to get married. Monday I'd be back to square one on that.

I found it amazing that Wayne put up with me sometimes. Time to find a way to enthrall him with a place to tie the knot. A place Mr. Easton wasn't involved in, that's for damn sure.

Chapter 24

"WHAT'S THE ETIQUETTE for a nude wedding?" I said from inside my walk-in closet, not having bought anything for this event, not caring about spending the money when I had no idea how long I'd have to wear it. It was eight thirty a.m. The wedding started at noon. We had to be there no later than eleven, Kaye said. Preferably sooner. "Do you arrive dressed then undress in the locker room? I doubt she has enough lockers for this many people." The last time I was there, there weren't more than sixty lockers. Maybe seventy.

Wayne appeared in the closet doorway, handsome in light-gray slacks, white shirt, and a soft peach-hued tie. Camel-colored Cole Hahn wingtips on his feet.

Heat rose in me. "Cowboy, damn, you look good," I said, sliding to him, arms around his middle while I wore nothing but panties and a bra. "Makes me scared to allow you in public."

He wrapped me in his arms. "Have to say, there might be a lot of temptation at this thing. Imagine all these ladies peeled down to the real deal. Beats picking and choosing from ladies all wrapped up in clothes, having to guess what's underneath."

I laughed once. "You clearly haven't been to a nudist resort when it's busy. I look like a million bucks compared to the average naked person there."

His brow rose. "Bragging or warning?"

"A little of both, Cowboy. Now, let me get dressed." I let loose of him but then turned back and looked him over. "Seems like you went through a lot of trouble looking so good when you'll only have to shed once you get there." The watch on his wrist looked . . . expensive. "Where'd you get that?"

"I save it for times like this."

What the . . .? "Is that a Rolex? If so, that's a five-figure watch, Cowboy. Hope you're not flashing that thing at work. They'll think you're on the take."

"Just use it making entrances," he said, disappearing back in the bedroom. "If it fools you, it'll fool a pickpocket," his voice rising to be heard. "Government property, Butterbean."

I didn't have anything that looked expensive short of my engagement ring that my finger didn't easily give up.

Back to the closet. I wasn't so eager to invest in the time to truss myself up to the nines then have to undo it. The makeup was justified, of course, and I even went for heels since they'd be coming off anyway. I nixed the sleeveless shift and jacket remembering the gauze and tape on my knees and forearms from the bumper-car action I'd endured earlier this week.

How stupid. We'd be bare once we got there. Now what?

The first aid kit lacked an answer, so I rummaged under the sink.

"Slade? Hurry up," Ally called from the kitchen.

When I didn't reply, Wayne came in, catching me on the floor, hunting a solution for my wounds. "What are you doing?"

I pointed at my bandages.

He didn't get it at first. He ran out and was soon back with big, flesh-colored adhesive bandages in his hand.

"Where did you—"

"Your sister. Come on, Slade. Get it together." He tossed them on the floor beside me and left.

My phone dinged with a message. Kaye was already there, per texts that asked when we would be, too. "Let's go!" Ally hollered again from the kitchen.

Throwing on dress black pants with a gray, summer-weight sweater, I added a pearl necklace hoping some pickpocket found it worth something, assuming the guy would show up at all, then joined Ally and Wayne in the kitchen. I smelled cookies.

"Isn't this thing catered?" I said, rushing in with my simplest clutch purse, already frustrated at trying to fit everything in it.

"Cookies are for the kids," she said. "A reminder that I did this for them, so they will behave while we're gone."

She was getting damn good at this mothering business.

The three of us piled into my truck, Wayne driving. Even with the tracker gone, I watched my rearview mirror for a tail. Wayne watched me watch. He didn't say a word; however I had a sense that we took my vehicle just in case someone did. He'd love the opportunity to confront them. We had one potential stalker for a couple miles, but it disappeared. After ten miles I was able to quit worrying, only to worry more about going naked.

The forty miles took just under an hour. The guard at the gate approved us to enter after a glance at our access pass for the event.

We slow-crawled by the forest, then the collection of campers where only three people stood outside in the buff. While one elder gentleman set up his grill, two middle-aged ladies, hands waving in the air, performed spirited chatter in the middle of the gravel route that connected the RVs.

"You ready for this?" I asked Wayne.

"Of course he's ready," Ally replied. "I can't wait!"

Wayne *humphed*, not interested in conversation about the experience we were about to have. I had agreed to do this for Wayne mainly, a close second reason being for Kaye. The moment we could leave, we'd be out of there.

We arrived an easy hour ahead of time, and a sixty-something gentleman already in place directed parking, standing there in all his sags, wrinkles, and glory.

My pulse amped up. "How cold is it?"

Ally showed me her weather app. "Seventy. Since we're in the sun, ought to be great."

I already felt my nipples shrinking, scared of who else might notice my assets once I offered them to public scrutiny. Then I reminded myself no one was supposed to be looking—nudist etiquette.

We piled out of the truck noting the arbors and floral arrangements in the distance. The colors were peach, brown, and a hint of gold. Leave it to Wayne to have asked about what color tie to wear so he'd match. He was fast becoming the tasteful one in our dynamic duo.

The parking attendant came up with a plastic box, asking for our phones.

"They're okay, Tom." Kaye came running over. "They're security. They keep their phones." Kaye wore an Oriental robe—and I mean robe only—its colors a soft teal, white, and, of course, peach. Sweet sandals to match. I could have dressed like Kaye if advised accordingly, but my trip down to Craven shorted Kaye's discussion about what to expect. I'd sort of lost the right to whine.

Pish posh. We'd all be peach, tan, brown, and blended together anyway.

"Hey, y'all. Finally," Kaye said. "Let me show you around so we can put you to work. This thing will leap to life before we know it."

She walked us toward the decorated area beside the pool. "The bride and groom and their families are milling around. They're wearing these little peach flowers to match, so they can be recognized. In their hair, around their neck, on their feet, on their wrists. They got innovative with it."

"Wear your tie," I muttered to Wayne, walking at his side. "You'll fit right in."

He gave me another *humph*.

Kaye escorted us in a whirlwind, showing off her first wedding event with pride while orienting us to the expected flows and gathering places. Someone came up to her every few minutes with a question or confirmation. The naked ones belonged to the resort. The clothed ones belonged to the caterer, snappy in the black-and-white formality of waitstaff.

"You didn't make the people supplying this wedding go naked?" I winced. "Never mind. Not sure I want that handling the bar or the hors d'oeuvres."

"Spoken like a novice," she said. "But you're correct in that they are dressed so that they stand out, such that guests can ask questions, ask for refills, and so on."

Made sense. That and going buff certainly wasn't in their job description when they hired on to the company, but I bet they had to sign something on how to behave on site. Bet they couldn't have phones or cameras.

We were reminded of the lay of the land. Kaye had indeed upgraded the place. What resources they'd given her, she'd used effectively. Since that dark time I'd been here, the place had taken on a glow, a freshness that enticed you to toss the dress and run barefoot across that grassy section that led to the cabins and woods, and ultimately, the river—body parts bouncing, free, and happy.

"Focus," Kaye said, when she'd called my name and I hadn't answered. "The people will stroll in here, from the back. The front is there, as you can see by the flowers. Wayne, you can stand over—"

"I'll decide where to stand," he said, motioning toward the decorated outdoor bar which stood about twenty yards from the ring of bistro tables around the cluster of tableclothed tables for four in the middle. "Slade, you'll stand the opposite of where I'll be, keeping an eye on the guests but not coming around me."

Ally popped up. "Where do I stand?"

"You float," Wayne said. "Mingle and watch. Don't cause a scene. If you aren't sure about someone, slip over to me and say so. I'll take it from there. Act like a guest."

Ally scrunched her shoulders, matching the scrunch of her nose, eager to get started. "This is indeed an adventure, isn't it?" Wayne understood my sister. Once she started chattering with guests, she'd forget the mission.

Kaye glanced at me, as if saying Ally was my sister and what was I going to do with her. "She's a force of nature," I said. "Don't blame me. I didn't birth her."

We headed inside the building, to scrutinize the locker rooms, and to see where the bride and groom were sequestered for the time being, changing and getting ready. The place looked spotless.

One of Kaye's assistants, co-nudists, whatever, came running up. "People are here," she said. Young enough to be in college, she had less give to her thighs and underarms than the rest of us, with some serious definition in her shoulders. Home girl worked out. But I wouldn't want to be that naïve again for a million bucks—the sentiment my way of justifying my age and muscle tone. "They aren't allowed to drink or eat yet, right?" the girl asked.

"The caterer handles that, Hannah. Just contain the people. Remember the floral stamp required on the back of their hand. If they stray, steer them back to the area we talked about. We don't need first-timers wandering in areas they have no right to. We still have residents and vacationers here. And vice versa as well. If someone doesn't have a hand stamp, ask them to wait until it's over."

Hannah held a deer-in-the-headlights look. "Thought everyone was invited."

"They were, but they were supposed to RSVP by a deadline so we had a head count. Don't need twenty unexpected people showing up to chow down on food prepared for sixty, do we?"

"Got it," she said, and disappeared, me wondering what she did for those glutes, and if I could learn that.

Wayne watched, too. "That's what we're protecting today?"

"She's staff, Bubba," Kaye said. "And trust me, Hannah's the best bod you'll be seeing, and that includes the bride."

Ally and I weren't insulted in the least. Truth was truth.

"Time to get this party started," Kaye said, turning on her heel and disappearing back outside.

I stood there in the hallway watching Wayne then Ally, my breathing heavier while trying not to show it.

"Come on, Sis," Ally said, snaring my arm. "You heard Kaye."

Wayne winked at me and disappeared into the men's locker room.

He suddenly didn't seem bothered in the least. How did arriving here calm him down but give me a panic attack?

Jesus, were we really doing this?

In our locker room, Ally promptly opened a locker and started shedding clothes. Three other women did the same, all older. None of them thought twice about exposing their crepe folds and middle tires in front of us.

Then it hit me. The pickpocketing could very well take place here first. Damn. Bet the dynamics of that was covered while I was gone, too. I moseyed to the mirrors on the far wall, then around the benches painted white with gold filagree and way prettier than your standard gym locker room. I eyed hands and waited for the feel of someone capitalizing on my pockets, easier than most to pick. I'd put money in them, just in case. After circling the room twice, I returned to the locker and counted my money. There'd been no attempts.

Ally motioned me over. "What are you doing?"

"Giving the pickpocket a chance to pick my pocket before the pockets are gone."

"Ooh, Sis, that was smart. Can I do it?"

"You've started to undress. People will notice if you're putting clothes back on."

"Point taken." She removed her blouse. Her slacks were already folded and stashed in the locker. "Here, one locker means one key and less chance someone takes our things."

"Don't leave anything of value in there, silly," I said. "Taking your purse outside will entice the pickpocket to show his hand." I pointed at hers. "Especially since you brought one with a gaped-open top." Mine was clasped shut, a choice intentionally made.

To think Ally had attended Kaye's lesson and still brought a gaped-top bag.

"Come on, we need to be outside," she said, her panties coming off, her bra already gone.

She was correct. While I had felt the hazard more in here, with clothed people, what if the pickpocket was male and wandering the crowd, hunting for a purse like Ally's.

With stiff legs, I moved closer to her. Four more ladies came in. Then two more. I could hear more in the hall. This gig was going down fast.

I looked at Ally, making a face when I noticed a tattoo on her shoulder. "Is that a gardenia?" The white flower had soft greenery and shadows of peach. "Hey, that's my second-favorite flower," I said. "Thought you were a rose person?"

"Reminds me of you," she said, and I couldn't tell if she meant that or not.

She leaned in, her boob sweeping my upper arm. "It's temporary," she whispered. "I wanted to give people something to look at." She giggled. "Now . . . speaking of flaunting skin, let's see yours." She eased my jacket off, then reached out for me to hand her my slacks. Like a mom undressing her child. Her doing it made the ordeal easier.

"Leave on the necklace," she said in turning me around. "It looks tasteful."

"I guess so," I hissed. "It's the only thing I'm wearing."

She gave me a thorough once-over. "You're having a good hair day, too, but you should've painted your toenails."

I hadn't thought of that.

"Well, you're stuck barefoot. Wear those heels and you'll look like a hooker, so stash those."

I scoffed. "Yeah, sure. Like strutting naked doesn't scream that."

"Hey, don't strut, either."

By now, the room filled with people peeling off clothing, checking their hair in the mirror, then hurrying out, chattering like . . . well, like anyone going to a wedding with clothes on. I watched for anyone to take advantage, but damn, it was hard to see past the bodies in a style you don't see every day.

I followed Ally to the door.

The hall teemed with people heading to the wedding. Funny how they all still smelled of hairspray and cologne. Women still carried their purses, but then, so did I, like a damn security blanket. Everyone had been given peach towels, the etiquette of any nudist resort. One regular sized, another smaller. Something to use strategically, if necessary, and another to sit upon.

We got swept up in the crowd, me using my five-by-nine-inch clutch as much as a fig leaf in front of my female parts as possible, in spite of the towels. Thank goodness my bag held my phone, in order to communicate with Wayne. It felt like an absolute lifeline to me for some reason.

Outside, the autumn sun hit us like a spotlight.

"Tell me this doesn't feel great on your skin!" Ally said.

"It doesn't."

"You prude. Go do your thing. I'm to mingle, Wayne said. You're to stick to the opposite side of the throng from where he is." She pushed me. "Let's go be security." She giggled then released a squeal. "God, this is so fun!"

She left me standing there with my clutch and my towels.

I tried to mosey as if I did this often, noting the various family members of the wedding party. Their little matching flowers did make them notable. Some on wrists, some in hair. One was anchored on a belly ring, another in a nipple ring. The older gentlemen had them on long chains around their neck, the flowers hanging mid-belly. They gave you something to notice instead of what they hung over.

This nude wedding motif fell outside my preference, and I suspected Wayne would agree with me. Speaking of Wayne, I hunted for him. Swept up in the arriving guests, I neared the main area, looking for his height, his beard, and that body I was intimately familiar with. For the life of me, I couldn't find him. Had he not left the locker room? Maybe he circulated in there, thinking the clothed people more at risk.

But we were told to be outside. Scan the attendees. Take note of who looked out of place or seemed too observant. I bet he had two towels with him, too, you know, just in case. I'd hate to be a guy out here, especially if there was more than one or two Hannahs.

There he . . . was. *What the hell?*

My lawman had found a place in the shadows, a few yards east of the bar.

He was totally clothed in the suit he'd arrived in. And he was talking to Mr. Easton.

Chapter 25

WITHOUT THINKING, I started toward Wayne. Why the hell wasn't he naked like the rest of us? And what was Easton doing with him?

As common-sense reasoning caught up with me, I stopped, pivoted, and put my back to them. Opening my clutch, I lifted my phone, then remembered they were taboo in the resort. I'd been granted carry permission only because of who I was and what I was drafted to do—be security.

Instead of pulling out the phone, I drifted to the other end of the pool, now off-limits because of the wedding, and pretended I was new, admiring the amenities. Then I ducked behind the corner of the main building. A long line of tinted picture windows accented the smaller, heated indoor pool used off season. I turned my back to them and texted Wayne.

WTF?

Not normally my vocabulary, but the message said it.

He didn't answer.

Well, crap. Of course he wouldn't answer. He was talking with Easton, and the guests would take issue with his having a phone just as they would have if they'd seen me with one.

I put mine back in my clutch, again, pretending to note the surroundings . . . and jumped. Two people observed me through the glass. One of them put their thumb and little finger up, resembling a phone, and mouthed a silent scolding. *No phone*, she mouthed. The other scowled, pointing at me to go to the office and turn it in.

I mouthed *Okay, I will, sorry*, and left.

The wedding was about to start. I hadn't done much for Kaye—namely the watching for pickpockets and thieves—because I was too distracted. But then, wasn't that what a criminal would expect? The guests would be too caught up in the nudity, ceremony, and joy of the occasion to think about the potential of grift.

Wayne wasn't far from where he'd been, and Easton wasn't with him anymore. I waved, but Wayne pretended not to see me. He didn't quite portray the Secret Service image he normally could, but then, he was supposed to be a guest and pocket bait. He mingled well, and from the way folks smiled, welcomed, and humored him, he was being charming. The clothes seemed to make people feel for him as many made comments, touching his coat, smiling with the understanding he was a newbie.

A woman in full garb approached him. He wasn't the only one who'd chosen to attend clothed. There were a dozen or more. And he gravitated to them, as would a non-nudist at a nudist event. It made sense that a pickpocket would wear something with pockets to squirrel away what they pilfered.

So why the hell was I standing here without a stitch on?

Ally. Damn it.

I found her about to assume a seat on the bride's side, near the back. She put her little peach towel on the chair, and I did the same, my clutch strategically in my lap. "What the hell, Ally. There are clothed people here."

"You didn't come to the meeting at home meant to prep us. Wayne argued that a pickpocket would be attracted to those with pockets, so he's over there with his finest on, in hope he's a target."

"Which means you and I aren't targets."

"Wow, Sis. Like I never heard that before." She nudged me. "You did it to yourself, girl."

"But you're not clothed. Thought Kaye told y'all—"

"I like going *au naturel*. We went with that."

Cue the music. I had no desire to be preached at again about what I missed last night.

Everyone stood as the bride appeared from behind us, bare except for her veil, accented with peach flowers, her bouquet in front of her private parts. Her father appeared, a braided peach rope of sorts around his neck. His privates weren't hidden, though they weren't that much out in the open, either.

I'd never be able to see the color peach again without memories of this sea of skin.

Even the preacher . . . not a fit older gentleman . . . showed his assets for God and everybody. The groom wasn't so bad, but that was because he wasn't older than twenty-five.

The crowd wasn't intensely large, but it bumped a hundred, enough to make petty crime a possibility.

A breeze went through, and goose bumps reminded me everyone

could see the parts of me that would respond to the chill. But the sun still beamed, coming out from behind the cloud that had allowed that breeze, and warmed us back up.

The vows took minimal time, and I thanked God for that. We rose when the happy hitched couple walked up the aisle to the open grass, and the celebrating began.

I tried sticking next to Ally, for reasons I could not explain. Talking to naked strangers made me feel barer still.

"Get away," Ally whispered. "I'm to *mingle*."

She'd used that word three times already. Whatever Wayne said, she did.

"You're to stand on the opposite side from Wayne," she repeated. "We are to observe. Go." She left me.

Nothing left to do but the job assigned. I laid eyes on the clothed souls more so than the not, which totally went opposite from what I thought would happen. Out of the blue, when I noticed a guest opening her purse for a tissue, however, I realized those purses made a great hiding place as well as target for the criminally inclined. Diligently scanning people, my clutch remained tucked close.

Many hugs took place between people with minimal space between them. This wasn't nearly as easy to monitor as I thought.

"Afternoon, Ms. Slade."

I would've jumped out of my skin, but it was all I had on. My purse instantly became my cover. "Why, hello, Mr. Easton."

I forced myself to look him in the eye. "I thought you only handled weddings on farms."

"Clay River wasn't a venue that many caterers are willing to serve," he said. "Not only is it rural and secluded, but, well," and he gave me a wink, "you know."

"Well, you look good," I said to him in his black-and-white formality, a white and lilac pin on his lapel. About a dozen workers in similar garb worked the crowd. "Is your mother catering this event?"

"She is. Why wouldn't I use her? Not only do I get a great discount, but I know the menu by heart . . . plus, I am her heart." He spoke like he'd said the line many times before.

I started to mention I'd met his mother, then thought better of it. Instead, I thought of something else, and the realization of its potential almost stunned me. "Are you trying to *bird-dog* this place for a developer, too?"

"It's a nudist colony," he said, as if the words were foul to say. He gave me an up-and-down scan. "You don't trust me one bit, do you, Ms. Slade?"

"You capitalize on weakness wherever you find it, don't you?" I said, fighting not to flinch at his obvious attempt to shame me. "You owned up to that in the Waffle House. You're sniffing out trouble."

"Is there a weakness here I ought to be aware of?"

God he was daring, but I'd said too much. This time I had to protect Kaye.

Clay River had enough legitimate frontage on an active flowing river to make some developer a pretty penny. Twenty-five miles from the state capital, on a road not as heavily traveled as others, and on a side of the metropolitan area least developed, it was considered cheap water frontage compared to that of Lake Murray. Within five years—tops— that lake acreage would be limited. A river would be a nice compromise for those unable to settle on Murray.

"It's nowhere near the lake," I answered. "And from what I hear, the business here is great. They're on a national database that keeps their cabins and RV sites filled."

His gaze took a quick circle of the place. "I could still sell it." One of his staff came up and whispered in his ear.

Easton whipped around, in angered wonderment. "What?"

The employee shrugged and cast a glance at me.

"I see you have work tugging on you. Go tend to your food and drink," I said. "Don't let me—"

But he sharply turned back to me. "You are a conniving bitch. You and your Mr. Largo." He marched off.

What had just happened?

Immediately scanning the crowd for Wayne, I couldn't find him. I hunted for Ally. She was off near the pool, chatting up a group her age. Walking, not to attract attention, I made my way in a circle, one eye on the people, one eye seeking Wayne. Even finding Kaye would be nice.

Had Wayne hit pay dirt with a guest?

I reached the bar, the lady behind it in a Miss Lily's black-and-white uniform, a lily on the collar. "How're things going?" I asked.

"Fine," she said. "Red or white?"

Limited bar, I guess. "Red."

She poured a cabernet, something I'd seen in the grocery store. "This is not quite the norm for us," she said, "but you live and learn, huh?" She gave me an eye roll, then at her realization I was one of the naked ones, she blushed.

"Hey, my first time at an event like this, too," I said.

She gave me a slight smile. "Kudos to you. I have too many surgical scars to do this."

I grinned back, holding up the goblet in thanks, then flaunting my bandages. "Scars or no scars, flab or no flab, my family sort of roped me into it. Funny how you quit noticing after a while, though." I looked down over myself. "Feels kinda good."

"Again, your game, not mine." She turned attention to the husband and wife behind me. The man lightly bumped me moving up as I veered right. The bump didn't bother me as much as the light grab of my ass.

Instead of jumping away, I stopped, seeing red. Leaning into him, I reached down to where he held his towel before him. A quick bump of my fist hunched him just enough to tell me I'd hit home. "The red sucks," I said. "Choose the white." Then I strode off, pretty convinced he wasn't the pickpocket.

Somehow, I felt more empowered now.

Clumps of people imbibed and munched on canapes, by now, the snacks all cold, I noted. I guessed anything hot or drippy was not wise in this audience. More comfortable I wove through people, finally more at peace, more able to pay attention to crime potential instead of being seen as a spectacle. With my purse clasped against my belly, however, the vibration within jerked me to attention. I fast walked to my spot behind the building.

The phone had stopped ringing. However, once secluded between a tall rose bush—*seriously?*—and the pool's security fence just in case people were admiring the indoor pool like before, I checked the phone. Caller ID said *Cowboy*.

I rang him back. "I ought to choke you for the whole clothes scam."

He wasn't in the mood. "Snared our pickpocket," he said. "One anyway. I'm in Kaye's office. Wanted to let you know."

"I'll be there in a second."

"No need. You're not clothed, and we don't need that in the equation. I'll call with what happens next."

"Was he clothed or unclothed? It was a *he*, wasn't it?"

"Yes, but keep an eye on the group. They often come in pairs." He hung up.

No wonder I didn't see Kaye. That left Ally and me to surveil the party.

Most of me wanted to be with Wayne. The logical side said to do what I was told, what I had agreed to do as security for Kaye. Tucking the phone away, I briskly made my way to the people.

I wove in and out hunting Ally, to cover the areas where they weren't, analyzing bodies to spot a petty criminal. Finally, I saw my sister, but I left her to her own devices. For a while I served as both Wayne and myself, on guard, but saw nothing.

On my third round and my second glass of red, Easton caught my attention. He half hid behind the tables of food, a makeshift wall of cloth on a frame flaunting the Miss Lily's Table logo. His arms waved at someone sheepishly trying to explain herself.

I closed the distance, hoping to hear, but the employee, a woman around my age, noticed me, cut the conversation short, and slid away, leaving Mr. Easton in mid-sentence, huffing, markedly disturbed.

His snap-to-laser attention in my direction took me aback. "You . . . again." He spat the words like they were ammunition.

I attempted to diffuse. "What's up?"

"None of your business."

He didn't want to be nice. "Maybe it is my business, Mr. Easton. I'm part of the security team. You left cursing me a few minutes ago without any sort of explanation, and add that to whatever you have going on with that one . . ." I pointed with my chin to the woman trotting off. "It would seem you aren't having a good day. That disturbance could affect the guests. As security, I ask that you share what's happened."

He scoffed. "Security . . . well, hell and be damned. I should've known if Mr. Largo was, then you might be as well. If I'd known before taking this gig that y'all were part of the package, I'd have turned up my nose, I'm telling you. You two are bad luck."

From what I'd been mulling around in my head of late, he was bad luck for a lot of people. "What, you didn't get the Oakley property like you'd hoped?" He'd brought out the cat in me.

"What? *Miss Detective* didn't hear? Oakley's will left the place to that farm coop. I courted the man for nothing."

A relief to hear.

"Thought you loved planning weddings more than anything," I said. "The bird-dogging was just gravy, if and when situations arose to steer prospects to developers." I leaned in, my nudity causing him to take a half step back. I sort of surprised myself at no longer caring about having no clothes on. Frankly, the fact he stepped back made me want to flaunt it more. I rested fists on my bare hips, towels clutched in one, the purse in the other, and my front exposed without a care in the world. "Were you trying to put those farmers out of business? Is that how you choose where to hold weddings?"

"What? Of course not." He tried to backpedal into a more genteel persona, his eyes unable to find a place to land. "It's just, if he was going to die, I'd hope to be a party to any kind of sale. Nothing evil about that."

"Nothing noble, either."

A dozen questions popped to mind along with a dozen nicknames for this bastard. Purpose outweighed setting. Clothing or lack thereof mattered none.

Then I noticed the leaving employee hadn't returned to her work. She headed to the parking lot, purse in hand. I ought to be asking her questions if Easton wasn't talking. Him I could find later.

Pickpockets had partners.

Easton followed my line of sight and waved his tight fist. "Your Mr. Wayne scared my other man off. This woman just quit. Now I'm short-staffed. It wasn't easy getting people to work this event, you know."

Easton had no idea Wayne had the waiter in Kaye's office, interrogating him. And there went the possible partner making tracks to her vehicle, hoping not to get caught. I took off toward the parking area, ignoring Easton's demands to be told what was going on, in a fast walk at first, but the closer the escaping woman got to the vehicles, the faster I had to make up ground. Thank God there wasn't a soul on this facility or around this place for miles but nudists and their guests. With nobody but me and this woman in sight past the hedges, I took off buck naked across the lawn.

"Ma'am," I called, the grass not bad on my feet as I advanced to a trot. In reaching the parking lot gravel, however, I slowed. In mid-stride, I dropped my towels, pulled out my phone and let loose of my purse, determined to at least catch pictures if she bested me. I should've followed her from the outset, damn it, leaving Easton for a later talk. "Ma'am," I hollered again.

She took off running. The pudgy thing had thirty pounds on me, and I caught up with her just as her hand touched the car door.

She spun, a hand balling up to make a point. "Get away from me," she said, peering down her nose, huffing from the run.

I snapped her picture. "I'm the one naked. I ought to be saying that to you."

"Give me that phone," she said, taking an adversarial stance, arm still reared back ready to follow through with her silent *or else* threat.

I held the phone in the air behind me, but that only made her jump for it. I leapt back. She launched for my arm, and I spun like a basketball center. "Stop," I shouted. "Your partner has been caught in the act, and you might as own up to what y'all were doing. He's ratting on you as we speak."

"Don't know what you're talking about," she said, though she hadn't hidden her instant of surprise. "And my leaving is none of your damn business."

"I'm security," I said. "So, yes, it is."

"Nobody takes my picture without permission."

Before I could lay further claim to authority, she leaped from talking to tackling me, and we went to the ground.

My writhing was meant to escape her. Her writhing was meant to seize my phone. The process, however, dug pieces of granite into me, neck to toes, top to bottom, literally.

Necklaces, rings, and wallets scattered across the rock from her apron pockets. She hadn't even realized, being more afraid of being memorialized in my phone. "Give me that!" she shouted, growling behind the words, the two of us rolling in the rock. I maneuvered on top, ripping off the bandages I already wore, but then we rolled again, giving her the advantage. She lifted herself to only drop on my gut, and the wind whooshed out of me . . . and wouldn't come back.

I could not suck in a drop of air.

Chapter 26

MY LUNGS FROZEN and flat out too stunned to work, I still held the phone over my head.

The waitress bounced again, squeezing out my last bit of wind. Stars flickered in my periphery. I seriously expected my ribs to crack, one of them piercing something vital. An effort to dig in heels for the traction to dislodge her weight failed.

Suddenly, she was off me.

I was grateful. So damn grateful. Still, I couldn't sit up. At any moment I expected her to come down on me again like some wrestler jumping off the ropes. *Get up. Get up.* Or should I roll? I seemed incapable of doing either.

One arm around my midsection, I fought harder to sit up and managed to do so, taking irregular gulps of air, taking stock of where the woman was. Reaching down for strength, I also found anger, and if the universe would give me a few seconds, I'd beat the ever-loving crap out of her.

The woman never returned.

Because Ally stood there, hands on naked hips, cheeks red and angry, inviting a fight. She'd yanked my adversary off, strong enough to send her rolling eight feet away. My sister stood ready and waiting, eager for another round. "Bring it, bitch. I'll take you on. I've studied every move in *Fight Club*, sweetheart."

Miss Lily's waitress clamored to her feet, not in a graceful way, and I was pleased as punch to see her elbows scraped all to hell. Light-gray grit covered her torn uniform, and the white blouse had pulled out of her skirt.

"You bringing it?" Ally said, going to the balls of her feet. "Yeah, come on. Bring it, honey."

Her anger had replaced mine. But as much as both of us desired to beat the snot out of the lady, we needed information.

"You're crazy," the waitress said, and moved toward her vehicle.

Ally danced side to side. "Yeah, that's right. Get out of here before the two of us whip your ass! I can call the cops, too. Yeah, we have security at this wedding. Let me go get him for you."

"Ally," I struggled to say. I needed to interview the woman.

"We have your name," I lied to the woman. "And we have your partner. Murder is a powerful charge."

The *M* word made both Ally and the waitress freeze.

"I never murdered anyone," said the woman. "I only took jewelry and wallets, and just this one time, too. Talk to Richard about the harder stuff . . . which I know nothing of . . . not that there is anything. And he answers to the Eastons, not me. I've only dealt with Hill and just this one time. None of this shit is worth the price of murder."

The waitress spun and retreated to her car.

"Wait," I tried to yell, but didn't have the lungs to talk, though I did have sense enough to attempt a picture of the tag before she hit the gas and sprayed Ally and me with rock.

"Read the tag, Ally," I managed while trying to do the same, in case my photo hadn't grabbed a clear shot. I noted make and model and the first three letters of the South Carolina tag.

Close enough. I sank back resting on my hands in the gravel, attempting to regain my senses.

Dust settled around us, Ally staring daggers at the car until it disappeared.

"Oh, good heavens, let's look at you," Ally said, hands out to assist me to my feet. The front of me had scrapes already oozing small spots of blood, one shin with an eight-inch scrape, the old wounds minus gauze . . . and their scabs. My toes shined from cuts with red outlining the nails.

Good thing I hadn't gotten a pedicure.

"Damn, Sis." She fussed around me, brushing dust, dirt, and bits of parking lot off my back, my hips. "Oh, honey. I'm not so sure you don't need a doctor. Does that hurt?" She pointed to a spot on my left pelvis, and I gave a wince as I looked.

"Not really, but I have a feeling it will."

She ran over to retrieve my towels and purse, returned to hand them over before placing an arm around me. "You need a shower, and I'll find you a robe. No way you want to put your clothes back on over that damage. Some of those cuts are deep enough to get infected."

Kaye came running. "Jesus, Slade. Do you realize what you've done to yourself?" Like I wallowed around on gravel by choice.

"Get her a robe," Ally said.

"There's one in my office."

I gave a knowing look at Kaye, hoping she was aware Wayne was in there. Her return glance told me she was, and we didn't need to share the intel with Ally. However, with an accomplice having attacked me and escaped, Wayne needed to know. I had the woman's picture, and looking down around us, thank goodness, we had what had to be most if not all of the loot she'd purloined.

"Ally." I swatted my purse with a towel, realizing the dry dust would never come out. "Kaye can take care of me. You, however, must continue to watch the crowd. This woman you threw off me so masterfully was one of the ones we were supposed to hunt for, I bet."

Ally looked dumbfounded. "Seriously?"

"They never work alone, remember? There's liable to be another, too."

Kaye took the cue. "That's right. I taught you that. We don't need to ruin the bride's wedding. Go take care of business."

"The show must go on," Ally said.

Kaye grinned. "There you go. I'll owe you bigtime for this."

"And with Wayne occupied . . ." I stopped myself before saying the wrong thing.

"What about Wayne?" she asked.

"Wayne would be proud of you for being his wing girl watching things like I was. At least until I get cleaned up to his satisfaction."

With both her sister and her bestie pushing the same, noble message, Ally conceded. She leaned in and whispered, as if anyone was near enough to hear. "I have my phone if something comes up. Stay in touch."

"Gotcha." I winked, and she left.

I gave Ally time to be gone. Kaye and I picked up the strewn valuables. She examined the two wallets. "I'll slip these back to the people. Tell them they were found and left at the bar."

"They're evidence. Proof that woman stole them," I said.

"Don't care, Slade. I'd rather my guests leave with their belongings and oblivious to the fact they've been taken advantage of. Don't even ask for them back. I'll tell Wayne the same thing."

Which meant we'd probably never snare and prosecute the escaped waitress. "What about the jewelry?" There were two necklaces and three bracelets. All tiny, the easier to snap loose or slip off someone.

"I'll wait until people have had a few. They aren't far from that now. Then I'll hold them up and ask whose they belong to, saying this kind of stuff happens." She held the bracelets and necklaces in one hand, the wallets in the other, clearly with no intention of giving them to me.

I had arrived at the belief that Easton's presence meant scam. On a farm, at a wedding, wherever. I honestly felt that to delve deeper into anything would reveal an attempt to steal someone's property. If he wasn't causing the bad reputation of a place, he was capitalizing on someone's poor luck. And with the employees belonging to his mother, with her having tailed me, with Easton being ever present at the right time, I sensed his momma in the mix.

He was slippery, but had badly had I overlooked her?

Kaye waited for me to make some sort of decision, but she'd lost her calm and couldn't stand still. This wedding could make or break her. No doubt in my mind now that this pickpocket situation was an Easton creation to mar the reputation of Clay River. He operated an enterprise with the innocent face of weddings and reunions, displaying a persona oozing fun and joy for one side and offering income opportunity for the other . . . helpful to one and all.

The wedding and reunion people would have their one-off affairs, with people only enjoying Easton's one, smooth side. The property owners hosting the events would never see him coming, especially with many of them dead and in the ground.

The problem was that every bit of this was conjecture.

Oakley's place had been willed to the young farmers' cooperative, thank goodness, but Easton was pissed about that, reinforcing my intuition. Mrs. Brooks was the wisest of the lot, not falling for Easton's ploy. He'd definitely read her wrong. The others, however, would end up at his mercy. But Clay River. . . .

"Kaye?"

"What?" she asked, waiting for what she hoped was instructions.

"Did Easton speak with you or the owner of Clay River to set up this wedding? Which one?"

"Both of us," she said. "Got permission from the owner, which I could've handled, but she turned things over to me."

So he'd gotten to both of them. That meant he was familiar with who was in charge, who had the most to lose, and whom he could manipulate. He was slick. Kaye was usually more street savvy than this, showing me just how much her heart was in this place. She'd become vulnerable and hadn't seen it coming.

Easton had already crossed into my beloved agriculture, but this time he'd trespassed into my family. If Easton ruined the reputation of this place, leading to Kaye losing her job, she'd fall back into thinking she'd failed and would disappear again. It took Wayne years to run her down before, and a year once he found her to help her regain confidence. Wayne would lose his mind all over again hunting for her, and I'd have a broken husband. My sister would lose her best friend, and my children would lose a revered aunt.

We all loved Kaye. She was good for all of us, and I wasn't letting this damn fool of an opportunist ruin that.

We hid behind a row of hedges that ran outside the pool fence. Blood ran down my shin now, clotting in places, and aches told me that bruises were coming to life on my backside. "I need to get to Wayne and let him know about this pickpocket, Kaye. But I can't walk past people looking like this. Not without upsetting your crowd." I had to let her be part of the solution.

"Extra robes are in my office," Kaye replied. "In my private closet. Stay here."

I held her back. "No. You'll be more missed out here." I wiped the drips from my shin with the small towel, then opened the big one and wrapped it around my waist, hanging it such that it hid as many scrapes on my rear side as possible. Kaye read what I was doing and handed me hers, and I draped it around my shoulders. "I need to get to Wayne and tell him what went down out here. Not sure why he has the other guy. We may have just identified our pickpocket team, and he needs to know, and best that be from me."

She rewrapped one of the towels that came loose. "There."

"Good. Now, I'll walk straight to the building. At the same time, you go to the opposite side of the crowd, meeting and greeting people openly, to distract them. Be seen and get as many people as possible to look your way."

"I can do that."

There was no good moment. "Then go," I said.

Kaye struck out, going by the bar to grab a wine glass and deposit the belongings under the bar, telling the barkeep to keep an eye on them. I prayed the barkeep wasn't in on the scam.

Then with a hop and some loud raucous laughter I'd never heard out of her before, Kaye stepped up on the platform where the couple were wed. "This way, people!"

The murmuring traveled like a wave, but everyone turned toward her. "A toast from Clay River to the bride and groom. Thanks for being our first-ever wedding. How about it, everyone? Hold up your glasses for a toast. Hurrah, happy couple!"

As people chanted in return, I scurried to the main building.

"Hurrah, Clay River!" Kaye shouted. The people shouted in kind, all facing toward her like sunflowers to a rising sun.

I ran through the front door, then reaching Kaye's office on the right, I jerked the handle. It was locked.

"Wayne!" I shouted, timing my call and three fast knocks to the reverberating shouts of toasting and cheers from the tipsy people outside.

The door opened a couple inches. "Slade, stop. Go back—"

I pushed into the room. Going straight to the closet, I grabbed the longest robe. It wasn't slinky silk like Kaye's, but I sought coverage, not style. Dropping my towels smeared with blood, Wayne gave a small, quickly controlled grunt of reaction to my wounds as I slipped arms into the sleeves, not caring who saw.

"We'll get to me and my mess in a second," I said, laying a gaze on the *prisoner.*

The waiter stared from his seat in front of a file cabinet, Wayne having positioned him away from outside views.

"Slade," Wayne started again.

"Now," I said, tying the sash around my waist. "Who is this gentleman?"

Wayne hesitated. I'd totally thrown him a curve ball.

The waiter was equally stunned.

Time to own the role. "I was working the crowd with Agent Largo here, sir." I had much to add to this conversation with no plan to go in any damn particular direction, running more on emotion than detail, but this was as close to answers as I'd gotten throughout this ordeal. I'd have to work this on the fly. I remembered my phone and retrieved it from my purse. "After a proper introduction"—I motioned to some of my wounds—"imagine what I learned from your compatriot."

The waiter turned leery. "Does she look like you?"

"Worse."

"This is Richard Hill," Wayne said, reluctantly going along. "He's admitted to robbing the crowd."

Oh, how fun. "How opportune. Your partner kept saying *Talk to Hill. Hill's in charge. Hill organized everything. Hill did more than just pickpocketing.* What a coincidence that we finally meet," I said. "By the way, I relieved your partner of the goods she stole, Mr. Hill. We've already returned them to their rightful owners."

Wayne's expression soured hearing the evidence no longer existed.

"But not before we took inventory and pictures. And, of course, we'll have statements from the owners that they'd been robbed." Assuming Kaye didn't run interference on that to save the resort's reputation.

"Where's Lisa?" Hill asked.

"Well, we certainly weren't bringing her in here," I replied. "She sure spoke a lot about you, though."

"Bitch."

I wasn't sure Hill meant me or Lisa, but this was good. We had a name. We'd get the last name from Easton, assuming she gave him her correct employment information, but first things first. "I am Carolina Slade, Special Projects Representative with the United States Department of Agriculture."

He wouldn't know what the hell my title meant, but the length of it sounded official. Partner that with acceptance by the Special Agent in the room, and I was solid. Plus, I'd tackled his accomplice, as if I was trained to do something like that and did it all the time.

"But you caught *her* with the goods," he said. "Not me."

"She admitted to working alongside you. And you've already confessed to . . . what?"

"Little to nothing," he answered, grinning like he saw an opening. "I'd like to know how the feds got involved. This ought to be a misdemeanor tops and handled by the county idiots."

Wayne held up the gold watch he'd been wearing. "This Rolex valued at twelve thousand rules out misdemeanor, wouldn't you say? We're in felony territory now."

I still had to hear the story about where Wayne got that watch.

"Guess that explains why the feds and why not the misdemeanor," I said. "And there must be history of you and your cohort's previous behavior or you wouldn't even have the feds on site. If you want to help yourself, what we'd really like to hear is who you picked pockets for and why, because you're definitely not acting on your own, and this isn't your first gig."

Wayne was blank as to where I was taking this, but he didn't interrupt. His slight squint, though, said we'd be having a serious talk. We'd been in this scenario before, where one or the other initiated a situation, a conversation, even a fight, the other having to play catchup without giving away they might be clueless.

This time, while I might not have a grasp of the details, I wasn't clueless. Wayne, however, had zero idea, but the only way to prove my theory was to act the alpha, then fill him in later.

He'd either be proud of me or read me the riot act once this was over.

"Mr. Hill." I paused, meaning for him to turn his attention to me. "You work for Miss Lily's Table. Yes or no?"

The forty-ish man scoffed. "You're a brain trust. Of course I do." He pulled the material bearing the embroidered emblem up from his chest to prove it.

"You've helped Mr. Easton, Miss Lily's son, in catering weddings at other places. Before you lie, there are ample documents to prove when and where."

"Yes, I have, but I never picked pockets at those."

"Were you told to do other things to deface, derail, or intimidate?" Wayne's expression said he liked the question.

When Hill hesitated, I added, "Lisa seemed to think you did . . . several times. Said you preferred the heavy-hitting tasks."

"Not my idea to do any of it, and I'm not admitting I was told to pickpocket, deface, or any of that other stuff, either here or the farms," he said.

"So you operated solo? Maybe you and Lisa made money for yourselves, meaning you hoodwinked Miss Lily and her son?" Was he this stupid? I mean, crooks were noted for not being the sharpest knife in the drawer, but he was sort of caught in the act here. And he'd segued for us by mentioning the farms.

His expression froze for a second. "Wait, no, I did not say I operated alone. I followed instructions, lady."

Better yet. "Let's say you didn't rob from the other venues, but you performed other duties at the request of Miss Lily or Easton," I said. "That sound like more the truth?"

He didn't answer, his expression showing he wasn't sure the right way to answer.

"Like maybe you harassed people. Maybe even tailed them," I said.

His expression barely shifted, almost at a micro-expression level, but I saw it. Wayne did, too.

"You've tailed me, for instance," I said. "We found your tracker in my wheel well." Then I added, "With fingerprints."

He fought making an expression, attempting to remain noncommittal. The effort was almost as good as confessing. We'd save that for later.

The funny part was Wayne fought making an expression, too. He tried to understand where I was going, afraid to interrupt and equally afraid to cut me loose with a free rein.

"You and your buddies did one or more of the following." And I waited to offer up the list.

The man sat on the edge of his seat, apprehensive and unsettled as to how and what I knew.

While I had proof of nothing, I had nothing to lose here. Once he lawyered up, which he stupidly and thankfully hadn't done yet, I'd be booted out altogether. I'd have to school Wayne on what I'd learned, what I suspected, and hand him all the research I'd done. Monroe would be asked why he hadn't called the Inspector General to start with. I'd be asked why I didn't recommend he do so . . . and I'd have to say I did, pushing responsibility ninety-nine percent onto Monroe's head.

Wayne's gaze said he was on the brink of stopping me, but I proceeded, taking a risk that the lawman gave me some benefit of the doubt, and there was a lot of doubt to go around here.

"You or your counterpart with Miss Lily's did one or more of the following," I repeated.

"I'm listening," Hill said, his impatience tickling the hell out of me.

"You antagonized a man to the point he hanged himself in Saluda. This gave his wife sole ownership. Then she was prompted to sell, which was the original goal of your boss." Empty eyes on that one. Wayne's said, *Surely you've got better than this.*

"You pursued a farmer in Richland, giving chase to him in his field, creating a dangerous situation which ended with him dead beneath his rolled tractor. You knew after that death, the estate would have to sell."

A clear flicker on that one. He might not be aware of the bigger picture, but he'd had a hand in that or knew who had. I tried another and kept it simple.

"You caused a farmer in Lexington County to die of methane gas poisoning."

A wince on that one. My guess was he'd been there or, again, was aware of who was.

Another one. "You killed a farmer's dog, leaving a threatening note, trying to push him to sell."

"I don't kill dogs," he said.

"But you know the person who did," I snapped back, to which he didn't deny.

My wounds began to sting, an ache creeping into my muscles, so I rolled Kaye's caster chair around and sat, going almost knee to knee with

Mr. Hill. Maybe a little too close, but I felt enabled with Wayne at my back.

"Do you fish, Mr. Hill?" I asked.

He acted afraid to answer, as if it were a trick question. It was.

"It's a simple yes-or-no answer, Mr. Hill," Wayne said. His deeper voice etched a weightier value to the question, and while I hated the fact Wayne had that tool at his disposal and I didn't, I was happy for him to ram the question home.

"Of course I do. Most people fish if they're within twenty miles of Lake Murray," Hill said.

"A drone puts someone at Mr. Homer Brooks's boat on the day he died, something they've held from the public. They're thinking of reversing their accident finding to one of murder. Manslaughter at a minimum."

Total bullshit, but that impromptu performance got us what I'd hoped . . . a look of fear. It stayed long enough for him not to be able to deny it.

"I want my lawyer."

Noise sounded in the hall. Voices raised. The words weren't intelligible until they stopped right outside the door. One voice belonged to Easton.

Chapter 27

"SOMEONE SAID they came inside," Easton said.

"You are not authorized here," said Kaye.

"I am if Largo kidnapped my worker!" Knuckles pounded on the door.

"Is Easton in on this?" Wayne asked me, having put together enough from my questions to Hill to ask one of his own.

"I believe so." I said, still not having all my ducks in a row, but Easton walked like the proverbial duck and quacked like the proverbial duck. I just hadn't nailed him down.

Hill watched us, chuckling to himself.

I wasn't happy with that. Wayne noted and silently threw concern at me. "All for one and one for all," I said. "Whatever one did, we can tie to the other." Then the rest I said more for the benefit of Mr. Hill. "From pickpocketing to murder, they're all involved."

Hill woke up. "Murder?"

"Murder, Mr. Hill," I said. "Let's hear you laugh now. Let them in, Agent Largo. Mr. Hill has lawyered up, so if he's silent, we can at least listen to what Mr. Easton says about Mr. Hill's involvement."

Wayne opened the door.

Kaye entered. "Do I need to prep guests for the police arriving?"

I loved that.

Wayne pierced Easton with a stare, as if Wayne's answer depended on Easton's response.

"You . . . you took my staff," Easton stuttered. "I'm in a bind."

This time I let the real agent take charge.

Lawman glowered at the fresh audience. "You two seem to want to join the party. Come in. But I'm setting the ground rules."

Kaye listened. She was no dummy.

Easton paled. "I have a . . . a right—"

"Mr. Easton," Wayne said, in his cop voice. "I ask questions. You answer. Disrupt this conversation and you're out of here or you're cuffed. That clear?" He looked around the room. "That means everybody."

Everyone, including me, nodded.

"Easton," Wayne said, motioning for the man to take a seat in the caster chair I'd abandoned when the two new bodies appeared. "Does Hill here work for you?"

"Technically, no," he said, as if he had an easy out on that one.

"You didn't hire him?" Wayne repeated.

"He works for Miss Lily, my mother, and I contracted with her for the catering."

"So, Hill is under your supervision."

"Well, yes."

Wayne did a light dip of his head in acknowledgement. "Well, Mr. Hill was caught in the act of stealing a Rolex. That puts part of the liability on you, doesn't it?"

Up went his hands. "I did not hire him. I could not vouch for him."

"We should pursue your mother instead of you. Is that what you're saying?"

Easton's mouth opened and closed like a Lake Murray bass hauled into the boat.

Hill chuckled. Wayne let him.

Now I dared to speak. I knew way more than Wayne, and hopefully my participation could underpin his actions. "How many other occasions have you supervised Hill?" I gave air quotes for *supervised*.

With a shrug, Easton assumed I meant catering. "A few times. Not much. I don't know him personally, but he's not exactly a stranger."

"Did Hill work on any of the farms I've questioned you about?"

Easton tried to appear lost. "I'm not sure which—"

"Don't dig yourself into a hole, Mr. Easton," I warned. "We discussed them at the Waffle House. We've already talked to Hill. So, which farms?"

Hill wasn't saying anything. With Easton floundering, putting on such a flubbed-up show, Hill was probably hoping that the wedding planner had forgotten or wasn't sure.

Easton rattled off the five, the fourth, of course, being Candleman, his hog farm not conducive to wedding entertainment. He'd even included Oakley.

Hill had already given us indications that he was familiar with Candleman.

Were the deaths—intentional or not—by Easton, or Easton's people?

I began seeing another hypothesis. Wayne was about to take over, but I needed to bring this around more, not just for him, but for me . . . before this case rapidly slipped away into the lap of the IG.

"Kaye," I said. She sat cross-legged against the door, as if serving as guard until we got this situation handled.

Easton interrupted. "Ask me all your questions for me so I can get back to the guests."

"In a second, Mr. Easton."

Wayne gave him a hard look for me.

I returned to Kaye. "Were all your conversations with Mr. Easton regarding today's wedding? Was there anyone else?"

"Nope. Just him."

"Were your conversations restricted to catering? Wedding supplies? Choreography? Music and flowers?"

She started to say yes, then it was like she read my direction. "No, as a matter of fact."

Easton stiffened, then he repositioned himself, attempting to appear amazed and lost as to her meaning.

"He asked if we'd be willing to sell," she said. "He asked my boss that as well."

He rolled his eyes. "Ms. Slade. I told you without reservation that I dabble in real estate."

"I believe you called it *bird-dogging*," I reminded.

"Which doesn't require a license," he reminded me back.

"How long ago did your conversation with him take place?" I asked Kaye.

She had to think. Then, bless her, she asked him. "When was it we had our first chat, Mr. Easton?"

"Um, a couple months ago?"

"More like four," she said, just as pretty as you please.

"Could be," he said.

I pulled things around a bit. "And when did the vandalism and theft begin happening?"

Kaye uncrossed her legs and rose, then took a step into Easton's space. "A couple of weeks after that," she said. "We had pickpocketing, cars broken into, theft in the cabins and RVs, and graffiti on the guard-house."

Hill stiffened in his chair.

Kaye noticed. "We had a rush of guests, and with it being still summer, I didn't think anything of it. The online site was alive and well, and the national system of making reservations worked smooth as silk. But we went from every two weeks to weekly to several times a week with something bad happening. We'd never had issues before."

"Before?" I asked.

"Before Mr. Easton," she said.

With that revelation, Wayne remained in the background, watching to see where I took this.

"Nobody died?" To an innocent on the outside looking in, that question sounded ludicrous. Even Easton blinked a lot, like he attempted to make sense of where I was going.

"No," Kaye said.

"Easton," Wayne said, moving nearer to his sister, laying a hand on her shoulder. "Sounds like she's lucky, huh? If we hadn't intervened, she may have joined those four farmers, huh?" Wayne had put pieces together.

"Five," I said.

"Five," Wayne repeated.

"What?" The word bounced off the walls of the small room, warmed by so many emotional people trapped inside. Easton's expressions flipped from amazement to wonder before resting on fear. "This . . . is about me?"

Kaye picked up on the script. "You . . . you were going to kill me, Mr. Easton?" She gave a pleading, desperate look at her brother like she couldn't believe what she was hearing. After years of working with, escaping from, and running from a criminal drug gang for close to a decade, she was capable of shifting appearance. Plus, she and Wayne shared enough DNA to almost read each other's minds. It was why she'd been so difficult to find all those years.

Easton's mouth flopped open. Hill's, however, didn't. "Tell them I didn't order you to do anything other than serve guests," Easton said. "I didn't tell you to do anything here, on the farms, anywhere, and I damn sure didn't direct you to harm people." He gasped, hand to his throat. "Kill people? Good heavens, that never crossed my mind."

His fluster ran red up his neck and into his face. His eyes held legitimate fright. I had to admit his shock was believable. Hill, on the other hand, remained silent, reading the room.

"Hill! Tell them!"

But the waiter remained quiet. I would too if I were him.

Wayne's critical attention stuck on the waiter. "Shame you lawyered up and can't tell us, Hill."

"I'll talk for the right deal." He grinned at Easton, but it fell short of the smugness he aimed for. The crook wasn't as emboldened as he'd hoped to appear.

Which made him malleable.

"I'm not involved in any of that," Easton said.

"You asked me what would talk me into selling," Kaye reminded.

"You asked all those farmers the same thing," I tacked on.

Arms out, flailing, he walked over. Why he came to me, I had no idea.

"You get agriculture," he said. "Farmers skate on thin ice. One year's disaster can set them back five years. Throw in divorce and bad health and progress—"

"Developers," I corrected.

His admission to that came in jerky nods. "Yes, developers . . . anyway, the farmers quickly get in over their head. You know, Ms. Slade. You know."

"Yes," I said. "I do know. And you ought to know better. You recognize the odds they struggle with, but, when you spot a weakness, you dive in for the kill."

"I don't kill people!" he screamed. "These farmers are lucky I understand! My parents almost wore themselves out scratching at dirt and selling livestock at a miniscule profit. When they went under . . . when he died, as horrible as this may sound, that was probably the best thing that could've happened to my mother."

He looked over his shoulder at Wayne but decided he preferred venting to me, his gaze pleading. Easton and I were more agriculturally oriented than the others in the room. Maybe that was it. Though we squabbled at Waffle House, we'd held a discussion. I'd tried to understand him. He'd tried to make me understand him.

Oh my God, was he crying? "I don't kill people," he whimpered.

"You just push them to suicide," I said softly. "And still, you crawl in the shadows to developers with your *bird-dogging*. Doesn't quite paint you so altruistic, does it, Mr. Easton?"

"I'm in a position for deals to fall into my lap. The developers came to me, at first. Now I have an open door to go to them."

Like any of that sounded any better.

"I'll talk for the right deal," Hill said again. "With a lawyer present."

A break. Thank God.

"Then I'm not talking to you," Wayne said. "We cuff you, take you in, and let you throw the dice with the United States Attorney."

Hill didn't like that. "Can you cut a deal?"

"No, but I can speak in your favor if you shed more light on how these events went down. Frankly, I'll be the most open-minded person you meet going forward. Answer my next question honestly and your odds go up exponentially. However, if you lie now, and I find out later, I'll use all the powers in my grasp to bury you."

I wished I could think of things to say like that.

Hill sat back, studied Wayne before studying Easton, who cringed. "Sure," Hill said. "Ask your question."

"Did you, in any way, facilitate any of the deaths?" Wayne asked.

If I'd been asked that, I'd have wet my pants. The answer had the power of making or breaking the rest of one's life.

"I didn't hurt or lay hands on anybody," Hill said, "but I might know things."

Easton went wide-eyed and paled. "No, I didn't order anything." The words came out almost in a whisper.

Wayne pointed at Easton. "Did Garrett Easton give any instruction that constitutes breaking the law, Hill?"

"No, I didn't!" Easton said.

But Wayne ignored him. "What do you say, Mr. Hill?"

Hill gave Easton a sneering grin, enjoying the stress he heaped on the man, feeling the ground he was gaining. "No."

Mr. Easton sank to the floor. Nobody went to his aid.

All of us stood there, a little shocked, waiting for where this story would pivot next. We thought we were cornering Easton.

"No," Hill began again. "Little Garrett's never told me to do anything. He'd shit himself sooner than get his hands dirty."

Easton's brisk little nods of agreement didn't earn him any of our pity.

"Well, you weren't on your own," Wayne said. "And you're shrewd enough to understand that without coughing up the leader, you won't get your deal."

Hill shrugged. "I'm not an idiot, Mr. Agent Man. The more I give you, the better the deal I'll expect."

And he would get it, too. Clearly, he wanted to get this ball started. He would be arrested. Like most criminals, he was eager to define what punishment he could escape, and what would stick.

"I work for the queen," he said.

Still in his kneeling position, Easton stiffened, tears still drying on his cheeks. "No. Don't."

With a bobble of his brow, Hill leaned elbows on his knees, intent on Easton. "How's it feel, baby boy?"

"I need a name," Wayne said.

He enunciated each part of the moniker. "Mrs. Lily. Mae. Chassereau . . . Easton."

Easton's posture melted.

"Did you know?" I asked Easton.

He shook his head.

"Did you suspect?"

He gave a mild shrug. "I liked to think I did all this on my own. The weddings, the real estate deals. It was rather easy." His voice reduced to barely audible. "I just didn't want to know why."

A machine-gun repetition of a knock beat on the door. "Where is everybody?" Ally cried from the hallway.

I went to the door, cracking it six inches, making it clear she couldn't enter. "What is it?"

Trying to peer around, she talked with her hands and spoke up loudly, expecting the others to be behind me. "Where have y'all been, Slade? People are asking. Guests, the bride, the wait staff . . . everyone is coming to me like I'm running the place. Where's more ice? When do we cut off the bar? Why aren't there any hot hors d'oeuvres? When do they throw the bouquet? How the hell am I supposed to cope here? I'm only the pickpocket watcher."

Kaye got up and came over. "Come on, girlfriend. Let's rock the rest of this party. Let me show you how it's done."

Chapter 28

WAYNE TOOK MY truck to deal with Hill's arrest. We three ladies stayed behind to fill in for staff, wind down the wedding, and clean up the resort, because Easton went along with Wayne and Hill.

An investigation was to be opened, directed by his agency, driven by him. In spite of or because of his connection to me, Agriculture's liaison to the Inspector General, I wasn't sure, but no point being too vocal about any of that tonight. While Wayne was busy with the arrest and formulating his plan for the week, I was in a dilemma about whether to feel stupid, guilty, or, dare I say, proud.

We three ladies arrived home close to midnight, Ivy meeting us at the door with grownup worry.

"I texted you," I reminded, hugging her before moving inside. "But everything's good."

"That's good?" she asked, pointing to my wounds and assorted bandages.

"I fell in the parking lot," I said.

She turned her worries toward her Aunt Ally, the least knowledgeable, whom we'd mostly kept in the dark. Ally shrugged, hugged, and escorted the child into the kitchen, away from the silent, deep-thinking adults. Zack had been asleep for two hours. We left him that way.

Ally had tried to talk to us in the car, attempting to understand, but Kaye and I weren't up to it, and I wasn't sure what could be safely said. Ally had learned some time ago to expect a certain degree of this sort of discretionary conversation when a case was involved.

Wayne had beat us home and gone to bed. Though tomorrow was Sunday, he'd hit the ground running on this case . . . or so I assumed. We hadn't spoken since the meeting in Kaye's office except for him to come up to me outside to say, "We have to talk."

"When?" I'd asked.

"Later," he'd said.

I'd been replaying that line in my head all evening long.

In an official capacity, I'd have to weather an interview. A big question was whether I'd acted properly in the Inspector General's eyes. The bigger question was whether I'd screwed up in Wayne's.

Wayne rose Sunday and took off, staying gone till dark, not wanting to discuss the case before he left and refusing to upon his return.

Then the week began, me in my role and him in his. He left before I did on Monday, and I stepped off the elevator at the office wondering if Monroe had been informed, and whether it was my place to inform him if he hadn't been. He'd be angry either way.

Briefly I thought of the half-dozen smaller issues on my desk awaiting my focus, plus whatever Whitney had saved for me. Big cases came directly from Monroe.

Whitney's sparkle wasn't there when I walked in, and she darted eyes toward my office. Wonderful. Someone waited for me. Monroe, probably. I took a breath and entered.

Wayne sat in my guest chair, taking notes in a notebook, looking like a federal agent.

I took my seat behind my desk. "You didn't tell me you were coming in this morning. You ready to talk the case?"

"I'm ready to interview you, Slade. Monroe's been informed. He will not bother you about it afterwards, and likewise, you will not discuss the case or the interview with him."

A part of me wanted to fuss. Another part of me recognized the agent doing what he was supposed to do. Again, I wasn't sure if I'd screwed up or had done what I was trained to do, to take things as far as I could take them before turning over a solidly suspicious case.

The part about Monroe is what niggled me. He'd told me not to tell Wayne. Now Wayne was in charge. I had zero idea if Monroe would feel betrayed. I also had zero idea if Wayne was angry at me, not necessarily betrayed but disappointed. Disappointed I had not confided in him.

I was damned either way.

"Here or somewhere else?" I asked.

"I have a meeting room reserved on the fourteenth floor," he said.

"When?"

"Now. I made sure your whole day was free."

He'd removed the chance of people knocking on my door, phone calls, and prying eyes. I hadn't brought lunch and wondered if he'd be allowed to have lunch with me. Stupid the things you think about when the feds want to pick your brain.

I slept with this guy. Why was I so nervous?

He left first. His suggestion. People might talk if we left together.

People saw us together all the time now. Why would they . . .? "That's fine," I said. "See you in ten."

He rose without a goodbye, with nary a smile, and left. I gave him the ten minutes then followed. The fourteenth floor. A federal senator's office occupied that floor. He was not there that often, but he kept a full-time staff of two for public inquiries. The senator must be out of town. No way anyone would interrupt us there.

Getting off the elevator, I forgot how this floor felt like a tomb. The two admin types didn't come close to filling up a space this size, and they kept to themselves. I could drop dead in one of these conference rooms and wouldn't be found for a month.

Wayne had put a note on the right door, saying *Do Not Disturb. Interview in Progress.*

Jesus.

I entered. He had his recorder set up, his notepad before him, already filled with questions for me and reminders to himself. I'd been trained in how to do this. He'd been trained, however, in how to do this better.

"Sit down, Slade."

He'd expect me to follow instructions without much explanation, and he'd expect me to understand the ritual. And since he was my lover, he knew me well enough to sense I was aware of how serious this was.

He read into the recorder the time, date, and named the people in the room, and off we went.

The first few questions anchored who I was, where I worked, for how long, etc., etc. What my duties were, then, finally, asked when and why I'd opened a case.

There was no way not to mention Monroe.

"Why didn't you contact the IG for guidance?" he asked.

A set-up question. And there was no way to avoid the correct answer.

"First, nothing seemed criminal when I started."

"Second?"

This was what he wanted. Oh, how I hated saying the words. "The State Director told me not to."

"Did you ask him for permission to do so anyway?"

"Yes."

"More than once?"

"Yes."

He'd just cleared me and put crosshairs on Monroe.

"However you chose not to tell the IG?"

"Agent Largo, I was caught in the middle. But honestly, there was no proof of criminal activity. No murder. No threats. The farmers were honest. Garrett Easton hadn't done anything criminal I could see. No coroners said there was a death by human hand . . . nothing by misadventure even."

"Yet you felt a pattern existed."

"I did."

His mouth held a flat line. "You didn't think to inquire of someone with more skill to pursue these matters, to assist you in investigating the potential of criminal activity?"

"I thought about it," I said, some steam rising. Was he making a legitimate claim or was he insulted that I hadn't brought the case home with me to talk over on the porch?

"And what kept you from doing so?"

"The firm belief that you . . . the IG would decline the case."

"You had no way of knowing—"

"Listen." For the first time I shifted in my chair, and I did so to lean forward, to rest on the table and lessen the space between us, and to make a damn point. "Your people trained me. I've handled more cases than all the people like me across the country. I may not carry a gun or be able to arrest the bad guy, but I recognize when something is unpalatable, when it is against the rules, and when it is against the law. You only come in when the case falls clearly into the last category."

"One call, Ms. Slade."

"No, it isn't about one call, Mr. Largo." I made his name formal like he'd made mine. "It's also about integrity. If it isn't criminal, I don't call. If I called every time I had a question, you'd lose respect for me and my abilities. Give me some credit, please. This whole case didn't start unraveling until the pickpocketing incident, when someone actually broke the law. Before that, nobody could pinpoint a thing. This pickpocket incident was the thread we could finally pick and unravel. The waitress I caught and the waiter you grabbed tied some things together. Both pointed to more than just stealing watches."

Wayne didn't show emotion. Even with nobody in the room, or even within hearing distance, he maintained his professional persona. That was his training, but it pinched my feelings. I got it . . . but I still wasn't happy. I wanted someone to give me some damn credit.

"Ready to go over the farmers?" I asked.

"I'll ask the questions," he said.

So I sat back and let him ask his questions. Finally he got to the meat of the issue.

"In your talking to Mr. Hill at the wedding, when he was pulled aside by me in an office, you said you had four or five questionable deaths. What happened to make you question these deaths when coroners had already determined them to be accidents?"

"I drove to Craven County and spoke to a police chief from Edisto Beach and a private investigator from Craven. You know Chief Callie Morgan. You know of PI Quinn Sterling. Since I was under orders not to talk the case with the IG, I asked them for advice. On top of that, Sterling would be aware of CDM Dorothy Bell's past since her uncle, the sheriff, investigated the accident. Just doing my job, Mr. Largo."

"That's when you started making connections?"

"I'd already had a conversation with Garrett Easton in which he'd admitted to working with them all. I took my details and thoughts to Craven when I sensed some dark direction to the farm deaths, and they helped me see that something or someone had to be behind this. Especially after I had been hit by a white SUV belonging to Miss Lily's Table, *after* I'd been watching white SUVs follow me for a week. Then on my way to Craven, I was followed by another, this time driven by none other than Miss Lily. Quinn Sterling found the tracker on my truck and disposed of it. Someone was worried I was investigating. If not for the information uncovered during the wedding at Clay River, I might've met with foul play."

"That tracker could've been used as evidence," he said.

Yeah, I'd realized that after leaving Craven County.

He took notes in spite of the recording. I'd just talked about getting hurt . . . his fiancé getting hurt, and he rocked on like it was nothing.

After a long moment, he looked back up at me. "I'll be interviewing CDM Delores Bell on the heels of your interview."

"Okay."

"Do you have concerns about Ms. Bell and Mr. Monroe Prevatte and a relationship? Is that why you went down to Craven?"

We were back to Monroe. My heart leaped at where this might be going. "She was difficult to speak with," I said. "And Mr. Prevatte seemed to be protecting her, so I wanted to find out the details as to why she left Craven, came to Richland, and was yet another connection to Easton." I dodged using the word *relationship* or anything like it. If the IG wanted to take down Monroe, I was not going to be a party to it.

Wayne would see that, too, but I didn't care.

"I'll be interviewing Easton after Bell," he said.

This second remark threw me off. An interviewer didn't tell an interviewee their plans. Maybe a sign of respect? The agent was supposed to say as little as possible, wanting the one being interviewed to do all the talking.

He wanted me to grasp the order of his interviews. A forewarning?

More notes. God, how the hell wasn't he showing any expression with me?

Flipping a page, he seemed to find a question he needed. "Why do you think Easton showed interested in Delores Bell when she arrived in Richland?"

"He had irons in the fire on several farms and couldn't afford for her to ruin his wedding and/or real estate endeavors. He'd done his research beforehand since she was a fresh factor in his business, going so far as to take a daytrip to Craven County where he learned of her affair with a farmer and the wreck that killed him. He spoke to several people, to include Quinn Sterling."

Wayne watched me hard. "Did he threaten Bell? Blackmail her?"

"I don't know. You'd have to ask her."

"I intend to, but what do you think?"

"I went to Craven to investigate Bell so I'd have firsthand information. I didn't want to guess then and I'm not guessing now like you're asking me to do."

He waited for me to say more. In the silence between us, I reminded myself this wasn't a competition. This was taking steps to nail the bad guys, so I spilled my thoughts just as I loved for interviewees to do when I was asking the questions.

"But, for the sake of . . . logic," I said, "I believe Easton was trying to hold onto either farm venues or farm sales. Richland is low in agricultural acreage. Bell needed enough clients to justify her job. Easton has an awareness of agriculture so was shrewd enough to know a CDM would have information he'd find helpful. She didn't want her indiscretions to come to light. Perfect for him to set the ground rules on their working relationship."

Wayne wrote again. He took a pause, which I'd come to identify as a *tell*. He would shift direction. "Why didn't you investigate CDM Delores Bell when the accident happened in Craven County?"

Oh, how I wish I had. "The State Director didn't assign me that investigation."

"Who did he assign it to?" Wayne asked.

I was unprepared for this. "Nobody that I'm aware of. The RDM, Bell's boss, was surely consulted, but as to an investigation, I'm not aware one was done. The State Director must've come to his own conclusion and acted how he saw fit, but I have no first-hand knowledge."

"Did you look at her personnel file?"

"Yes."

"Was there, say, an accident report from the Craven County Sheriff's Office?"

"No."

"Was there a write-up by anyone about her situation in Craven?"

"No, there wasn't."

"What did the file state was the reason for the transfer?" he asked.

Heck, he knew. He'd already seen her file. Sometimes these questions seemed so cat-and-mouse and unnecessary. My saying it, however, made me look less culpable . . . and Monroe more so. "It said she asked for a transfer for personal reasons."

We both knew that answer, but he had to have it for his damn formal interview. He had to confirm I'd had the file and read the file.

"Are you covering for Mr. Monroe Prevatte in any way, shape, or form?" he asked.

"No."

"Do you feel Mr. Prevatte is covering up anything regarding either Ms. Bell or Mr. Easton or Mr. Hill or anything regarding these farmers?"

How did I answer that?

"I don't like answering questions that don't concern fact," I replied.

Wayne's right brow lifted. Admiring me . . . I could hope.

"Would you have investigated CDM Delores Bell if the choice were yours?" he asked, again. I would have asked the same.

"Yes, I would have."

"Would you have called the IG if you were Mr. Prevatte?"

I didn't want to answer. Shuffling ideas, I realized I only had one reply if I were being honest. "Yes, I would have. Maybe after doing some research first, but yes. The numbers alone would've given me pause."

"Did you push for him to call the IG?"

No, Wayne. You are not pushing me into that corner.

"I asked if I could call the IG. Twice. At two different meetings." There. Let's move on.

But he didn't. "Did he say why you couldn't call the IG?"

Damn it. Yes, Monroe had. He'd been clear as day about why. "Because the case or cases might be taken out of our hands," I said.

"And out of your control," he added.

It wasn't a question. I didn't bother to answer.

The next shift was abrupt but welcomed. We dove into the farmers. The CDMs. The causes of death. The facts without the coating of assumption or interpretation.

Then he asked me about various ways in which Miss Lily's flunkies could've intimidated farmers, nudged them to despair and fear, or achieved the deaths. If one looked at each death through the right lens, there was a way each could've been murder, with the exception of the hanging. Even then, the farmer could've been harassed into his demise.

Like I said from the outset, no proof of a crime.

The interview took three hours including a ten-minute break during which we still didn't talk. Wayne appropriately closed the recording. I didn't totally relax, but the stress in my muscles slowly slid away.

"It's eleven thirty," he said, looking at his watch. "Want to grab lunch?"

I didn't know if I wanted to or not. That hurt. "Let's just see each other at home," I said. "I've missed half a day's work."

Wayne wasn't surprised, though he seemed a little pained. I sensed something personal and sad coming off the lawman. "Fine by me if we take a break during lunch," he said, "but I need you back here at one."

I frowned. "Why? We covered everything."

"With your interview, yes, but I want you here for CDM Bell's. With you here, she won't be inclined to alter anything she told you, or debate what you learned down in Craven."

I hated this side of Wayne. I hated watching him wall off his feelings for me behind his professionalism, because it was scary . . . and quite convincing.

Chapter 29

I ATE ALONE IN my office, having grabbed an egg salad sandwich from the canteen, then finding myself with no appetite, threw it in the trash. It might smell before the day was through, but who cared since I expected to be at Wayne's mercy all afternoon on the fourteenth floor.

It was that kind of day.

CDM Delores Bell beat me to the conference room, waiting with hands in her lap, staring at anything but Wayne seated on the other side. The clock said two minutes to one, so I reminded myself I was not late. When she threw her blue-eyed daggers at me, I reminded myself I was only doing my job, wishing I could commiserate with her by telling her I'd just been in her chair an hour ago.

But she couldn't know that. And I couldn't feel sorry for her. Interviews were meant to be unbiased collection of information giving direction to the investigator down paths that led to suspects, motives, methods, or corroboration. Which meant the questions could be rather cold at times. Harsh at other times.

Wayne opened with more explanation than I'd received on how interviews were done since Bell was not accustomed to such rituals. But he leaped right into the meat asking why she was transferred to Richland County, right off the bat putting her on the defensive.

Interviews could be designed to make the participant cooperative or defensive. Guess Wayne was going for the latter. Bless her, she owned up to it.

"I fell in love with a man in Craven County who happened to be one of my farmers," she said, rigidly holding that pose. "He received no extra assistance or compensation because of our relationship. On the contrary. He declined to come in for some programs because of his concern for appearance."

Wayne threw a look my way. This was the sort of investigation I was supposed to do. He could interpret this as Monroe having hidden the affair on purpose. I mentally fought not to agree with him.

"Why do you think Mr. Prevatte concealed your affair?"

"I have no idea, but I'm grateful he did. I threw myself on his mercy, and that's what he did." She tried to sit up straighter. She was already stiff as a board.

"Did you ask him to conceal it?"

"Thought about it, but I didn't. He was already being nice enough."

"Nice, huh? Are you in a relationship with Mr. Prevatte?" he asked.

I tried not to cringe for her. Interviews like this could get personal, sensitive, embarrassing, and some agents were quite adept at popping you with a question that splayed you open and bared your soul but asked like they inquired about nothing more than the weather. She'd be stunned. Wayne, however, could've come at her so much harder than this.

"No, sir. The State Director and I do not have a relationship."

Tensing, I waited for Wayne to come at her from other angles.

"Did he come down personally to see you?" he asked.

"Yes."

News to me.

"Did you meet him in your office?"

"No. We met at a restaurant in Charleston."

That wasn't good either. Purposely hiding someplace to hold their discussion.

"Did he ask you to sleep with him?"

"What? No!"

"Did he attempt to kiss you?"

"No!"

"Did he promise you a comfortable job, away from the stigma of Craven County, in exchange for personal favors?"

Each question was meant to chip at her. "God, no."

"Would you like to be in a relationship with Mr. Prevatte?"

Eyes wide, mouth the same, she hesitated. "How can you ask me that?"

Wrong answer.

"You deflected, Ms. Bell, and you didn't answer the question," he said. "Do you find Mr. Prevatte attractive?"

She teared. I was surprised she hadn't before now. A tissue box was on the table for moments like this, and I moved it to her.

"He's a kind man," she said. "He's noble. Mr. Prevatte cared about my career while being worried about how what I'd done would impact the agency. He could've fired me. He could've let the story explode and mar the agency across the state, but instead he sought to salvage me, protect Craven County, and shelter the agency. I admire him for how he handled things."

"Which was his greater concern, Ms. Bell? Concealing your dirt for your protection or concealing the dirt for the agency's protection?"

Stick a knife in her, Wayne. Damn.

She winced, and as hard as she tried, she couldn't stem the tears. "I'd like to think it was a balance, but if I had to select one, I'd say he might've wanted to protect the agency a little more, but still . . . like I said, he was better to me than he had to be."

Wayne stared deeply at her, waiting for her to get ahead of the crying, dry her face, and make eye contact again. "Are you ready to continue?" he asked.

She nodded.

He pointed to the recorder.

"Yes," she said.

But before he could continue, she spoke up. "For the record, I do not admire you and how you are handling this interview, Agent Largo. Mr. Prevatte did nothing wrong. If you want to crucify me, go ahead, but he was totally unselfish in his choices."

Wayne was unphased, highly unreadable, having been chastised before by targets, victims, suspects, and the innocent. Bell's hands trembled as she struggled to keep herself collected. He acted like he didn't see them.

"Were you familiar with Garrett Easton before you arrived in Richland County?" he asked.

One could see her shoulders ease as Wayne crossed into her life post-transfer, and the conversation with Easton when she became more the victim. He'd approached her, made his introduction, said he was aware of her past, and explained that he only wanted to be left alone when she dealt with the farmers he was also in business with.

She had no idea what Easton meant and was afraid to ask for specifics with her being so raw about her recent past. Kudos to her, though; she said if she'd seen anything criminal, she'd have turned Easton in. No one thought an overturned tractor on a farmer living alone looked like anything more than an accident. The coroner deemed it an accident. What was there for her to fear from Mr. Easton after that? She'd heard nothing of his other businesses. Couldn't name another farmer they shared.

"One last thing, Ms. Bell," Wayne said, after having gone through at least six pages of notes with her. "Don't tell anyone, including Mr.

Prevatte, that we talked. No vague reference, nothing. Steer clear of him until told otherwise. To discuss this case with him means I would seek your termination, and depending on how this investigation goes, prosecution for obstruction."

A hard shiver ran through her. "What if he calls me in? What if he asks what we discussed?"

Reaching into his shirt pocket, he drew out his business card, the embossed gold badge on the snow-white paper shouting law enforcement. "Show him this. Tell him you're prohibited from talking. You get up, leave, and call me."

He made her say she understood. When she stood to leave, her gaze shot hatred at me as if I'd been every bit as penetrating as Wayne. He'd kept me there to keep her honest, yes, but in doing so, he'd painted me as an ally in his raking through her life and career.

Delores Bell would absolutely hate me for the rest of that career.

I didn't blame her.

When she left the conference room after what had dragged into three hours, I worried from the way she walked that her legs would give out, but she rallied. Once the elevator dinged, and we heard the door close behind her, I turned to Wayne. "That woman—"

"Had to be interrogated," he said. "She's key to Easton who's key to the farmers. She's key to Monroe who may have made some bad choices. That's to be determined."

Bell had to be a mess now, and she'd be a mess for some time to come. She'd fallen in love with a man with complications but nothing unusual there. Then she'd lost him in an accident that she'd survived, which was tough enough. Then after being transferred across the state, fearing she'd lose her job at any misstep, she was threatened by Easton. Now she was being investigated.

We'd learned of no close family, so she was going home to an empty house. I'd be knocking back a bottle of Old Forrester if I were in her shoes.

My heart ached hard for the woman. A damn hard urge to plea for CDM Delores Bell coursed through me like a current. I'd been interrogated once upon a time like she had just now, and it had about done me in.

"Wayne, she's been hushed by Monroe, then sworn to secrecy by Easton. Now you threaten her within an inch of her life to be quiet. My being here indicates she's answerable to me as well. Damn. She doesn't know which way to turn." Unable to bring myself to say she didn't need to be alone, I still thought it. Alone in a small place with no relatives or close friends. Monroe might have even been her only go-to person.

I'd wanted to do investigative work to follow the law, protect the innocent, and put the criminals away. This interview with Ms. Bell didn't seem to fall under any of those categories.

"She still has her job, Slade," he said.

"She isn't so sure about that," I replied. "She's on the edge of having nothing left."

"This is part of investigations, Slade," he said, peering down at his briefcase, putting away the recorder. "You know that. You have to distance yourself from the emotion."

I did know that. Didn't mean I liked it. The wrong people were being hurt, in my opinion, and we still didn't have people we could lock up except for Richard Hill for his pickpocketing. Maybe his accomplice. "Has Hill given up names? Ratted out any of Easton's people? Fingered Easton enough to do anything? What about old lady Easton?"

"We're just getting started, Slade. Don't overthink this." He rose, this time his gaze on me. I hoped the agent had been locked up in the briefcase with the recorder.

Here was the man I fell in love with going after Monroe, my friend of twenty years. Wayne still functioned on zero assumptions, meaning Monroe would be questioned not only about Bell but also about how he tried to use me to investigate on the sly. Admittedly, all Wayne's thoughts had flitted through mine, but I'd continued investigating on Monroe's behalf as requested instead of going to the IG.

With an investigation, you hunted facts, but the part they don't tell you is that you usually begin with an initial target. The facts might change your target or acquit them, but you have one. This could be two cases. One of impropriety and another of murder. They brushed each other, but did they overlap? Monroe could be considered in both cases, and surely felt the bullseye on his back.

I wanted to hear what Wayne thought about Mrs. Easton, too, but he wasn't allowed to tell me. He hadn't even mentioned her name to Ms. Bell.

"Going home?" he asked.

"Got another hour," I said, neither of our words scratching the surface of what we were thinking. "You?"

"I've got to meet with Monroe."

He had to get to Monroe quickly, too. That interview would go into the night.

We stood there, unsure what to say.

I turned to leave, him following. He held the elevator door for me to exit first when we reached Agriculture's headquarters on the tenth floor, then he followed.

"Gotta stop in here first," I said, reaching the restroom.

"Okay. See you at home," he said. "Gonna be late."

There was no way I could stand watching him walk into Monroe's office, and I disappeared into the restroom. In a bathroom stall, I sat and passed time thinking of kids, thinking of the lake, thinking of family . . . trying not to think of Monroe.

Thinking of my family made me think of the other families swept up in this mess, and the permanent damage that had been done to them as well as their rural communities. That didn't count the deaths, deaths I was just about positive we'd never chalk up to anything. They'd likely go down as dying by chance, by fate, and by depression.

I looked at my phone. No updates from Wayne. Too early for the family to be expecting me. A half hour since I came in. Leaving the stall, I was forced to see myself in the mirror. Cheeks swollen from crying, I figured I'd better fix that before others saw me.

Chapter 30

CALLIE CALLED ME before I ever called her. It had been a long week since my interview on the fourteenth floor.

"How's it going?" Callie asked. She'd called after work hours, but Wayne wasn't home. As usual. We'd hardly seen him as he interviewed farmers and CDMs, met coroners, and ran down people affiliated with Richard Hill and Miss Lily's Table.

"He's not telling me much," I replied, foregoing coffee for a bourbon this evening, with barely a splash of water.

This week had been awkward. Not just with Wayne, but with everyone. Kaye felt guilty at being some sort of catalyst for the troubles with Wayne's and my jobs and what everyone was perceiving as trouble in paradise. We hadn't seen her since last Saturday night. Ally kept the kids out of our way. The kids weren't asking questions. At least of me.

"I'm sure he's up to his neck in the case," Callie said. "How are you? I mean, personally?"

That prompted a draw on my drink. If I talked too much about it, I'd be craving a second pour. Good thing she was there and not here in person. I wouldn't be able to drink around her.

"Have one for me," she said, reading me through the air waves.

"Be glad to. You, and Quinn, and everybody I can think of," I said.

"Slade," she said, not scolding, but more a form of pity. Then she didn't say anything.

"What, Chief?"

"Want me to drive up? You need company?"

"I have company. They're just not talking to me."

Her offer touched me, and I started to take her up on the visit, but she had a job, and she'd get here and get pulled into the sidestepping everyone was doing.

A pressure built in my chest, and I took another sip to stop the chance of tears. "No. Appreciate it, but he's living here, too." I started to add *for the time being*, but was that what I really meant to think? Or was I being dramatic due to the alcohol?

Over and over in my head I asked wasn't Monroe just doing his job and I doing mine?

"Wayne has to perform this case by the book," Callie said. "Especially with you involved. Especially with one angle of it lasered on Monroe. Try to understand that. This is his job on the line, too."

"I know."

"Give him space. Give him . . . grace," she said.

Callie Morgan was one of the most level-headed people in my world. What she said next summed it all up.

"This is why couples in law enforcement don't work together. The ability to read each other and feel each other can override the black-and-white structure of procedure."

Sensible, but that's not what I needed in the here and now when I felt like shit.

"I'm not criticizing either one of you," she said. "I love you both. I also know you both. I don't see either of you being in the wrong. There's a struggle to do right . . . while at the same time respecting the other. There's a clash of professions going on here."

A clash of personalities, and feelings. . . . Time for a refill. I got up and went to the kitchen.

"You're welcome to come down to Edisto any time," she said. "Sit on the sand, watch the waves."

I poured a double this time. "Scout for the sharks." An escaped drop of bourbon rolled across my finger. *There, promptly licked off.*

She chuckled. "You and your phobia. Still, you can always sit on my porch with me."

I found my way back to my own porch. "That would be nice," I mumbled, propping feet, looking over my toes at the lake, sighting a mallard as if looking down the barrel of my .38.

"Take care, and don't overdo the booze."

I thanked her for reaching out, and we said our goodbyes.

She must've talked to Quinn because a half hour later, the PI phoned. "You still sucking down on liquor, or have you sobered up?"

"The former," I said, seeing two geese instead of one when I attempted to sight down across my feet to one on the dock.

"Quit feeling sorry for yourself," said the private-investigator-turned-therapist.

"But I'm so good at it."

"That's the drink talking. Been there. You can't get to the bottom of this with Wayne until you two have a sit-down peace talk."

"We aren't fighting," I said, feet down to the porch floor, sitting up like that made me think better. "We aren't anything."

"Then take the effort to do something," she said. "He's on a case. He's focused. Good agents do that. They put the personal aside, tuck it as far away as they can in order to channel their energies. Been there on that, too. It's how they solve cases better than the next guy."

Now I studied my toes, swirling the half inch of bourbon around the glass, creating an eddy. "Don't want to interrupt all that focus, Quinn. He has to let me know."

Like Callie had, it was Quinn's time to chuckle at me. "He hasn't figured out how, Slade. Be the bigger person."

"He interviewed me, Quinn. No, he *interrogated* me. You weren't there. Then he made me sit through the one with Delores Bell, making me the bad guy along with him. That sucked even worse. He's talked to Monroe several times from the comings and goings I'm hearing about, and I'm banned from talking to Monroe until this is over." I started to finish the remnants in my glass and threw it in the flower bed instead. "I'm in limbo, like I'm in some investigation hell."

"Wow, you've definitely had one too many, girl." She laughed a little, more empathetic. "Give him time. I'd say you might offer to assist him, but he can't let you. Surely you saw this coming."

I had. This shouldn't bother me as much as it was. Guess seeing Monroe in trouble for the exact thing I worried he'd get in trouble for laid a guilt on me for not controlling things better. Naïve choices. But Wayne would argue that Monroe got paid the big bucks in his role as State Director, and he should know better.

He was right.

ANOTHER WEEK came and went. Wayne and I were talking, but the investigation remained the elephant in the room. I still wasn't allowed to see Monroe. This investigation wasn't long as far as investigations went, but it felt like forever.

Finally, one night, Wayne leaned over and kissed me on the head as he left the room. I sighed at the relief, but that was the beginning and end of his feelings.

I reported to work every day, but there was nothing *as usual* about it. My casework consisted of misuse of the government credit card each office had, and someone drove their government car on vacation. Someone screwed a contractor who'd gotten loans from us, giving the appearance of a conflict of interest. Stupid for them. Simple for me.

Their discipline would be up to Monroe. He'd discipline them less than I would, the softy, but he wasn't contemplating such triviality these days, leaving such cases in limbo in his in-box.

I hoped he had a good attorney. I seriously hoped he didn't need one.

Eleven o'clock in the morning on a Wednesday the lawman waltzed into my office unannounced. His smile wasn't his usual but enough like it to be a welcome sight. Every time I saw him these days, it felt like anything he said or did might have a *but* on the end, as if there was business still hanging, secrets he still had to keep from me. This time I sensed a genuine heart behind the smile, and I laid down my pen and spoke up loud enough for Whitney to hear, "Hold my calls, please."

"Yes, ma'am," she said.

Wayne closed the door.

He sat in my guest chair.

My heart pounded. On whom had the IG decided to lay blame? What was he breaking the ice about?

"The case took a turn," he said.

My heart flipped, and I set my hand over my stomach, hoping he didn't see. "What does that mean?"

He settled in the chair like he needed the rest. Like he wanted to be there a while. Like Quinn said, this had to wear on him with being familiar with some of the people involved. There wasn't as much pity in his expression as there was weariness, telling me maybe this turn wasn't directed at me.

However, I couldn't help but wonder what I hadn't seen and did it impact someone like it shouldn't have?

This second-guessing had taken up residence and twisted my gut since the wedding at Clay River. I'd make a terrible criminal.

"It's coming out in the papers tomorrow," he said. "Online any time. Didn't think you needed to learn about it from other than me."

It. What the hell did *it* mean? *It* could mean anything from Monroe to Easton to whatever they'd uncovered I'd missed. Would my name be mentioned?

Were Monroe's days numbered?

Had they snared that old bitch from the restaurants?

"So, tell me," I said, resting back in my chair, not nearly as nonchalant on the inside as I attempted to show. I wanted to scream, *Spill it, for God's sake.*

"Lily Mae Chessereau Easton confessed to telling her people to lean on these farmers in order to broker their land to developers," he said.

Questions popped into my head. Was Easton involved? Did any of them literally commit murder? Did they catch the flunkies she ordered to do it?

"Did you look at the developers?" I hadn't had the chance to. Honestly, I hadn't thought of checking them out until after the case had been taken from me.

"Looked at two. It became clear they weren't too proactive. Didn't have to be. The Eastons made it so easy they didn't have to get their hands dirty. We nixed that line of inquiry early on."

"We?"

"They sent another agent to shadow me, Slade. Wouldn't you if you were them? I'm a tad close to a couple of the people involved."

Wayne had gone by the book, to the nth degree. But that also meant the other agent had heard my interview and deemed it above board and thorough. I'd have hated being interviewed twice. I was familiar with a good number of Wayne's peers. Honestly, I didn't even want to know who this particular agent was.

"First, what about Monroe?" I said.

Wayne had a tolerance of my relationship with Monroe.

Wayne wouldn't be living with me, however, if he wasn't certain he was my number one.

"Neither Delores Bell nor Monroe is germane to the case," he said. "They won't be referenced in my report short of in relation to the list of farmers you were given." He stopped, watching for my reaction.

My exhale escaped with a long hard *whoosh,*

He grinned that half grin of his. "Thought you'd like that."

Tears dripped before I could grab a tissue. "Thank you." I blew my nose, thinking he still hadn't addressed the side issue. "What about him and Bell? Were they a thing? He may not have broken the law, but did he . . . mess up?"

If Wayne had found basis to an affair between a director and a subordinate, the case wouldn't be criminal. It would be sent to my agency's higher-ups in Washington DC. He might be disciplined or more, depending on the morality concerns of the current administration. Monroe deserved to be happy, but not this way. The agency was everything to him.

"They didn't screw each other, Slade."

I rose and came around. He leaned back in his chair as I rested my backside on the front of my desk. "If he had, I wouldn't care," I said, rubbing my knee across his boot. "He needs somebody."

"Other than you."

"Better than me."

A softness came out in another grin. "He could do no better than you, Butterbean."

Which made me tear up again. My gaze wandered from him to the door.

"Nobody's coming in. Not even Monroe," he said, waving for me to come sit in his lap.

Once I'd settled on his legs and in his arms, he said, "I just finished with Monroe, so he's relieved. But I told him I had to meet with you for a while, to discuss how you handled things, so he'll keep his distance. Plus, I told Whitney not to interrupt. I might've put chocolates on her desk to enforce that."

I hugged him, relishing the missed, familiar aroma of his neck, his beard. Most women hated beards. I loved this one.

The silence we'd endured for the last few weeks had been unbearable. My repeated conversations with Quinn and Callie had sustained me, them telling me to hold fast and give Wayne the space he needed to do the job that needed to be done. I was in the way, they said. I'd done what I was supposed to do, and maybe more than I should have, which left him to do the dirty part of things that wrapped up the case.

"The dead farmers?" I asked, putting that on the table. "Miss Lily tried to kill them, didn't she? For Easton?" Through all this solitude and distance, I'd woven many scenarios. The one that made the most sense was the mother taking care of the son and them being in cahoots with each other. Even as stupid as Easton could act, I couldn't fathom him not knowing his mother *took care of business.*

"She professes to have pushed these farmers on her own, yes. Easton would come home and tell his mother about his business, naming farmers, bragging about the connections he was making, talking about the potential of acreage for development. She put developers onto him to start with, making them promise to commission him, but they soon skipped her to tap into him directly, inquiring as to what might be coming available. Mommy, of course, kept up with her son, and as potential land grabs showed potential, she used staff to coax farmers to sell."

"Farmers don't sell easily, though."

"As they found out," he said.

"So she had them killed?" I asked.

"Pushed to their death, you might say, but yes, she fessed up to me, loud and clear on a recording, Slade." He'd gone somber. "A confession that she sent people to harass, in hopes that the farmers gave up. 'If they died, they died,' she said." He shook his head. "That's a cold damn woman. She had a strategy and she pulled it off, and we can't touch her son. He honestly thought he was that good at finding real estate opportunities. And she didn't pull the trigger on the farmers. Odd deal, but it worked. For a while."

"Well, give him some credit," I said, sitting up to see him better. "He set up wedding venues and did have an inside track on the ones in trouble."

"She caused some of the trouble, Slade. Most of it, actually. Easton fed her the names. She took the reins. The problem is we can't prove attempted murder."

I wasn't liking where this was going. "What can you prove?"

His clipped laugh was melancholy. "The closest we can get to her is through Hill and his friend. We are damn lucky we did that wedding for Kaye, you know it?"

Yeah, I saw that now. "Fill in the holes, Lawman. Hill talked . . . Miss Lily confessed . . . Easton's stupid. Who goes to jail? That's what I want to know. And for how long, and for what charges?"

He pushed me until I slid back to my feet. "You're not going to like it."

None of this affected me personally, yet my blood still chilled. "Not going to like what?" I returned to my seat, as if I needed the support of my executive chair and the feeling of being in charge from behind my desk.

"Miss Lily has pancreatic cancer," he said. "She was setting him up financially in preparation for her death."

My chair popped as I snapped forward, seeing where this was going. "He's got his wedding work, and he's an only child. He'll inherit a damn restaurant dynasty. Why the hell did she have to ruin these farmers . . . these farms." I could see the problem now. I didn't even want to ask, but I did. "You aren't doing a damn thing to her, are you?"

"She wanted him to feel he'd created something on his own. And she'll be dead within three months. We had that confirmed. I've seen her deteriorate in the few weeks I've met with her."

Heat climbed up my neck, my jaw tight, and my temper needing a place to spew. "I have not one drop of sympathy for the bitch."

"Neither do I," he said. "She's got a rotten core for sure. I'll let you read the interview. Listening to it will infuriate you."

Like that wasn't a trigger for curiosity. "Why, what else did she say?"

"She bragged about never seeing a courtroom, saying she'll die first. She confessed to making farmers' lives harder with threats, then arrogantly boasted about how it could never be proven. She could name the farmers. Two of them you didn't even look at."

"Wayne," I said, leaning on my blotter, fists tight. "An overturned tractor can't be proven. I get that. And Dewey Anderson hanging himself was his own doing, even if someone taunted him to do so. But the methane gas? That's just not common. Livestock farmers understand the dangers there, and they have safeguards not to mention experience and sense. To check a pump and just fall in? That I can't swallow."

He let me vent, his expression solemn but in agreement.

"The guy in the fishing boat. Yes, he was dying of cancer, but he was a lifelong fisherman. Nobody would've seen another boat come up and do him in."

Wayne gave a gentle nod.

"But"—and I held up a pointed finger—"I'm still not believing Al Blanchard. He got drunk and overdosed on insulin? Both actions just weren't something he'd do. Get with that coroner. She seems to have her act together."

He patted the air with a palm. "Slade, simmer down a notch. These doors were installed by the lowest government bidder."

Yes, the doors were thin. I lowered my voice. "So, she professes to telling people to mess with farmers and sending developers to her son. So who are the harassers . . . besides Hill?"

"He claimed to be the only one. She claims he's the only one who did anything . . . proactive. The others just reported to her."

"Can you lock him up?"

Wayne just watched me with what could only be called pity. I hated pity. It made me mad, and I was getting madder by the second. "What don't I know?"

"He volunteered the information that took us to Miss Lily. Armed with his confession, we collected hers."

Falling back I spun to look out the window at the capitol building. "He got six months or probation or whatever, didn't he? She gets her own death penalty. Nobody gets justice. What are the charges?"

"The United States Attorney hasn't decided. Maybe manslaughter, but there's no forensics to win that. Hill admitted to being compensated for making the farmers' lives miserable, and when the farms got sold, he got a kickback."

"He killed the Brooks's dog, then."

"He did."

Bastard.

"Don't forget Clay River," Wayne said. "Hill was on task to come for that resort like the farms. Vandalism was just the start. That's a positive, Slade. We saved Clay River. We may have saved Kaye."

Amen to that at least.

"Well," I said. "I'm guessing from what you've said that the US Attorney wants to collect pleas and move on."

Wayne's lack of response gave me my answer.

"I hope she takes ten years to die," I said. "Ten miserable, painful, sleepless, agonizing years. I want to see her—"

"Yep," he said, mainly to stop me from winding up and going nowhere with my anger.

Two, three, maybe four minutes passed. Me wondering what could've been done to catch these people. Wayne letting me.

"I went through all this for nothing?" I finally said, low and, for lack of a better word, broken hearted. "*We* went through all of this for nothing?"

We, meaning Wayne, me, my family, the farm families, the farming community, Monroe, and the CDMs and others peripherally affected. Miss Lily was the hurricane that came ashore, caused the devastation, then lost energy and died.

Wayne took my question as rhetorical because there really was no answer.

Chapter 31

WAYNE AND I had left at dawn, him urging me to get on the road early. Guess he forgot to tell all the other drivers that.

"It's the wrong time of year for there to be this much traffic on the interstate," I said, the glut of cars on I-95 South slowing what should've been smooth sailing to Craven County. Snowbirds making their way to Florida for the winter, maybe, which was fine with me, as long as they weren't looking for new subdivision developments in our state. I loved South Carolina. Guess it had been only a matter of time before others discovered it and learned to feel the same.

Quinn had invited us to some shindig at Sterling Banks to celebrate the pecan season. "Y'all need a party," she had said. "With you two being agriculture people, you'll appreciate what we do around here."

A last hurrah, she'd explained, before the nuts started falling at which time they'd be operating almost twenty-four-hour days to honor requests through their website, and the commercial needs throughout the three-state area.

"You'll like Sterling Banks," I said.

"You sure seem to be enamored by it."

We hadn't been this relaxed in a long time, nor this happy. With the case closed, we'd tried to focus on us, on family, and we hadn't discussed even the simplest case since the Eastons were dealt with. So, when Quinn had extended this invitation, we'd looked at each other and said, *Why not?*

Wayne sped around another semi. "Still, like I said, though she offered, we aren't staying the night or anything. They have a tight agenda down there. We're lucky she squeezed us in to their little kick-off party."

I'd sort of hoped we could spend the night, but I too was aware of the tight schedule a nut farm had in the fall. "Can't wait for you to see the place," I said. "Imagine trees as far as you can see. No weeds. The scent . . . that house. And on a branch of the Edisto River, no less. Hope no developers get a hold of that."

He gave a short laugh. "Not as long as a Sterling breathes, I imagine."

"Callie might come, too." I hoped she did.

Then I sat back and watched the scenery pass. Once off the interstate, we made good time, and soon we pulled through the iron gate of Sterling Banks Farm.

The vision stole my breath. "Oh my God, look at that."

The leaves hadn't fallen, but they were barely a week from doing so. However, that meant an endless sea of bright golden leaves stretching as far as one could see. Sunglasses bright. Exquisite, making the sun seem that much brighter.

"Wow," Wayne added.

I rolled down the window, letting it impact all my senses.

A quarter mile in, an open field of ten acres appeared, not full of cars, but there were enough to indicate an event. A dozen. We were probably early. Good. We could offer to help.

More cars were at the house. Wayne parked. "Give me a sec," he said, returning a text or two. It might be a weekend, but he usually remained on call. They'd promised him a partner one day, but after his last was killed a year ago, his bosses hadn't been too keen on replacing her very fast. Wayne had lost two partners in his career, both since we'd met. Neither when he was around and neither his fault, but you couldn't tell him that.

"Done," he said, and got out, coming around to open my door. *Yeah, nothing beat a Southern gentleman.*

Quinn came running out of the house.

And on her heels came Callie.

We rejoiced, squealing almost like schoolgirls in a group hug.

"This is great," I said. "So, what do I do? Let me help set up, dole out food, whatever you need."

Wayne stood to the side grinning, watching us.

"Mind if I steal her from you a bit?" Quinn asked, already pulling me by the hand toward the house.

He held up hands in defeat.

She pointed further up the drive, where the goat keeper lived. "Go find Jonah. He's in the house right through there, about a quarter mile. He's waiting for you."

Wayne struck out, walking the dirt in those boots like he belonged here. Though ten years younger than Wayne, Jonah shared fiancé status as well, both their ladies being crime solvers. With that and agriculture, they had a lot in common to talk about.

"Mark's down there, too," Callie said, following as Quinn dragged me through the door.

That thrilled me. The only thing better than girlfriends getting together was for their guys to get along, too. It was like the universe had decided we'd had enough crap in our lives and we deserved some fun.

Inside, the house seemed more subdued. I wondered why, then noticed the drapes were pulled over all those glass doors that spanned the back of the manor that oversaw the grove.

"Those leaves," I said, wanting to peer out and see how it looked from that incredible slate porch.

But Quinn redirected me toward the kitchen. "What do you want to drink? Too early for you or are you willing to crack that bottle of bourbon I set aside for you?"

I cringed, with a glance at Callie, the woman on the wagon.

"I'm fine with it. Go ahead if you like."

"Yeah," Quinn said. "I stocked up on that spicy ginger ale she drinks."

It was going on ten thirty. "Might be a tad early for me, but once the clock chimes twelve, I'm your girl. Coffee will do me now."

Jonah's mother stood in the kitchen, with all kinds of food cooking away, other dishes already prepared and covered, waiting on counters. "You remember Jules?" Quinn said, stealing what appeared to be a pecan cookie out from a covered plate.

We smiled at each other, Jules pouring me a coffee laced with the obligatory goat's milk.

"Hey," Callie said, looking a bit apprehensive. "You can say no, if you like, but I took the liberty of bringing that dress you asked me to pick out. I know that was a few weeks ago, but no way I was going to think your wedding plans had just disappeared. I considered them set on the shelf for later. When Quinn told me about today, I brought everything here. Wanna see? I can always take it back if you don't like it." She turned to Quinn. "We've got time to try on a dress, don't we? You can go on out and tend to the party if you need to."

"Nah," Quinn replied. "That's the luxury of owning the place. You hire people. Come on. I want to see what kind of taste you have."

"Not yours, for sure," she said.

Quinn shook her head in jest. "Mine consists of jeans, scarves, and boots. Takes an act of God to get me in a dress."

Callie was already on her way up the stairs.

"Sure," I said, curious what Callie had settled on.

I so needed this. Not that things hadn't smoothed out at home. On the contrary, Wayne had been super sensitive to my needs since the case wrapped up. We'd gone on dates again, held barbecues with the sisters and the kids, and laid out on my lakeside dock, sometimes till midnight, admiring Lake Murray. This time of year was my favorite, shining with blue skies, pregnant clouds, and every autumn color possible reflecting in lake waters almost too cool to swim.

One of those evenings, Wayne had re-proposed, asking for a do-over. We didn't talk venues. We just talked about forever. He said if I wanted to go to the courthouse and do it, fine. He'd drop whatever he was doing and do it. Whenever I wanted. I said if he wanted a wedding in a church, fine. We laughed, we cuddled, and we decided how we got married really didn't matter anymore.

We still, however, hadn't decided on where . . . or when. We were okay with that, interested more in making up the ground we'd lost in our relationship than beginning the formality of an event. Recently, my mother had suggested the family church down in Ridgeville. I was even willing to do that now, just hadn't talked it over with Wayne.

Quinn took us down the hall to a bedroom. She opened the door but didn't go in, instead backing away for me to enter first.

My breath caught in my throat; my heart stopped.

The bed had been removed; the other furniture pushed back. A rack of dresses stood to one side, at least twenty. Three tables held an array of shoes, slips, veils, and jewelry.

"What . . .?" I looked to Callie first, but the extravagance of the arrangement, the larger-than-life assortment screamed Quinn.

"Both of us," Quinn was quick to say.

"Her charge card," Callie was quick to say on her heels.

I was almost afraid to go further. This was . . . insane. "I don't know where to begin." But this was supposed to be Quinn's celebration. "Don't let me take you away from things, seriously. Your people probably need you."

"Like I said, not a problem, honey." She reached for my top, pulling it over my head. "Kick the shoes off."

There wasn't a white dress in the lot, thank goodness. I started with the first one on the rack, feeling obligated to try them all. We giggled, we laughed, and somewhere in the mix, Quinn brought out a bottle of non-alcoholic champagne.

My hand fell upon the next one, and the feel of the material made me stop. Soft but with a firmness that held its form, creamy beige with embroidery around a lapel, falling just below the knee. Tiny, covered buttons down the back. None of the others had fit me nor my taste, but this one called my name. The tag said eleven hundred dollars. I jerked my hand back like it had scorched my fingers.

"I should've cut off the tags," Quinn grumbled. She reached over, pulling a pocketknife out of her pocket to whack it off. "We can tell you like it. Try it on."

"This is too much," I mumbled while falling in love. If it fit. . . .

And it did.

"Okay," Callie said. "No doubt this is the one, but since we have all the accessories, let's do this right." She helped me out of the dress.

"Put these on," Quinn said, holding out panties, bra, and slip.

"Nah." I took another sip and glanced at the rest. "It fits. Too expensive, though. Let's see if we can find another that's less . . ."

Callie maneuvered me back to the table of shoes. "Did you shower this morning?"

Giving her a weird look, I scoffed. "Of course."

"Then put on the underthings." Quinn started disrobing me down to the skin.

Clearly they'd planned this surprise, and who was I to ruin their festivity? I was their Barbie doll, and I went with the flow.

It took them an hour, but at the end, they finally allowed me to pose before a full-length mirror they'd covered until they were through.

"What do you think?" Quinn turned me to the mirror as Callie removed the drape.

"Oh," and I couldn't say more.

I'd never looked so put together, and—dare I say—pretty, in my life. My hands raised over my mouth, stunned, gratified, and moved so deeply I couldn't speak.

"We did good," Callie said, nudging Quinn.

"Damn good, I say."

Callie peered out the window. "What time is it?"

"A little after noon."

"We've got time."

"Time for what?" I asked.

Quinn flopped into a golden-lemon upholstered chair, then immediately sat up. "Hand me that bottle."

I did. "Time for what?"

She refilled her glass and passed it to Callie, who did the same and found her own seat. "Time to decide how you're going to get married," she said. "We wanted you to feel it. Here you are, all dolled up, with an idea of how cool you'll look. Now, how are you going to get married?"

I found my own seat and sat carefully, not wanting to wrinkle anything. "Wow, this is a lot of effort to make me commit to a date and place."

Quinn spoke with her fluted glass. "You didn't seem to be getting anywhere, Slade. When Callie told me she'd been entrusted with picking out a dress, I sort of tagged along. We brainstormed and went a little wild with the choices, but then we decided, hey, why not throw a hen party and get you to try on everything instead of us betting on one? Have to admit it's fun, right?"

I started tearing. "This . . . is incredible."

Callie leaped up. "No, don't cry. You'll ruin the makeup job. Stop it." She handed me a tissue, then snatched it away and dabbed for me.

Quinn looked at her watch. "Can you sit here a few minutes? I really need to check on a few things."

"And I promised to call the beach," Callie said, rising and finishing off her glass. "I kind of left them in a lurch about something. You'll be okay here, right?"

"Yeah, I can change without your help."

"No, no," Quinn said. "Stay as you are. I want some pictures, and I'm thinking about getting you to still try on that peach number down there on the end."

I didn't tell her that peach was indelibly stained in my brain as Clay River, but I promised to wait. They ran out, leaving me to sit there alone. The mirror beckoned me again, and, rising, I gave my polished image another analysis.

They'd made me so damn gorgeous. Wishing Wayne could see, I reminded myself such an image was to be introduced to him going down the aisle. The girls had done a good job. Now I really did want to get married. The sooner the better.

Chapter 32

FOOTSTEPS SOUNDED in the hallway—rushing footsteps. I went toward the door only for Quinn to push it open. "Come on."

She was decked out in emerald, her red hair in a braid accented with flowers.

Callie came around her and reached out a hand. "Yeah, come on, girl. You'll be late." She looked exquisite in a sage pantsuit, with beige beads running around the hem of the sheer long coat over it.

"What kind of damn party do you throw for your pecan business?" I asked.

"A mind-blowing one," she said. "Besides Callie said you wanted something you could wear for more than just a wedding." Then she dragged me out of the room and down the hall.

At the bottom of the stairs, Callie stopped me and reapplied my lipstick. Quinn, however, went to the sliding glass doors. "Ready for this?"

Nerves shot through me. But before I could analyze why, she slung the drapes back. Someone on the outside slid back the doors.

Music from somewhere struck up. Daddy was waiting on the flagstone porch, beaming ear to ear, dressed to the nines in a brown suit that couldn't have matched my dress any better.

My knees went weak.

Callie had been ready for that, a grip on my elbow. She whispered, "We did the dresses, Slade, but Wayne organized this for you." This time she had to wipe away a tear.

I almost said, *I can't do this*, but that wasn't so. Realizing how hard he'd had to think details, coordinate, and get me here . . . my heart swelled ten times its size. Of course I could do this. This . . . was as good a wedding as anyone could ask for.

Callie passed me over to Daddy. Ivy handed me a bouquet of fall colors, designed to match whatever shade of outfit I would've chosen, and I beamed so wide at her. She was proud to be a part of this, and bless her, Ivy had had something to do with the flowers, just as Callie had recommended.

Daddy escorted me down the aisle of pecan trees, the white fold-up chairs arranged in lined clusters to enable everyone to see past the massive trunks, each tree on the aisle wrapped in a wide ribbon and accented with flowers to match those I held. Overhead, the yellow leaves shone so bright, reflecting the sun from a cloudless sky, giving the setting an illumination unmatched in any type of church.

Callie and Quinn had assumed their seats alongside Mark and Jonah, respectively. Tyson Jackson, Quinn's childhood friend who'd worked with us once. Jules, of course. Kaye was there, Ivy having made her way back to sit beside her soon-to-be aunt. Kaye needed a partner. A guy, a girl, my sister.

God bless him, Monroe came. And Whitney, along with a handful of other Agriculture people. Savannah Conroy! My longest friend and CDM from Beaufort. Then from Callie's island were Deputy Raysor; Stan Waltham; Callie's old boss from Boston; and, goodness gracious, Sophie—all from Edisto.

Mom sat in her chair up front, an air of peace about her, and pride. If this didn't make her weepy, nothing would.

If someone had told me this many people, numbering sixty, seventy, or more, would come, I'd have denied the likelihood. For them to come and me know nothing about it . . . I wasn't sure what that spoke of. Loyalty? Respect? Maybe love?

The lump in my chest grew larger. But the second I laid eyes on Wayne, everyone else melted away. Suited up, of course, but in fresh-out-of-the-box boots, his beard trimmed, his eyes trying not to rim with moisture.

A warmth swelled inside me, and I could stand it no longer. "Thank you so much, Daddy." I kissed him, pulled my arm out of the crook of his. Walking, then walking faster, I trotted the last ten feet, and threw my arms, flowers and all, around Wayne's neck, laying a kiss so fine and passionate to leave no doubt in anyone's mind that no wedding could be more perfect than this. Nor a husband.

His low laugh filled my ear, barely heard over the laughter of the guests, and I threw my head back and laughed louder.

"You're supposed to wait for me to kiss the bride until after the vows are exchanged," he said.

"Then let's fix this," I said, turning to the minister. "The short version, sir. No sermon."

"And to think I had this inspiring message planned," he said, with an ample dose of humor. "At least allow me some scripture."

"Done," I said, and rubbed a hand over the front of me, smoothing out a dress so refined it wouldn't wrinkle if I'd done somersaults and squats coming down the aisle.

"You look fine," Wayne said, chuckling.

"I ought to," I said. "This bloody thing costs somebody eleven hundred dollars."

His brow raised, but while he registered the price tag, I did a point and tongue-click to the waiting minister. "Time to raise the curtain, preacher. Let's do this."

And do this we did. Afterwards, I couldn't tell you a word the parson said, but I did remember the party afterwards.

Food galore came out in a synchronized order under Jules's command, onto tables that appeared out of nowhere under the trees. The music morphed from the wedding march to background elevator stuff, until we emphasized to them that to get tipped well the musicians better know some Southern rock. They immediately cranked out Marshall Tucker Band.

I made the rounds. Crying with some, laughing with others. Not sure you would say I dodged him, but finally I faced the inevitable. Coming up behind him as he spoke with a gathering of Agriculture people, I rested a hand on his shoulder. "Hey, my friend."

The employees filtered away. His turning to face me might've been slow, but I also could've misinterpreted the moment.

"Congratulations, Slade," he said, and we came together in a hug. We held it hard, and we held it a while. Today finalized what had been coming a long time; the conclusion to Monroe having a chance at me.

"I still love you, Monroe."

His smile held genuine pleasure, but I could still see the hint of sadness.

"I'm so happy the investigation worked out," I said, keeping an arm around his waist, at the same time thinking this was more the type of topic we'd be discussing from here on out. Sure, he'd be a friend, and he'd come over to the house and he'd go out to dinner with Wayne and me. Lunch at times with only me. I'd make sure of that.

"Sorry if I did anything wrong, Monroe. Wayne said I didn't, but I didn't keep you informed like you wished, though I really couldn't—"

He reached around my waist and squeezed. "Listen. Let me clear up some things, Slade. I couldn't before while the IG was involved, then Wayne informed me about today and its being a surprise, and I didn't want to go into it with you. At least not until after the wedding."

Oh, my sweet Monroe. He'd also not wanted to see me knowing the wedding was pending. He'd have acted differently. I'd have noticed.

"Bell went through a bad time after that accident," he said. "She messed up, and you might've done worse to her in my shoes. You're a harsher taskmaster than I am, Slade. I couldn't, however, let her lose her career."

I saw where this was going and couldn't find a way to interrupt.

"She was shaky in the beginning, and I told her my door was always open. Accidents happen. But when she came back, saying she'd been threatened by Easton, I got worried. She said someone was going to expose her, and maybe me for hiding her past. When nothing happened that seemed like much of a threat, I told her to keep quiet and refuse to discuss Craven with anyone. Send them to me."

Again, sweet Monroe. "Did you . . . did you two . . .?" Then I regretted even asking. It wasn't my business,

"No, Slade. I hope you didn't believe that."

"No, I didn't," I said, telling myself I'd never let that concern totally take root.

"But then came the two in Lexington. Then Saluda. When CDM Blanchard called me, with the message Troy Oakley left for him, I knew something had to be done. See, I'm not a bad investigator."

He made me smile at that one.

"So I did the best thing I could do and put you on the case," he said. "Not just about the farmers, but about Bell, too, because I felt them possibly connected. I had confidence in you to shake loose anything. I wanted someone whose heart was in agriculture, not some agent following the law. You would be more inclined to save the farmers, root out what was happening but still with care about saving agriculture at the forefront."

"You told me they'd committed suicide, though," I reminded him. "Only one of them did."

He looked at me knowingly. "To catch your attention, Slade. In the end, we weren't too far from the truth, were we?"

He looked like he had more to say, and I regripped him around the waist again, putting a head on his shoulder to let him know I was patient. I was here.

"Don't think I didn't have doubts about Bell," he said, "but I prayed she was worth saving. Falling in love isn't in a person's control. Sometimes you have to take whatever happens, whether it favors you or not." This time his grin melted all over me. "Bell, like me, has a lot to offer agriculture. That's the only thing we have in common, Slade. The only thing. I've been mentoring her, to keep her on track, and to avoid her being another casualty."

I swept away a tear. This was the Monroe near and dear to me. The white knight of the agency. The man, who like me, worried about protecting what developers craved to destroy. On this issue, Monroe outshined Wayne to heaven and back. On this issue, we would champion the state together to the end of our days.

ALL TOO SOON, I was returned to my Barbie status and redressed by my two ladies and escorted to Wayne's SUV, a few streamers out the back but nothing to embarrass us.

"Where are we going?" I asked, still high on the joy.

"Where do you want to go?" he answered, then suddenly I was faced with a decision I'd given little thought to. The wedding plans had stymied me enough these last few months.

His laughter stilled any concern. "Just sit back and enjoy the ride, Butterbean. You have a week off, and I have it all planned."

Of course he did.

"You're mine now," he said.

Yes, I was his and was thrilled at the title of Mrs. Largo. But he was also mine, and I'd always be called Slade. We both knew that our union would not come with instructions nor would be easily predictable, but the unexpected was what introduced us, and the way we fought through it was what told us we worked well together.

"Don't care where we're going, Cowboy. Just leave the criminals behind."

Chapter 33

Epilogue

EASTON WALKED through the dining room, asking random diners if everything tasted good. When he stopped at my table, he about choked on his own spit. "What are you doing here?"

"Eating lunch," I said.

Having come alone, I didn't want anyone else to be aware of where I was and my purpose for being there. It had taken me six lunches here over a period of three weeks to finally find him on site of the original Miss Lily's Table in the heart of the capital.

I'd allowed a few weeks to pass after Easton's mother died before I decided to entertain these lunches and hope to find him. While my preference was to locate him in the field, where nobody could hear us, he'd inherited the restaurants, and chances were his wedding business might be on hold. Besides, it was December, most likely a slow month for rural outdoor wedding events.

I reached over and patted the other side of the table. "Sit. Tell me how it's going. I wasn't able to attend the funeral, but I also wasn't sure you wanted me to."

He slid in, pouty with his genteel manner of putting on a face. "Before she died, she asked me not to sue you," he said.

"Smart woman. You ever tried suing the federal government? By the way, the collards are great. The biscuits, however, might be a tad dry." I ate a spoonful of mashed potatoes, took my time tasting them, then nodded. "These aren't bad."

"There are so many other places for you to eat, Ms. Slade, so state your purpose."

I put down my fork and washed down my last bite, then pushed the plate back a few inches to make room for elbows. "Came to see if you're still in the wedding business."

Mouth agape, he sucked in air and held it, as if he was so stunned I dared ask. "Not for the winter," he said.

"The spring? Surely if you're planning spring weddings, you're making plans now. With you owning Miss Lily's Table, the catering ought to be a cinch."

He scouted the room in case he was needed . . . or could find an excuse to leave. Then he leaned in—way in—giving me a nasty squint. "I'll be damned first before I handle your affair."

I held up my ring finger. "Been there, done that, Easton. Two months ago. A shindig you'd be out-of-your-mind jealous of. On a farm, no less, and that farmer would've seen you coming a mile away and shut the door in your face."

"Humph." Likely thinking about how much time he'd wasted with me talking wedding, talking farmers. He wasn't sure what to say, nor could he fathom why I'd even want to talk to him. He probably considered me history . . . a bad dream he hoped he'd never have again.

"The reason I'm here is to find out how much future time I'll need to set aside to continue watching you," I said. "If you work with farmers . . ." I waited for him to acknowledge that one way or another.

"I might," he said, biting on the two words.

"Then I'll be keeping an eye on you. And the farmers I hear doing business with you will be getting visits from me, at which time I'll talk about your track record. Not much got out to the public about this case, Easton, and you got off easy."

"I didn't *get off*," he said. "I had no idea what was happening. Mother pulled the strings and kept me out of it, to protect me."

"So she said."

"And you can't prove otherwise."

The table to my left had recognized Easton and noted his rancid expressions. It wouldn't take long for a few others to do the same. I didn't care. Easton would, though.

I lowered my voice such that only he could hear. "Mommy is gone, Easton. Anything that happens will have your name all over it. No excuses. No protection. Nothing but suspicion, and me coming after you."

Breathing hard, he presented a frozen, wrathful mask of hate, and I let him sit there and hold it a few moments. I wanted him to think about what I'd just said. He needed to run the scenarios through his head. His habit of seeking farmers with weaknesses, or creating weaknesses to capitalize on, might paint a whole different future for him. He could lose more than his wedding business. I'd do my damnedest to see that he lost everything he owned.

"Be happy with your restaurants," I warned, even lower . . . leaving no chance of misunderstanding about how hard I meant the message. "Agriculture struggles enough without scum like you making lives more difficult. The second I hear about you irritating a single farmer, I'll make you wish you hadn't."

"How dare—"

"You won't see me coming," I said.

The heat in him almost reached me across the table. "Don't come back to any of my restaurants. You or your Mr. Largo."

"Deal," I said, reaching across the lunch dishes to shake his hand.

He refused, got up, and left.

I was one person with Agriculture, but I had a little extra power than most, a State Director in my pocket and a federal agent by my side. Farmers didn't have a ton of allies these days, but they had us. And we were damn good at what we did.

THE END

Acknowledgements

As always, the top person to thank is Gary W. Clark, Sr., who constantly tells me how proud he is of me setting sights on something big and going after something that was anything but certain. As he continually tells me, "I shall forever be in your corner."

I want to thank the baristas of The Coffee Shelf who have my large hot latte with light whip ready by the time I walk from the door to the cash register. They endorse my books to patrons as if they had a hand in writing them. And I bless Anne Shon, owner, for being such a fan, such a supporter, and such a sweet person.

I'd be remiss not to thank wholeheartedly Karen Carter at The Edisto Bookstore on Edisto Island. She has believed in me since the first book, and that means the world to me.

This time I want to thank Carey Nelson Burch Leo and Rosemary Tarquinio for everything you are doing to take my stories to another level. We'll just leave it at that, fingers crossed.

Thanks for the support from my sons, Matthew and Stephen, and the ladies behind them, Ashley and Tara, for endorsing me to others and being proud of what I do. And of course love to Jackson and Duke for thinking I am the smartest and greatest grandmother in the world.

And I'd be nothing without my readers. You keep me going, and I never tire of being asked, "When's the next book coming out?" That is as good as any hug.

About the Author

C. HOPE CLARK has a fascination with the mystery genre and is author of the *Carolina Slade Mystery Series*, the *Craven County Mystery Series*, as well as the *Edisto Island Series*, all set in her home state of South Carolina. In her previous federal life, she performed administrative investigations and married the agent she met on a bribery investigation. She enjoys nothing more than editing her books on the back porch with him, overlooking the lake, with bourbons in hand. She can be found either on the banks of Lake Murray or Edisto Beach with one or two dachshunds in her lap. Hope is also editor of the award-winning FundsforWriters.com

C. Hope Clark

Facebook - facebook.com/chopeclark
Instagram - instagram.com/chopeclark
Author website www.chopeclark.com